A clammy mist hung ove... in May as Tay gunned the black Ferrari onto the streets of Nob Hill heading toward downtown San Francisco. The expensive sportcar had been Bren's college graduation present two years ago. Tay would have preferred something more practical and less conspicuous, but by now she understood that Bren took perverse pleasure in contrasting the extreme luxury she could provide with the abject poverty Tay had left behind. And Tay had since discovered she wasn't immune to the thrill of driving the Ferrari, just as she had also gotten used to living in the mansion. A year ago, when she had talked of moving out to her own apartment, Bren had promptly called in a contractor and turned several ground floor rooms into a spacious maisonette with separate entrance. Tay felt obligated to stay.

It was not the only way in which she had failed to free herself from Bren's control.

Also by Jessica March

Illusions
Obsessions
Sensations
Temptations

Visions

Jessica March

CORONET BOOKS
Hodder and Stoughton

British Library Cataloguing in Publication Data

March, Jessica
Visions
I. Title
823.914 [F]

ISBN 0 340 59554 4

Typeset by Avon Dataset Ltd, Bidford-on-Avon

Printed and bound in Great Britain by
Cox & Wyman, Reading, Berks

Hodder and Stoughton
A division of Hodder Headline PLC
338 Euston Road
London NW1 3BH

For Giorgio Verrecchia,
A Medicine Man for all who knew him

BOOK I

Ohitika Win
Brave Woman

1

South Dakota – Summer 1956

'For godssake, Cori, have some fun!' Brenda Hartleigh cried out with exasperation through the wind rushing across the open convertible. 'The motor on this thing must have three hundred horses. We oughtta be going ninety miles an hour at least, but you're driving like it was some old jalopy.'

'We're coming to a town, Bren,' Corinne Hartleigh said in the sensible tone that made her sound the older of the two sisters, though she was younger by six years. 'You'd zoom right through at top speed, I know, but I don't want to see anyone getting hurt.'

A moment later the fire-engine red Cadillac cruised past a roadside sign that read 'Welcome to Rapid City, Pop. 32,500'. Cori slowed the car to exactly twenty-five miles per hour.

'Sure as hell *looks* a place I'd go through fast as possible,' Bren remarked, her cool green eyes scanning the roadside shacks and gas stations on the town's outskirts. Under the noon sun the shabby scene looked especially harsh and unappealing.

'Oh, don't always be such a darned snob.' Cori's tone was more good-natured than scolding. 'Even Washington and San Francisco were small once,' she added, a pointed reference to the two places that were the current poles of her older sister's glamorous life.

Brenda went on eyeing the sights sourly. 'Christ, if I'd known this was what most of America looks like, I'd never have agreed to take this trip.'

'Bren, you really are being awful. We've seen plenty of exquisite scenery.'

' "Amber waves of grain" and crap like that.' Brenda emphasized her disdain with a swish of her long golden hair before putting her head back on the seat and closing her eyes. She hadn't the least interest in seeing one more dingy main street of one more pathetic small town along one more dusty highway. Nor even one more majestic landscape. Her own idea of beautiful scenery was the twinkling lights of a big city sprawling below a luxury penthouse . . . or the view of a man's body, young and strong with a hard muscled stomach, stretched out either above or below her, the position didn't matter. Of course, for Cori it was different, Bren knew. Cori had always been the poetic one, who wore dresses of floating chiffon and appreciated art and good books and used words like 'exquisite' . . . and believed in waiting for the man of her dreams to come along before she gave her heart – or her body.

'Hey, *look*!' Cori yelped suddenly.

Brenda Hartleigh sat upright. The highway had taken the convertible into the center of Rapid City, but she saw nothing out of the ordinary for a western town. Just the usual row of stores that sold boots and hardware and ladies' clothes two years out of fashion, lined up with the usual quota of bars.

'What are you shouting about?' Bren asked.

'Right up there, straight ahead! See . . . ?'

Now Bren noticed the banner suspended high over the main street, yellow letters on a crimson field: RODEO, SAT. 13 AUG. 2 P.M.

'Shit, Cor',' Bren erupted, 'you're not thinking of holding

us up in this godforsaken place to go to a rodeo?' Cori had always loved horses.

'Bren, it's *today* – starting in just a couple of hours!'

'So by the time it's over we'll be stuck here for the night,' Bren objected.

'Please, Bren,' Cori pleaded. 'I haven't seen a real rodeo in so long . . . not since that time—'

'When G.D. took us to the Cow Palace,' Bren supplied. Hard to forget since it was the only time their father had ever taken the two sisters and their brother on a family outing in San Francisco. Even then, it hadn't been purely to entertain his children. G.D. Hartleigh was interested in horses, too, and admired cowboys since they were rough and ready and independent as he was himself. It was the reason his favorite among the family's several vacation homes was the ranch in Jackson Hole, Wyoming.

'C'mon, it'll be fun,' Cori persisted. 'Weren't you just saying I should have more fun? I'll start right now.'

Bren sighed. The way she recalled that day at the arena, the whole place had smelled of manure and horse piss and she'd been bored silly watching dumb cows chased by men on horses twirling ropes. Not her idea of fun at all. The only part she'd enjoyed was watching the cowboys saunter around in jeans so tight the crotches bulged, imagining which ones she'd enjoy fucking. She'd been sixteen then, no longer a virgin, while Cori would've been only nine. Even today, she guessed, it was the men she'd enjoy looking at, while Cori would still have eyes only for the horses.

Cori had pulled over to the curb under the banner. 'C'mon, Bren,' she insisted, 'just this one stop. We've been driving straight since we left Washington—'

'Because you wanted to spend time at the ranch before we go home.' Bren didn't care for vacations on the ranch, and she was impatient to get to San Francisco. There would be lots of action already as the fat cats geared up for the presidential nominating convention starting in ten days. But since the drive was taking them practically right through Jackson Hole, she couldn't deny her sister a short stop-over.

Cori was still gazing at her older sister with pleading eyes. 'Oh, what the hell, kiddo,' Bren said, 'if it'll make you happy.'

They didn't want to get back on the road after the show was over, so they checked into a suite at the best hotel they could find on Main Street. Cori unpacked her clothes, then took a bath before donning a demure cotton summer dress of pale blue printed with tiny daisies. Bren pulled a hot pink rayon blouse and a pair of sheer white linen slacks out of her own valise, leaving the rest of her clothes packed.

'Don't you want to bathe first?' Cori said, as Bren slipped into her slacks.

'Jesus, I showered this morning and all I've done since is breeze along in a car. I'm fresh enough to sit and watch a bunch of smelly men tangle with a bunch of smelly animals.'

Cori shook her head. 'I can't change clothes without bathing,' she said absently, as she checked herself in a mirror.

Don't I know it! Bren thought to herself. During the few months they had lived together in Washington, Bren had become even more aware of the differences between herself and Cori than when they were growing up together. Cori's fondness for classical music contrasted with her own liking for jazz and pop. Cori's dislike of the constant parties which were a natural part of the city's political scene, while Bren always felt at her best in a room crowded with powerful people. And Cori's uneasiness with Bren's frank appetite for sex, whether it meant unplanned nights out, or bringing men back to the apartment. With all their differences, it was soon clear that living together was a disaster, and that it had been a huge mistake for Cori to come to Washington.

Not that the idea had been either of theirs. In advance of Cori's graduation from Wellesley last June, G.D. had phoned Bren to insist she invite Cori to Washington for the summer. 'Give her a chance to see the way the country works,' he'd said. 'And meet a few nice young men – the kind with good prospects.'

'There are no nice men in Washington,' Bren had observed, 'or nothing would get done. Let Cori come home after college, G.D. Washington is too rough-and-tumble for a woman alone.'

'Doesn't bother you,' he said. To which Bren said nothing. Her father damn well knew she and Cori were cut from different cloth. 'Anyway,' he went on, 'she won't be alone. You're there to watch out for her.'

'I have work to do – *your* work, in case you've forgotten. I can't be playing nursemaid to—'

'Look, I want your sister to get some experience,' he cut her off sharply. 'If you've got so damn much to do, then Cori can help. She'll work in the office with you.'

The thought of sharing the office with Cori had seemed twice as onerous to Bren as merely sharing her apartment. Having carved out her own niche, she didn't want anyone trespassing on her territory. Yet Bren had called Cori at college to invite her for the summer.

Cori's own plan had been to go home; she'd been thinking she would enjoy teaching young children. 'Summer's the time I should be looking for a position in a school,' she said. 'I don't want to start too late and spend next year sitting around. I want to do something useful with my life, Bren.'

Bren held back a retort to the implication that what she did was less than useful. 'At least come for a few weeks before you travel all the way back across the country,' she coaxed. 'You'd be helping me out – the work's been piling up.' In truth, the office was headed into the summer doldrums, with Congress soon to recess and everyone preparing for the two presidential nominating conventions. But any of G.D.'s orders, Bren knew, was also a test of her ability to carry it out. If he wanted Cori to have some exposure to Washington, so be it. Anyway, it wouldn't last the whole summer. The Republicans would be nominating a President in San Francisco late in August, and G.D. naturally wanted her there to lobby the delegates, protecting Hartleigh interests during the elective process. Cori could be shepherded home by then, at the latest.

Bren had decided, too, that it wasn't impossible she might learn something from being around her little sister. With all the sharp differences in personality that had kept them from becoming close in the years of growing up, there was not only a degree of mutual respect, but some mutual envy. Cori wished she had more of her big sister's daring, spontaneity, and irrepressible high spirits; Brenda admired Cori's warmth, sensitivity and insight. Though when it came to looks, Bren was content she'd been dealt the better hand. She liked being a statuesque stunner whose greater height, emerald eyes and mane of golden hair got noticed as soon as she entered a room. Cori was beautiful, too, with chestnut hair and hazel eyes, but her pale skin, frail body, and the short hair she favored added up to a porcelain-doll effect that too easily faded into a crowd. Still, Bren recognized that her sister possessed some mysterious inner quality that made her the more appealing of the two. Both had always been popular, but Bren collected friends by winning them; Cori, on the other hand, was surrounded by friends simply because they were drawn to her. The difference wouldn't have irked Bren so much if it also didn't noticeably affect their father. *She* was the one who'd always had to work to win his love, demonstrate over and over that she, more than the other two children, was his true kindred spirit. Still, Cori had always been the unquestioned favorite.

The Cadillac convertible was just the latest proof. 'You'll need a way to get around Washington,' G.D. had said when he handed the keys to Cori as a graduation present, 'and it won't do any harm when you offer one of those Congressmen or Senators a ride.'

It galled Bren, since she'd had to buy herself a car – and it was already nearly five years since she'd convinced her father to send her to Washington to work with the lobbyists for Hartleigh Mining. It was an important time to keep a closer eye on new legislation, Bren had suggested. The gold mined from Hartleigh's South Dakota fields had always been the primary source of income, but in recent years – since the Second World War had been ended by a new kind of bomb – the company's uranium deposits had become equally valuable, and now laws were being passed to keep atomic power under safe control. It wouldn't be good for Hartleigh Mining Corporation if there were *too* many restrictions, or government went so far as to decide uranium couldn't be left in private hands. G.D. had seen her point, and Bren had served so well in the office of the established Washington lobbyist whom the company paid half a million dollars annually, she had soon won approval to set up on her own as *the* Hartleigh lobbyist. She had proven far more effective at winning government favors for HMC than her predecessor. All the free champagne dinners, theatre tickets, and Caribbean holidays the old Washington insider had bought for members of Congress didn't accomplish half as much, Bren had found, as the occasional blow job for one of the young Congressmen she enjoyed dating.

As they drove into the rodeo parking area, the two women in the open red Cadillac instantly attracted attention. Many of the contestants, identifiable by number sheets pinned to the back of their shirts, were there standing around their pick-ups and horse trailers, trading stories while they hand-rolled cigarettes. They all stopped to stare as Bren and Cori got out of the car.

One cowboy, wearing an electric-blue western-style shirt with pearl buttons said, in a drawl loud enough to make sure he was overheard, 'Couldn't imagine a better ride then bein' bucked around on that palomino.'

He meant her, Bren knew – a palomino was a horse with a blond hide. On her way to the stands, she paused to give the cowboy a direct look. He was young and attractive, lean and sinewy with a lick of straight brown hair that hung down under the rolled brim of his hat. 'You might have trouble staying on,' she said.

The cowboy in blue raised an eyebrow while the men around him laughed and gave him jovial nudges.

'Bren!' Cori admonished in a sharp whisper, as she pulled her sister along. 'You'll get us in trouble. You better fasten another button on your blouse, too. I can see your bra.'

Bren shot her sister a pitying glance: could she really understand so little?

They gave the ticket-taker three dollars each, and climbed up in the wooden grandstand overlooking a section of railroad stockyards cordoned off to make an arena. In the background stood corrals full of cattle waiting to be shipped to slaughterhouses. Nearer, some of the stock pens had been set aside to hold the broncs, calves and hump-necked brahma bulls used in the rodeo events. Beside the stands were chutes from which the animals would be released into the arena.

The grandstand filled quickly with local families, groups of high-school girls, and old-timers looking for a taste of the old west. About a thousand in all. Mimeographed hand-outs showed a roster of the standard events – calf roping, steer wrestling, bronc riding, and bull riding. Prize money of between one and three hundred dollars for the winners.

The bull-dogging began, chutes releasing heifers that scampered across the dirt arena chased by hooting cowboys on horseback twirling lassos. The calves had to be roped, brought down and hog-tied; the man who could do it in the least number of seconds was the winner. Before each attempt, a voice boomed through a loud-speaker identifying the contestant. 'Here's Dusty Loggins, over from Salinas, Kansas. Dusty won this event last month down in Houston . . . Next up is Chance Stover from Montana's "big sky" country . . .'

Dusty. Chance. Windy. Smoky. The cowboy names, thought Bren, were so perfect as to be almost a parody of the real west – though there was no doubt the rodeo riders had to be genuinely gutsy and strong and adept at these special skills. Men took hard falls from bucking horses, or got spiked nastily by a steer's horns. To distract animals that had gotten out of control, a clown in cowboy clothes occasionally ran out into the arena.

Having developed a taste for men who were more polished and powerful, Bren was no longer distracted by fantasizing about these rodeo riders, most of them grubby and unappealing. She was soon anxious to leave.

But Cori was unbudgeable. Sitting on the edge of her seat, she clapped for each contestant, and constantly made excited comments on the spectacle. Her enthusiasm encouraged a grizzled old man seated next to her – evidently a one-time rodeo hand – to start offering insights into the tricks of the trade. During the bull-dogging event, the old man pointed out that the contestants who were fastest in wrestling the calf off its feet would take the animal's lip between their own teeth and bite on it; the lip was one of the animal's most sensitive parts, so the pain would cause it to surrender quickly.

The lesson delighted Cori, but disgusted Bren. 'Just proves it's true what they say about cowboys,' she remarked. 'They'd sooner kiss a cow than a woman.'

During the event that featured the bucking broncos, Bren saw the cowboy in the electric-blue shirt climb onto the side of a chute, preparing to ride. Cleaner than the others, younger, quite good looking, he was a little more in her league. If she did have to be stuck here for the night, Bren mused, she could do worse than spend it with him. Just as the thought entered her mind, he turned and locked his eyes on her, having evidently noted her location in the stands.

Now he shouted up to her: 'Just watch how well I stay on!'

Bren tossed her head in a laugh, and he hopped down onto the back of a horse waiting in the chute.

'On deck now,' came the announcer's voice, 'is last year's champ up and down the circuit in both the bronc and bull riding – Charlie Mills, riding Hellfire.'

The chute sprang open and the bronc charged out, bouncing crazily up and down on its kicking legs while Mills, reins in one hand, raked his spurs over the horse's flanks. Previous contestants had been bucked off after a few seconds, but Mills stayed in the saddle eight, nine, ten . . . and was jolted off just before a horn brayed over the loudspeaker. The crowd cheered. The old-timer nudged Cori and pronounced the ride a sure winner.

As he walked from the center of the arena, Mills looked toward Bren again and lifted his white Stetson. She gave an approving nod, and he walked off to the side and vanished through a gate.

Other contestants followed, but all were bucked off their mounts long before the horn sounded. Bren wasn't bored anymore. She had something at stake now; she wanted Charlie Mills to win.

'Now our final entry,' the voice came through the loudspeaker, 'Ed Black, riding Red Rocket. Ed's by way of Rosebud, right here in the state, and this is his first year competing.'

This entrant was already having trouble, his horse jumping around so viciously before the chute was opened that the cowboy couldn't drop down into the saddle.

The old-timer beside Cori chuckled. 'Red Rocket looks to

be a "draw-around",' he said. 'This new fella'll be on his ass soon as he's out of the chute.'

'What's a draw-around?' Cori asked.

'Riders get their horses by draw. When an animal's so mean it's almost unrideable, that's a draw-around – 'cause the men all want to draw around it, see. If you got a friend runnin' the draw, then a horse might be held back to help you out. But this Ed Black don't have no friends here.'

'Because he's new?' Cori said, as she saw the cowboy finally managing to drop into the saddle.

Before she received an answer, the chute opened and the horse shot out in a writhing, leaping, kicking blur of movement. The cowboy's body bounced furiously up and down in the saddle – but as the seconds passed he remained astride the horse. He was a big man with broad shoulders, obviously extremely strong.

'Hold on!' Cori yelled. Bren gave her a hot glance, but Cori couldn't help rooting for the newcomer underdog who'd been stuck on the wildest horse.

The horn blared, but the horse went on bucking so wildly that it took Ed Black a few more moments to find his chance to leap off safely. Meanwhile, his hat flew off his head. At last he jumped, landed on his feet and walked over to retrieve his hat from the dirt. As he did, the applause was sparse, nothing like the cheers Mills had received. Without the hat and its shadowing brim, it was easy to see not only the man's strong handsome face, but the coal-black hair gathered into a long braid that trailed down his back and the reddish caste of his skin. This was the answer to her question, Cori realized: Ed Black hadn't been sabotaged with a "draw-around" because he was new – but because he was an Indian.

At the end of each event, the prize-winners were announced. For the bronc riding, only Ed Black had stayed on for the full ride: he received first prize of two hundred dollars. Charlie

Mills took second-place money of a hundred and twenty. Unhappy with the result, the crowd booed when Black's name was announced.

The next event was bronc riding again – this time 'bareback'. Without a saddle, and nothing to hold onto but a rope halter – and only with one hand, according to the rules – most of the cowboys didn't last more than a few seconds. But Charlie Mills stayed for nine seconds. When his turn ended, he strolled to the edge of the arena below Bren's seat, tipped his hat back and called up to her brazenly, 'That one was for you, darlin',' as though dedicating a sure winner. Bren acknowledged the gesture by casually blowing the cowboy a kiss. But Cori guessed Ed Black would do better when his turn came. Indians grew up riding bareback.

However Black didn't appear among the riders before the event ended. Mills was announced as winner of the first-prize money.

The performance moved on to the wild-cow milking, a comical free-for-all of cowboys working in pairs to rope a calf, collect a squirt of its milk in a bottle, and race to a finish line first. Bren looked for Charlie Mills, but he hadn't entered the event.

'And now, ladies and gentleman,' the announcer declared dramatically after reading out winners of the comical cow-milking, 'the climax of our show, the wildest, rip-snortin'-est thing you'll see today – the brahma bulls!'

The massive cream-colored long-horned bulls were ridden bareback. Instead of the basically up and down bucking motion of the broncs, the brahmas also twisted and spun as they reared, tossing their haunches around almost as if they were disconnected to the front of their body. Their backs were broader, too, making it difficult for a cowboy to grip the sides of the animal with his legs. Three or four seconds was considered a good ride. The horn signalling a complete turn went off after only eight seconds. Once a rider was thrown the animal often went after him, viciously attempting to gore him. At this point the antics of the rodeo clown became life-saving, diverting the bull while fallen riders ran to safety. To save himself from being gored by the charging animal, the clown jumped into a padded barrel. It frightened Cori to see the barrel being sent tumbling into the air by a bull's horns, and tumbled over and over with the hapless clown inside. The old-timer next to Cori offered the fact that it was 'a brahma' that had ended his own career of rodeo-riding. 'Got throwed and the critter crushed this-here leg,' he said, clapping one thigh.

'That's awful,' Cori purred sympathetically.

'All in the game. There's a sayin' round here: never was a critter couldn't be rode, never a cowboy couldn't be throwed.'

The first three bulls threw their riders almost at once, and one cowboy went off over the animal's head, a horn tip catching the man's leg so that his pants tore and blood flowed from a minor gash on the inner thigh.

'I'm ready to leave,' Cori said, clutching Bren's hand. 'This isn't fun anymore.'

'Wait outside if you can't take it,' Bren shot back. 'I want to see Charlie ride again.'

So it was 'Charlie' already, Cori thought. 'Bren – you're not going to . . . do anything with that cowboy, are you?'

'Will you calm down?' Bren said. 'I'm enjoying this, that's all.'

Cori was debating whether to stay or wait outside when the next contestant was announced through the loudspeaker: 'Well, here comes that new fella Ed Black back again to try his luck. Let's see if the bull's as good at throwin' an Indian, as Indians are at throwin' the bull.'

The crowd laughed, but Cori gasped. 'That's an awful thing to say.'

'Hell, it's a joke,' the old-timer said. 'Old one at that.'

Cori's attention was caught by the sight of Ed Black as he climbed the side of the chute preparing to take his mount. One sleeve of his buckskin shirt was torn, and a red welt was visible on one cheek since he was no longer wearing a hat, but only a leather band of brightly-colored beadwork wrapped around his head. 'Look at him,' Cori said to Bren. 'He's had an accident—'

'Probably took the prize money he already won, went for a few slugs of fire-water, and fell on his face,' the old cowboy put in.

'Maybe he shouldn't be riding,' Cori said.

'Oh hush,' Bren snapped impatiently. 'This isn't girls volleyball, for godssake.'

In the next moment, Ed Black had slipped down onto the bull, the chute opened, and animal and rider were sent on their mad, spinning trip around the arena.

Black seemed to be glued to the back of the animal. As if he could predict each movement of the bull, he appeared to adjust for it, shifting his balance, leaning this way or that to compensate, rather than being tossed at the whim of the animal. There was an almost magical quality to the vision of him astride the beast, Cori thought, an illusion that they were not locked in angry combat as the other bulls had been with their riders, but that they had made a respectful compact to join in demonstrating their strength and skills.

The horn sounded, but Black stayed on the animal's back as the bull continued his furious writhing leaps around the whole arena. Five more seconds, ten. The horn sounded again. But Black kept riding, all the while his handsome face turned to the crowd, his black eyes glaring with burning defiance. It became clear that the Indian's feat was his proud answer to the crowd's hostility.

The horn blared for a third time, a long insistent blast. Finally Black jumped from the bull's back, landing on his feet with the grace of a gymnast. At once he began walking to the sidelines with not even a backward glance to check for danger from the animal. The rodeo clown charged out to do his job of distracting the bull.

The crowd watched in stunned silence, but Cori couldn't keep herself from showing her support. She jumped to her feet and clapped her hands. After her solitary applause broke the silence, just a dozen other spectators joined in, Bren among them.

'I thought you were rooting for Charlie,' Cori said.

'In Washington,' Bren replied, 'you learn to switch fast to winners.'

The old-timer overheard. 'That redskin didn't win nothin' yet,' he declared.

'No one else is going to stay on that long,' Cori said.

'Don't have to. It was his own idea to show off after he did the eight-second limit. If Mills makes it to the first horn, too – and shows better form – he can take first money.'

The next three riders lasted only a few seconds each. Then Charlie Mills was announced. Before climbing into the chute, he looked up toward Bren as if hoping for encouragement. But her allegiance had changed; she pretended not to notice him.

Mills lasted seven seconds before finding himself in the dirt. He dusted himself off, collected his fallen hat, and limped out of the arena.

When Ed Black was announced as the winner, the boos were louder and more numerous than before.

'Never let injuns in the rodeo in my day,' the old-timer grumbled, 'and they shouldn't be in now. Rodeos is for cowboys.' He got up and shuffled off. The show was over, the stands were emptying out.

'That *was* fun,' Bren said as she stood. 'I'm glad we stopped.'

'I'm not,' Cori said. The blatant prejudice she had witnessed against the Indian left her feeling almost physically ill.

Outside the arena, the rodeo cowboys were loading horses into vans. As the sisters walked toward the convertible, Cori saw Bren scanning the area. She was pretty sure she knew who Bren was trying to find. But they reached the car without encountering Charlie Mills, and as they drove away Cori breathed a sigh of relief. She knew how easy it would be for Bren to have a fling with a man like that; and Cori had a powerful intuition that it could have led to a very bad end.

2

'Feeling better?' Having showered off the dust of the arena, Bren sat now at the dressing-table in the hotel room brushing out her long blond hair. In the mirror, she looked at the bed where Cori lay in her slip. 'We'll take a walk, find a nice place to eat.'

Cori pulled herself up listlessly. 'I'm not hungry, but I'll sit with you.'

Bren put on a swirling red silk dress with a low neckline – too jazzy for this hick town, she thought, but she owned none of the very simple things that Cori wore.

Cori took another bath first. Reclining in the warm water, she went on brooding over the prejudice she'd witnessed at the rodeo. She wondered now about her family's share of responsibility for mistreating the American Indians? In this very state, eighty-five years ago, the Hartleigh Mining Company had been founded with a large gold strike on a claim staked by G.D.'s grandfather. Expanded many times, Hartleigh property in South Dakota had come to abut reservation lands of the state's predominant tribe, the Lakota Sioux. In a number of cases, Cori knew, the tribe had contested ownership of large tracts containing valuable deposits of gold-bearing ore – and, more recently, uranium. HMC had always proved in court that it operated only within its legal rights. But, as Cori had seen during the recent month of observing her sister's work in Washington, the way those rights were defined was shaped by the lobbying influence wielded by Hartleigh Mining.

In the past Cori had never assumed anything but that the company did its business legally, contributing in an important way to the strongest economy in the world, building on the independent tradition that had allowed her grandfather, a poor but adventurous Irish immigrant, to head for the frontier, stake a claim to a plot of scrub ground no one else wanted . . . and turn it into a fortune. That was how Cori had been brought up to think of it: the American dream fully realized. Whatever the inequities she sensed behind the way her family's company did its business, she had managed to overlook them. She'd never seen the mining operations; even on this trip, driving for the first time across the country, she was glad that Bren, who had made several visits to the mines since starting work with the company, had not suggested making a stop. Cori felt that if she looked too closely at the way the family had acquired the wealth that provided her privileged life, she might find it hard to reconcile with her belief in fairness. Yet she could not imagine ever rejecting her alliance to the family, or taking issue with her father about business practices. Though Cori didn't kid herself: G.D. was a tough man, even sometimes ruthless. If he was known to friends and enemies alike – even to his children – merely by his initials, they were also known by all to stand for 'God Damn' Hartleigh, because of the curses he swore at others, and those they swore at him. But she loved him unconditionally; he had never been anything but kind and gentle and generous with her.

Yet today she felt the dam of indifference she had constructed against the truth suddenly weakened – the result of one small example of wrath and scorn she had seen turned on a man solely because he was an Indian. That one man, Cori realized, stood for many. How many thousands of Indians might have suffered even greater indignities because of the way her family made its money?

As she dressed after the bath, Cori wished she could share these troubling thoughts with her older sister. But she knew it would only lead to fruitless argument. Bren's job, after all, was to defend what the company did – indeed, to persuade the government to align itself with Hartleigh interests.

They went out and walked along the main street looking for a restaurant. There were a couple of diners and coffee shops, but Bren peered through the windows and pronounced them all 'greasy spoons' where the food was sure to be awful. They also passed by a few unsavory looking bars. Affixed to the door of one, Cori saw a placard etched with the words 'No dogs or Indians allowed'. Cori felt sick all over again. She'd have to talk to Bren about it, she decided.

They came to a place called the Last Sunset. Men and women dressed in casual western style spilled out onto the sidewalk through swinging café doors. The babble of a crowd inside mingled with lively honky-tonk piano. Bren paused to look at a menu posted outside. 'Ribs, chicken, and steak,' she read aloud. 'Sounds okay.'

'Bren,' Cori said, 'this is a bar.'

'No . . . a *saloon*,' Bren corrected, pointing to the gold stencilling on the large front window.

'Bren, I don't think—'

'C'mon, it must be good. This is the biggest crowd we've seen.' Before Cori could protest again, Bren had pushed through the café doors. Cori trailed along.

Inside, it was the image of the old-fashioned gathering places that catered to cowboys in any Hollywood 'western'. A long polished oak bar with a mirror behind it, round tables with checkered table-cloths, and chandeliers with cut-glass globes.

21

But this was no stage set. It had the authentic air of a place that had served outlaws a hundred years ago.

Men only were lined up at the bar, and as soon as she saw them Cori recognized several as rodeo cowboys. They all paused to take notice of Bren. Cori didn't begrudge her striking sister the attention she always attracted, but tonight it added to her malaise. These men were a different breed, formed by rules and customs as old as the saloon. It hadn't been so obvious when they were participating in a sport, but in this setting they looked more ominous. Many wore gun belts complete with holstered six-guns that they hadn't worn while riding. By walking in here, Cori felt, her sister had wilfully been asking for trouble. She reached for Bren, to make a more forceful appeal to leave, but Bren was already moving toward an area of tables at one side, some occupied by groups of men and women – girlfriends who also followed the rodeo circuit – others solely by men sipping beer or whiskey.

As Bren headed for an empty table near the wall, an attractive cowboy in a sleek cream-colored shirt with black piping and onyx buttons rose abruptly from his chair, blocking her path. It took both sisters a moment to realize it was Charlie Mills.

'Well, looky-here,' he said, 'the golden angel from the grandstand. I was hopin' you might come lookin' for me . . .'

Bren eyed him coolly. 'I came looking for a nice juicy steak, that's all. Even charcoal grilled and well done, you look too tough for me to chew on.'

Mills laughed. 'That bein' the case, how 'bout I buy both you gals a couple of nice tender T-bones?' He gestured to his table. All but one of the six chairs were occupied by men he'd been drinking with. 'Jody, Fred,' he said, 'clear out, make room for the ladies.' Two of the men started to rise.

'No,' Cori murmured, turning to Bren.

'Keep your seats, fellas,' Bren said drily. 'My sister and I

22

would rather dine alone. We have family business to discuss.'

Cori gave Bren a grateful glance. It seemed she had realized Cori's need to talk about what was troubling her.

Mills shrugged. 'Nothin' more important than family,' he said gazing straight at Bren. 'Too bad, though. It would've been a powerful pleasure to make your acquaintance, Miss . . .' He let the pause hang in the air, fishing for her name.

Cori hoped Bren wouldn't tell him.

'Hartleigh,' Bren said. 'Brenda Hartleigh. And this is my sister, Corinne.'

A lift of one eyebrow gave a tell-tale hint that Mills recognized the name, though he said nothing about it. 'Nice meetin' you girls,' he said, smiling as he moved out of Bren's path. 'Hope we cross paths again some time.'

'I doubt we will, Mr Mills,' Bren said, sidling past him.

When they were seated at their own table, Corinne hissed at Bren in a whisper. 'Why did you tell him our names?'

'Just being polite,' Bren said.

A waiter in a white apron arrived at the table with two shots of whiskey on a tray. He set them in front of the sisters, and said it was 'the best stuff in the house' courtesy of gentleman at the nearby table. Looking around, they saw Charlie Mills raising his glass in tribute. Bren smiled her thanks, and tossed her shot down in a swallow. Mills approved with a nod. Cori forced a smile, but pushed the whiskey aside.

The waiter asked for their orders. When Cori said they hadn't looked at a menu yet, he smiled tolerantly and said there were no menus. 'Steak, chicken, ribs, burgers, all broiled. And anything you want to drink, exceptin' fancy cocktails. That's it.'

Bren wanted steak and a beer. Cori felt the stirrings of an appetite, and ordered chicken and a glass of ginger ale.

For a minute or two after the waiter left, the sisters sat taking in the atmosphere, listening to the songs being played on the old piano. Facing toward Mills, Cori saw him constantly glancing over at Bren, hoping for some reciprocal interest, but Bren ignored him.

'Want your whiskey?' Bren asked. 'Shame to waste it.'

'Bren, don't drink any more,' Cori said.

'Hey, Miss Straight-and-Narrow, I'm a big girl now.'

'I don't like it here,' Cori blurted.

'Then go back to the hotel.' She picked up Cori's neglected whiskey, and took off half the shot in a swallow.

Cori would have liked to go, but she didn't want to lose the opportunity to talk. Pulling closer to the table, she prepared to explain how upset she had been by the way the Indian had been treated this afternoon – and to probe for the truth of Hartleigh Mining's relations with the local Indian tribes. But now she saw that Bren was staring intently at something over her shoulder. Glancing around, Cori saw that Ed Black had entered the Last Sunset and was headed toward an empty table right behind them.

Up close, the Indian was even more impressive than he had seemed before. Broad-shouldered and narrow-hipped, with a bearing that could be summed up as 'noble' – cliché though it might be. Remarkably handsome, too, with a straight nose, strong jaw, and intense black eyes emphasized by heavy brows. The headband adorned with vividly colored beadwork was still wrapped across his forehead, but his long shining black hair was no longer braided, and hung down loosely around his shoulders. His shirt looked to be an article of traditional dress, soft tan leather decorated with folk designs of animals painted in a brown dye.

Following him was another man – not an Indian, Cori thought. The faint tinge to his skin was not so decidedly reddish, just the ruddy weathering of an outdoor life. He was almost as tall as Black, but thinner and less muscular, with light brown hair and pale blue eyes. His clothes were more conventional, pants and shirt of blue denim. As he sat with Black, the second man caught Cori staring and their eyes held for a moment. He smiled nervously, and she smiled back, eager to convey that she felt none of the animosity already evident from others in the bar. At Black's entrance the noise level had fallen sharply, and many of the cowboys were glaring at him with undisguised anger and contempt.

Black seemed oblivious to it, however. Cori overheard him say to his companion, 'What'll you have, Abel? C'mon, I'm buyin' – two firsts today calls for a celebration.'

As the two men conferred on their order, Cori turned back to Bren. 'It's rotten,' she said.

'What?' Bren murmured absently. Her gaze was still directed over Cori's shoulder at Ed Black.

'The way they're being treated. Did you see that sign outside another one of the bars, "No dogs or Indians allowed"? Imagine putting that right out in public. Gosh, they've got as much right to be here as we do. More . . .'

'This is the west,' Bren said flatly, looking now at Cori. 'This is how it's always been.'

'It's time things changed.'

Bren shrugged. 'They will someday. But it can't happen overnight, here or anywhere else.'

By 'anywhere else', Cori realized, Bren was referring to someplace quite specific. Since the Supreme Court had declared segregation of blacks and whites in the Southern states to be unconstitutional and ordered it ended, no bigger domestic issue had preoccupied Washington than bringing the laws into line. It was only in April that more than a hundred Southern Congressmen had publicly endorsed massive resistance to the Court's rulings.

After a moment, Cori said, 'How badly are we involved, Bren?'

Bren looked at her blankly.

'The company, I mean,' Cori added. 'What's Hartleigh Mining's position?'

'About what?'

'The way the Indians are treated.'

Bren stared at her. 'Why are you concerned?'

Cori replied thoughtfully, 'I'm aware there have been problems between the company and some of the tribes, and I don't like to think we – I mean the family would be—'

Bren cut her off. 'We have a lot of Indians working for us. If anything, we're giving them jobs, helping them earn a living. All right? Now, I don't think you ought to be worrying about it, Cor'.' Bren patted her sister's hand.

The patronizing pat would have made Cori angry, except she was more relieved that Bren's response had been so mild. Bren had a streak of cruelty inherited from G.D.; she could come down very hard when she wanted. For now, Cori felt encouraged to think the subject could be raised again, explored further – not now, but as they traveled.

The waiter returned with their order. When he started away after setting down the plates, a voice spoke nearby – softly, yet it carried: 'We're waiting to order drinks.'

Cori saw Ed Black and his friend still sitting at a bare table.

Acting as if he'd heard nothing, the waiter walked away, stopped at another table and jotted down orders on his pad.

'Did you see that?' Cori whispered hotly to Bren. 'He's not going to serve them.'

Bren was stoic. 'It's a little nicer than putting up one of those signs, I suppose.'

'Can't we do something?'

Bren gave her a lingering look. 'You really want to get mixed up in this?'

The question had the inflection of a dare, Cori realized, offering a last chance *not* to get involved. It seemed Bren had already formed some notion of what might be done.

Cori nodded.

At once Bren pasted a glowing smile on her face, leaned forward and called to the table behind Cori. 'We saw you ride today . . .' Ed Black looked at her. 'You were wonderful.'

The Indian was silent a moment, his glittering obsidian eyes shifting from Bren to Cori and back. 'Thank you,' he said.

Cori understood the tactic now. Join forces. Make a group. 'It was so exciting,' she chimed in. 'I haven't been to a rodeo since I was a little girl.'

Black stared silently at Cori. Then his eyes went again to Bren, and he nodded silently. He seemed to understand the women's intention, weighing the consequences of accepting it.

'Where was that?' The other man spoke up, smiling at Cori.

'San Francisco,' Cori replied, 'where my sister and I grew up. We're driving there now, but when we saw the sign for the rodeo we had to stop . . .' She was babbling, nervous about what they had started and unsure of how to continue. The background noise had softened even more, she was aware, everyone watching them.

'Have you been doing this a long time?' Bren said to Ed Black.

They stared hard at each other. Cori sensed the electricity passing between them.

'This is my first year,' Black said at last. 'They don't like us to ride. But I thought it was a chance to earn some money for me and my people. As good a way as any other we're given . . .' His voice took on a bitter edge.

Cori noticed that the second man's eyes hadn't left her, and each time her own glance went back to him, he smiled gently. He was very pleasant looking. 'Do you compete, too?' she asked.

He shook his head. 'I was in the rodeo, though. I'm the clown.'

Cori gazed at him admiringly. She had seen the daring chances the clown took to divert the bulls from harming fallen riders. It looked like bumbling clumsiness, but it took skill and courage.

'They don't mind us being clowns,' said Ed Black. 'They just don't like us to win.'

He had said 'us', Cori noticed. So were they both Indians? 'You won everything you were in,' she said to Black, to keep from staring at the second man.

'Everything they couldn't keep me out of,' Black said with a hard edge.

She recalled that he had missed the bareback bronc riding, then appeared later with bruises. Now it struck Cori that he must have been forced out of the event after his first win – must have had to fight some cowboys to get into the bull riding.

'Would you and your friend like to sit with us, Mr Black?' Bren asked.

The men exchanged glances. 'We'd better not, Miss,' Black replied.

Cori sat forward eagerly. 'Please. We saw the trouble you've had, and we'd like to help.'

The second man said, 'That's very kind of you. But it's not a good idea.'

Bren persisted. 'Why not?' She waggled her head invitingly at Black, her long blond hair falling over one eye. 'C'mon. A man who can ride one of those crazy bulls the way you do must really enjoy shaking things up.'

For the first time Black's lips curved in a thin smile. 'You are positive?'

'Yes, we know what we're doing,' Cori said, directing herself to Black's companion. 'Please.'

The men traded glances again, then stood from their table. Bren pushed back a chair. 'Sit by me, Mr Black.'

He still seemed hesitant. 'If you wish to know me,' he said, standing by the chair, 'call me by my name.'

'Ed . . . ?'

'No. It is Black Eagle. And this is my cousin, Abel Walker.' He gestured to the other man. They were still standing.

'Hello, Abel,' Cori said invitingly. 'I'm—'

She got no farther with the introduction before Charlie Mills came up beside the table. 'Pardon me intrudin' on you, Miss Hartleigh, but this just can't be allowed. Women of your calibre can't be drinkin' with their kind.'

'It's not for you to decide who I'll drink with,' Bren said calmly. 'I've invited Black Eagle and his cousin to sit down.'

Mills smiled thinly. 'Black Eagle, is it? So we're on a first-name basis now with the animals.'

Cori gasped. She hadn't imagined the show of sympathy would develop in one leap into an ugly scene. Turning to Black Eagle she saw his eyes blazing as he rose and stared at Mills. He was taller than the cowboy and appeared much stronger, but he stood rigidly, apparently determined to maintain control.

The men who'd been drinking with Mills stood and moved up behind him. The whole bar had gone as silent as a desert.

Abel Walker stepped to his cousin's side and put his hand on his arm. 'Let's go,' he said quietly.

The Indian kept glaring hotly at Mills. Abel Walker tugged at him.

Cori's heart was pounding so hard she could feel the pulse in her throat. 'We'll all go,' she said, starting to rise.

'No need for you to leave, Miss,' Mills said. He laid his hand on Cori's shoulder, firmly pushing her back into her chair.

'Keep your filthy hands off her,' Bren snapped.

Mills pulled his hand back with an exaggerated mime, as though he had burned himself. 'Oh, too hot to handle, is she? I might've said that about you, maybe, not your little sister. But redskins got such thick hides, I suppose it wouldn't burn 'em much if a couple of hot girls like you let *their* filthy hands give you a feel.'

Bren laughed defiantly. 'Might not at that,' she said, and Cori threw her a shocked glance.

Black Eagle remained silent. Motionless.

Abel Walker glanced at Cori, then came around Black Eagle to confront Mills. 'We'll go. First I think you'd better give these ladies an apology.'

'If that's what they really are, there wouldn't be a problem. But ladies don't fuck around with 'skins.'

Finally, Black Eagle spoke. 'Yes,' he said to Mills, with a studied calm, 'you will apologize.'

'Fuck you, redman. Now get outta here.' He gave the sisters a sneering look. 'And maybe I should let these rich bitches go with you, after all. I guess you can be a Hartleigh, and still be a whore.'

Like a snake striking, the Indian's arm suddenly shot out, his large hand viced around Mill's neck just under the jaw. The cowboy's wind was choked off. His eyes bulged.

A pair of his friends came flying out of the background. One threw an arm around Black Eagle's throat, the other swerved to the side and hacked his fist down on the Indian's arm, breaking his grip on Mill's throat. While the first man kept his strangle-hold on Black Eagle, Mills collected himself then stepped up and threw a vicious punch squarely into the Indian's face.

Cori screamed as Black Eagle staggered backward a couple of steps, blood flowing from his mouth and nose. Yet he remained upright, even with one cowboy still adhered to his back, his windpipe cinched shut by the man's forearm. Mills lunged again for Black Eagle, who somehow found the strength to swing a fist that caught the cowboy in the ribs.

Abel Walker had joined the fray. Grabbing the hair of the man strangling Black Eagle, tearing at it, he pulled him off, then delivered a roundhouse punch that sent the man sprawling onto the table where Bren and Cori were seated. They sprang up and pressed themselves against a wall.

'Stop . . .' Cori whimpered.

But Bren remained silent, watching with wide sparkling eyes like a spectator at ringside of a prizefight.

Other cowboys had left their tables. One grabbed Abel by a shoulder, spun him around, and swung a fist, but Abel deflected it and delivered his own punch. Once more Mills and his two cohorts went at Black Eagle who now stood back-to-back with Abel. With a lightning move, the Indian spread his arms, grabbed the edges of the nearby round table, and swung it up so it became a shield.

'Stop, no more, stop!' Cori shrieked, hands pressed to her head as if to keep it from splitting. The shrill pitch of her hysteria pierced through all the other noise and movement. Everyone froze and turned to her.

'Please,' she called out in a quavering voice. 'We'll go.' She glanced at Bren, then at Abel Walker, and Ed Black. 'We'll all go,' she repeated, pleading with them.

There was a frozen silence.

'Yes,' Abel said. 'We will go.'

Slowly, Black Eagle lowered the table, setting it back on its legs. The cowboys with Charlie Mills opened their fists.

Black Eagle swiped the back of one hand across his mouth, and looked at the smear of blood it collected. His black eyes went back to Charlie Mills, and it seemed he might explode again, but then the coiled tension of his body eased visibly. The truce had been accepted. The Indian started to raise his arm, and Mills flinched suspiciously. But Black Eagle kept his movement slow, unthreatening . . . and extended his hand toward Bren, reaching for her to leave with him. Abel reached out similarly to Cori.

'No,' Mills said. 'I changed my mind. The women stay.'

'It's not up to you, is it?' Bren snapped. She started moving toward Black Eagle.

'I think it is,' Mills replied. 'Up to me and any man here who cares about what's right.' His hand closed around the butt of the revolver in his holster, and he lifted it out, aiming straight at Black Eagle who stood ten feet in front of him. Over his shoulder, he said to Bren, 'You don't belong with him, Miss, you or your sister. This red trash should know better than tryin' to take you outta here.' He twitched the tip of the revolver in Abel's direction. 'Git! The both of you!'

'C'mon, Cori,' Bren said. 'They can't give *us* orders.'

'Stay put!' Charlie Mills roared, and thrust the gun in the direction of Black Eagle. Bren stayed where she was, and put out her arm, signalling Cori to stand back as well. It wasn't hard to see that Mills's control was teetering on a knife-edge, his hatred compounded by the humiliation of losing to the Indian at the rodeo. 'You know what's right,' Mills said to Black Eagle. 'You and your half-breed friend can't be mixin' with these women. So walk on out. And don't let me see y'again – ever!'

Cords of muscle in Black Eagle's neck stood out as he clenched his jaw, and held his hands at his sides. For ten seconds there was hardly a sound or a movement anywhere in the bar. Then Abel Walker moved to Black Eagle's side, and laid a hand on his shoulder, urging him to leave.

Very slowly the tall Indian raised his hand again, reaching for Bren.

'No,' Abel said, clutching now at his cousin's sleeve. 'It's not worth it.'

'I'm warning you,' Mills shouted shrilly.

'Go,' Cori called out. She was desperately sorry now that she had encouraged Bren to interfere.

His arm still extended toward Bren, Black Eagle took a step in her direction.

'If you wish to come,' he said, 'my hand is open.'

'Last chance!' Mills hissed. Around him other cowboys were murmuring. 'Never mind, Charlie.' 'The injun's loco.' 'Cool off, boy . . . have a drink and forget it.'

Black Eagle took another step toward Bren.

Suddenly, a desperate cry rose from Abel Walker – a few words, but in a language that only he and Black Eagle understood. The Indian glanced back at his cousin, and shrugged. Then he faced Bren again, and took one more step toward her.

The sound of the shot seemed as loud as a bomb detonating within the bar. The shock was such that for an instant none of those watching had any comprehension of what had happened, no trust in their own senses. They stood in a frozen tableau, waiting for a clue to reality.

It came, the stain of blood spreading across Black Eagle's chest, reaching to the shoulder of the arm that somehow he was still holding out. Cori wanted to scream, but her throat was paralyzed.

Black Eagle pitched forward, face down.

Abel Walker fell to his knees, and turned Black Eagle over. The shining onyx eyes stared up sightlessly. Cradling him, Abel looked up toward Cori, a desperate beseeching look as though of all the people there he thought she was the one who could take away his pain. 'He's dead,' Abel said, the tone somehow mingling disbelief and misery with a declaration of fact.

Cori felt he expected something from her. But she was frozen, unable to act. She turned to her sister.

Bren stared in horror at the dead man, the blood from his wounded heart puddling on the floor around him. It was the first time Cori had seen such confusion engraved on her sister's face. For once in her life, even Bren didn't know what to do.

3

Cori couldn't stop shaking. It was two hours since she'd seen a man she barely knew needlessly shot down in front of her, but the shock was no less fresh and devastating than if it had happened to a close friend only moments ago. Moment after moment, it went on happening in her mind. She heard the percussive bang, saw the red stain spreading across the pattern of dyed animals on Black Eagle's rawhide shirt, perceived the pain in the eyes of Abel Walker as he cradled his dead cousin.

She sat alone now in a small bare room at Rapid City police headquarters. Immediately after the shooting, Bren had grabbed her and urged her to leave the saloon. 'We mustn't get stuck in the middle of this,' Bren said. 'The police will want our statements, then the newspapers will get hold of our names, and that means trouble for the company. G.D. will blow his stack.'

But Cori refused to leave. She had seen a man slain in cold blood. She couldn't run off without telling the police exactly how it had happened.

'Damn it, Cori, the police don't need us for that,' Bren argued. 'A hundred other people saw it, too.'

Yes, Cori thought, a hundred others who didn't find anything wrong with forbidding dogs and Indians from entering a bar on signs that made no distinction between the two. Those people wouldn't have seen the killing the same way as she did. 'Go if you want,' she told Bren, 'I'm staying.'

Seeing Cori's determination, Bren stayed too. And when the police came, she had stepped up with Cori to say they had been involved in the incident. They had been taken to the police station to give their written statements. For more than an hour, while Charlie Mills was put through the procedures of being charged and Abel Walker was interviewed, the sisters had been left together in this waiting-room. Bren paced and went through a full pack of Lucky Strikes while Cori sat with her arms wrapped around herself, occasionally breaking into a spasm of crying that would last a few minutes. Finally, feeling protective of her delicate, less experienced sister, Bren lost patience. Yanking open the door of the room, she said to Cori, 'You need to get out of here and get some rest. Take it easy. I'll be back soon.'

That had been an hour ago, though the time mattered little to Cori. In a way, she felt she belonged here – imprisoned in this cell-like space. She deserved to be punished as much as anyone for what had happened: the murder would never have happened if she had not begged her sister to go to a rodeo.

Bren came briskly through the door. 'All right, it's settled. I phoned one of the company lawyers, after all; he spoke to the Sheriff and smoothed things out. The Sheriff is coming any minute to release us.'

'But I haven't told them anything.' Cori said.

'No need. I gave them a statement.'

'But mine might not be the same.'

'We were side-by-side. What could you see that I didn't?'

'He looked at me, Bren, not at you. I saw his eyes, the pain . . . the way he was begging me to do something about it, to tell the truth and make sure they get justice.'

36

'What are you talking about? Who looked at you?'

'The dead man's cousin, Abel Walker.'

Bren stooped in front of Cori and grasped her arms. 'Listen, I'm no doctor, but I can tell the shock of this has stretched you to the breaking point. They're ready to let us go, and that's what you need – to get out of here, and put this behind you.'

Cori looked bleakly at her sister. How could she ever put it behind her?

The Sheriff barged through the door, trailed by a deputy, both in silver-gray uniforms, stars pinned to their chests. 'Here I am, Miss Hartleigh,' he said to Bren, 'good as my word.' He was a large man with a foghorn voice and a belly sagging over a belt studded with cartridges for his revolver.

Bren stood. 'Thank you, Sheriff Winston.' She gave him the broad smile Cori had seen her use when she greeted Congressmen at her office. 'This is my sister, Corinne. She's ready to cooperate, too.'

The Sheriff nodded to Cori. 'Howdy, Miss Hartleigh. Got your statements all typed up. Soon as you two gals sign on the dotted line, you'll be outta here and on your way.'

His deputy, a thin man with a moustache, laid two sheets of paper on a small table in the corner of the room. The Sheriff pulled a pen from his breast pocket, and held it toward Bren. She took it, wrote her name at the bottom of one paper, then turned and held the pen straight out to Cori, as if it were a wand she were using to control her will. 'Come and sign,' she said.

Cori scanned the statement laying beside Bren's. Glancing from one to the other, she could see the language was identical. Each a single paragraph to testify that on the evening of 13 August, while visiting the Last Sunset saloon, they had witnessed a fistfight between Charles B. Mills and a Lakota Sioux Indian named Edward Black Eagle Crying Wind, a.k.a. Ed Black, that ended with Mills fatally shooting the Indian. That was all.

Cori glanced up at Bren. 'It's not that simple. Didn't you tell them, Bren?' She turned to the two lawmen. 'The fight was over. Black Eagle and his cousin were willing to leave the bar, but they wanted us to—'

'They know all that, Cori,' Bren said.

'Yes, indeed, Miss Hartleigh,' the Sheriff jumped in. 'Your sister gave us the full picture. For legal purposes, though, what really counts is who shot who and what was goin' on at the time. All that's right in there.' He pointed at the statement waiting for Cori's signature.

'No, it doesn't tell the story,' Cori insisted. 'There was no reason to shoot. Mills started the fight because he hates Indians and he was mad about losing at the rodeo, and when he tried to force us—'

The Sheriff moved up right next to Cori. 'Listen here, Miss Hartleigh.' His deep voice took on a strained edge. 'This situation is plenty bad enough without addin' extra problems. Let's face it, Hartleigh Mining's an important name in these parts. If it gets played up that you two girls were right in the middle of this thing – that we had white man and red man fightin' over ya – won't do nobody no good. Don't ya see? It'd get the Indians more stirred up against the Hartleighs. Then we'll get all kindsa people takin' sides. Could turn into a lot more'n a shooting.' His voice softened. 'Now, there's a bunch of newspaper fellas outside tryin' to find out what's what. I've kept 'em coraled 'til now, and I'd dearly like to get you out the back door before you get spotted.' He glanced to Bren. 'That's what I promised your lawyer fella.' His eyes came back to Cori. 'But you gotta do your part.'

'Cori,' Bren pleaded gently.

Where did her loyalties lie, Cori asked herself, to a stranger – or the family? She glanced at the statement again. If too little was explained, still there were no lies. And the single most important thing was there: Mills had fired the fatal shot.

The rest could come out at the trial.

Cori took the pen and signed. The Sheriff immediately swept up the papers and passed them to his deputy. As he guided the two sisters out into a corridor, he assured Bren that the statements would be photostatted and duplicates sent to Hartleigh Mining's legal counsel.

'One more thing, Sheriff,' Cori said. 'If Abel Walker is still here, I'd like to see him for a minute.'

'Oh, he's here, Miss Hartleigh – fact is, he'll be right here for a while. But it wouldn't be wise to let you two talk while we're holding him.'

'Holding him?' Cori repeated. 'He didn't do anything wrong.'

'Well, he was fightin' along with the rest. But the reason we're gonna keep him is he's a material witness; we can't take a chance he'll disappear on us before we've got our facts straight. Let these kind wander off, you never know if they'll come back. Slippery as a 'skin can be, it's even harder to trust a breed.'

'A breed?' Cori echoed questioningly.

'Half-breed. This Walker fella's a peppermint stick, see – white mama and a red daddy all spun together.'

Behind the Sheriff, the deputy snickered.

These men were no different in their prejudices than Mills, Cori realized. So what was the real purpose in getting her to sign that bland statement? She thought back over its meager facts – one man had shot another after a fight. Suddenly it struck her: the way it was worded, there was nothing to prevent Mills from pleading self-defense.

'Are you holding Charlie Mills, too?' Cori demanded abruptly. When the Sheriff didn't reply, she turned to Bren. 'What's going on, Bren? Didn't they arrest Charlie Mills?'

'Yes, they arrested him,' Bren said.

But Cori heard an ironic twist in her tone. 'Where is he now?'

'Can't hold a man if he makes bail,' the Sheriff said.

'But you'll keep Abel Walker?'

'When a man's bein' held as a material witness,' said the Sheriff, 'that's not open to bail.'

It was crazy, Cori thought: the innocent man was kept in jail because he was a witness; the murderer was already free. 'I want my statement back,' Cori erupted. 'I shouldn't have signed it!'

They had reached a door at the end of the corridor. The Sheriff pushed it open. It led outside to a dark lot where several police cars were parked. 'Walk across this lot, Miss Hartleigh,' the Sheriff said to Bren, 'that'll bring you to—'

'It was murder!' Cori shouted. 'I won't let you call it anything else.'

Bren touched her arm, 'Cori, we're finished here.'

'No! We can't let them do this!'

Bren grabbed Cori's wrist, locking her fingers onto Cori's delicate bones with a painful grip. 'They're not doing anything wrong, Cor'. Mills has been charged, but he made bail, so he's out. They'll keep Walker a day or two to make sure they get all his testimony.'

'And give him a chance to cool down,' the Sheriff added.

'Don't want him scalpin' anybody for revenge.' The deputy spoke up for the first time.

Cori felt desolate. There was little she could do now, she decided, unless she went directly to those newspaper reporters the Sheriff had mentioned. But that would betray the interests of her family. Bren had done everything possible to keep the Hartleigh name out of the incident; by calling a company lawyer, it was probably being handled so G.D. wouldn't learn about it.

The Sheriff seemed to know Cori had surrendered. He pushed the door open wider. 'G'night, Miss Hartleigh,' he said curtly to Cori. 'And Miss Hartleigh.' He smiled at Bren.

Cori hesitated only another second before stepping outside. The air, surprisingly cool for a summer night, gave her a bracing lift. She let Bren steer her away, across the parking lot, into a street that led back to the hotel. In the room, she obliged her older sister by taking two of the tranquilizers that Bren always traveled with, and getting straight into bed.

But all the time until sleep came, she kept thinking about the 'half-breed', Abel Walker, seeing in her mind's eye the way he had looked at her after Black Eagle was shot.

They left Rapid City the next morning, Bren driving; Cori felt too shaky to take the wheel. Before midday they had crossed the state line into Wyoming. Cori insisted they keep the convertible top up. Today the sun hurt her eyes, irritated from the tears she'd shed last night.

Bren tried to keep the atmosphere light, tuning the car radio to stations carrying the latest top-ten hits, singing along with Patti Page, Perry Como, and the Ames Brothers. But the songs did nothing to dispel Cori's rage and despair about the killing, and the attitude of the police, which gave every indication that Charlie Mills was going to be let off easily.

'I can't forget that sign I saw outside a bar,' Cori said bitterly at one point. ' "No dogs or Indians allowed" – as if they were the same. Those policemen acted as if they thought so, too. As if shooting an Indian was no worse than shooting a dog. Imagine, an hour after the killing, the murderer was already walking around free.'

'That's the system everywhere,' Bren countered. 'A man's innocent until proven guilty. But posting bail isn't the same as going free, Cor'. For someone like Charlie Mills, that five hundred dollars they made him put down, is a fairly heavy—'

'Five *hundred*?' Cori echoed. The figure was so ludicrous, she was sure she'd heard it wrong, or Bren had made a mistake. 'The charge was murder, Bren. Bail for murder couldn't be set so low. You mean five thousand, don't you?'

Bren busied herself looking for a new radio station with less static. Only when Cori persisted did Bren tell her that five hundred dollars was indeed the correct figure . . . and the actual charge brought against Charlie Mills was not murder, but second-degree manslaughter. The lesser crime allowed for the possibility that the shooting had been negligent or accidental.

'There was nothing accidental about it,' Cori said indignantly. 'Bren, we can't let him get off so easy.'

'It's not our battle. These stupid cowboy and Indian fights have been going on for a hundred years. Certain things are forbidden, but that Indian went after them anyway. He should have done what he was told, just walked out of that bar without trying to take us along. If he had, he'd still be alive.'

'How can you say that?' Cori cried. 'The reason Ed Black didn't leave is because you played up to him, led him on! And that made Mills burn because you'd also flirted with him.'

Bren tossed her head. 'Christ, you expect me to blame myself? That big Indian practically dared the cowboy to shoot him. Not to mention that you were the one who pushed me into talking to him.'

'That's true,' Cori murmured guiltily. 'That's why I *do* feel responsible.'

'Well, you're nuts. Nobody's responsible except the bum who pulled the trigger.'

'And nothing will be done to him,' Cori muttered dejectedly. But it was pointless to go on discussing it. Not that Bren held any sympathy for the hatred and bigotry that inspired and condoned the Indian's murder. To Bren, Cori knew, a man was a man; if Black Eagle hadn't been shot, Bren would have probably ended up going to bed with him. But Bren's work as a lobbyist had also accustomed her to working within the system, accepting things as they were and finding a way through all the loopholes to get whatever G.D. and the company wanted, so that she never stood back to see what was right or wrong, never thought there were things that ought to be changed. As long as she made the system work for her, Bren never gave a thought to whether it was corrupt.

Even without asking for the details, Cori was certain now that the Hartleigh company must have conducted its business to take advantage of a status quo which paid little respect to the rights of the Sioux tribes who claimed ownership of the South Dakota mining lands. Hadn't the Sheriff mentioned something about the potential for Black Eagle's killing to get the Indians even '*more* stirred up' against the Hartleighs?

For too long she had turned a blind eye, taken the comfortable easy path of keeping herself ignorant of the company's practices, lived off her father's wealth without caring how it was acquired. But last night her conscience had been aroused. Now it wasn't going to be easily pacified.

The family's Golden H Ranch in Jackson Hole consisted of a compound of large log-sided buildings set at a picturesque turning of the Snake River, facing across its rushing rapids to vast meadows and rolling ranch land that stretched away to the foot of the Grand Teton mountains. The Hartleigh property was more than twenty thousand acres; it was possible to ride all day without reaching the boundaries. Inside and out, the houses and outbuildings were designed in a rustic style in keeping with the rough-and-ready image of ranch life. Rooms filled with rough-hewn furniture and local crafts, bathrooms with old-fashioned fixtures, in the dining-room a long table of varnished pine planks which could sit twelve on a side. All this quaint rusticity was only a mask, however, for the same luxury that prevailed in all the Hartleigh homes. The ranch, though used by the family no more than eight or nine weeks a year, had a domestic staff of five always in residence, keeping the house always ready for visitors, right down to vases of fresh 'wild' flowers – actually grown in a greenhouse on the ranch – in each of the ten bedrooms. There were gardeners, and a man who tended the pool and tennis court, and ranch hands detailed to keep the riding horses in good condition. The few hundred head of prize cattle that could be seen grazing in the pastures across the river were not there to make the ranch a paying proposition, so much as to complete the living painting G.D. liked to see from his rustic log porch.

Nevertheless, from the earliest times that Cori had been brought here, she had always treasured the ranch as a blessed relief from the stiff gilded refinement of the Hartleigh mansion on Nob Hill, the Fifth Avenue duplex in New York, the Caribbean beach retreat in Jamaica's Round Hill, and the one hundred and eighty-foot yacht that cruised the coast of California and Mexico. The ranch brought out the independent tomboyish streak that had been smothered by the finishing schools and debutante cotillions Cori had been forced to attend. From the time she had demonstrated a love for horses, Cori had been given one for her own at the ranch, a spirited roan she'd called 'Peg', short for Pegasus. There was no greater pleasure in her life than to climb on Peg and gallop out across the meadows, up into the foothills of the Tetons, to ride for hours along a crest looking out over a landscape as unspoiled and breathtaking as it had been a thousand years ago. At those times, life could seem so heartbreakingly simple and beautiful that Cori invariably wished she could stay forever.

Once, when she was twelve, and had just taken Peg up into the hills by herself for the first time, she had ridden home at dusk to find her father waiting for her where the horse waded back across the river shallows.

'I was worried about you,' he said.

She had apologized for worrying him, and explained she had gotten lost in a daydream. The land was so magically beautiful, she said, she had never experienced anything more exhilarating than being in the middle of it, alone except for the horse to take her as far and as fast as she wanted to go. 'I like to pretend I'm a pioneer woman,' she had told her father, as she took Peg to the barn and he walked with her, 'seeing it all before anyone else. It must have been wonderful to be the first . . .'

He had laughed. 'Wonderful? There were murdering Indians behind every tree, and wolves and rattlesnakes and diseased water, and a girl wouldn't ever get a chance to go for lovely joy rides alone, she'd be so damn busy from sun-up to sundown washing and cooking while the men tamed the land. It's a pretty dream, Corker' – his pet name for her – 'but, I doubt you'd have liked being a pioneer woman.'

'I wouldn't have minded all the problems, either,' she insisted. 'It's solving problems that makes life interesting. Life's too boring when everything's easy.'

'Are you bored, Corker?' he asked with concern. He had done everything possible to make her life easy.

'I didn't say that,' she replied, anxious not to hurt him. 'I was just saying I wouldn't mind living here all the time.'

He had laughed again.

Since that time, though she never failed when she came to the ranch to take one of her long solitary rides, and pause at the peak of a ridge to consider what it must have been like when the land was empty and play with the notion of making a life here now – she always ended the fantasy by hearing that memory of her father telling her what a grinding, dangerous place it had been.

She heard it now as she rode back across a meadow toward the compound after being out in the hills with her horse all morning. Yesterday evening, after she and Bren arrived at the ranch, the shock that had gripped her since the killing had culminated in an exhaustion so complete it bordered on paralysis. When she'd awakened this morning, though, with the first rays of a rising sun shining straight through a window onto her face, her energy had been fuelled by a desperate impatience to see Peg and go for one of her long rides into the hills. She'd dressed, collected some fruit and biscuits and a thermos of orange juice from the kitchen, and ten minutes later she was on Peg, galloping full tilt toward the hills. The wind rushing in her face seemed to carry away with it every burden, every worry, every bad thought. Now, coming back, she felt miraculously restored.

As she cantered her horse toward the stable, Cori saw Buck Stovall waiting for her, and she broke into a broad smile. Buck was one of the first men who had been hired to work on the Golden H fifteen years ago, a cattle wrangler whose job was to tend G.D.'s herd of prize steers. Buck was a cowboy in the true mold of the old west, a nomad who'd gone from one job to another for thirty-five years taking nothing with him but his horse, bedroll and a few weeks' pay. When he'd picked up news somewhere that a ranch called the Golden H was looking for an experienced wrangler, he hadn't realized that he'd be signing on to be more of a pet handler than a real ranchhand. When it did become clear that the Golden H was only a show operation for the man who owned the biggest gold mines in the country, Buck had thought of quitting. But two things had made him stay. One was his age; at fifty-three, it was time he settled somewhere. The other reason was purely sentimental. In his first month on the ranch, the Hartleigh family had visited for a couple of weeks, and one afternoon, passing the stables, he'd seen the little seven-year-old daughter getting a riding lesson from a fancy-pants instructor in jodhpurs who'd flown in from San Francisco for a couple of days. Buck had seen right off that this little girl, small and delicate as she was, had an easy confident manner in the saddle, a natural affinity with the horse. The only thing that made her appear stiff and uncomfortable was that she was being taught in the refined

English way – posting up on the trot, reins held separately in both hands – never mind that all the saddles and bridles for the ranch horses were the western variety.

Later, when he'd spotted the kid practicing in a ring on her own, Buck had wandered over, and offered a few tips about riding western style – 'plant your butt firmly in the saddle and stay with the movements of the horse, and hold those reins in one hand, so you can steer the animal with just a touch of the leather to one side of the neck or the other.' The looser style of riding had suited the kid perfectly.

In the days that followed, he became the one who took her out on trail rides, and showed her how cattle could be herded on horseback, and – so he claimed – taught her how to talk horse language, so it would do what she wanted with only a click of her tongue or a soft crooning sound. It was Buck who had first taken Cori out to show her the trails that led up into the hills.

At the end of that two weeks, before their private plane would fly the Hartleighs back to San Francisco, Cori had sought him out. 'I'll see you when I come next time, won't I, Buck? We'll go for some more long rides.'

'Sure, kid. I'll look forward to it.'

He hadn't been sure he'd meant it at the time, but it had become a reason to stay, after all. When he thought about what he'd seen of the Hartleigh family, it was obvious the father didn't have time for the kids. The little girl had always been so desperately eager for time with Buck, so ready to take him on as a substitute father. And for Buck, who'd always been a loner, the adoration of the beautiful little girl had given a lift to his heart that became surprisingly important to him.

So he stayed for the next time she came . . . and then the next after that. Though they had never said a word about it in such terms, over the years Buck and Cori had become close. With everything else Cori loved about the ranch, Buck was at the heart of it. He seemed to know her as no one else did, and he treated her not as the reserved, delicate 'baby of the family' which had become her role with her parents and siblings, but as strong and capable and adventurous – a pioneer woman.

'Well, look what the cat drug in,' he said now, as Cori trotted up to the barn. 'Or should I say the Cat-illac? I seen that shiny new buggy o' yours sittin' out front.'

He often kidded her about being spoiled – not in a mean way, but because he knew so well that she preferred the simple things.

'My graduation present from G.D,' she said, a bit defensively as she hopped down out of the saddle.

'I should've remembered, you're a fully educated woman now. Let me look at ya.' He took her hands in his, and raked his eyes up and down. 'Yes, indeed, you do look a whole lot smarter.'

She laughed, and kissed him lightly on his rough unshaven cheek, and he hooked an arm half around her and patted her on the back. He never gave her a full embrace, always careful not to step completely over the boundary between himself and the daughter of his employer.

'And you don't look a bit different, thank God,' said Cori.

'Dumb as ever, y'mean.'

'Oh, no, Buck. You've got to be the smartest man I ever met – at least, the only one who knows how to talk to horses.' Looking at him, her eyes shone with affection. In the time she'd known him, he'd gone from being fifty-three to sixty-eight, and yet he hardly looked a day older. Dressed as always in frayed denims and scuffed boots, a two-day growth of stubble usually frosting his chin, his shaggy graying black hair poking out under the brim of his ancient stained Stetson, Buck was still one of the most attractive men Cori had ever seen. He resembled Clark Gable – without the big ears – but much more weathered, the lines around his pale blue eyes more deeply

48

etched into skin made leathery-brown by wind and sun.

Cori led Peg into the barn, and Buck followed along. While she watered and unsaddled the horse, he asked how she'd liked her stay in Washington – she'd sent him a postcard of the Lincoln Memorial – and what her plans were. From her listless answers, he soon suspected that, while she was politely honoring his interest, something more serious than general news was on her mind.

'What's wrong, Corinne?' he asked – he'd always addressed her by the full name. 'You in some kinda trouble?'

'I'm not in it myself, Buck,' she said. 'But it seems to be all around me.' She told then what had happened in Rapid City. While she curried the horse, she talked steadily. After filling him in up to the time she'd been allowed to leave the Sheriff's headquarters, she said, 'All these years, Buck, I've never thought much about how my family got rich. Sure, I knew all the stuff about my great-grandfather coming west without a penny and finding gold . . . but I just kept my eyes closed to everything else that had to be involved. Then this summer, I saw the way my sister worked to make sure the government does things in a way that's best for us. And when I put that together with the way I saw those Indians treated, I wondered if we were any better than that murdering cowboy, and the police who let him go.' She was having trouble holding back tears by now. 'Buck, it's my family. But now I have this terrible feeling that maybe we've been lying and stealing to get what we have. And I don't want to be part of it. Suddenly, I don't want to be who I am.'

She put her face down onto the soft hide of the horse's flank, and surrendered to the tears.

Buck got up from the stool where he'd sat listening in the corner of the stall. 'Corinne, honey,' he said, laying a hand on her shoulder, 'there's no way to get out of bein' who y'are. And that's nothin' to mind about. No matter what name you go by, you're a might good person. And bein' such, it's just as well you are a Hartleigh. That puts you in the best place to change things the way you'd like to see 'em changed. If you're all tore up by what you saw a coupla days ago, seems to me you're never gonna feel right about it, unless you stay with it. Don't close your eyes no more – startin' with what happens about that killin'. Keep right in there, and be at the cowboy's trial and make sure the truth gets told.'

'It's no use, Buck. Bren won't back me up, and there'll be twenty or thirty other witnesses – friends of Mills's, people who think Indians are worthless – who'll all tell it another way.' After a moment, she said, 'The scariest part is what G.D. would do to me. He'd see it as being . . . well, a traitor to the family. You know my father, Buck. When he's mad—'

Buck gripped her shoulder, and pulled her around to face him. 'Honey, you can't let that stop you from doin' what you know is right. Not you, Corinne, you're just not the kinda person who'd be able to ride on easy if you didn't at least try. It's not your style.' He smiled at her. 'It'd be like someone tryin' to ride English in a western saddle.'

She nodded, and her own smile broke through.

'I know how tough it is to think of doin' anything your daddy wouldn't like. But remember, if there's anybody G.D. Hartleigh's ever had a soft spot for, it's you. He's the one bought you that shiny red car . . . and this fine horse here,' he slapped Peg on the rump.

Cori looked lovingly at Buck, 'But you're the one,' she said, 'who taught me not to fall off.'

4

Balloons and confetti rained down inside the cavernous Cow Palace, and the orchestra went into the fifth repeat of the song Irving Berlin had written to promote the man who had won the presidency four years ago and was being renominated tonight.

> I like Ike
> 'Cause Ike is good on a mike
> I like Ike . . .

As the thousands of delegates sang out heartily, Dwight David Eisenhower stood on the podium with his Vice-President, Richard Nixon, and their wives. All were grinning and waving, but it was Ike's beaming smile that had all the genuine candlepower. He was an easy man to like, and he was a war hero, the man who had overseen D-day; there was no doubt he'd be re-elected.

In a box overlooking the podium, Cori sat with her mother and father, Bren and Chet, the brother who had been born between them. A younger version of G.D. in almost every way, Chet was tall, and broad-shouldered, with full brown hair framing a handsome square-jawed countenance. He looked especially like G.D. tonight, Cori thought, as they sang out support for Ike together. Cori had rarely seen her father sing – not even 'Happy Birthday' at their parties – but tonight he was booming out every verse of 'I Like Ike'. His voice surged after Ike looked directly up at the box, and gave G.D. a personal wave. As one of the largest financial backers in the Republican party, George Dennis Hartleigh had been invited to the White House numerous times during Ike's administration.

'He looks great, doesn't he?' G.D. enthused as the rest of the crowd went into a sixth repeat of 'I Like Ike'.

'Mamie's looking a little better, too,' Pamela Hartleigh responded to her husband. Thin and poised, always sleekly coiffed and decorated with just enough jewelry to parade her wealth without being vulgar, Pamela Hartleigh regarded Eisenhower's wife with more pity than admiration. It was well known among political intimates that Mamie had become a chronic alcoholic during the war years when Ike was overseas and carrying on an affair with the woman army officer who had been detailed as his driver.

'Let's hope they can keep her dry through a few big campaign appearances,' said Chet Hartleigh. 'Women might be turned off if they learn the First Lady is a falling-down lush; the women's vote is getting to be a real factor in these elections.'

' "Getting to be," ' Bren mimicked sharply. 'Where the hell have you been, Chester? Women have had the vote since 1912.'

Chet hated being called Chester, a name given in tribute to G.D.'s father. 'But they haven't used it much as a group,' he shot back at Bren. 'The essence of voting is making up your mind – something you women have a notoriously hard time doing.'

'Is that so?' Bren countered. 'Back in Washington, I don't

just make up my own mind, I get plenty of weak–minded men like you to make up theirs exactly the way I tell them.'

'And we all know how you do that, don't we?' he sniped.

'Children, please,' Pamela's genteel voice cut through the singing crowd.

'If this shithead is going to run me down,' Bren snapped.

Chet fought back. 'I'm not going to let her tell me—'

'That'll be enough of that, both of you,' G.D. commanded. Instantly Bren and Chet retreated to silent fuming.

Cori gave her father a timid sidelong glance. Under his full mane of white silky hair, above the black and white of his tuxedo and tie, his square chiseled face looked especially florid. Was it from anger, or the August heat in the auditorium? She wondered how he would deal with her if he knew what she'd been busy doing since coming back to San Francisco. How quickly and furiously would he tell her 'that'll be enough of that'?

Determined that the murder of Black Eagle should not be unjustly dismissed, she had obtained a list of Rapid City lawyers from the South Dakota Bar Association, and begun calling cold, seeking one who would keep track of the case and report developments to her, and also locate Abel Walker to protect his interests.

The first lawyer she'd contacted had dismissed her. 'I don't like the idea of being a snoop, Miss Hartleigh. And, frankly, I don't want this scalphunter for a client. Around here, people think he and his cousin picked the fight. I can't represent anyone if I don't believe in their case.'

She had gotten similar replies to the first dozen calls. Then she found a man who said he'd do the job, but only on condition that some work for the Hartleigh company was also steered to him. His pressure offended Cori, all the more since what she was doing was personal, probably at odds with what the company would want.

Calling down the list, she connected at last with a lawyer named Steven Nevelson. As he answered his own phone, not a secretary who reeled off the string of names usual for a law firm, Cori guessed he might work alone and need the job she offered. When they talked about the case, he sounded young and genuinely sympathetic. She agreed to a retainer of two thousand dollars.

'One more thing,' she told Nevelson. 'If you think it will help Mr Walker to have a lawyer, give him all the help he needs and I'll cover the costs. But my part in this has to be kept strictly confidential.'

'Even from the client?' the lawyer asked.

'Especially from him,' Cori answered. 'I'm afraid he'd be apt to refuse help if he knows it came from a Hartleigh.'

The lawyer seemed to accept her reasoning. 'He's bound to ask the source, though. How do you want me to explain it?'

'Can't you say that the case interests you personally as a matter of principle?'

'I can do that, yes.'

Cori arranged to contact him at the end of each week to get his report. She didn't want him calling her, that would increase the chances G.D. might find out.

The first time she checked back, Nevelson told her he had learned that Abel Walker lived two hundred miles from Rapid City on the Rosebud reservation, one of several in South Dakota assigned to the Lakota Sioux people. He had also discovered that, while Mills had been charged with second-degree manslaughter – 'that applies to a killing done with reckless disregard for human life,' the lawyer explained – charges of disturbing the peace and assault had also been filed against Walker. The lawyer had gone to the Rosebud reservation to offer his help in fighting the unfair indictments, free of charge. But Walker had turned him away. 'He thinks I'm being sent in to undercut him,' Nevelson told Cori, 'paid by friends of Mills. It'd be much easier for Mills to win acquittal if the charges against Walker stick.' To overcome Walker's resistance, the lawyer urged Cori to allow him to reveal who would be paying the bills.

Still, she refused. 'I can't let my involvement be known, Mr Nevelson. But keep trying, please.'

Cori had called him again just yesterday. Nevelson reported that he had returned to the reservation and had persuaded Abel Walker that he was sincere in donating his help as a matter of principle. 'It was tough getting him to trust me, but I think he does now.'

Knowing that she was helping justice to be done made Cori feel better than she had at any time since the killing.

Now, as she sat in the Cow Palace, watching the self-satisfied celebration of the politicians looking forward to four more years of power, she felt the stirrings of disgust and rage. There was so much wrong with the country when such injustice could be done to its original citizens, who had roamed the land freely before anyone else, wisely used its natural resources to support themselves, while preserving its beauty. Would these politicians do anything to change the situation?

Cori glanced again at her father. Among the thousands here, he was one of the richest and most powerful. If only she could bring him around to her point of view, he could do so much – particularly with the influence he had in South Dakota.

He caught her looking and winked. 'Having fun, Corker?'

She forced a smile. Yes, she was his favorite, she knew. But did she dare take the chance of telling him the truth?

To cap the close of the convention week, G.D. Hartleigh gave a large party at his Nob Hill mansion for all San Francisco's richest Republican campaign contributors. Many had already given generously, but G.D. knew that by setting the example of waving another twenty-five thousand dollars contribution of his own, he could probably shake loose a substantial sum to help the party defray expenses. Campaigning was getting to be a much more expensive proposition. In the old days, you could put your nominee on a train, the newspapers would write about his whistle stops, and that would provide all the exposure needed. Now there were planes to charter, hotel rooms for big staffs required everywhere – and it was beginning to look like paid advertisements on television might deserve a big chunk of cash. You could make people believe anything if you said it the right way on television. It might not be long, G.D. thought, before television would be the whole ball game. He planned to tell Eisenhower the campaign should film some ads and pay the networks to run them. Shots of Ike standing on Omaha Beach after D-day, that sort of thing – images of the natural leader.

Always a perfectionist, G.D. went downstairs half an hour before the party was to start and wandered through the mansion's huge living-rooms, library, and ballroom, making sure everything was ready. Overseeing such preparations was Pamela's province, and she always did a fine job, yet G.D. never delegated anything one hundred per cent. He made sure there was enough champagne and that it was being properly chilled, he took a tiny taste from one of the mounds of caviar in silver bowls to be sure it wasn't too salty, he surveyed the floor in the ballroom to be sure it was polished but not too slippery. Then he lined up the servants to make sure they understood their duties. Eisenhower would be at the party, he reminded them, but there was to be no gawking or breaking ranks to ask for an autograph. G.D. detailed his own English butler to stand by Eisenhower, and serve him exclusively.

That done, he glanced at the platinum Rolex on his wrist and saw that he still had fifteen minutes before the first guests would arrive. Time enough, he decided.

He rode the elevator up from the large entrance to the third floor of the mansion, where each of his children had a suite with bedroom, sitting-room and bath. At the end of the long corridor he knocked loudly at Cori's door. 'Corker?'

She opened the door wearing a dressing-gown, her hair still damp from bathing.

G.D. frowned. 'Not ready yet? You know, I like you girls down there to help your mother greet the guests.'

Cori moved back into the room. 'I'm sorry, Daddy. But Bren's so good at parties, you don't really need me.'

G.D. followed her across the sitting-room, back into a bedroom where she sat down at a dressing-table and started brushing her hair. 'I know you're not as much of a social animal as your sister, Corker,' he said gently. 'But you've got your own way of charming people. Every bit helps set a mood so everyone feels good, and that makes it easier to get them to part with a bit more money.'

'I'll be there, Daddy,' Cori said. 'I'll just be a few minutes late.'

'Good, Corker. You really *do* add something, you know.'

She smiled at him in the mirror. He sat down on a corner of the bed from which he could watch her reflection in the mirror. What was it, he wondered, that made him love this child the most? Perhaps it was because she was the most unlike him, a testament to the fact that even if he knew himself to be a tough bastard, and his wife a vain slave of status, something in the genes had enabled them to produce a person of tenderness and intelligence and extraordinary goodness – as if rough engineers had turned out a delicate work of art. If only, he thought, he was able to govern his own actions by her example. But he found it impossible to go against the iron in his own nature.

'There's been so little chance to talk,' he said, 'since you and Bren got back. You know I don't mean to ignore you, Corker, but with the President himself here in town, and all the parties and convention sessions . . .'

'I know, Daddy,' she said understandingly. Not that they ever sat down for great long chats. He was always busy with something.

'If we'd had a chance, I suppose you would have told me all about your trip across country . . .'

She turned from the mirror to regard him warily. Was he testing her reaction? Could he know what had happened in Rapid City? Expecting G.D. would be furious at the negative potential if the Hartleigh name became embroiled in the murder of an Indian, she and Bren had sworn a pact that neither would tell. Bren had been especially concerned, since G.D. might assume it was her flirtatiousness that precipitated the incident. But knowing how ambitious Bren was, Cori didn't rule out the possibility that she could have decided to make points with G.D. by parading her honesty, being the first to confess. Yes, she realized as she saw the way he was looking at her now, G.D. knew already.

'No,' she answered him contritely. 'I didn't plan to tell you everything.'

When he nodded as if sympathetic with her answer instead of showing any surprise, she knew she'd been right. She had been foolish to imagine he wouldn't find out somehow.

'Protecting your sister, is that it?' he said. 'From what I've heard, this whole thing might not have happened if—'

Cori broke in. 'No, Daddy, it was my fault. We saw these two men being humiliated, and I thought we should help them, and . . . it all went wrong.' The memory was suddenly so fresh, Abel Walker cradling his cousin and gazing up at her beseechingly, that she started shaking again, and tears sprang to her eyes. Putting her face down into her hands, she murmured brokenly. 'It was so terrible, the worst thing I've ever seen . . .'

G.D. rose and came over to the dressing-table. Stroking her hair, he said, 'You should have told me.'

She looked up at him. 'How did you learn about it?'

From the inside pocket of his tuxedo jacket, he brought out and handed to Cori a long letter from a lawyer employed as outside counsel to Hartleigh Mining. The lawyer began by reporting that he had been asked by Miss Brenda Hartleigh to act secretly for her, but that 'on due consideration', he had decided his primary responsibility was to the company, and accordingly it would not be outside the bounds of his duty to inform G.D. of all the details.

The letter went on to describe fully what the lawyer had done, proudly mentioning that, with the cooperation of police and newspapers, he had managed to keep the Hartleigh sisters from being named as witnesses in the case. Finally, he reported that one of the principals in the incident, a Sioux of the Rosebud tribe named Abel Walker, was being defended against related charges by a Rapid City lawyer named Steven Nevelson. 'There has been some question about who is bearing the cost of Mr Nevelson's representation,' the letter continued, 'but I have ascertained that these expenses are being paid by Miss Corinne Hartleigh. This may be with your knowledge and consent, but in my opinion it could jeopardize my efforts to keep the family and the company from being placed in a very unpopular position. Accordingly, I thought it essential to keep you advised.'

Corinne looked up from reading to meet her father's eyes. She felt better knowing that at least it wasn't Bren who had betrayed her.

'Is it the truth?' he said.

She nodded. He lifted the letter out of her hand, and tucked it back inside his jacket. After a long silence, he said, 'When you were a little girl, you were always the one who'd come home with some sick animal you'd come across, a bird who'd fallen out of a nest, a stray cat. But one time you brought home a pigeon you'd found lying somewhere, and it turned out that it didn't have a broken wing, it was seriously diseased – with something that could even affect humans. I got the thing out of here fast, and had it destroyed . . . and you cried. But the important thing was to keep you well, and to protect the family.'

Cori looked away. She hadn't forgotten it either. In her own recollection, the pigeon hadn't actually been 'destroyed'. It had been taken away by a maid and thrown, alive, into a garbage bin.

'It's no different with this, Corker,' G.D. went on. 'You always want to do good. But when it has the potential to hurt you and the family, I can't allow it.' He fixed his gaze at her, expecting automatic agreement as usual.

But this time she couldn't give it to him. The analogy he'd used had touched a nerve, reminding her of that hateful sign she'd seen outside the Rapid City bar. 'Daddy, we're not talking about an animal! Abel Walker is a *man* – a victim. His cousin is the one who was murdered, but the way he's being treated, it's as if he's a criminal – as if any Indian who gets shot deserves it.'

'Corinne, I told you I understand why you want to help. But it doesn't change the fact that we simply can't afford to take sides in this.'

'There's right and wrong,' she cried out. 'Why can't we afford to be in favor of what's right, and against what's wrong?'

He stared at her, not stumped by the question so much as simply amazed: his children had been taught never to argue with him. Under his accusing gaze, Cori herself became aware of the gravity of her transgression.

'Daddy,' she appealed, 'if you'd been there—'

'It must have been awful,' he said flatly. 'But it's in the hands of the law now, and you're out of it, and that's the way it will stay. First thing in the morning, you'll dismiss this lawyer, Nevelson, from the case. Is that perfectly clear?'

'Yes, Daddy.'

He hesitated a moment. 'I've always depended on you to obey me, and I expect you will now. But if I learn you've disregarded my wishes, I will take measures that would make it impossible for you to direct any more funds to this cause.'

She signaled her understanding with an obedient nod.

Still standing over her, G.D. stroked her hair once more, then glanced at his wristwatch. 'Guests will be arriving any minute. I'd better go.' He moved to the door of the bedroom. 'Don't be late coming down, Corker.'

'I won't, Daddy,' she murmured.

He went out.

Cori turned to the mirror and looked at herself. So good, so nice and respectful, so refined and delicate, such a good daughter – she ran down the list of things she knew people said about her. Nothing bad in any of that. So if she couldn't change, maybe that was no reason to feel ashamed.

She picked up her hairbrush and began stroking it across her hair. How bad would it get if she actually disobeyed G.D.? He'd spoken about cutting off funds, but what else might he do? Wasn't she his favorite?

Her hair was done. She put down the hairbrush, and picked up an eye pencil, her hands beginning to move more quickly and deliberately. G.D. had said she really would add something important to the party. She mustn't be too late.

5

Cori hated to abandon her help to Abel Walker, but she feared the consequences of defying her father. It was obvious that Steven Nevelson must have violated her confidence; she doubted now she could go to any lawyer without G.D. learning about it.

She informed Nevelson by letter that 'due to unforeseen circumstances', it would be impossible for her to cover any fees beyond the retainer, but she hoped he would ration his work so that the initial payment would cover some continuing help to Walker. Though she was angry at the lawyer for failing her, it wasn't Cori's style to scold or complain. She conveyed her feelings in the letter's chilly tone, and concluded – because G.D. must not ever see mail coming to the house from a Rapid City lawyer – 'if the wishes of a client, even a former client, mean anything to you, please do not even reply to this letter, but regard our business as terminated'.

With the political convention over, life settled into its usual routine. G.D. and Chet went to work at HMC's new skyscraper headquarters, Cori's mother busied herself with social engagements, and Bren returned to Washington. Cori started looking for a job teaching children, though Pamela thought her younger daughter should be leaving herself free for the more important task of finding a husband. Bad enough that Bren was almost thirty, and still single. Cori persisted, however, and her qualifications, coupled with her prominent name, were enough to win her a position teaching second grade at Wickham-Hunt School, a private institution that drew its enrolment from other Nob Hill families.

It took Cori a few weeks to get a full grasp of her job, but she had a knack for communicating with children, and was soon at ease in the classroom, and adored by her young students.

She wondered occasionally about the case in Rapid City, but it receded from her thoughts as she became engrossed in her teaching, and reabsorbed into the pleasant social rhythms of the city. Though known to be shy, Cori received a constant stream of invitations to parties and requests for dances from the sons of men in the same tier of wealth as G.D. Hartleigh. Many of them, she found an excuse to decline. She preferred being home evenings, designing projects for her students and assessing their homework, to the empty babble of a party.

There was one man, however, with whom she always enjoyed spending time. Frank Patterson, whose family owned the *San Francisco Observer*, the city's leading morning paper, had been her classmate from kindergarten through graduation from high school. As children they had often played at each other's houses, in later years they had been able to rely on each other for advice and solace at any time relationships with other peers became too difficult or intense. While Cori was at Wellesley, Frank had been at Princeton, and they had kept in touch with letters or phone calls. Though close friends, it had never occurred to them that they could be more than platonic. Once, when Frank had come up to Cambridge with the Princeton crew rowing against Harvard, he had invited Cori to the race, then had taken her for dinner at the Ritz, and afterwards to a nightclub in Boston. She had felt so comfortable with him every moment, even in his arms as they danced at the club, that it only consolidated the bond of friendship. With other college boys, she always felt tension, some sense of danger or risk which Cori perceived as what she should expect with anyone who might attract her as a possible husband and future lover. How could Frank be either when she'd known him forever? Though she believed any man she chose to marry would have much in common with Frank. Kind, smart, interested in the world and the arts, he was also very nice looking – with straight, sandy brown hair, gray eyes, and a strong chin.

Since her return to San Francisco, Cori had seen Frank Patterson only a few times. She was wrapped up in her teaching, and he was busy with the job he'd been given on the newspaper – city news reporter – a rung up the ladder on his way to someday taking over for his father as editor and publisher. Also, she knew from their conversations when they had been together, he was dating a couple of girls fairly seriously. Sometimes he talked to her about the problems they gave him. For her part, she confided in him that she had still met no one who interested her as a potential husband and lover. Long ago, she had told Frank she intended to remain a virgin until after she married.

'What a wonderful old-fashioned girl you are,' Frank had said then.

Why did it have to be called old-fashioned, Cori wondered, if you believed that sex was a gift to be saved for the man with whom you intended to spend your life?

On the night of the presidential election, there was a party at the Patterson home to celebrate Eisenhower's resounding victory – their newspaper had strongly endorsed Eisenhower. The Hartleighs were invited, and Cori happily went along, always eager to see Frank. She was less pleased to see that his date for the party was a young woman who, as the evening went on and she drank more champagne, began openly nibbling on his ear and sneaking her hand across his crotch. She was beautiful, but obviously a slut, and Cori had to repress the impulse to march up to Frank and tell him he deserved better.

Nevertheless, Cori held her tongue when Frank left the girl to come over and talk. 'You should be happy,' he said. 'Another term for Ike means another four years of your father being a frequent guest at the White House. Four more years that are bound to be good for Hartleigh Mining.'

'What makes you so sure that everything good for my father and the company should make me happy?'

He knew her very well, and it was obvious from the remark that she was hinting at something troubling her. 'What's wrong, Cori?'

For all the honesty that was common between them, she hadn't previously mentioned anything about the shocking events that had occurred on her trip across country. Not mentioning it was part of smoothing it out of her life, and she also hadn't been certain that Frank wouldn't agree with G.D. about staying clear of the situation. The politics of the Pattersons had always been similar to those of the Hartleighs.

But the celebration around her made it that much harder to bear the things about the country she wished she could change. So she told Frank now. He listened intently, leading her away from the noisy party to the quiet of his room as the story went on.

'I feel like such a coward,' Cori said, when she came to admitting she had withdrawn her help to Abel Walker. 'I should be doing more, but I'm afraid to go against G.D.'

'Cori, your father is just trying to protect you. The way that killing is being handled isn't fair, I agree. But you'll only make yourself unhappy by getting in the middle of it, maybe even put yourself in danger. You have nothing to be ashamed of –

you've paid to provide legal help for that Indian.'

'It's the least I could do. Frank, I never thought about it before, but over the years Hartleigh Mining has probably been responsible for a lot of injustice to the tribes in South Dakota.'

'You don't know that . . .'

'I've seen the attitudes that prevail. I've seen how easily we could take advantage of them.'

'Cori, whatever the truth is, you're not responsible – and you can't change something so big single-handed.'

She was ready to accept that as the last word. But as they returned to the party, Cori realized she might feel better if she didn't have to go on guessing about the company's policies. And Frank was particularly well situated to help her. Would he be willing, she asked, to use his position at the newspaper – access to back files, contacts to other news services and information sources – to compile a picture of the way Hartleigh Mining Company has dealt with the South Dakota Sioux over the years?

'I don't mind doing it,' Frank said. 'But think, Cori: do you really want to know?'

'Maybe not,' she said. 'But I *need* to.'

On Monday of the following week, she came home after school to find an envelope in her mail marked with the Rapid City return address of Steven Nevelson. The letter informed her that the trial of Charlie Mills for the killing of Black Eagle was scheduled to begin in Rapid City two weeks hence. Though attached to neither side in the case, Nevelson wrote, his concern for Abel Walker made him anxious to see Mills suitably punished, and Cori's testimony about events leading up to the killing could make all the difference in whether or not the trial resulted in some degree of justice being done.

'Your sister's testimony would also help,' Nevelson went on, 'but she claims that her work in Washington makes it impossible to leave. Lawyers for your family have obtained consent for the written statements signed by you and your sister to suffice in place of an appearance in court by either of you. But your past interest in helping Mr Walker leads me to hope there is still some chance you might be willing to come and testify in person, although I am aware it would put you in a difficult position.'

The letter alarmed Cori. The family mail was always sorted by servants, left in separate places for each family member. It was possible that G.D. had mentioned to the staff that he wanted to be informed of any indication that Cori was still following the case. The fact that company lawyers had already arranged, without her knowledge, to relieve her of the necessity to testify left no doubt that G.D. was keeping aware of the case himself.

Yet Cori was also puzzled. She had assumed it could only be Nevelson who had betrayed to G.D. that she had helped Abel Walker. But that didn't tally with the sensitivity he expressed about her position, nor with the fact he had obviously continued working independently on behalf of the Indian.

For the next few days, she agonized over how to respond to Nevelson's plea. Even Frank had told her she was better off to stay clear. She watched for any sign that her father knew she had been contacted, but she saw none.

On Friday, when all her classes were done, she went to the school offices. Using a telephone there, she called Steve Nevelson. As usual, he answered the phone himself.

'My father has forbidden me to become more deeply involved,' she explained to him, 'and I can't go against his wishes. I'm sorry. I might have been freer to act if he hadn't found out I hired you, but you have only yourself to blame for that.'

'Myself? In what way?'

'I asked you to keep my involvement with the case strictly confidential, but—'

'I did,' the lawyer insisted. 'Absolutely.'

'Mr Nevelson, do you have a secretary?'

'No,' he said pridefully, 'not yet.'

Cori couldn't prevent a faint smile. The answer bespoke youth and ambition. 'Then only two people knew I hired you, the same two people talking on this telephone. And I didn't tell anyone—'

'Nor did I!' he declared. It sounded like he was getting angry.

She let it rest. No one else could have given her away – she hadn't even told Bren – but there was no point in arguing about it. 'Mr Nevelson, all that matters now is that as much as I wish I could help, I can't. Please don't contact me again.'

'Don't you even want to know what happened to Abel Walker? You paid me to defend him . . .'

Yes, she realized, she wanted very much to know. 'Tell me,' she said quietly.

'Only a few days after you last wrote me, he was prosecuted for trespassing, disturbing the peace, and assault. I got the assault charge dismissed. He was sentenced to six weeks in jail on the other charges.'

Cori expelled a sigh. It was so massively unfair. 'Is he still there?' she asked.

'No, he got out a week ago. If you come to the Mills trial, you'll see him. He'll be testifying for the prosecution.'

'I'm sorry, Mr Nevelson. It's not possible for me to come.'

But after she hung up, Cori could not chase from her mind the memory of the man who'd been called 'a breed', lanky and blue-eyed, the gentle smile he'd given her when they met, the anguish on his face as Black Eagle lay dead in his arms.

As she came down the ramp from the commuter plane, Cori knew instantly that the man standing halfway between the landing area and Rapid City's small air terminal must be Steven

Nevelson. There was a general air of 'lawyerness' about him – stolid medium build, dark hair in a no-nonsense trim, spectacles with tortoise-shell rims. And of course the bulging briefcase he held in one gloved hand. He wore a squarish blue-serge overcoat buttoned up to the collar against a November wind that seemed to grow more biting minute by minute as the sun sank closer to the horizon.

He stepped up to Cori as she reached him. 'Miss Hartleigh?'

'Yes . . . Mr Nevelson.'

'I can't tell you how grateful I am that you agreed to come.' He smiled warmly, the first crack in his lawyerly façade.

'It's not a gift or a favor,' Cori said as she followed him into the terminal to await her baggage. 'I'm here because I felt there wasn't any choice but to come and tell the truth.'

In order to tell the truth, however, she had first needed to lay down a path of lies. At the school, she asked to have a few days off so she could travel east to interview at a graduate school she might enter to obtain a master's degree in education. At home, she said she was feeling worn out by the stresses of controlling a roomful of seven-year-olds day after day, and that she had been granted some 'sick days' which she intended to spend on the ranch at Jackson Hole. She told G.D. and her mother not to worry, she would call them daily, and telephoned Buck to instruct him that if any telephone calls came from her family, he should cover her absence – say she was out riding, taking a nap, gone to bed early. Because of Buck's seniority at the ranch, and the fact that the family visited there only rarely, Cori felt certain the staff would follow his lead before any loyalty to G.D.

She drove with Nevelson to the hotel where he had reserved a room for her. During the ride in his old wooden-sided station wagon, he brought her up to date. The trial had been in progress two days; a jury had been empanelled, opening arguments had been heard, the prosecution had presented most of its witnesses.

'I hope you'll testify tomorrow,' he told Cori. 'I've informed the prosecuting attorney you'll be in court, and willing to take the stand.' After a pause, he added. 'But it's not certain you'll be called.'

'I don't mind if I have to stay a second day. But if it goes beyond the weekend—'

'Miss Hartleigh, I can't guarantee the prosecution will call you at all. I have no official capacity in this case.'

'But you asked me to come!'

'I asked you because having you here gives Abel Walker and all his people their only chance that you *might* be used.'

Cori was bewildered. Believing she might bring insights and information no one else could provide, she had taken the risk of defying G.D. How could her testimony *not* be used? Was this all a trick? She still hadn't completely recovered her trust in the lawyer.

Nevelson reminded her of the hard facts: the prosecution was not particularly eager to mete out the harshest punishment to Charlie Mills.

'So I came for nothing,' Cori muttered in dismay.

'That's not certain yet,' the lawyer said. Her presence in court would make it harder for the prosecution to avoid calling her. Especially if local newspapers raised questions about it: Nevelson said he had friends among local reporters who were primed to do just that.

Leaving Cori at the hotel to settle in, he asked if she would have supper with him later in the hotel dining-room. 'I wanted some time with you to prepare in the event you do testify tomorrow, and I thought that would give us an opportunity . . .'

She acceded.

Later, after they sat down to dinner, he said, 'Before we go any further, I'd like to clear the air between us on one very important matter. I fully understand why you wanted your interest in the case to be kept confidential, Miss

Hartleigh, and it should have been. But—'

She cut him off. 'Mr Nevelson, my father is a powerful and influential man in this state, and I can see you're a young lawyer trying to build a practice. I suppose it was only human for you to feel you might score a few valuable points by letting it be known you were representing his daughter. I can forgive you now that I see you're truly dedicated to helping the Indians.'

He stared at her coldly. 'You can forgive me, can you? That's so kind of you, Miss Hartleigh.'

Cori was taken aback by the acid twist he had given his words.

'But the fact is,' he went on, 'you have nothing to forgive. As I tried to tell you, I honored our agreement absolutely.' He had been no less disturbed than she was, he said, that their confidence had been breached. He had spent some time investigating the matter, and the answer had finally occurred to him when he was making a routine stop at the bank one day to withdraw some funds for his office. 'I remembered then that the check you wrote to me for my retainer was printed with your name and address.'

'That's right!' Cori exclaimed. 'So if my father had people from his company snooping around, that would be enough . . . Oh, Mr Nevelson, I'm the one who has to be forgiven. Can you ever? Blaming you, when all the time . . .'

His cold manner melted at once. 'It was an easy mistake to make,' he said. 'Ever since Shakespeare wrote something like "kill all the lawyers", people have had a hard time trusting us. Now let's order something to eat, then we can run through your testimony. I want you fully prepared for anything the defense might throw at you.'

As he sat across the table, listening to her story, coaching her on how to present the facts for maximum effect, Cori became steadily more impressed by his sincere devotion to obtain a fair result in the trial.

By the time they were having coffee, they had worked their way through the coaching session, and they were on a first-name basis.

'Tell me, Steve,' Cori asked, 'did the retainer I paid end up covering the time you put in defending Abel Walker?'

He shrugged. 'I didn't really keep track.'

If he hadn't, she suspected, it was because he had put in so much time. 'If I hadn't fired you,' she said, 'I imagine I'd owe you quite a bit of money. I'll try to find a way to pay my bill.'

'Never mind. I went on with this case as much for myself as for you. There *is* a matter of principle involved.'

Cori felt a fresh pang of guilt for the way she had misjudged him. 'At least,' she said, 'you can let me pay for dinner.'

But he wouldn't even let her do that. 'You've done more than enough just by coming,' he said. 'Now let's hope we can get you on the stand.'

There were six rows of spectator seats in the courtroom, divided into two sections by a center aisle. When Cori walked in the next morning escorted by Steve Nevelson, she saw that both sections were nearly filled. As faces on both sides of the aisle turned to look at her, she also realized that each section was occupied by a different faction of opposing interests. To her left, the seats were filled by cowboys and the women who had been with them at the Last Sunset the night of the shooting. On the other side of the aisle were a group of approximately fifty men, women and children she had never seen before – though they all eyed her with a friendly combination of sympathy and hope. They were all from Black Eagle's tribe, Cori realized. Many wearing beaded leather dresses or vests, their shiny black hair adorned with feathers or other traditional ornaments of horn and turquoise and leather, they had evidently dressed to draw proud attention to their shared heritage, and that of the dead victim. Gathered in tribal dress as if for a ceremony, they clearly meant to put the court on notice that an unjust verdict would be taken as one more crime against their people.

Nevelson led Cori to the front of the section occupied by the Sioux, and they sat down in two open places, apparently saved for them. They were the only whites on this side of the aisle. Glancing around the courtroom, Cori saw that Abel Walker wasn't there. When she asked Nevelson about it, he explained that Walker was scheduled to appear as a prosecution witness, and was thus barred from being present for the questioning of other witnesses.

'Then how can I be here?' Cori asked.

'Because you're not a scheduled witness – and the whole point of having you in the courtroom is to show you are available, to embarrass the prosecution so much for not using you that they have to relent.'

'Will I be allowed if I've heard other testimony?'

'You can be – with a ruling from the judge.'

Cori could guess that the judge might have his own political motives for ruling against her.

Just before the judge entered to take his place at the bench, Charlie Mills turned from the prosecution table and caught Cori's eye. He grinned at her no less smugly than if he had already heard himself pronounced innocent.

The trial resumed where it had left off the preceding day with the state attorney for the prosecution questioning a man Cori recognized as a friend of Mills's who had joined in the fight with Black Eagle. His testimony established that Black Eagle had been shot when Mills's gun 'just went off'. In the cross-examination that followed immediately, however, the defense attorney drew out the fact that Mills and Black Eagle 'barely knew each other', implying that there was no motive for one man deliberately to shoot the other, thus it could only have been accidental.

Of course, Cori reflected, true motive didn't require any relationship beyond racial hatred to exist. Not to mention the fact that Mills probably bore a grudge against the Indian for beating him earlier in the day in two rodeo events. None of this was brought out, however.

The next witness was a specialist in ballistics from the state crime laboratory. His brief turn for the prosecution verified that Charlie Mills's gun had been fired only once, and the bullet discharged was the one removed from the dead man. But on cross-examination, the defense attorney got the expert to state that his testing of Charlie Mills's Colt revolver revealed that it had a sensitive trigger that might have gone off accidentally.

Next, the prosecution called Abel Walker to the stand.

When he faced the courtroom to take the oath, his soft blue eyes found Cori in the gallery. He looked lankier than she remembered him – thinner perhaps from the stresses of his own prosecution and the ordeal of jail – and his face still reflected all the sadness she had seen at the time of the shooting. She ached to help him, but all she could do for now was give a smile of encouragement, which he returned with a small nod.

The events he described were exactly as she would have told them herself, Cori thought. But on cross-examination, the defense attorney managed to discredit him completely. Was it not true, Abel Walker was asked, that he had been sent to jail himself on charges arising from the incident in which his cousin had been killed? Didn't that prove that neither of the two men was a wholly innocent victim, and that they must share responsibility for any outbreak of violence?

As the defense attorney raised these points, Cori could see Abel fighting to control his temper. The muscles in his jaw knotted visibly as he clenched it tight before delivering each calmly measured answer. The section of Sioux who had come to support him were also making an effort to control their emotions. Around her, Cori heard them muttering angrily about the badgering to which Abel was being subjected. But outwardly they, too, maintained their composure.

Then Abel was asked a question that pushed him over the edge.

'Even in the version of events you've given us, Mr Walker, it seems your cousin had many chances to walk out unharmed. By staying and challenging Mr Mills, wasn't he deliberately taunting Mr Mills into shooting him, almost as if he had . . . a death wish.'

Abel Walker repeated the phrase very quietly. 'A death wish. Perhaps,' he continued, his voice growing steadily louder, 'perhaps, then, it's fair to say that every time an Indian fights a white man it must be because of a death wish. Every time we have fought to keep land, to keep what is ours, every time we have fought to keep our basic rights and our self respect, it is proof of our death wish. Because we have never had an equal chance, have we? And we should have known that even to fight for what is ours would bring death.' His voice had risen nearly to a shout, his control shattered. 'We should know that the white man has always wanted us to fight because then he can shoot us down, kill us off, clear the land, take our treasure, take our souls!'

In the gallery of Sioux, some had gotten to their feet, and begun crying out in their own language, agreeing with Walker's bitter denunciation. The judge began bánging his gavel, calling for order.

Abel went on roaring above the tumult. 'The *wasicuns* can eliminate us as they wish, without any consequence – just as is happening here!' He bolted up and pointed at Charlie Mills. 'Just as that man can commit murder without being—'

The shouts of the judge drowned him out. 'Bailiffs! Remove that man from the courtroom!'

A pair of armed court officers had rushed in from the corridor at the outbreak of the commotion. They seized Abel Walker by his arms, and dragged him off the stand toward a side door. As he went past the gallery, Cori thought she caught his eye for a fleeting moment, and she tried in that instant to send a silent message of sympathy. But he was gone before she could even be sure he had seen her.

As the courtroom returned to order, the judge announced that Abel Walker's tirade would earn him a citation for contempt of court punishable by ten days in jail. The gallery was warned against any further demonstrations, then the judge told the prosecution to call its next witness.

'No further witnesses, Your Honor,' said the state's attorney, giving Steve Nevelson and Cori a boldly defiant glance.

Seized by fury, Cori sat forward, a shout of indignation starting to rise in her throat. But Steve's hand instantly viced on her arm, pulling her down.

'It's no use,' he hissed. 'You'll only get charged with contempt yourself.'

The trial proceeded to Mills's defense, a few witnesses who testified that 'Ed Black' had been asked to leave the bar peacefully, but had refused, escalating the situation to violence. As proof of Black Eagle's violent nature, one rodeo cowboy testified that after winning the saddle bronc riding event, the Indian had gotten into a fight with a couple of other contestants which had prevented him from riding in the bareback event.

If there had been a fight, Cori knew, it had been initiated by the cowboys to prevent Black Eagle from entering an event he was sure to win.

After the court returned from a lunch recess, Mills's defense was completed. There were quick summations by both sides, then the jury was sent out. They reached their verdict in an hour. Much to Cori's surprise, the jury foreman announced that Charlie Mills had been found guilty of second-degree manslaughter.

The defendant was instructed to rise to hear his sentence. The judge then intoned a few words about the gravity of the offense, and explained it was within his discretion to decide the term of imprisonment based on an assessment of mitigating circumstances, and the character of the defendant. 'From what I have observed in this court, Mr Mills, I believe it is reasonable to sentence you to prison for a term of one-to-three years.'

The gallery of Indians stirred. It was a kind of victory – a white man actually imprisoned for killing one of their tribe.

The judge continued, 'However, as the court feels that you are not a danger to society, and have expressed remorse for these unfortunate events, I am exercising my prerogative to suspend sentence.'

Instantly, the Indians' murmur of pleasure changed to a low angry growl. The judge banged his gavel loudly once more, and declared the trial at an end.

Cori sat in stunned silence. She glanced to Steve. He was also in shock, his body rigid, face gone pale. Then Cori turned and saw Charlie Mills receiving congratulatory slaps on the back from his friends. And on the other, the Sioux were muttering in futile anger. Abel Walker would spend another ten days behind bars, the man who had shot down Black Eagle in cold blood would not spend even a single one.

As the monstrous injustice sank in still deeper, it was not fury that overtook Cori but grief. Putting her face down into her hands, she cried as pitifully as if she was mourning not for a stranger but for someone she had loved all her life.

6

Cori stopped the rented car where a metal sign, weathered letters stenciled on a rusted white background, was planted amidst a stand of sagebrush on the dusty shoulder of the road. She got out and stood in front of the sign to read it:

NOTICE

YOU ARE ENTERING THE ROSEBUD SIOUX RESERVATION.
WITHIN RESERVATION BOUNDARIES ALL ARE SUBJECT TO
TRIBAL LAWS AND MAY BE PUNISHED ACCORDINGLY.

It was almost as though she were crossing the frontier into another country. Except here there were no barricades or passport checks. In fact, there was little besides the sign to mark any boundary. Stretching ahead were fields of dry sunburnt grass undulating in low hills and valleys dotted with an occasional lone tree, a landscape no different than what she had just driven through. The only other demarcation was a change from the smooth well-maintained concrete of the state highway to the cracked, pitted asphalt of the road continuing onto the reservation.

Cori got back in the car, and sat for a minute, gathering fresh resolve. Every step of the way – leaving the Nob Hill house, at the airports where she departed and landed – she had stopped to question why she was making the trip, what she hoped to accomplish, what meaningful words she could say when she arrived at her goal. She had no certain answers, yet each time she had pushed ahead. As now she turned the key in the ignition and drove on.

After returning from the trial, she had been plagued all through winter and spring by a guilty sense that she might have done more to get her own version of events placed into the record, and her memory that the confrontation leading to Black Eagle's death and the injustice meted out to Abel Walker had begun with her attempt to show them friendship in the midst of hostility. She had felt a growing impulse to do something – anything – to purge herself of the nagging self-recrimination.

The desire intensified after Frank came to her with the result of his research into the land battles between Hartleigh Mining and the tribes collectively known as 'the Sioux Nation'. As he outlined the history, the seven separate tribes of the Lakota Sioux had once roamed freely through the Black Hills and millions of acres of plains as far south as Texas, drifting in the wake of the great herds of bison which provided their food, clothes, the hides for their shelter and many other needs. In the mid-nineteenth century the miners had come, gold had been found, and the battle lines were drawn. As the pioneers moved west, extending the size and reach of the American republic, the government in Washington seized jurisdiction over these rich mining lands, and a long effort had begun to settle peacefully the conflict between Indians and settlers. It was never possible, though, that the government would fully grant the Indian claims; the need was too great for precious metals coming out of the same earth the Sioux claimed as tribal hunting lands. Each promise made to the Indians was broken as miners kept making new, more valuable finds. The Indians were forced to battle for their land. Through the decades up to the turn of the century, there was a steady cycle of fighting interrupted by efforts at peaceful settlement.

The claim staked by Cori's great-grandfather, Eamon Hartleigh, had contained the richest veins of gold yet discovered. This gave him the means to buy up surrounding claims, and absorb profitable mines started by others. Eventually Eamon, then his son Chester, came to personify the mining interests protected and advanced by the policies coming out of Washington and enforced by the US army. The Hartleighs had consolidated their hold on vast tracts that were formerly Sioux territory by the time an agreement was reached to carve out a separate reservation for each of the seven tribes. None included any of the land valued for mining. Later, as veins of ore were discovered extending across boundaries, the Hartleighs had extended their operations, and the company had beaten the Indians in court whenever ownership of these resources was contested.

'So we've stolen from them,' Cori said after listening to Frank. 'A lot of what we have should be theirs.'

'That's not how the courts saw it, Cori. It was all done legally. You don't have to feel guilty because your family is in a business the government views as vital to its economic health.'

'What about the health of those people? Most are very poor. Black Eagle was competing for rodeo money so he could bring it back to his tribe.'

'So? Don't the cowboys compete for the same reason – to make a living?'

'Frank, don't you have any sympathy for these people?' It was the only time Cori had ever thought of Frank as being insensitive.

'Sure. There's a lot we should do to help. But trying to turn back the clock isn't one of them. The Apaches used to roam over a part of Arizona where Phoenix now stands. The Seminoles had the land which is now Miami. And wasn't it the Iroquois who got talked into selling Manhattan for twenty-four bucks? What should we do now? Give back the cities? Let them have the resort hotels? Or fill in mineshafts so the buffalo can roam again?' Frank's questions were no easier to answer than the ones she asked herself. The one thing Cori did know was that she couldn't do nothing.

A friend from her dorm at Wellesley, Valerie Barton, lived in Denver. The Bartons were in the oil business, the sort of wealthy family G.D. would feel comfortable having Cori pay a long visit. Cori phoned Val Barton and asked her help in constructing an excuse for a trip away from San Francisco.

'You want to say you're visiting me,' Val ran back the story, 'but you're going somewhere else? Cori, what are you up to?'

'I'd just rather not have my family know where I really am.'

'Oh, I get it. There's a man involved . . .'

'That's right,' Cori said to satisfy her friend's prying. It was, in a way, true.

To extend the time she could be absent without G.D. objecting, Cori said that after the Bartons she would go to the ranch in Jackson Hole, maybe even spend the rest of the summer there before returning in time for school.

Now, as she drove across the reservation land, Cori wondered why she had made plans that would permit her to stay away so long? Certainly, the sights that were unfolding around her made it look like an unpleasant place to spend time, much less inhabit. Here and there, houses stood at the end of dirt tracks that led off the cracked asphalt road, but none of them was large or attractive. Most were no more than shacks with tar-paper siding and tin roofs, the best were pre-fab huts with only a few rooms, or trailers cemented onto cinder-block foundations. Between these dwellings were smaller huts that Cori guessed were outhouses. Rusted car wrecks littered the dusty infertile areas around many of the houses. There were few trees to provide the relief of shade from the summer sun, few flowers to add a refreshing touch of color to the sere brown of dried grass, the pale powdery earth. Where the houses stood near the road, Cori could see children toddling around, the younger ones usually only half-dressed, the older ones in frayed hand-me-downs. There were also many dogs, scrawny animals Cori spotted wandering far from any house as if abandoned to fend for themselves.

It occurred to her suddenly that while she had been taking in these impressions of the general poverty, she might have already traveled past the place she was seeking.

After driving another few miles, she saw a roadside shack behind two gas pumps. A painted sign hanging from the eaves read simply 'Reservation Store No. 2'. She pulled into a small parking area of cinders fronting the small building, and stopped by a battered pick-up truck.

Inside the small store, the walls were hung with shelves crammed with canned foods, clothing, rifle ammunition, and motor oil. A stocky middle-aged man in a lumberjack shirt sat behind a counter wedged into one corner. From his features, Cori guessed he was not an Indian. His eyes narrowed suspiciously as she entered, but he said nothing.

'I'm sorry to bother you,' she said, 'but I wonder if you have a telephone book or any kind of directory that would give me the address of someone on the reservation.'

His face didn't change, but there was a small movement of his head as though he had stifled a laugh. 'You think these folks got addresses for their houses, or phones hangin' on their walls? Got a phone in the store they can use for a price, that's about it.' He pointed to the wall phone by the door. 'But no such a thing 'round here as a die-reck-tory.'

'Well . . . how do I find someone?' The reservation covered many hundred square miles.

'Ask around.'

The man seemed so gruff and unfriendly Cori almost left, but she decided not to waste the opportunity. 'Do you know where I could find a man named Abel Walker?'

'Walker . . .' he murmured the name to himself two or three times, before shaking his head. 'Not one of my customers.' Cori turned to go. 'Hold on,' he said then, 'I'll call one of the other stores. You could travel around here for days, and these 'skins'd tell ya nothin' if they weren't in the mood.'

The storekeeper used the wall phone to make a series of calls. Evidently there were several stores like this one spotted around the reservation. From what Cori could hear of the conversations, the first two calls led nowhere. But on the third the storekeeper's reactions indicated he was getting useful information.

'Oh, *that's* the guy . . . didn't connect it with the name . . . yeah, well that explains it, I guess. Tell me that again . . .' The storekeeper took the nub of a pencil hanging from a string tacked up near the phone, and scribbled on a scrap of paper from his counter. 'Thanks, Hal,' he said at last. He hung up and turned to Cori. 'Got your man.'

'Thank you.'

He studied her up and down. 'He's said to be a dangerous type, though. Didn't connect it with the name at first, but I heard the story – some months ago him and a friend almost killed a cowboy up in Rapid City.'

Cori drew in a steadying breath and said nothing. She didn't have the time or energy to correct the misconception seeded by the previous injustices. It was only Abel Walker to whom she owed explanations or apologies.

'You seem like a nice quiet lady,' the storekeeper went on, 'not what we usually see 'round here, so I wanted to be sure you know what you're in for.' He handed over the paper with his notes. 'Those are your directions where to find the fella.' She thanked him again.

'Oh,' the storekeeper added as Cori reached the door, 'I wrote his name down there, too.'

She stopped, confused. 'But I have his name.'

'What you told me is the name he uses off the rez – his white name. Around here, you'll get farther knowin' his Indian name. It ain't Walker. It's Walks-Through-Fire.'

The directions sent her five miles farther on, past Reservation Store No. 3 and a small clapboard building marked 'Rosebud Post Office', to a crossroads marked by a wooden church. Turn left, another two miles past Store No. 4, to the next dirt road on the right. All along the way, she saw more shacks, rusted car hulks, dogs and children. Sometimes, too, there were groups of men standing and talking at the roadside, or around a car pulled up at a store or the post office. But there was little industrious activity, little evidence of anything *happening*. Of course, Cori realized, people had to be doing things somewhere – building, working, accomplishing. Perhaps the sense of stillness and languor was natural for a day like this, the sort of lull that might descend anywhere in the heat of summer.

Taking the last turn, Cori found herself on a dirt road that snaked up a low hill to end at a pair of shacks with raw plywood siding, and roofs that were a crazy quilt of tile, tin, wood, and asphalt shingle. There were many figures moving around the bare ground outside the shacks: several young children and a couple of toddlers, a woman standing over a washtub, another elderly woman knitting as she sat in a dilapidated easy chair that was placed by itself on the hillside, a man wearing jeans and an undershirt who was planing a piece of lumber propped on a pair of sawhorses. Here, too, several gutted car wrecks were scattered not far from the shacks, their doors hanging open, the seats pulled out and lying on the ground nearby. Some of the kids were scampering through the car bodies, or bouncing on the seats outside – their playground.

As soon as they saw Cori's car approaching, the children stopped playing, the older women and the man turned to look at her. Their eyes stayed on her as she got out of the car and walked up the hillside to the crest. Cori felt their suspicion, but she forced herself forward.

She thought the old woman in the easy chair might be the easiest to talk to. 'I'm looking for a man named Abel Walks-Through-Fire,' she said, stopping by her chair. 'I was told this is his home. Is he here?'

The old woman stared back with rheumy eyes as she picked up a smoldering cigar from a plastic ashtray perched on the arm of her chair and took a puff. She said nothing. Then Cori became aware of the children, pooled into a group at one side, giggling. She glanced at them, embarrassed yet warmed by their innocent mirth. They were all unwashed and shabbily dressed – and all beautiful, with huge glittering black eyes, and shining black hair, and faces that glowed in the sun as if a reddish light was shining within just under the skin. Cori smiled at them, and their giggling increased.

The man in an undershirt working at the sawhorses set his plane down and came over to Cori. 'She doesn't speak your tongue,' he said, nodding at the old woman.

'Oh. What I told her was—'

'I heard,' the man said. He was short and wide, though not fat, just solidly built. His face was owlish, the eyes narrowed in a constant squint, yet he didn't seem suspicious or unfriendly. He pointed a finger across the crest of the hill. 'Walk that way. You will find Abel.' He turned without another word and went back to his task. Cori called her thanks after him.

She set out in the direction he'd pointed. The giggling children pursued her until the man barked out a couple of words Cori didn't understand. Then they stopped in their tracks, and she walked on alone.

As she came over the hill, she saw a long slope leading down to a shallow stream, with a couple of stubby trees providing two pools of shade. She could see a man sitting with his back against one tree, facing toward the stream. As she went nearer, she saw he was busy with something in his hands. She was only a few yards away when he became aware of her. He looked up, then rose to his feet, but not quickly, not as if he was surprised. He stood up like a host greeting an expected guest.

'Hello,' he said simply.

Cori echoed the word and smiled nervously. She had come not knowing what she would say when they met, how to explain her impulse. Having him behave as if no explanation was necessary did not make it easier to speak. As she stared at him, she saw he was holding a child's white leather moccasin in one hand, a threaded needle in the other. An unfinished pattern of red, turquoise and yellow beads was sewn across the front of the moccasin.

Her words came unthinkingly now. 'That's beautiful work.'

He glanced down at the moccasin. 'It's a traditional pattern. I've done this one many times.'

She guessed it was another way to earn money. Perhaps he could no longer work the rodeos, or didn't want to.

While she was still groping for a way to explain her presence, he said, 'Would you like to sit down?' He gestured to a shady spot under the tree as if it was a chair in a living-room.

Cori hesitated only a second before lowering herself to the grassy ground. He settled back where he had been sitting before. There was a cloth sack on the grass, and he dug into it, pulled out a handful of small beads, and began feeding them onto a thread.

'It's so strange,' she said in amazement. 'You haven't asked me why I'm here. You . . . act as if I *should* be. As if you knew I was coming . . .'

He looked up from his task and smiled at her. 'Perhaps I did.'

Cori thought in that moment how much she liked his lean face, more plain than handsome, but a kind of plainness that made it easy to see his honesty and sincerity. She had liked the face from the first time they had looked at each other. If such horror hadn't followed so soon after that moment, she thought, she would never have forgotten how pleasant it was to look at him.

'How could you know?' she asked.

'*Cante ishta*,' he said softly. 'In the Sioux language, this means "eye of the heart". What we see in this way sometimes can tell us not only what is happening, but what will happen.' He shrugged. 'Sometimes.' He looked back to his work.

Cante ishta. Cori repeated it in her mind, committing it to memory. Eye of the heart. Knowing the phrase, she thought, could be like an incantation that enabled her to use the faculty. For it occurred to her now that, if she had been aware sooner of *cante ishta*, she might have known – as he seemed to – that there was an inevitability in being here.

'Also,' he went on, 'I saw you at the trial in Rapid City. You wanted to help, didn't you? As you wanted to help the night we met. I felt you might not stop wanting . . .'

'Yes,' Cori said. Suddenly it was easy to speak. 'I've felt so badly since that night. The things that happened to you afterwards . . . I felt responsible. It's worse, I suppose, because of who I am – who my family are. I feel responsible for so many things that have made your life difficult.'

He went on applying beads to the leather so steadily and

intently that she wasn't sure he was really listening. She wanted to use his name, to call him to attention, but it seemed so awkward to address him as 'Mr Walks-Through-Fire'. In spite of the curious familiarity in his company—or perhaps because of it – she was also shy about using his first name.

'I guess I had to come finally,' she said, 'just to tell you how terribly sorry I am.'

When he raised his eyes this time, they were flashing with anger. 'So that's why you are here? To say you're sorry? Well, thank you for your apology, Miss Hartleigh. But what will it do? There are so many *wasicuns* who tell the Indians how sorry they are, but that gives back nothing of what has been taken away. And for me, it means only half as much.' He waved a hand toward the hill that led back to the houses. 'Go back there. Tell *them* how sorry you are. Perhaps it will mean more to them. I'm only fifty per cent a victim, you know – *iyeska* – or as the *wasicuns* call it, a half-breed.' He dropped his eyes to concentrate again on his beadwork.

The sting of his attack left her paralyzed for a moment. How terribly wounded his pride must be, she thought, that it took so little to make his pain and bitterness overflow like this.

'I wish I could give back what's been lost,' she said at last. 'But you're right – saying it is an empty gesture, meaningless unless it leads to *doing* something about it.' She started to rise from the ground. 'I'll try . . . Abel. I don't know how much I can do by myself, but I promise you, I'll try.'

On her feet, she looked at him for another second, but he kept staring at the work in his hands.

Cori turned and began walking back up the slope. Tears flooded her vision. She had come so far with only a desire to soothe him, to make amends and ease his mourning, and for a moment it had seemed so right to be here. But it had turned bad no less suddenly than if a bolt of lightning had cracked down from the sky. Now she wanted to go as quickly as possible. Her feet started to move faster, faster, until she was running, the air rushing against the tears spilling down her cheeks—

Then she felt her arm caught, she was being pulled around, and he was there behind her, panting from his pursuit. She turned her face away, as if she could hide her tears.

'Forgive me,' he pleaded. 'The last thing I mean to do is chase you away. You've done a brave thing to come here, I know. I have no right to be angry with you, no right at all. But inside me, there's always such a storm of feelings it breaks out like a wind crashing through a wall, even at the wrong times. Please don't go.' He leaned sideways to look into her face. 'Please.'

She stopped resisting, and he loosed his hold on her. She brushed the tears from her face. Then he held out his hand – the gesture mirroring the way Black Eagle had held his hand out to Bren. When Cori put her hand in his, it was as though a touch that had been interrupted by the murder had finally been completed, and, in some small way, the injuries of that violent act were partly healed.

He led her back to the tree beside the stream, and they sat together for the rest of the afternoon. While he went on beading the pair of child's moccasins, they spoke of their lives, exploring together the mystery of how such diverse paths could intersect, listening to themselves as much as to each other for clues to understand fully what the eye of the heart had already seen.

The central defining fact about himself, Abel explained, was that he was an *iyeska*. He suffered all the indignities that any other Indian man was forced to endure, and he felt his own alliance to be with the Sioux. Yet even among them, there was not total acceptance because he also carried the blood of a *wasicun*. His father, known only as Walks-Through-Fire, had been a pure-blooded Sioux with strains on the maternal side of his family that went back to Red Cloud, the great Sioux chief who had negotiated for the tribe in its dealings with the government in the 1860s and 1870s. Walks-Through-Fire had also been respected as a man of power, but not as a chief. He had been a tribal magician and healer, a *yuwipi* man, as the Sioux called it. In the summer of 1921, the daughter of a prominent Boston surgeon named Claire Eaton, a graduate student at Harvard in the field of anthropology, had come to the Rosebud reservation to study the Sioux culture. At the time, it was thought that the customs and traditions of the Indian were on their way to dying out completely – it was, in fact, the policy of the government for all the Indians to be assimilated into the 'white' culture – and it had been deemed a worthwhile intellectual pursuit to record the Indian ways before they disappeared. Claire Eaton had not been welcomed at first by the tribe, but gradually she had persuaded the inhabitants of the reservation she was sincerely interested in preserving a valuable culture. Among the aspects of Sioux life that interested her most were its medicine and magic, so she had come to know Walks-Through -Fire, and they had fallen in love. When Claire Eaton informed her family that she was pregnant and intended to become the wife of a Sioux medicine-man, she had been disinherited. She and Walks-Through-Fire were married according to Indian custom.

'I was born the next year in the Month of Changing Colors,' Abel told Cori. 'I was not yet three years old when my mother became ill. My father trusted his own medicine, yet he was wise enough to know that she had a condition that might be better treated with white medicine. He sent a telegram to my mother's father, asking for his advice, perhaps a reference to a doctor in the west. No answer came back. Perhaps my father should have gone then to any local hospital, but after the insult he was determined to cure his wife by himself with his own medicine. Two weeks later, she was dead.' By all accounts, Walks-Through-Fire and the genteel young woman from the east had been deeply in love. With her death, he had lost faith in his power and knowledge as a *yuwipi* man. Lonely and aimless, he had resorted to the common escape of others on the reservation who had no purpose or self-esteem – alcohol.

'He was very good at drinking,' Abel said with grim humor. 'He died of alcohol poisoning when I was six years old. But I wasn't left completely alone. Already I was being raised in my father's *tipospaye*.' This, he explained, was the Sioux word meaning 'those who live together', which referred to the extended family group that was a customary unit in the tribe. Parents and grown children, brothers and sisters and their mates often lived together, cousins being raised almost as brothers and sisters. 'My father's brother, Brave Wolf, was father to Black Eagle, and we all lived in the same *tipospaye*. He raised me as his own. Just as some of the children you saw when you arrived are my cousin's, and now I help to raise them.'

In defining herself for him, Cori did not have to talk about her origins. She was a Hartleigh, he knew what that meant – he knew how much wealth had been taken out of the Black Hills that had belonged once to the Sioux, and he knew that generations of her family had battled generations of his to keep the source of that wealth. Cori spent her time talking about the things that were not common to all the Hartleighs, the things she liked to do, the feelings and beliefs that made her different from the others in her family. She talked about her love of horses and nature and the ranch where she spent time with both, and the pleasure it gave her to teach young children, and the poetry she liked to read. She talked about her romantic notion that she could have been happy living in these hills as they had been hundreds of years ago, before they were mined and fought over.

And she confessed to a secret fantasy that she'd had as a child. It was when Buck had been teaching her to ride western style instead of in the English manner. As part of getting her accustomed to the natural movements of the horse, he had put her onto a pony without a saddle – bareback – and let her trot around on it. 'That's how the Indians ride,' he had told her, 'no saddle at all – no stirrups to stand in for all that fancy postin' up – and the Indians are the best.' Think of herself as an Indian maiden, he'd told Cori, learn to sit on a horse as if it had no saddle, that was the way to do it. For weeks afterwards, she'd fantasized about being an Indian maiden, believed that she'd been one in some earlier life.

'Then I grew out of it,' she said to Abel. 'Funny, I haven't thought of it again until today. Yet now . . . I'm wondering again if it might not be true.' What else could explain how she felt as they talked that she belonged here with him?

The sun was dipping onto the horizon when he sewed the last line of tiny turquoise beads into the pattern and held up the pair of moccasins to show Cori they were finished. She told him they were exquisite, and he dangled them in front of her. 'Try them on. See if they fit.'

She guessed his intention. 'No, Abel . . . I couldn't.' He had told her earlier that doing beadwork on belts and shoes and purses was an important source of income for the *tipospaye*.

'I want to give you something, and I have nothing else of value.'

She would not injure his pride – and, besides, she was happy to have something from him.

But when he set the moccasins on the ground, and she tried to slip them on, they were too small.

'Too bad,' he said, as he bent to pick them up, 'it seems you are not Cinderella, and I am not your Prince Charming.'

There was such a look of sadness on his face as he stood staring down at the shoes in his hand, that she felt like crying herself. 'But I think you are,' she murmured quietly. 'Believe it, Abel. Believe in us . . .'

He raised his blue eyes and they gazed at each other for a long moment. Then he held out his hand, but this time not to lead her anywhere. He brought her closer, slowly, purposefully until she was against him. Still, he hesitated as though reluctant to take the next step to possession. So she lifted herself up on tiptoes because he was much taller, and raised her face, bringing her mouth up until their lips brushed.

The first kiss was so soft and light she was barely sure when it began and when it ended.

But there was no doubt about the next. Passion unleashed, he enfolded her tightly in his arms, and pressed his mouth firmly over hers, and they devoured each other. Cori wanted him as she had never wanted any man before.

And all of this, she knew, all that was to come, was only the fulfillment of a vision she should have seen before with the eye of the heart. *Cante ishta.*

7

In the grip of passion for the first time in her life, Cori forgot the firm rule she'd once set for herself that she would be a virgin when she married. She wanted Abel to be her lover.

At the end of her first day on the reservation, when he asked if she would like to stay the night with the *tipospaye*, she knew he also wanted to sleep with her. To justify his boldness, though, he said, 'There are no hotels anywhere on the reservation, and you would have to drive a long way back.'

He took her back to the property on the other side of the hill. The people Cori had seen earlier were all gathered in the largest of the three tar-paper shacks, which consisted essentially of one rectangular room that ran its entire length, with doors leading off from one side to a line of narrow bedrooms. At one end of the large room stood a wood stove, iron sink, and an old-fashioned ice box, forming a rudimentary kitchen. A trio of gas lanterns suspended from the ceiling provided light as the two women, the young one and the old one who only spoke Sioux, cooked the evening meal. The short man who'd been planing lumber now sat on a stool in a corner, tinkering with a part from a car engine. The children were all over the place, a couple of the older ones involved in assisting with preparing the food, the rest chasing each other, or turning the pages of tattered year-old fashion magazines, or bouncing on a pair of huge unmatched sofas from which loose white ticking billowed like milk boiling over.

Entering the shack with Cori, Abel announced that he had invited her to be his guest. He did not say her name, but he pointed around the room identifying each person for her. The short solid man by the stove was Emory Fast Horse, and he was the son of another brother to Abel's father than Brave Wolf, who had been Black Eagle's father. The old woman who spoke Sioux was Bessie Appearing Day, and she had been Brave Wolf's companion after his first wife died. The younger woman was Bessie's married daughter, Ada Crying Wind. Of the dozen children in the *tipospaye* some were Ada's, others were Emory's – his wife had deserted him, Abel explained, and was said to be working in Las Vegas serving drinks in a gambling hall – two little boys and a girl were Black Eagle's, and a couple belonged to a sister of Ada's.

Appearing Day, Fast Horse, Crying Wind – how poetic and magical all the names were. Meeting them again, looking at them more carefully, Cori recognized Emory and Ada as having been in the gallery at Abel's trial. So they had not needed to be told who she was, and what part she had played in Black Eagle's death. She expected she might catch a hint of hostility to her, but there was none. Not that there was any welcoming warmth, either. She was greeted merely with placid, unquestioning acceptance. From what Abel had told her, Cori understood it was the nature of the *tipospaye* to take in any person connected to someone who was already a part of it.

They all sat down to eat at a long table, a meal of beans and fried slices of tinned luncheon meat and potatoes. The children drank half a glass of milk, and the adults took beer from an iron keg. While they ate, two other young women arrived and sat down at the table. Able introduced them as Annie Lone

Dog, who was Ada's sister, and Kate Highwalking, who had been Black Eagle's lover at the time of his death.

It became apparent to Cori that all the women were living apart from men who had fathered their children, and the two men – Emory and Abel – were also alone. Yet what might have been classified elsewhere as 'broken families' were mended by being included in this larger group.

Keeping order among the many young children occupied the adults enough so that Cori wasn't singled out for questioning at the table – a relief, since she did not feel confident that she could talk about herself in this company without arousing some negative sentiment.

The meal ended with a berry pudding called *wojapi*, a traditional dish. Cori began to join in cleaning up, but the other women said her help was unnecessary. As the others set about doing dishes, and putting their children to bed in the adjoining bedrooms, Abel led Cori outside again.

With nightfall, the empty landscape no longer seemed so forlorn and scarred everywhere with the signs of poverty. From horizon to horizon a blue-black dome was dotted with stars, the multitude casting a silvery light over the contours of the earth. It was dark enough that the ugly car hulks became nothing more than black boulders.

Alone with Abel, Cori no longer felt the sense of alienation that had overtaken her while she was among the others. She reached for his hand, and pulled him into a kiss. The fever to have more of him was rising in her again.

'I want you, Abel,' she confessed as soon as their lips parted. The words seemed to come of themselves, as if a spirit was speaking through her.

'But don't you see how hopeless it is?' he answered. He glanced back at the shack. She suspected now that he had invited her not to keep her there, but to illustrate that neither of them must be swept into the impossible.

'That isn't what you saw in the eye of the heart,' she said.

He let out a breath as, still holding her hand, he ambled further from the group of shacks, gazing up at the sky. 'There are dreams for which we do not see the end, sometimes they are gifts . . . and sometimes they are warnings.' He stopped walking, but his gaze remained on the stars as he resumed. 'I had a dream . . . a few nights before Black Eagle and I went to Rapid City for the rodeo. I told Black Eagle about it, but then he forgot. We both did . . . until it was too late.'

'What was the dream?' Cori asked.

Keeping his eyes on the dark sky, he told her. In the dream it was the Old Time, and he was one of the braves taking part in the great hunt the tribe undertook every year in the Month of Grass Appearing, when the animals emerged after their winter sleep to roam everywhere across the unspoiled land in great numbers. He was hunting in the old way, bow and arrow in his hand . . . and he was naked, riding a pinto *sunke-wakan* – the 'holy dog' as his people called the horse – and his beloved cousin Black Eagle was on the back of a *sunke-wakan* right beside him. Ahead of them, up in the sky, *wanjbli* – the eagle – was gliding in a wide circle, and directly below *wanjbli* was a herd of buffalo. Though it was night, under the silver light cast over the land by the moon, the two braves could see the animals and were galloping forward to make a kill.

But all at once, the herd was gone, vanished . . . and now there were only two white buffalo, each a sacred prize. He rode faster, Black Eagle staying beside him. But as far and as fast as they rode, they came no closer to the two white buffalo. The night went black, and instead of any animal all he could see ahead was a single glowing point of light, like a star that had come down from the sky. They rode still faster toward the pinpoint of shimmering light.

And suddenly he was not in a dream but a nightmare. Turning to look at Black Eagle, he saw his cousin still astride his horse, but a gigantic black mountain lion had leapt onto his back. The huge black cat was biting and clawing into the flesh of Black Eagle, slashing him apart and devouring him, making his blood fountain everywhere.

Then on his own shoulder, Abel had felt the agonizing grip of talons. When he forced his head around to look, he saw no beast attacking, only *hinhan* perched right there next to his head, the owl's glaring golden eye staring straight into his. Most frightening of all, he saw *hinhan* begin to open his beak, saw the fat tongue within, wormlike, begin to curl backward, as if the bird was preparing to screech—

He fled from the horrible vision into consciousness, and went the next morning to visit Nellie Blue Snow, the medicine woman who was also an interpreter of dreams. She had told them that if they continued to pursue what was forbidden, they would be destroyed.

'You see,' Abel concluded, 'we should have known what would happen. But we didn't understand then, and we went ahead, and Black Eagle died.'

In the darkness, she moved closer to him. 'So you believe the white buffalo in your dream, the thing you were forbidden to have . . . that stood for my sister, or me?'

'Or perhaps any white woman,' Abel said. 'I am one proof that it brings misfortune. Black Eagle is another.'

She was quiet a minute, looking up at the stars with him. 'Have you had the dream again?' she asked.

'No.'

'Then isn't it possible, there's nothing more to fear? For Black Eagle there was . . . but not for you.'

He turned to her. 'I wish it could be so.'

She gazed up at him, his features faintly visible in the silver-blue night. Far over his head, a circle of stars floated in the sky like a crown. 'We can make it so, Abel,' she said softly.

He brought his hand up to the side of her face and caressed

it lightly. 'How smooth and soft you feel,' he said. 'But you are strong, aren't you? You are what we call *ohitika win*.'

'*Ohitika win*,' she repeated. 'What does it mean?'

'A brave woman.'

She leaned her face into his hand. 'I don't think I'm brave. I only know that I want to be with you, and I can't believe there's anything wrong in that.'

He stood motionless beside her. The only sound was a slight wind brushing across the open land, whistling faintly through the clumps of sagebrush. She waited, praying he would dare to cross the gap between them, knowing if she tried to pull him across he might only retreat – for her sake if not his own.

Finally, his hands slipped down over her shoulders, grasped her arms and pulled her near. When his mouth came down onto hers, Cori kissed him hungrily, the desire raging through her even more fiercely than when he had kissed her before. She had never before felt her body so completely sensitized over every inch. His lips on hers, his hands moving across her back, the fabric on her stomach where he pressed against her, the dampness welling between her thighs, every separate sensation added to a flow of thrills sweeping over her. 'Take me, Abel,' she said.

She would have lain down for him right there. But he lifted her swiftly up into his arms, and it seemed only a few seconds later that the sky full of stars overhead was gone. He had pushed her through a door, and they were in one of the smaller shacks. A glowing kerosene lantern hung from a hook on a low ceiling beam. By its light Cori saw the interior consisted of no more than a room with two beds, one against each of the side walls, placed under a window. Emory Fast Horse was seated on the edge of one bed, still fiddling with the same engine part. He glanced up as Abel entered carrying Cori in his arms.

For all her propriety, Cori only wished that the second man would evaporate, leave so quickly and soundlessly that the spell would not be broken. After staring at them only an instant, he rose from the bed, and went straight out into the night.

The lovers continued as if they'd seen nothing more than a fleeting apparition. Abel laid Cori down on one of the beds, then moved to the lantern, and lifted the glass chimney, preparing to blow it out.

'No,' she said urgently, 'I want to see you – to see *us*.'

He came back to her, and they undressed each other in an impatient flurry, their kisses moving to each new patch of flesh that was bared to the other. How wonderful his lips felt on her breasts, how much she loved the warmth and the smell and the faint salty tang of his skin. Cori was astonished by her own brazenness as her lips and tongue roamed over his body, yet she felt no shame or regret. She could see and feel him, at the same time, exploring her, tasting her, looking at her. Then he pushed her back, and her body uncoiled, legs stretched wide apart, so she could give herself to him. She ploughed her fingers into his thick hair, and held his head while she felt him breathing into the core of her, his tongue thrusting, drinking from her. A wave of shocking thrills convulsed her body, and a sound rose out of her throat, a low purr of pure carnal delight that became a cry.

'Oh . . . Abel, now . . . now!' Her hands clawed at his back, pulling him up over her until she felt the hard length of him plunging down inside her. There was an instant of pain, as though an arrow had been fired into the core of her, and then the hurt was gone and there was only the most intense pleasure she had ever known. Her arms tightened around him, pulling him in deeper, deeper, as the miraculous flowering she felt within went on and on and on until she was at the summit of the ascending thrill.

Then she went limp, and her eyes closed, and in that inner darkness she realized she was staring into the eye of the heart.

The tide of sensations receded at last, and she was back in the arms of a man she had just come to know – and had loved all her life.

Now the habits that she had cast aside in the heat of passion reasserted themselves. 'Your cousin, Emory,' she said, 'he saw us together. He'll know we've been lovers.'

'Does that bother you?'

'I don't know. I mean, I'm not sure how it will affect what happens to us. I suppose he'll tell the others . . .'

'And you wanted this to be a secret,' he said with a tone of pained resignation. 'I'm sorry.'

'Abel. It's not because I'm ashamed.'

'Then what worries you? I can promise you no one would use what they know about us to hurt you, or try to gain anything from you, or—'

He interpreted her propriety as suspicion, Cori realized. 'Abel, I'm not worried about any of that. You need to understand . . . I've never been with a man like this before, any man.'

'I had guessed that,' he said.

'I just wish it could have been more . . . private, that we could be alone.' She rolled over and looked across the shack to the other bed. 'Right now I want to make love again, all night if we can, and I keep thinking he'll come back any minute.'

He pulled her around to face him again. 'Emory won't come back tonight. We respect each other's privacy.'

So tonight they would be alone. But Cori realized that she was actually thinking far beyond one night. Bren could have stayed with Black Eagle for a single hour, then left and never given him another thought. For herself that was impossible. Rashly as it might have been done, when she had given herself to this man, she had made a choice that she imagined would shape every decision, every day that followed.

She dared to let him know what was on her mind. 'This is where Emory lives, though. So if you and I were going to be together for more than just tonight . . .' She had courage enough to say only that much.

'Can you really want that?' he asked. 'Coming from your world, can you want this kind of life?'

'What I want,' she answered, 'is that tomorrow, and for as long I can, I'll feel the way I do right now. In my own family, all my life I've been weak and timid and obedient. But somehow that's changed – began to change from the moment I first saw you. What did you call me – a brave woman? No one else I know would ever call me that. But tonight, I think maybe I'm becoming brave – and I feel like a woman, not a little girl. I don't want to go backward again. As for the life here, I see how difficult it is. But I can't think of anything more worthwhile I could do than stay and work to make it better.'

His hand played over her body, his touch an expression of appreciation for her pledge. 'Many people, for many years have wanted to make it better,' he said, 'and they haven't been able to. I wouldn't want you to waste your life that way.'

'Nothing can be done if people don't try. As long as they try, it's not a waste.'

His hands stopped moving and he pulled back to look at her through the golden lamplight. 'I suppose the same ideas and feelings brought my mother here. But she paid the price of losing her own roots – her family – and her life. It could happen again.'

'No. It doesn't have to be the same.' Cori pushed back the long mahogany hair that had dropped to curtain his eyes. Studying his lean face, she was reminded that his mother's people had been proper Bostonians, and that the rejection of their daughter had occurred more than a generation in the past. Also, she thought, the father of that woman couldn't have adored his daughter as much as Cori knew G.D. doted on her.

But however she discounted such risks, Cori believed the choice she needed to make depended more on an answer she still needed from him. 'Do you want me to stay, Abel? If you do, I will.'

He hesitated only a moment. 'Yes . . . very much,' he said, his voice throbbing with the intensity of the wish. 'I want you to stay.' As he rose above her again, and moved to join with her, she heard him whisper, '*Ohitika win.*'

They had made love until dawn, and when she awakened she found herself with the desire to feel him inside her again. She would have forced him to take her, if he hadn't already left the bed, and gone outside. She found him putting up a *tipi* on a grassy strip beside the stream. If she was going to stay, he said, then the *tipi* would be where they slept. In the old days, too, he explained, *tipis* were built whenever a couple wanted to live by themselves.

Cori offered to help, but he said it was something he had to do by himself, for her, so she sat on a rock by the side of the river and happily watched. He built it in the traditional way, a conical framework of long saplings bound together at the joints with leather strips. It was not as naturally finished as it had been by his ancestors, however. He had to use a combination of blankets and tar-paper for the covering rather than buffalo hides, and the bindings were from old belts and worn boot tops he sliced into strips.

Sitting on the rock, Cori stretched and, as though looking at a silly picture of herself in an album of childhood snapshots, she smiled at the memory of the frightened virgin she had been until last night. When he glanced over and saw her smiling, he asked why.

'I'm just happy,' she said. 'I'm as happy as I've ever been.'

That night, when they made love in the *tipi*, she felt it was part of a ceremony in which she had given herself completely and irrevocably to him.

Later, after he fell asleep she lay wide awake, finally seeing beyond the romantic phenomenon to the thousand practical problems it created. When and how would she explain it to her family? Bren should be the first to know, of course; she could understand, and she would be an advocate when G.D. was told. There was also the problem of how to deal with Abel's *tipospaye*. She must convince them that she belonged here, that she was not just an adventuress prowling among them on a whim.

After her first night with Abel, she encountered the others at the meals that were taken communally in the largest shack. Starting at breakfast, after the children had gone to play outside, the other women had openly displayed their doubt about her motives, not in a nasty way, so much as by plying Cori with bemused questions, most of them targeted frankly on sex. Did she find her night with Abel was worth coming 'all this way'? asked Ada Crying Wind, a petite woman with a very pretty face and straight black hair that hung down her back to her hips. Wasn't it better with Abel than with a *wasicun* man? Annie Lone Dog wanted to know. Even Bessie Appearing Day, the old woman who smoked cigars, had a question. She asked it in the Sioux language so Cori didn't understand, but it made the other women roar with laughter.

When Abel first heard such questions touched upon at breakfast, he had tried intervening to protect Cori. 'Is that all you can think about?' he chided the women. 'Miss Hartleigh is well educated, she has been to college; you could ask her about many more interesting things.'

'Aha!' said Ada 'So you are afraid to let her tell us if you were good! Perhaps an *iyeska* is only half as good.'

Cori was stunned to hear Abel mocked for his mixed heritage, but he took it good-naturedly, so she guessed it must be done often and without malice.

'That depends,' he said, 'on which half of me is which.'

'Remember, Black Eagle was called *che maza*,' said the murdered man's last companion, Kate Highwalking. A statuesque woman who wore her long hair in a ponytail and had the classic high cheek-bones characteristic of the Sioux, she worked as a nurse at the small health clinic on the reservation. 'Abel has much to live up to.'

'What's the meaning of *che maza*?' Cori asked.

The women broke into happy bubbling laughter.

'*Che maza*,' old Bessie chortled, until her laugh was strangled by the phlegmy cough produced by her constant cigar-smoking.

Abel hesitated, and Cori saw he was actually blushing, his skin turning the same reddish tinge that came naturally to the others.

'Tell her or I will,' Emory prompted.

'It means . . . iron prick,' Abel said, and laughter filled the room again. Cori found herself laughing, too. Rather than embarrassing her, the honest curiosity expressed by all the other women seemed to liberate her from her habitual modesty. When the laughter faded, she didn't mind confessing to the plain truth. She couldn't be sure Abel was better in bed than another man, because she'd never been with any other – and the way she felt today she would never need to be.

Reading the emotion behind her words, the others around the table made eyes at Abel, and gave him coy looks. Despite her inability to speak English, old Bessie had no difficulty interpreting these signs, and she murmured something that made the others explode with the loudest laughter yet, also bringing the flush back to Abel's face even as he chuckled.

Cori glanced around waiting to have the joke translated.

Abel buried his laughing face in his hands.

'Tell me!' Cori insisted.

Ada leaned over to her. 'Seeing the way you look at Abel, Bessie thinks he deserves to be called something better than iron prick.'

'What?'

'*Golden* prick!'

Cori's jaw dropped. For a few seconds she was frozen in mortification. But then, like a casing of ice cracking and falling away, she felt suddenly unbound from her old reflexes and poses, and her own laughter rose up, loud and free as the others'.

Once they saw she did not mind their frankness, their interest turned at last from sex to broader subjects. On the second night, after the shared evening meal when the children were in bed, glasses of *mni-sha* – a wine home-made from herbs – was poured all around, and they stayed at the table asking Cori about San Francisco, and her family, and what the house in which she had grown up looked like. They asked her what had made her leave such a nice place to come to *this*. And they asked her what she would do, since she was a Hartleigh, to change the policies of the mining company. It was the company and its hold on the land, they all knew, that had been one of the most powerful influences on their lives in the century since gold had been found in the Black Hills.

Cori replied honestly to everything, but when she spoke to this last question her answer was obviously not what they had hoped to hear. There were disappointed expressions all around the table when she said, 'I don't approve of everything the mining company has done, and I'm going to try and bring about changes. But I can't promise things will be different overnight. The most I can do is speak to the people who run the company – speak for you. Also, I'd like to help organize here on the reservation so that your point of view can gather the support you need to—'

'This is bullshit double-talk!' Annie Lone Dog erupted hotly. She was a very thin woman, underweight, and the strained intensity of her outburst was emphasized by the way the cords of muscle on her neck stood out. 'If you want to help us, why should it be so hard? Your people own the company. They own *us*.'

It was the first time Cori had been challenged by a show of anger, but she met it sympathetically, both because she was aware of the role Hartleigh Mining had played in local history, and because she had seen Annie helping herself to more of the *mni-sha* than anyone else. 'No one owns anyone else, Annie. And I don't own the company. The men in my family run it, and they don't listen to the women about *how* to run it anymore I expect the men around here take orders from you.'

There was a heavy pause in which Cori realized she had made a bad comparison. In fact, there were less men than women in the *tipospaye*, and Cori had seen that the women were required to be independent and forceful. She had noticed, too, that both Emory and Abel were sympathetic and respectful in dealing with the abandoned women who surrounded them.

Yet Cori's forceful defense of herself blunted Annie's attack for now, and the evening ended with quiet 'good nights' as Abel and Cori went out to go to the *tipi*.

Apologizing for Annie's hostility, Abel explained that her husband had gone to work in one of the Hartleigh mines to support her and their children. When he had become sick on the job a few years ago, the company fired him, providing no compensation. Joseph Lone Dog had come home to the reservation, and had wasted away, unable to afford any treatment but the rudimentary care offered at the clinic run by the Bureau of Indian Affairs.

The sad story led Cori to ask why the other women in the *tipospaye* were also without men. Abel told her that, especially after Indian couples had children, it was common for the men to leave the reservation. The women could then claim to be abandoned, which made them eligible to receive money the federal government provided through the BIA specifically for 'aid to dependent children'. And while the women collected ADC money, men might also send home some of what they were earning elsewhere.

'Of course, that's not the only reason the men go,' Abel said. 'They go because there's so little they can do here, and because they don't want the women and children they love to see their pride dying before their eyes. Some go because they've lost all hope that life will get better here, and they decide it's better to join the white world and get lost in it.'

'But you've stayed,' Cori said.

'I was born on this land,' Abel replied. 'My people are buried here.' They were nearing the *tipi*, and he paused to scan the dark contours of the land mantled again under a clear sky speckled with stars. 'I do not leave . . . because this is my home, and because I do not want to get lost.' He pulled back the blanket that formed the flap over the entrance to the *tipi* and motioned Cori inside.

When he lit the lantern that hung on a rope from the frame of saplings, Cori saw that he had found time to bring in some carpet remnants to cover the earthern floor, and placed colorful woven baskets and pottery jugs around the perimeter. Where they slept, a mound of fur pelts was arranged, the skins of coyotes that Abel and Black Eagle had hunted together. To Cori, the *tipi* now seemed cosy rather than confined, a place where she would not mind coming at the end of each day, a nest.

As always now, she and Abel moved easily and naturally into an embrace, and lay down on the bed of fur as they undressed each other. Soon they were in the throes of passion, and Cori was reassured once again that whatever ordeals she might have to meet, whatever hard feelings and mistrust might rise against her from those like Annie Lone Dog, in Abel's arms she would find the strength to triumph over them.

8

Naturally fascinated by anything new and unfamiliar, the children of the *tipospaye* followed Cori everywhere. She enjoyed their attention, and her teaching experience made it easy for her to keep them amused. Within days, impromptu sessions of story-telling had evolved into formal classes under a tree or inside the *tipi*. As she probed their general knowledge, Cori perceived that the reservation school had provided a very poor quality of education to the children. Science, math, English, in every subject there were broad gaps in learning that didn't exist in children she had taught in San Francisco. Cori resolved to visit the school and see what she could contribute to improving the children's education.

Abel's dedication to supporting the extended family group involved him in several different kinds of labor. He did traditional beadwork and leatherwork which he sold to traveling dealers who then wholesaled it to city stores; he put in half-days at two reservation stores unloading new shipments; and he did carpentry. Cori had been with him for a week when Abel and Emory went off for three days to build an extension on a meeting hall in a settlement on the far side of the reservation. There were numerous such settlements with names

111

like Black Pipe, Two Strikes, Upper Cut Meat and He-Dog, random groupings of shanties around a church and a store or two, not large enough to be called a town.

Cori hoped the time Abel was away would be an opportunity to get closer to the other women in the *tipospaye*. Though she had been with them at mealtimes, it was obvious that they continued to hold themselves somewhat apart. Her offers to help with the cooking and cleaning up were always refused, and if she came upon them talking in a group and joined them, they greeted her cordially but then the group would dissolve and drift away. She wanted to believe that it was not unfriendliness; even Annie had not shown her further hostility since the night she'd had too much wine. It simply took time to penetrate such a close-knit group.

But with Abel gone, the situation became even worse. The ribald joking and tolerant questioning that had been common during meals when Abel was present gave way to a harsher, less sympathetic kind of interrogation. Not all the other women were as deeply hostile as Annie, but even those of gentler nature, like Ada and Kate, seemed to harbor a deep suspicion of Cori. They asked constantly why she had *really* come, what she was trying to prove, who she was running away from.

Patiently, Cori explained that Black Eagle's murder had touched her as nothing else in her life, at the same time as it had brought her together with a man to whom she felt mysteriously bonded. That part of it could never be logically explained, she said. But did they not all know about *cante ishta*?

'Sure, we know,' Annie answered sourly, when they were all together at supper the second day Abel was away. 'There's all kinds of legends and magic and wonderful stories. But if our magic was truly so good and strong, would we be so low-down poor and hungry? Would we have lost so much to the *wasicuns*? We had our wonderful legends . . . but they had guns and money. So don't tell us it's *wakan tanka* that brought you to Abel.' *Wakan tanka*, Cori had learned, was Sioux for 'the great mystery', the force of nature that ruled over everything. 'Once we believed *wakan tanka* meant for us to hunt forever as far and wide as we wished,' Annie concluded. 'No more.'

The other women didn't so completely reject their traditional beliefs as Annie, yet one way or another they all urged Cori to understand that she would be better off leaving the reservation.

Late on the night before Abel was to return, Ada came alone to the *tipi*. She brought a red clay pitcher filled with *mni-sha* and two pottery cups, and she asked Cori to drink with her.

'You like sleeping here?' she asked after they were seated cross-legged on the floor of the *tipi* sipping wine. Her eyes scanned the inside of the *tipi*, as though its construction was strange to her.

'Yes, I do,' Cori said. 'But I've always liked camping out.'

Ada smiled. 'For now, for all these sunny summer days, you may think our life is not too hard for you to share. But when winter comes, it will not be easy to rest on frozen ground or wash outside in the icy stream, or to use the outhouse to relieve yourself. Then you will decide to move inside with us . . . and there you will find yourself shivering in bed, wearing gloves even in the lodge so your hands don't get too cold to hold a knife or fork. Your fine rich living in big warm houses never prepared you for that, *ohitika win*.' When Ada used the term she'd heard applied to Cori by Abel it was not meant as mockery. Ada acknowledged that it had taken a measure of courage for Cori to break away from her comfortable and secure existence.

Cori thought of saying that she planned to improve conditions; she could afford to have heating and plumbing installed, buy more bedding, have everyone better clothed and fed, buy toys for the children. But to defend herself by saying she would arrange a more comfortable existence would only justify Ada's doubts. 'Abel's mother came from a background similar to mine,' Cori said, 'and that was a time when conditions here must have been even worse. If she lasted, so can I.'

'She became ill,' Ada said.

'What I've heard about her shows how determined she was. Even when she was sick and dying – though her father was a doctor – she stayed here and relied on her husband's medicine.'

Ada studied Cori for a moment. 'I think Abel has not told you everything. His mother did not die of a sickness – not in the way you talk of it. She took her own life.'

Cori's head lifted sharply, and Ada affirmed the statement with a slow nod before resuming. 'One night she rose naked from her bed, climbed on a horse and rode for a few miles. Where she found a tall tree, she threw a rope over a branch, and hanged herself.'

The revelation stunned Cori. 'Why?' she murmured.

'She was sick, yes,' Ada replied. 'But with an illness of the mind. From the time she married Abel's father, she had done many things to hurt herself; she cut herself with a knife, or made herself sick sitting naked in winter snow. After Abel was born, she took a stick from a fire, and put the glowing end inside herself, making it impossible for her to bear another child.'

Even the imagined pain left Cori too breathless to speak.

Ada went on in a low, steady voice. 'Abel's father, Walks-Through-Fire, was a *yuwipi* man. He believed at first that his wife had been taken over by the *wanagi* – ghosts, dead spirits of our people who did not want the tribe to be corrupted by her white blood. After his most powerful magic failed to cure her, he realized the cause of her problem was not so mysterious: she was sick in her mind – crazy. He wanted to send her for proper treatment, but he did not have the money needed, and could not get it from her family. To send her to one of the free

114

state institutions was a sentence of death anyway. Thirty years ago, they were all filthy places – especially those to which one of us would be sent. So Walks-Through-Fire kept her here, and he did his magic, praying he might be wrong, and a *wanagi* could be forced to flee from her body. But, of course, there was no evil spirit. The disease killed her, and at last the tribe understood what should have been clear from the first. She had not gone mad while she was here; she had been insane even when she came.'

'But you said the symptoms started after her marriage,' Cori observed.

'The little ones,' said Ada Crying Wind. 'The biggest was there the day she arrived – but so large that those who saw it were as blind as if they were staring into the sun.'

'What was it?' Cori said.

'She came . . . and she stayed,' Ada said. 'Madness enough.'

Cori understood now why Ada had told the story. 'You think anyone who comes here to help has to be insane?' she demanded, her voice rising. 'You think there's something sick about my feelings for Abel? Why shouldn't I love him? He's a wonderful man.'

Cori stopped to listen to the echo of her own words. It struck her that this was the first time she had actually given definition to her feelings. Even with him, when they clung together in the dark, hot and damp with passion, she had yet to say 'I love you'. Other things, yes. 'I'm glad I found you.' 'You're wonderful.' But not that total declaration of self.

'If you are not crazy,' Ada said, 'you are most certainly very foolish. What sensible woman would leave the life you've had for this one?'

'If Abel wants me,' Cori declared, 'then this life gives me more than I've ever had before.'

'Perhaps his wanting you is because he is the son of a crazy woman, half crazy himself.'

Cori's patience was exhausted. She would be able to prove herself only with actions, not words, by sticking it out in this hard life through winter as well as a summer, and winters to come. Rising to her feet, she remarked that it was late, and said she wanted to sleep. She needed to be well rested, she said, because she hoped to take the children on a hike the next day to teach them a bit about the way the earth had been formed by examining rock formations, and to hunt for fossils that would help them understand human evolution. Cori knew there were places in the Black Hills that had already yielded troves of fossils, even dinosaur bones.

'The children already know how the earth was formed,' Ada said, as she stood and made ready to leave, 'and they understand the beginnings of man.'

'I don't think so, Ada. I've noticed—'

The Indian woman talked on. 'They know we are all descended from *we-ota-wichasha* – the blood-clot boy who was formed out of the blood that fell to earth from the first woman in her moon-time. They need to know nothing else.'

'Ada, your legends are beautiful,' Cori said evenly. 'They must be learned and preserved. But they are not the same as true knowledge.'

A steely undertone crept into Ada's soft voice. 'Do what you wish with Abel. If he wants to keep you, then you will live among us, and eat with us, and we will share what we have with you. That is our way.' She had moved to the open flap of the *tipi*. 'But the minds of the children we will keep for ourselves. If you try to steal them with your *wasicun* ideas, we will send you away even if it means losing Abel as well. Do you understand, *ohitika win*?' This time when Ada used the phrase, it had the dark shading of a challenge.

Before Cori could add a further plea for the children's sake, Ada was gone.

The encounter left her mired in despair. What could she

offer to prove her sincerity if she was not allowed to teach? And how could she teach if they thought of her as a crazy woman stealing the minds of their children?

Lying sleepless through that night, Cori thought about the story of Abel's mother, and pondered the riddle at its heart. Had Claire Eaton been crazy to come here? Or had she been too fragile to withstand the stresses that followed from her choice?

Still awake at dawn, she had no answer. But she had realized that the riddle was more than an unsolved mystery of the past; it was also the key to her own future.

'I would have told you,' Abel explained when he returned. 'But in my own time.' Wouldn't she have been scared off, he asked Cori, if he had instantly poured out all the tragic details of his family history? And he wanted her to stay.

They were lying naked on the bed of furs after making love, her conviction renewed that it was no weakness of the mind that made her want him. 'I'm not scared of you, Abel,' she said, 'no matter what was true of your mother.'

'You might be, though, if I told you the story myself.'

He revealed now that the 'truth' Cori had heard from Ada was only the popular version – with some of the facts left out.

His mother was somewhat sickly, it was true; she was a nervous woman who had found life on the reservation taxing, and as much as Walks-Through-Fire loved her, he had failed to cure her. But the extent of her mental problem had been exaggerated over the years. Had she scourged herself with fire, tried to burn out her womb? Never! – a tale made up by vicious gossips. Yes, his mother's nude body had been found hanging from the end of a rope tied to a tree branch. But it was never established that she had killed herself. From the day her body was found, there were whispers that it was not a suicide.

'My father was not the only Sioux *yuwipi* man,' Abel said.

'But until he married, Walks-Through-Fire was the most famous and respected, the one who had never failed to bring relief to those who were ailing or troubled. Then, after my mother came, he could help no one – perhaps only because he was so consumed with trying to help her. But many in the tribe believed his magic had been weakened by loving a *wasicun* woman, and would never come back while his heart was hers. So they killed her . . . for their own good.'

'So that's what you thought would frighten me?' Cori said, her tone dismissive. 'That I'd worry about being murdered, too?'

'I should have known you better.' He ran a hand lightly down her body, tracing its contours. 'My *ohitika win* . . . you are too brave to be scared away by old tales and rumors.'

'The only thing that scares me,' she said, as she pulled his body over hers, 'is that you'll stop wanting me.'

For the next week, he stayed close, loving and protective. Cori had also told him that Ada had warned her to stay away from the children.

'Give them time to know you,' Abel assured her, 'and you will be allowed to teach. The mothers will realize how much their children need what you could give them.'

But seeing how unhappy it made her not to have the freedom to speak or play with the children, he suggested a camping trip to distract her, a few days in which he could show her the beauties of the *Paha Sapa* – the Black Hills – especially its holiest place, the caves his people called *wamaka-og'naka-icante*, 'the heart of everything that is'.

They drove first to a ranch owned by Michael Strongheart Bear, an elder who loaned them a pair of pinto horses. Camping on horseback made the trip all the more exciting to Cori. This landscape was not as dramatic or majestic as in the Grand Tetons around Jackson Hole, an endless panorama of gently rolling hills rather than the horizon of soaring snow-tipped mountains, even so Cori felt nothing less than a dream fulfilled as she and Abel set out, riding side-by-side. Out of sight of any house or road, they were pioneers again in an unspoiled land; as lovers, she felt, they were the hope of the future, a living testament that the battles that had once divided this frontier could be erased.

No less accomplished on horseback than she, he outraced her again and again as they galloped full out across miles of open meadow. When they slowed their horses to a walk, he told her more of Sioux history, and began teaching her the language. The name of the tribe, Cori learned, derived from their own word for snakes, *nadoeuissiw*, as it had been shortened and pronounced by the early French traders. The negative attitude embodied in the French name was matched by their treatment of the Sioux, hunting them as though they were animals to be trapped. A century ago, Sioux scalps had sold for two hundred dollars apiece in Yankton, the capital of the Dakota territory.

When he saw that these stories upset Cori, Abel reverted to relating more colorful tales from the tribe's folklore. Riding through these lands, however, the history he came back to telling her was inevitably an account of the battles that had been fought between such great Sioux chiefs as Red Cloud and Big Foot and Crazy Horse, and the army generals who had been sent out to suppress them and their followers. It was on a mission to take possession of the Black Hills, that General George Armstrong Custer had been slain with most of his troops by Sioux warriors.

When the sun turned orange and winked down over the lip of the farthest hill, they made camp, laying out bedrolls and leaving the horses to graze. They were in a valley beside a wide shallow stream where there had been a Sioux village long ago, Abel said; it had vanished after a massacre.

Abel's whimsical romantic side replaced the grim historian

when they sat down to the supper he prepared. Simple food, ham from a tin, canned carrots, a fruit salad made from fresh grapes and bananas, but he dressed up the presentation with candles in pottery holders, and a bottle of Spanish champagne chilled in the icy stream. Afterwards, he took her on a long walk under starlight to the top of an isolated knoll. Here, he said, was the last remnant of the village that had vanished, and he showed her a deep, bowl-shaped concavity that had been dug out of the rocky summit and outlined in rounded stones. It was a holy place, he explained, where men of the village would come for a special time of communing with the spirits of nature to arrive at the answers to great individual problems, or even to understand the purpose of all human existence.

'You mean "a vision quest",' Cori said. She had heard of the Indian equivalent of a spiritual pilgrimage.

Abel nodded. 'The *hanbleceya*. It means "crying for a vision".' A man on a vision quest, he continued, would come here alone, without provisions except for some water, and sit naked in the vision pit, sometimes through several days and nights of the most extreme temperatures of heat or cold, until a vision came.

'So visions were probably just hallucinations,' Cori remarked.

'That would be the scientific explanation,' Abel agreed. 'But why does the hallucination take one form or another? We believe it is a message from the spirits.'

Cori wondered silently why, if there were visions of truth to be found here, the people who had come to this place to receive them had suffered a massacre.

The summer night was warm. When they returned to the campsite, they stripped and waded naked into the cold, shallow river. In the water, they began their touches, caressing skin cold as marble, statues coming to life, until he cupped his strong hands under her thighs and lifted her up. Speared on his hard hot muscle, arms looped around his neck, she rode him, until she threw her head back and cried out with joy to the stars. 'I love you, Abel.'

He whispered the same words back to her again and again as he carried her out of the stream, laid her down atop the bedrolls on the ground, and straddled her.

'What message do you think they'd send us,' Cori said, 'if we went to the vision pit? Are we fools or dreamers? Can we go back and ask the question?'

'It's a very holy place, Cori. Not a fortune-teller's booth at a carnival.'

'I didn't mean any disrespect,' she said contritely. 'But I do wonder, Abel: what's to become of us?'

As though the howl of a beast had knifed into her sleep, or a crash of thunder, she bolted up in the dark already in terror.

But the night was still warm and quiet, the sky clear except for a nearly full moon and the bright frosting of stars. She looked over at Abel to assure herself he was lying quietly beside her. At that moment, he let out a startling sound, a keening whine from low in his throat. He was still asleep, but he was not in repose. He thrashed within his bedroll as though trying to break loose from something holding him in a painful grip.

Her first thought was that he'd been bitten by a snake or a scorpion. She shook him. 'Abel! Wake up! *Abel!*'

His eyes snapped open, and at last he stopped flailing and relaxed onto his back. For a few seconds he lay gasping for breath as though he had collapsed after a desperate run to save himself from a pursuing pack of demons.

She leaned over him. 'What was it, Abel? A bad dream . . .?'

'Yes.' At last he focused on her. 'Very bad.'

'What did you see?'

'I saw that we must go.' He rose to his feet as he answered and began rapidly gathering his clothes, slipping into them.

She stared at him. 'Go? Now?'

'Get up, Cori. Get dressed.' Clipped commands, like military orders.

'But it's the middle of the night . . .'

He did not reply as he picked up her clothes, and tossed them to her in a ball. Baffled as she was, his momentum pulled her along. She put on her jeans and pullover while he started packing up their bedrolls, collecting all the cooking gear. By the light of the moon, she watched as he went to saddle and bridle the horses that had been left untethered to graze by the river.

It was not merely a dream that had frightened him, she realized, but another of those prophetic visitations like the one he had seen before Black Eagle's death. He was moving all the more quickly to heed this warning because he had ignored it last time.

When he brought her horse, she took the reins and mounted it without a word. She could not hope to live his life if she argued with his spirits. But as she watched him kick ashes over the last smoldering embers of their campfire, she shivered with an intuition that an inner glow had been extinguished as well.

In the darkness, they rode the horses at a walk, heading back again toward his reservation. At last, she tried again. 'What did you see in your dream?'

As he answered, he kept his eyes fixed on the horizon where the sun was rising. 'There were many *tipis*, enough for all the tribe, standing together – a village, at peace. Then you walked into the center of the village. In the dream you were a stranger, but I knew you'd come looking for me. So I walked out of one of the *tipis*, and went toward you . . .' He faltered, and she could hear a trace of the same breathlessness that had overtaken him in his sleep. 'Then suddenly all the *tipis* were in flames, people running out of them with their skin on fire – children, too, crying terribly, their bodies charring. I moved toward you, faster, thinking to save you – or perhaps you would save me – but my father appeared between us, and he waved at me to go back, away from you. I wouldn't, I kept going forward. And then, as though he were made of straw, he burst into flames. I went right through the flames though now I was burning, blinded, my flesh melting. I kept trying to reach you, groping. I was just about to touch you when my sight came back, and I saw *wanjbli* swooping down out of the flaming sky, his huge claws grasping you, ripping away your face as he started to fly upward . . .' He fell silent again.

'Who is *wanjbli*?' she asked.

'The eagle. One of our most sacred guardians.'

The rest was easy to understand. By loving a *wasicun* woman, he had become his father, Walks-Through-Fire. As it had destroyed one, it would destroy the other. The spirits, if one believed they spoke through dreams, were telling him that he was blind to all the dangers of loving her, and that he had to let the spirits take her away – obey their warnings to *send* her away – or many people would be hurt.

They rode in silence the rest of the way, her heart breaking, her world darkening even as the sun rose higher. Yet she was oddly unable to cry. The wound was so sudden, so huge, she was in that state of trauma where the nerves shut down against a pain too great to bear.

His own pain was no less, yet he bore it like the wound of a soldier. He was responding to a command of the spirits; no matter how great his suffering, it had to be borne.

It was late afternoon by the time they returned the horses and drove her car back to the *tipospaye*. He left her to go alone to the *tipi* to collect her belongings. As she carried them back to her car, she saw all the members of the *tipospaye* lined up outside the large shack, watching. None of them waved or called, not even the children. Abel had obviously explained her sudden departure.

He helped her place things into the trunk, then opened the door for her. 'I'm sorry,' he said. 'But you must see that staying together would be crazy.'

'Not crazy,' she objected. Whatever reasons he gave himself, she could not let it be described that way.

'Then say . . . unreal. What we thought was possible for these few days was only a dream. And it's the dream that told us the truth.'

'I understand that's what you believe,' she said, hopeless against the grip the spirits had on his being. She longed to reach out to him, to kiss him once more, but she feared he might step back or push her away, and she did not want the last memory she took away to be that. Better save the memory of how he had touched her when he had desired her.

Cori stood for a few moments, waiting – praying – that he might reach for her. When she searched his eyes, she thought she saw hints of doubt, signs his resolve might fail. If only there were no spirits to appease – at least, if his belief in them was not so great – he would never send her away.

But he said nothing, and made no move as she started backing away.

He hadn't taken a step by the time Cori reached the car and looked back once more.

She got in behind the wheel, and drove away without even a glance in the rear-view mirror. Only when she had gone past the rusted sign, and knew she was outside the boundaries of the reservation did she stop at the side of the road. She covered her face with her hands, and put her head down on the wheel, her body wracked by such convulsive sobs, that by the time she was done every muscle ached.

Still, that was easily tolerable compared to the boundless hurt in her soul.

9

She spent the next week at the Golden H in Jackson Hole. It gave her the time she needed to recover from the worst of the trauma. She went on trail rides during the day, and sat by a fire in the big lodge at night, eating dinner from a tray brought by one of the servants. Buck Stovall rode with her sometimes, and while he had no trouble perceiving that something serious was weighing on her mind, he didn't push her to explain, simply kept himself handy in case she needed to talk. Eventually, she told him what had happened.

It was all for the best, he assured her. She'd broken out of her cocoon of privilege to see the hard daily grind that was the lot of most people, and she'd had her first love affair. In short, she had grown up. Better that it ended than she had to reshape her whole existence to endure a harder life. Wasn't it easier too, that the whole episode could now remain a secret, and she would never have to confront G.D.?

Reviewed in the sensible perspective supplied by Buck, Cori's sadness was replaced by a philosophical appreciation of what she had enjoyed, however brief. By the time Cori returned to San Francisco, she had recovered her equilibrium. She did not doubt the truth and purity of the feelings that had consumed her while she was with Abel: she had been in love. But the whole experience seemed contained and complete, a bubble in time she could remember and examine as though it had happened years ago, instead of just weeks. She felt no bitterness toward Abel. It hadn't been his choice to send her away, she told herself, but a command given to him by a power greater than himself.

'There's something different about you,' Frank said. 'I can't put my finger on it, but you've definitely changed.'

They were sitting over a late supper at Ernie's, the most popular of the city's restaurants which preserved the atmosphere of San Francisco at the turn of the century. Frank had called at the last minute offering to take her to the symphony's first concert of the season and dinner afterwards because his date for the evening had come down with a stomach virus. 'If I was a gallant gentleman,' Frank had said on the phone, 'I'd give the tickets away, and go to the lady's house to feed her warm soup and read her the funny papers. But I'm more in the mood for Mozart than gallantry. And to get right down to the nitty-gritty . . . I've missed you, Cori.' He had called a couple of times over the past few weeks while she had been away.

Something different about her, he'd said. Cori toyed with an urge to burst out with the truth. *Of course I'm different, I'm not a twenty-two-year-old virgin anymore.* If there was any man beside Buck that she ought to be able to tell it was Frank. Yet Cori was reticent, no longer able to regard him as merely a buddy. Having slept with one man, her sexual curiosity about others was piqued. What would it be like with Frank? she wondered several times during the evening. In fact, she guessed that the crux of what Frank sensed as different was that she was no longer *in*different to him.

'Maybe it's you that's changed,' she said coyly. 'Since

you've become a reporter, always looking behind the scenes and digging for a "scoop", maybe you're starting for the first time to get a better idea of what's under the surface of me.' His work on the city desk had gone from basic ambulance-chasing to the investigative side. He had been responsible for uncovering evidence – published in a headline two days ago – that an official in the building department had been taking bribes to overlook enforcement of some of the rigorous codes that San Francisco had put in place since the great earthquake of '06.

Frank picked up his glass of wine and sipped from it, watching her over the rim. 'I don't think that quite explains it.' He put his glass down, but his eyes stayed on her. ' 'Matter of fact, I've been paying more attention to the surface than ever. Quite a lovely surface, I must say . . .'

He had never been so openly flirtatious before. 'Frank,' she muttered disparagingly, though she didn't really mind. She couldn't deny that she'd given more than the usual attention to how she dressed and made herself up, playing with the notion of attracting his interest. Unlike Bren, she didn't own anything with a plunging neckline, but the plain black Dior sheath she'd worn had a sinuous cut that showed off her neck and shoulders.

'Hell, Cori,' he said. 'We're not just playmates anymore. At least, I'd like to think we're not. You're one of the most . . .' He paused, obviously searching for a word that would not go too far all at once in shifting the ground of their relationship. ' . . . most *appealing* women I know. We've been friends so long that I've seen you pass through all the awkward stages – from pesky little girl, to a gawky tomboy with braces on your teeth, to that all-too-serious co-ed always carrying around an armload of books on renaissance art and modern poetry. It took me a while to adjust my eyes and notice that you've entered a new stage.'

'Oh? How would you describe it?'

'*Femme fatale,*' he said.

She laughed. 'That's going too far, Mr Patterson. Everybody knows Bren got all the *femme fatale* genes in the family.'

His handsome face settled into a more earnest expression. 'Okay, let's just say "woman".' He leaned closer across the table. 'I'm seeing you for the first time as a woman, Cori. And I'm wondering . . .' He paused.

She felt nervous suddenly, afraid he might ask what had brought about the change. If he had some blossoming attraction to her, she doubted it could survive finding out too much about her recent love affair. From his perspective it might make her appear flighty and sluttish – even unstable.

'I'm wondering,' he went on, 'if you'd have any trouble thinking of me as . . . something more than a friend.'

Cori's answer didn't come automatically. Even if she'd let herself toy with the idea of going to bed with him, as it moved out of the realm of imagination, she wondered if it would be possible. Could she ever depart from the shy, demure pose she'd taken with him to reveal the kind of passionate abandon she'd discovered when she was with Abel?

Even if it was possible, she needed more time to mend. 'I like you so much, Frank – I always have – that I wouldn't want to close the door on any possibility. But I don't want to move so fast toward something else that we leave the friendship behind. Having you to lean on has always been important to me.'

'To me, too. I wouldn't want to jeopardize that, either.'

They smiled at each other awkwardly. 'So,' he said, with a shrug, 'we'll just see how it goes.'

They sipped from their wine. Casting her eyes down demurely, Cori said, 'I never thought I was your type. The girls you took out were always more . . . you know . . .'

'Taller?' he teased.

'You know what I mean – you told me enough about them.'

'Blonder?'

'Sexier,' she said, half whispering as she leaned across the table. 'Slinkier. With bigger boobs. More like Bren, come to think of it. That's the type you were always with.'

'That was okay when I was interested in "types". But I'm ready for something – someone – unique.' His gray eyes fixed on her. 'I guess you could say I've grown up.'

Him, too. Perhaps it was even a sign they belonged together.

Over the following weeks, they spent all their free time together. On nights Frank was assigned to the city desk, he often asked her to come to the newspaper. While he wrote up his story, she would sit nearby reading a novel. She was pleased that he showed her the first drafts; a couple of times he'd incorporated the suggestions she made.

On a Tuesday night when the city was cloaked in Pacific fog, a report came in of a fire in a wooden tenement building in Oakland. A family with several children was trapped on an upper floor. Frank invited Cori to come and watch him work. In the past she would have been reluctant to put herself in the midst of a situation fraught with so much potential tragedy. But she was taking every opportunity to get closer to Frank, ready to move their relationship to an even deeper level. Their explorations of physical intimacy had only been tenuous so far. Holding hands, good night kisses.

Outfitted with a temporary press card, Cori arrived with Frank and was passed through the fire department cordon. Looking up at the burning building, Cori saw tongues of flame spouting from rows of windows across the top two floors. Two ladders were fully extended up to a couple of the highest windows from the back of a pair of fire trucks. Atop one ladder a fireman was hosing water into the building. The other ladder was empty. Even at a distance of forty yards, Cori felt the heat tightening her face and drying her eyes.

'The children,' she burst out, clutching at Frank's sleeve. At the same moment, Abel's dream came suddenly into her mind – he had talked of children in flames.

Frank stepped away and spoke to a fire marshal.

'They've brought most of them down safely on a ladder – all but one little boy. They're in there now trying to find him.'

The word had spread. Behind the cordon, rows of people were watching, all staring up at the window at the end of the empty ladder. Cori also saw a man and a woman by an ambulance peering up with stricken eyes. The mother and father, she suspected.

A stir went through the crowd as a fireman climbed out of the building onto the empty ladder, then a second fireman came to a window and passed a small figure wrapped in a blanket to the first. Frank stepped away to talk with a fire marshal holding a walkie-talkie. Concerned for the child, Cori drifted toward the ladder truck. Her attention fixed on the fireman who was rapidly descending the ladder with a bundle in his arms, she was barely aware of the intensifying heat as she went nearer the building. She was only a few yards away when the fireman reached the bottom of the ladder where a pair of medical orderlies waited with a stretcher. Exhausted from the ordeal of his search, his face singed and blackened by smoke, the fireman said nothing as he handed the bundle to the orderlies. But Cori saw him give a hopeless shake of his head. She couldn't tear her eyes away as the figure was laid down on the stretcher, the blanket peeled back. Enfolded within was a boy of no more than five or six. The skin of the face and upper torso had been so severely burned in some places it was black and flaking like burned paper. Charred. As Abel had said of the children in his dream.

She might have screamed if she'd had the strength. But as though the fire had broken through a nearby wall, there was a sudden burst of heat that seemed to billow out and consume her. She spun around to escape from it, but then she felt too weak to take a step, or even stop the spin. She went on, spiraling faster and faster, and at the same time falling as if from the top of that tall ladder into a deep black well.

Only a fainting spell brought on by the heat and the shock of seeing the dead boy, the ambulance crew said. But because she continued to feel some dizziness, a young medical resident urged that Cori spend a night in the hospital for observation and a routine check. Frank concurred; he felt guilty for exposing her to the gruesome scene. Fire department officials were also concerned lest G.D. Hartleigh hold them accountable for being careless about the treatment accorded his beloved daughter.

At two a.m., after seeing Cori comfortably settled in a private room at San Francisco General Hospital, Frank returned to the newspaper to file his story about the fire for the morning editions. He had already called Pamela Hartleigh to report what had happened, and assure her Cori was fine and there was no need for her to race to the hospital in the middle of the night. Fortunately, G.D. – who would have raised havoc – was out of town, in Washington to appear before a Senate committee considering new regulations for the atomic energy industry.

In the morning, Cori felt fully recovered. After a hospital breakfast, she showered in her private bathroom, then found her clothes in a closet. The ivory linen dress she'd worn last night was smudged and smelled of smoke, so she thought of calling for the chauffeur to bring a fresh change. But her usual fastidiousness was overruled by impatience to be released. It wasn't yet nine o'clock; if she hurried she could be home before her mother's usual waking time.

She had finished dressing, and was brushing her hair at a mirror opposite her bed, when the young resident who had been at the fire scene strolled into the room. He was short and heavyset with a mop of curly brown hair, adding up to a sweet

131

teddy-bear aspect that made him instantly likeable. 'You're not supposed to get dressed,' he said, 'until you've been examined and officially checked out.'

'But I felt so well, I didn't think you'd have to—'

'You're perfectly fine. I think we can dispense with another examination. We did a good work-up last night when you were admitted, including a comprehensive blood test . . .' He looked at her expectantly, as if he thought she might have a question. But Cori said nothing; he had already said she was fine.

'Miss Hartleigh, would you mind sitting down?'

The request made Cori a little anxious, but she lowered herself onto one of the straight-backed chairs supplied for visitors. Keeping the mood informal, the doctor perched on the edge of the bed at the foot. 'Have you ever fainted before?' he asked.

'No.'

'Can you think of anything that might have made you a little more susceptible than usual?'

Cori shook her head.

The resident nodded, as though he had confirmed a private diagnosis. 'I had a hunch you might not know.'

'Know what?'

'Miss Hartleigh . . . I mentioned that we took a small blood sample for routine testing. The results show that you're perfectly healthy – and something else: the enzyme levels clearly indicate that you're pregnant.'

Cori stared at him. The solidity of the chair beneath her seemed to disappear. She was going to faint again. But then her mind started racing, pulling her back to full awareness.

It had never been a habit of hers to keep track rigidly of her period, and she'd been so preoccupied anyway, coming to terms with Abel's rejection, then by the onset of a new relationship with Frank, that she hadn't given a thought to measuring time. Now she realized it had been about six weeks since she'd gone in search of Abel . . . a little less than three weeks since she'd returned. She wasn't just pregnant, but possibly advanced as much as a month. A reflex moved her hand to lie flat over her stomach, as if trying to sense that barely formed life. 'What am I going to do?' she said, looking around blankly.

The doctor didn't attempt to answer the question. 'Miss Hartleigh, I think you might like to know that I haven't discussed this with anyone else.' Just as he'd suspected that Cori might not be aware of her condition, the resident guessed she might want the information to remain secret. It didn't take a genius to figure that getting knocked up might create some nasty problems for the unmarried daughter of one of San Francisco's richest, most prominent families.

'I'd be very grateful if you'd keep it that way,' Cori said.

'I understand. But you also have to be aware that this is in the hospital records, and the case relates to an incident involving the city authorities. If I was your private doctor, I could guarantee confidentiality. Under these circumstances the records aren't under my control.'

Cori fought to keep her anxiety from escalating to panic. Frank! They had just crossed over the threshold into a lovely new kind of intimacy. Could that possibly survive his learning about this? He was a newspaperman. Would he – or anyone from the paper – come to the hospital to get details for a report on the fire? Could a fact like this find its way into the gossip column?

With an effort Cori pulled herself up from the chair. She couldn't sit here all day, frozen by the dilemma. She had to figure out what to do, get it done – whatever it was. 'Thank you again, doctor,' she said. 'You've been very considerate. I appreciate it.'

'Not at all, Miss Hartleigh.'

'Can I leave now?'

'I just have to walk you out to the desk and sign a couple of papers. Then you'll be free to go.'

No, Cori thought. I can go . . . but I won't be free.

Bren's voice came back over the telephone line after a long silence. 'Shit, Cor',' if you felt so goddam sorry for that Indian, why didn't you send a few thousand bucks to some charity, or collect canned goods, or . . . Jesus, I don't know. Why the hell did you have to go and fuck him? Your first, for godssake! What a crazy, stupid—'

'Damn it, Bren,' Cori erupted. 'I called for advice, not to get bawled out. The way you fling yourself at men, you're the last person who should be acting holier-than-thou.'

'Kiddo, all I'm acting is less-pregnant-than-thou. Sure, I fuck like a bunny, but at least I've learned to take precautions.'

For a moment, neither sister spoke. Cori glanced anxiously toward the closed door of the library, wondering if her raised voice had carried to other parts of the mansion. She had waited to make the call until this evening, when her mother was out at a dinner with friends, but there was always a chance Pamela would return unexpectedly – or even that one of the servants would eavesdrop. At least G.D. was away, though he was right there in Washington. Cori had made Bren swear up and down five times that she wouldn't breathe a word to G.D.

'Bren, what can I do?' Cori asked plaintively. 'You're the only person I felt I could tell. I was hoping you'd have some ideas. I'm so lost.'

Bren's voice came back on the line, more sympathetic. 'Sorry, kid. You're right, I've got no business reading you the riot act. Fact is . . . I had to learn to be careful the hard way.'

'What do you mean?' Cori asked.

'I had an abortion myself.'

'You did? When?' There had never been the least hint of Bren being in trouble.

'My first year here in D.C.,' Bren answered, something like

jauntiness in her tone. 'I had quite a thing going for a while with a freshman senator from Massachusetts, a cute guy, great in the sack. But one day I read in the paper he'd gotten engaged; all the time, he was fucking me he'd been squiring around some deb from Newport. That was the end of our afternoon tea parties, right there. But then I found out he'd left me with a souvenir. Well, it suited us both to . . . take measures. I didn't want his kid, and he's got plans to be President some day.'

'So how did you do it?' Cori said in a hush, still worried about being overheard through the closed door.

'Went to a first-class doctor down in Puerto Rico. Five thousand bucks, I was in and out in a day. Lay on the beach a few more days at the Hilton. I could set it up for you, Cor' . . .'

Cori went down that path in her mind, imagined the masked doctor leaning over her, hands probing, plucking out the seed of a life. 'No,' she said. 'I don't think I could do that.'

'Baby, you've got no choice. I mean, otherwise G.D.'ll have to know the works, and you'll have to take the incredible amount of crap that comes with that.'

Cori rehearsed that scenario in her mind, too. Worse than the first.

'Unless . . .' Bren's voice lifted optimistically as she let the word hang in the air.

'Unless what?'

'When we talked a few weeks ago, didn't you tell me you'd been seeing a lot of Frank?'

'Oh gosh, Bren, he's the last person I'd ask for help with—'

'Who said anything about *asking*? You want his help, you can have it without saying a thing. Have you slept with him yet?' Bren asked. Just checking. With Frank, who had known Cori forever as a strait-laced virgin, Bren was fairly certain her sister would have reverted to living by her old rules.

'No . . .'

'Perfect. Now all you have to do is move things along a

little faster. Then Frank'll think he's got to make an honest woman out of you. G.D. would be tickled pink, too, if you married a Patterson. Nothing better for the company than having a family connection to the city's most powerful editorial page.'

Cori had hardly heard a thing past the point where she understood Bren was talking about maneuvering Frank into thinking he was the father. They had reached the point where it would be easy . . . if only her conscience would allow it.

'Cor', are you there?'

'Yes,' she said softly.

'You see it, don't you? It's the perfect answer.'

'I see it,' Cori said absently. 'Thanks, Bren. I knew you'd help.'

'Keep in touch, kid. I'd like to hear the blow-by-blow . . . so to speak.'

Cori didn't rise from the chair at the big desk in the library after hanging up. It had indeed helped to talk to Bren; at least she saw clearly what the choices were – and, reflecting on them in the context of her sister's preferences – was quite sure of which she would be capable of living with, and which would destroy her.

In fact, she concluded, if she had ever deserved to be called *ohitika win*, then there was really no choice at all.

10

From the back seat of the family's Chrysler limousine, Cori watched the Lockeed Constellation taxi along the sunlit runway to HMC's private hangar where a stepped ramp was rolled up to the rear door. As the propellors feathered to a stop, the roar of the engines was replaced in her ears by the pounding of her heart.

Perhaps, Cori thought now, it had been a mistake to break the news to her mother first while G.D. was still away. But she had counted on more sympathy from her mother, as well as a more level-headed practical response. Pamela Hartleigh had always been so cool and well-organized when it came to solving problems. Though Cori realized now that what had been called problems in the past were minor nuisances compared with this crisis. This time her mother had been thrown into an absolute tailspin.

'This will *kill* your father,' Pamela had cried, dabbing a handkerchief at her eyes as if already in mourning. 'It wouldn't matter if it was Bren. But *you*. This will tear his heart out.'

That was only the beginning of her mother's litany of disaster. There was the effect it would have on her own social standing; she'd hardly be able to go anywhere in town without

137

the whispers following her. *Poor Pamela . . . did you hear about that daughter of hers*? And what about the effect on Cori's life? It had always been assumed Corinne Hartleigh would make a desirable marriage. But *now*? If Cori married it would be to someone *outside* the proper circles – assuming anyone would have her at all.

The situation would be better, of course, if Cori didn't have this wild notion about having the baby. Even if she went through with giving birth, that could be managed. If she went abroad soon, that could be covered with some story about wanting to study art in Italy, *cordon-bleu* cooking in France, whatever. She'd be out of sight until after the baby was given up for adoption. Not the first time a young lady from a gilt-edged family had engaged in that subterfuge. But *keeping* it, letting the world see this proof of the crazy fling with an ill-bred aborigine, and then raising it . . . that would destroy them all. If Cori persisted in such an insane idea, then her mother wanted no part of it, none at all. 'I won't have a daughter,' Pamela Hartleigh proclaimed, 'toting around a bastard papoose to make *me* the laughing stock of everyone on "the Hill". My God, if anyone knew it had gone even *this* far, I'd never be able to leave the house again!'

Cori hadn't been present when her mother had phoned G.D. in Washington, but she guessed last night's revelations had been relayed with the full measure of hysteria. 'Your father is flying straight home,' Pamela had told Cori this morning. 'You are to meet him with the car at the airport this afternoon.'

A pretty young stewardess appeared at the top of the ramp, in position to give G.D. a fawning farewell.

Finally he stepped out. Pausing in the sun, he brushed his full white mane back with his hand, then exchanged a few words with the stewardess. As they talked, Cori saw him smile. He didn't seem grim at all. When he proceeded down the ramp, he moved quickly with a light step. No sign of being worried or disappointed or fatigued. He looked dapper in charcoal slacks and a pearl-gray blazer.

She got out of the car to greet him.

Seeing her, his expression changed, but only to a look of the mildest reproof, as though he was walking into the principal's office at grade school after she'd been sent out for passing silly notes in class. He opened his arms as he came toward her. Relief came over her like a cool breeze. She relaxed into his embrace while a steward brought his luggage from the plane. He stepped away to confer for a second with the chauffeur as the baggage was loaded into the trunk of the car, then he got into the back with Cori and they started the ride into the city.

'I've never heard your mother so upset,' he began. The soundproof panel between the rear compartment and the chauffeur was fully raised.

'I know,' Cori said contritely. 'She kept saying it would kill you. I'm glad it didn't,' she added with an earnestness that seemed funny in view of his obvious vigor.

He smiled thinly as he regarded the passing view. 'That's called emotional blackmail, I believe. She knows you love me, and wouldn't deliberately do anything that hurt me so terribly.' He turned to her. 'That's true, isn't it, Corker?'

'Daddy, do you even have to ask?'

He gave her a warm and paternal smile, and turned again to the window. 'It does seem, though, that you have no trouble lying to me.' His tone had gone suddenly cold. 'You knew my wishes. You weren't supposed to go near this man's trial, much less let him between your legs!' His voice fell to a scornful hiss. 'My God, Corinne. How could you do it? A common Indian, of all people, throwing yourself at him for a few cheap thrills—'

'It wasn't like that! We cared for each other.'

He looked around stiffly. 'Did you? You went on some sort

of . . . errand of mercy, and spent a couple of weeks "going native", and now it qualifies to be called – what? – a love affair?'

Cori looked down as her eyes filled and she replied, barely audibly, 'I thought I loved him, yes.'

'That almost makes it worse,' he said. Then he shrugged. 'At least it's over. From what your mother told me, you don't intend to have any further contact with the man involved. Correct?'

Head bowed, Cori nodded. Tears dripped onto the hands crossed in her lap.

G.D. Hartleigh pressed back into the plush seat of the limousine, overcome for a moment by a wave of turbulent conflicting feelings, remorse and disgust and fury and defeat. This child of his, this pristine jewel – as he'd thought of her once – had been soiled, defiled. By her own choice. As she sat brokenly beside him, he was surprised to find that any desire to comfort her was overridden by a rising sense that he simply didn't want to touch her again – she was unclean. All love hadn't deserted him, but his most powerful urge was to do whatever was necessary to restore her and bring her back into his caste. 'You're mother also told me,' he resumed, 'that you were playing with the notion of keeping this child.'

She raised her head to look at him. 'That's not what I told her.'

'Oh no?' he said with a hopeful lilt.

'It's not a notion I'm "playing with",' she threw the words back at him with a bitter edge. 'It's a decision I've made. I want this baby.'

He arched an eyebrow. 'I see. And you think that's fair and sensible?'

'How is it unfair? It's *my* baby, my choice. As for sensible, it's too late to fit that into the equation. There wasn't anything sensible about getting myself into this mess. But now it goes against my grain not to accept responsibility for it, especially if the alternative means . . . taking a life.'

'Don't give me *that* crap! We're not Catholics, that's not an issue. Medically, too, there's no substance. Whatever you've got growing inside you right now has no heart or brain.'

'It will, though. It *is* the beginning of a life. What's more, I have an intuition it's a life that will be important.'

'More crap – the standard maternal pride. The reality is that the only lives at stake right now are all of ours, the family's. What about your responsibility to us?'

'This can't threaten you in any way that matters,' she said, a tinge of fear replacing the resolve in her voice. When G.D. raised the family flag it was a sign that he was prepared to do battle with all his weapons.

He was ominously silent for a while, regarding the scene passing outside. At last, he said, 'Listen to me, Corinne: I will not have a little bastard with an ounce of Indian blood for a grandchild. I suppose you think that's ugly and extreme. But whatever the Hartleigh's are, whatever we have, was built on knowing that we're on one side – and *they*'re on the other. I can't go back on that. And they wouldn't either.'

'For godssake, Daddy,' she burst out, 'the frontier's gone, the battles have been fought – and you won. There's no reason to go on hating—'

'It's not hate, Corinne, no more than what a spider feels for a fly is hate – or what water feels for fire. We just can't occupy the same space without one turning on the other, and whichever is the stronger or the better adapted is the winner. But it's not over. Maybe we're not using arrows and guns any longer, but there's still a fight going on. Christ, don't you know these damn Sioux have brought the company into court the past year? They claim the treaties by which they gave up our mining land are null and void because they were forced to sign? Hell, those treaties go back seventy, eighty years. Damn it, of course

141

they were forced to sign. We beat the shit out of them when they were trying to take every scalp in sight. But suddenly I have to defend my rights again! They talk about taking it all the way to the Supreme Court. Just another form of Indian ambush. Well, how the hell do you think I feel about even the possibility that another round might be launched against me someday by my own grandchild!'

The substance of his argument had gone from family loyalty to company policy. It did nothing to change Cori's mind. She forced herself to respond coolly and rationally despite his rabid tone.

'Daddy, I *am* going to have this child. I'm not doing it to hurt you – and it doesn't have to. You have a choice just as I do. If you're able to bend, there's even a chance that someday you'll feel I'm doing the right thing.'

His stoney expression momentarily softened. 'You have such a good heart, dear girl, such admirable faith in the future.' The moment ended. 'But I don't see it your way now, and I'm sure I never will. I've made it plain that I won't have this mongrel in my family. If you insist on bringing it into the world, then you won't be part of the family, either. I'm not making an idle threat, Corinne. You'll be cut off. Absolutely and irrevocably.'

The pronouncement hit Cori like a punch to the stomach. She slumped back, barely listening as G.D. hammered on with the specific terms of disowning her, the loss of inheritance rights and allowances, the reversion of trusts, the closing of bank and charge accounts, a demand for her to leave his house at once – and his expectation that she would move far from the city, so that neither he nor her mother would need to be embarrassed by any possible contact, or risk the damaging truth of what she had done being spread. He mentioned, finally, that he hoped she would cease to use the Hartleigh name. He would fight her legally, if need be, to keep her bastard from using the name Hartleigh.

He had thought it out in detail, obviously; there was no doubt he meant to carry through – if she did.

When she could draw breath again, Cori said, 'So you'd abort me, too, cut me out of yourself unless I do what you want.'

He was watching the view again, the bayside towers of the city looming larger. He said nothing.

'I imagine you've made the plans already, got me booked on a flight to Mexico or some Caribbean island . . .'

'Not at all – nothing tawdry like that. As long as you are my daughter, you shall always have the best. It'll be done right here, in a hospital.'

'It's against the law,' she observed.

'Not if a reputable doctor attests to the likelihood that a full-term pregnancy would be life-threatening to the mother.'

G.D. wouldn't have any trouble finding a cooperative doctor, Cori realized, not after all his years of being a major donor to more than one of the best hospitals in the city.

She retreated into silence. When she had told her mother she wanted to keep the child, Cori hadn't believed that it would conceivably lead to this impasse. Yes, Claire Eaton had been disinherited. But that was in another era. And could that puritanical Boston surgeon have been as adoring of his daughter as Cori knew G.D. was of her?

She balanced the alternatives. Keeping the life she had with all its comforts and privileges, or being orphaned and impoverished with a baby to raise – a child cut off from all its roots on both sides.

Ohitika win – she taunted herself ironically in her mind. Are you *that* brave? She knew she wasn't. Yet she couldn't yield to him outright, not because of pride, but something more primal. 'How soon do I have to choose?' she said.

He gave her an astonished glance. 'I can't believe you still think there *is* a choice.'

'How soon?' she repeated.

Held by his furious glare, it was a few moments before Cori realized that the limousine was no longer moving through traffic. Then she became aware that G.D.'s gaze had drifted from her face to look over her shoulder. Cori turned around.

The car was standing at the curb in front of the private patients' entrance to San Francisco General Hospital. The chauffeur came around to open the door.

'Go ahead,' G.D. said. 'They're waiting. I think it's better if I don't come in with you, under the circumstances. But it's quite a simple procedure, I'm told. Gannon will be here with the car again in a few hours to bring you home.'

Gannon, the chauffeur, offered a hand to help her out of the car. Numb with shock, Cori acted by reflex, laying her hand in his, stepping out, walking across the sidewalk. She kept going through the door, and entered the lobby.

'Miss Hartleigh?' a woman's voice hailed her before she had walked more than a few steps.

Cori saw a stocky nurse in a starched white uniform. She froze for an instant. The nurse smiled and moved toward her.

Cori whirled and ran in the opposite direction, back into the street. The limousine was gone, thank God. G.D. would have probably ordered the chauffeur to stop her – would have had her carried into the operating room, if necessary.

Behind her as she kept going, Cori could hear the shrill calling of the nurse who had followed her onto the street.

'Miss Hartleigh . . . where are you going? *Miss Hartleigh*!'

She kept running ahead, plunging blindly across the street as traffic halted to avoid hitting her.

'Miss Hartleigh!'

She never looked back. It wasn't her name being called – not anymore.

Resentment prevented her from taking any of the sensible steps that, months later, she would wish she had. She made no hurried trip to a bank to withdraw money from her own account, nor raced home to collect clothes and valuables – the jewelry her father had given her, assets that could have been sold. Didn't even try to get her convertible from the garage. What did she want with any of G.D.'s gifts? His love had been exposed as meaningless, so every vestige of it was equally without value. No point asking her mother's help, either. Cori wanted nothing from either of them. She would have emptied her purse of the ninety dollars she was carrying, but she couldn't leave herself without the means to escape, to run to where she could be reborn, begin to believe in her new name and new self.

Her last concession to the bonds of the family was to telephone Bren in Washington from the bus terminal – collect.

'Cori, dear, you're over-reacting,' Bren said after Cori reported G.D.'s edict, and explained she was calling to say goodbye as she set out for parts unknown. 'Go to the ranch and stay there. Give G.D. a week or two to cool down.'

'Cool or hot, Bren, he's not going to change how he feels about this baby.' Cori didn't bother mentioning that she had previously called Buck to ask if she could stay at the ranch, and he had told her that G.D. had already sent individual telegrams to every member of the staff with orders that, if Cori came, she was to be turned away as though she were a stranger. Anyone who ignored the order or tried to help Cori in any way would be fired. G.D. would not only deny them future references, but would make it his business to see that they didn't have an easy time finding work elsewhere.

'That sonofabitch,' Buck said. 'I would've told him off good if he'd gotten me on the phone instead of the housekeeper. Doin' this to his own flesh and blood. Never you mind, though, honey, you come straight here and Buck'll see you're looked after.'

To stem any further argument, she told Buck she would

come though she knew it was no longer possible. He was devoted to her; he wouldn't think twice about giving up his job. But she cared too much about him to make him the target of G.D.'s wrath. With Bren, Cori knew better than to expect her to intercede. Bren would not risk getting cut off as well.

'Cori,' Bren said as a final attempt at peacemaking, 'why do you have to force his hand? Is having this baby worth losing everything else? Do what he wants, for godssake. You can have other children, lots of others, once you get married. And it'll be with someone who'll make the right kind of father.'

Slumped in the phone booth, Cori stared out at the bus terminal and searched for an answer to give her sister – or just to give herself. There was no doubt in her mind she must have this child, whatever the cost to herself. But why?

'Bren, I wish to God I could do what G.D. wants. It hurts like hell being locked out, and I'm scared about what could happen to me.' She was trembling as she spoke, fighting back tears. 'I've never had to make my way alone, support myself, much less solve a problem like this one. But as hard as I know it's going to be, I don't seem able to stop moving ahead, doing what has to be done to have this child. It's not just biological, Bren, not maternal instinct . . .' As she tried to explain, it became less hazy in her mind. 'We've taken so much from them, Bren, don't you see? All of us have taken – but our family more than most. For so long, taken what's theirs, killed them when they fought back, and let so many die from starvation, or poor medical treatment—'

'My God, Cori, is that what this is about? You have to live in poverty and give birth to a mixed-breed baby . . . as a penance for winning the west? Jesus, you've always been a starry-eyed little jerk, but this takes the cake. This time—'

Cori cut her off. 'It doesn't surprise me that you can't understand. You do G.D.'s work. Well, I can't. I have to give something back. Even if it's nothing more than . . . a life.'

Quietly, Bren said, 'You poor kid.'

It galled Cori to hear more pity than sympathy in her sister's words, but she clutched at the phone through a silence, unwilling to break the connection.

'Listen, if it really gets tough,' Bren added, 'don't push it too far. You know what I mean, Cor'? And let me know where you are. I'm going to talk to G.D., and see if I can't get him to . . . make a few concessions.'

'Thanks, Bren,' Cori said, though without hope. It was probably a sincere gesture on Bren's part; that was what Bren did, after all, she lobbied in the halls of power for a concession here, an amendment there. But it was G.D. who had taught her the ropes and paid her to do the work on others; no lobbyist could make him ease the laws he made himself.

Portland, Oregon. Cori made the random choice at the bus ticket window because the fare would not use up too much of her money, and it was a large enough city so she expected there would be a choice of job opportunities.

She found work right away as a salesperson in a book store near the campus of the University of Oregon, and rented a room with a pullman kitchen from an elderly lady who had divided up her large, well-maintained home on a street lined with plum trees to provide inexpensive housing to students and young teachers. To her own amazement, Cori was content. She read the novels she borrowed from the store, welcoming the tribulations of beknighted heroines as testimony that her own problems were not really so terrible. In late autumn, the plums fell from the trees onto the sidewalks, so many that anyone who wanted could pick them up and take them. She brought home bagfuls and made delicious jam in her kitchenette, reveling in the discovery of how easy it could be to provide a small luxury for herself. If she could save some money, she thought, maybe she'd buy a small house and some land on a mountaintop somewhere, and raise the baby there.

But then she had several mornings of nausea so severe that all she wanted to do was stay in bed. When she called in sick the first time, the store owner was very understanding. Probably a twenty-four hour stomach virus, Cori said. But it struck her now that a time was coming, not so far off, when she *couldn't* work and earn enough money to support herself.

Only a few days later she wanted to stay home again, but she was reluctant to claim another sickness too soon. So she went to work, and did her best to stay on the floor and take care of customers . . . until she threw up over a huge stack of *Peyton Place*, the year's big best-seller.

After staying out sick two days the following week, the store owner let her go.

She found a job after a couple of weeks at a small movie theatre showing a constantly changing program of revivals and foreign films, also near the university campus. The job allowed her to stay off her feet, sitting in a booth to dispense tickets and count receipts. Like the bookstore, the movie theatre offered her a parade of tragic dramas against which to compare her own situation. Things could certainly be worse, she thought, whenever she used free a pass to sit and watch a *film noir*. She had no lover who beat her, no husband who wanted her dead.

But as the north-west autumn turned damp and cold, the ticket booth at the entrance to the movie theatre became an unhealthy place to work. The small radiant heater was little help in driving back the chill. Cori came down with a bad cold. Terrified by the prospect of losing another job if she stayed home, she came to work anyway. Once she had thought of herself as frail, but having gotten through the bout of morning sickness, she felt all she had to do was just keep going. So far she had even put off seeing a doctor for routine monitoring of her pregnancy. She did all the sensible things – no drinking, no smoking, eating well, drinking milk – that was all.

Then, on a Monday morning in late November, after a restless feverish night, she found herself lying twisted into bedclothes damp with sweat, feeling too weak even to make the trip to the coin-phone in the downstairs hallway of the rooming house to call the theatre and say she wouldn't be coming to work.

She lay sapped by the fever for the whole day, dozing on and off, dragging herself to the bathroom for water to slake her raging thirst. At twilight she was awakened by a loud knocking on the door. When she answered weakly, the door was opened with a key by her landlady. During her last trip to the bathroom, only half-conscious, Cori had plugged the sink while she cooled herself with a few splashes of water, then hadn't turned the tap off completely. The floor was flooded, water dripping through the ceiling.

Seeing how ill Cori was, the landlady phoned a doctor who came at once to the house. As soon as he started his examination, Cori told him about the baby. When he heard that she was past the first trimester, and had yet to see a doctor, he urged that she visit an obstetrician the next day, and said he would arrange for her to see a colleague. Her present condition, he described as being 'on the brink of walking pneumonia'.

Cori gave up her job at the theatre, and for the next ten days she stayed in her room except to make a trip to the obstetrician. He found that she was anemic, and warned that she must start taking better care of herself if she wanted to carry a healthy baby to term.

Mrs Twinem, Cori's landlady, shopped for her, and brought meals until Cori could manage to get up and prepare her own, and brought bunches of wild flowers she picked from the borders of her own yard. But on a Sunday morning, after returning from church, Mrs Twinem came to Cori's room only to talk.

'I prayed for you this morning, my dear,' she told Cori.

'Thank you. I can use your prayers.'

The elderly woman went on to explain, apologetically, that Cori should think about organizing another place to live – no rush, really, she could take five or ten days – but a single woman expecting a child wasn't the sort of tenant Mrs Twinem felt she could have in her rooming house. The rest of the tenants were young students, after all – what were the parents of those students to think of Mrs Twinem's standards if they learned about Cori?

Cori offered no argument. Of course she would go within the next week, she said. She felt no bitterness toward the landlady. Why expect her to jeopardize her livelihood by rebelling against the prevailing conventions?

As Mrs Twinem was at the door, she paused. 'I've spoken to my pastor,' she said. 'If you are alone, he knows of some charitable institutions for women in your situation. They can even help find a home for the baby, if you have to give it up . . .'

Was this what it had come to? Cori thought after the landlady went out. Being a charity case? There wasn't a doubt that she had to go where she would be sheltered and cared for. But the price of admission back into the family still hadn't changed, and she would never surrender her baby.

Aside from charity only one option remained. And at the very moment it occurred to her, she felt the first jolt of the separate life inside her, a kick within her womb.

Even the baby was reminding her that it was his child, too.

11

As she drifted half-conscious in a haze of faintly aromatic smoke, a great rush of relief swept through Cori. None of it was real – not since the rodeo. She had simply dozed off while napping at the hotel in Rapid City waiting for Bren to get ready for dinner. The rest was a dream. Concocted by her subconscious in league with guilty conscience. No murder, no painful banishment from home and family, no time of illness and loneliness.

Then, through the haze, she heard a chorus of voices murmuring *'Mitakuye oyasin'*. The Lakota phrase was commonly spoken during rituals, or after the sacred pipe had been smoked, or when arriving at ceremonial places like the birth lodge. 'All my relations', it meant. Its common use served as a reminder that among the most central of all the tribe's beliefs was the direct personal kinship of each and every individual with all other things that exist in nature.

But how had she acquired this knowledge of the language and tradition?

She remembered, then: she was in the birth lodge. The haze in which she seemed to float was the smoke from the dried sweetgrass smouldering in a corner of the ceremonial *tipi*, a tradition when a child was being born. As dreamlike as it all seemed – as she might wish it to be – it was real.

'*Mitakuye oyasin.*' It came this time from a single voice, close beside her. Opening her eyes, Cori saw the medicine woman, Nellie Blue Snow, leaning over her. Nellie served as a midwife at most births on this part of the reservation, and Cori had seen her many times over the past few months to obtain herbal remedies that relieved muscular aches and the cramping in her legs. Nellie was very old, her face etched with deep lines that ran in every direction, her long white hair divided into twin braids that trailed down her shoulders, their ends twined around a clutch of different feathers, some solid black, others black striped with white. The feathers were not merely decorative, Cori had learned. Taken from creatures who could fly through the air, travel high up into the sky, feathers were like antennae to the spirits. They were sacred talismans that enhanced different powers depending on which bird they were taken from. The black-and-white feathers of the magpie aided in curing and relieving pain, the pure black feathers of the hawk heightened intuitive understanding.

'How is the pain, *ohitika win*?' asked the medicine woman.

It was what they all called her now. The bravery Cori had shown in coming to the reservation the first time had been outdone by returning. The tribe understood that the decision of this *wasicun* woman to bear this baby must have already forced her to endure great loss and hardship.

'Not too bad,' Cori answered.

'*Lila washte,*' said Nellie Blue Snow. Very good. Then, in Sioux, she spoke to the shadows that were lingering at the edges of the birth lodge. As they came to life, responding to Nellie's instructions, Cori realized they were other women from the *tipospaye*, Ada Crying Wind and Kate Highwalking and Annie Lone Dog, and even old Bessie Appearing Day.

And Abel. He had been watching from near the entrance

flap, but now Nellie told him to leave. He paused to give Cori an anxious smile, then he was gone.

No matter what dire prophecy had once caused him to send her away, he had received her back without objection. The night she returned he had told her contritely that if he had known his own child was at stake, of course he would never have let her go.

The others in the *tipospaye* had accepted her back, too. It was the custom willingly to shelter anyone with a blood tie to the family, and now the rule extended to Cori. Strangely, this time there was none of the resentment previously encountered, and she was soon integrated into the daily routine, helping with the meals and laundry and caring for the children whenever she felt strong enough. And when she didn't, the other women took care of her. Annie Lone Dog, who had been the least friendly of the other women when Cori first came to the reservation, had been the most attentive during the pregnancy. It was Annie who had been with her this evening when the contractions came, and had brought her to the birth lodge Abel had built – a special *tipi*, with little pouches of tobacco strung along some of the supporting timbers, 'prayer ties' displayed as symbolic offerings to the spirits.

'Do you know the meaning of *ma hiyopo*?' the medicine woman asked now.

Cori shook her head.

'It means "help me". Say it.'

'*Ma hiyopo*,' Cori murmured weakly.

'Yes, I am here to help, and so are the spirits of those born long ago and those yet to be born. If your pain turns very bad, *ohitika win*, hold tightly to my hand, or to one of your sisters who stand by you, and cry out loudly *ma hiyopo* – shout through your pain loudly as you can to be sure every spirit hears you.'

As Cori nodded, Annie and Ada moved in from the sides

and grasped her hands, while Kate stood with Nellie at the foot of the blanket-covered platform on which Cori lay.

The birth took hours. Two or three times, the spasms of pain were so excruciating they knocked the breath out of her. She could moan or cry, but she hadn't the will or the wind to form words.

'You must not stop speaking to the spirits,' Nellie told her.

She forced herself to take in enough air to call it out, syllable by syllable. '*Ma . . . hi . . . yo . . . po . . .*' Again and again.

Later she would realize that the Indian words provided a natural form of breathing exercise.

When the baby girl finally slipped free into the hands of the old medicine woman, she cut the cord and bathed the child in warm water infused with herbs and swaddled her in a blanket. Then Nellie stepped outside the birth lodge for a moment and stood under the night sky. When she came back inside she explained that she had wanted the spirits of the night to see how beautiful the baby was. Also, from her glance at the stars, the medicine woman was able to discern – though watches or clocks were not allowed in the birth lodge – that the child had been born at the moment when one day ended and the new one began. There was no better time to be born, said Nellie Blue Snow, placing Cori's newborn daughter in her mother's arms; it was a sign this would be a special child.

Abel was summoned to return to the birth lodge, and the women all left so that he could be alone with Cori.

They were shy with each other now, had been since her return. He had taken her back not purely for herself, they both knew that, and they were both equally confused about what had occurred between them in the past. They remembered loving each other, all the more as they were reunited by the result of that love. Yet the memory was overshadowed by a realization that their passions had not been strong enough to defeat the power of ancient beliefs that had separated them.

Together again, neither doubted the choices of the past, yet they felt no confidence in the future. They had not dared let passion re-ignite.

But now, as Cori held in her arms the miracle they had made together, she felt her feeling for Abel flowing back into her. He seemed to feel it, too, gazing at her adoringly as he came to her.

'Look at your daughter,' Cori said quietly. 'She's beautiful, isn't she?'

'Very beautiful.' His fingertips lightly touched the baby's cheek then trailed down to caress Cori's arm. 'So is her mother.'

'I want you to name her,' Cori said. 'I want her to have a magical Indian name.'

He nodded. 'I have thought about it. If it was a boy, I would have wanted to call him Black Eagle.'

She smiled. 'A good name. We'll use it someday.'

'For our daughter, I would like to use the name Tayhcawin. It was my Indian grandmother's name.'

'Tayhcawin,' Cori repeated. 'It's lovely. What does it mean?'

'The young offspring of the deer. I cannot think of the word in English.'

'Fawn,' Cori offered.

'Yes, the fawn.'

'Tayhcawin,' Cori tried it on her lips again, as she looked down at the baby and found that her eyes, wide and blue, were staring back at her with a directness that seemed oddly aware – almost as if there was a spirit inside her that already knew the name belonged to her.

For several weeks Cori and the baby were the center of attention. She continued to be fussed over by members of the *tipospaye* and Nellie Blue Snow, and now there were also visits and gifts from many people she'd never met. Medicine men and women came from other settlements on the Rosebud reservation, and even from other Sioux reservations farther north, Pine Ridge and Teton and Standing Rock. There were also very old men who came dressed in the full traditional regalia with elaborate feathered headdress and gorgeous beaded jackets – members of the tribal council. They brought pottery or food, and lit up ceremonial pipes which they silently passed back and forth, until Cori insisted to Abel that it was unhealthy to smoke in the presence of the baby.

They did not come because there was anything rare of itself about a child being born on the reservation. What fascinated the tribe about this baby was, of course, that its mother was a Hartleigh, a princess of the family that had warred against them for generations, and won, and ruled over their lives. There had been stories going around for a year that a Hartleigh woman had spent two weeks in a sexual adventure with one of their men, and had recently returned. But until the baby was born, the news had neither spread so far beyond the bounds of the *tipospaye*, nor provided proof of what many had dismissed as impossible.

With the existence of the baby established, a current of hopeful new rumors began to flow across the reservation. The tribe and the rich family were joined in blood, now surely there would be an end to the exploitation of one by the other. On a couple of occasions, when some expensive black sedans were seen parked here and there on the reservation with a pair of men in business-suits seated in front surveying the scene and occasionally taking down notes, reservation dwellers surmised they had been sent by the Hartleigh company to make lists of needed improvements to the reservation, things that might be donated now that a descendant of the company's owners was sheltered here.

Cori knew better. Some men might have their angriest vows undone by no more than a first look at their grandchild. But

G.D. had left no doubt that seeing this child in the flesh would only repel him. Those men in the shiny black cars had been sent by G.D., Cori guessed, to keep him informed, and by their conspicuous presence also keep her aware that, though he'd cut her off, it did not prevent him from exercising an inescapable power over her if ever he chose. Even knowing this, however, Cori wasn't prepared for what happened in the third week after Tayhcawin was born.

Kate Highwalking brought the news one evening when she came home from her nursing job at the reservation clinic. The women were all together in the main lodge, but Abel and Emory had not yet returned from a carpentry job they were doing some miles away. As soon as Kate entered, she stalked over to a cupboard, took out a bottle of whiskey stashed there by Emory, and swigged down a mouthful. The others were stunned to see her drinking. Kate's work at the clinic exposed her to so much of the alcohol poisoning common on the reservation – some so horrible in its effects, as when the men desperate for a cheap form of intoxication drank Lysol instead of liquor – that she sermonized about the evils of *mini wakan*, 'the water that makes men foolish'. Alcohol, she said, had been the *wasicuns'* deadliest weapon in defeating and controlling the Indians, far more powerful than the rifle.

'What's wrong, Kate?' asked Cori, as she sat on the sofa feeding Tayhcawin.

Kate stared at the wall as she spoke, tightly gripping the neck of the bottle in one fist as though holding a snake. 'We do so little already compared to what's needed . . . and now we will only be able to do half as much.' She lifted the snake and put its head in her mouth.

'Stop, Kate!' Ada rushed to her and grabbed the bottle away.

As the stinging liquid spilled down her chin, Kate looked around at the others. 'They were giving us money . . . I never

knew until today, until the administrator told us they stopped
– they will no longer pay.'

'Who?' Annie demanded. 'What money?'

Kate glanced at Cori before answering. 'The mining
company. For the past few years they have made an annual
contribution to the clinic – I'm told the amount is one hundred
thousand dollars. Now, suddenly, they inform us they can no
longer afford to give this help. A lie, of course. This sum is
only a tiny part of their profits, though it can make a tremendous
difference to the care we offer. That much money pays for
many vaccinations, for new equipment . . .'

Neither Bren nor her father had ever mentioned this charity,
Cori reflected. At least their policies were not all bad.

But Kate gave Hartleigh Mining no credit for its charity.
'For them, though, it was just a bribe. Some of the tribal elders,
people who knew about the money, held back on criticizing
the company because they were grateful – and because they
knew if the company got too angry the donation would stop.'

'But during these same years,' Cori pointed out, 'the tribe
has gone on suing the company to recover land. And the
contributions continued anyway.' In spite of the way G.D. had
treated her, Cori couldn't stop some family loyalty from
asserting itself.

'Sure,' Ada put in, 'that was a good trick. With one hand
they took away hundreds of millions of dollars, with the other
they gave back a little. So in front of the *wasicun* judges they
could say, "Look how good we are, we would never steal from
our red brothers, we take care of them." Bullshit!'

The obvious next question was why had the contributions
stopped now. But it didn't have to be asked. G.D. Hartleigh
needed to go on reminding his daughter of the cost of her
rebellion, needed to vent his hatred of the very idea that any
generation of Hartleighs would mingle Indian blood. It was no
coincidence that a principal service provided by the reservation

clinic was post-natal care, and Cori brought her baby there for routine examination.

Cori could feel a chill mood of resentment begin to form against her. A whole tribe was punished as a result of the personal bitterness between herself and her father.

The mood had thickened by the time Abel and Emory returned, though nothing was said openly against Cori.

'It may be for the best,' Abel said after the situation was explained. 'When our people learn what the mining company has done, the anger will spread. It will help us wage our battle.'

The argument made little impression on the others. For a century, far greater reasons to unite in anger had existed, but the will to fight had been so thoroughly crushed that a broad popular movement could not flourish.

'Perhaps I should go,' Cori said that night when she lay alone beside Abel. They had been given one of the smaller shacks to share with the baby, and Emory had moved to a room in the big lodge with several of the children. Now that they had privacy, and were bonded by their child, they had begun to make love again.

'I was wrong to let you go the first time,' Abel responded to her. 'It will not happen again.'

'But as long as I'm here,' Cori said, 'my father will do whatever he can to keep punishing me – and all of you.'

'Are there any punishments left?' Abel said drily.

'He's rich and resourceful. Have you seen those men in a car parked down the road, watching?' She had not mentioned it before, not wanting to alarm him.

'I won't be intimidated by him or his goddamn company.' It was obvious from his answer that Abel had spotted the surveillance, and had said nothing to Cori for the same reason.

'Abel, remember your dream – the prophecy that if I stayed here, everyone would suffer. The danger is no less now.' She put her arms around him. 'G.D. would be just as happy if this child didn't exist.'

Abel gazed at her intently. 'Are you saying he would do something to harm the baby?'

'He has already. What does it mean to our child – as well as all the others here – if the clinic is less able to provide treatment? When that money stopped coming, it was a message that my father doesn't care about the health of the child. I ask myself now why those men from the company are lurking around. If they were given orders to take Tayhcawin, make her disappear, would the law protect us? Look what happened to Black Eagle's murderer.'

Abel rolled onto his back. 'I will admit I have been worried. At times, I have wanted to say take the baby and go – but then I remember your family will not take you back. As brave as you are, *ohitika win*, you are not strong. You came back here because you became ill. So then I think you must be protected. If your father could be so evil as to hurt Tayhcawin, it is all the more reason you and she must not go off alone.'

Cori took a deep breath, fortifying herself. 'If I go, Abel, I will leave the baby with you.'

He glanced at her sharply. 'You do not want her?'

'Of course I want her,' Cori replied in a pained cry. 'But as long as I'm with her – as long as I acknowledge her and give her my love, my father will go on despising her. If he believes I've renounced her, that might satisfy him.'

'And then what would happen to you?' he asked.

'Without the baby, he'd take me back. I'm almost sure he will once he knows I'm beaten.'

Abel lay still and quiet for a while. 'I will go along with your wishes, whatever they are.'

'Wishes,' Cori echoed in despair. 'My wishes are so different from what I think needs to be done. I'd wish to have Tayhcawin with me, and be able to give her everything, comfort and security and good health. And I'd wish . . .' She stopped, defeated by the futility of her desire.

But he urged her on. 'Tell me.'

'That you and I could feel again what we did at the beginning – feel it so strongly that we would risk anything to be together.'

He smiled, as he embraced her again and pulled her body close against his. 'I have the same wish.'

She saw the true longing in his dark eyes, and pulled him down into a kiss. But as their lips touched, she knew that even if they shared the wish, it was not enough. They were wiser now than to let themselves be swept away.

Still, Abel wasn't ready to surrender. 'Don't go,' he said softly as the kiss ended. 'Don't give up . . .'

She was not so certain of her choice that his plea couldn't tip the balance. But the fear that G.D. would never leave them in peace, always brought her back to the idea of separating herself from Abel and the baby.

Through the night Cori wrestled with the dilemma. Near dawn, still unresolved, it occurred to her that the Indians had their own way of finding the right course when they faced crises. Abel had once explained it to her: *hanbleceya* – 'crying for a vision'. In the morning, she told Abel that she wanted to go on a vision quest to decide what would be wisest and safest for her, the baby, Abel, and the tribe. She would leave Tayhcawin with him and go to the vision pit he had shown her, and spend a night and a day and a second night there alone, sitting naked in that damp, dark place as it had always been done. The next morning she would return to him. Depending on her vision, she would either go or stay – would either take the baby with her, or leave her behind.

Abel did not argue with her terms. Whatever the spirits decided, he said, he would accept.

Later that morning, he drove her to the small ranch of Michael Strongheart Bear where they had borrowed horses in the past. Cori brought along only a blanket and a canteen of water – no food, no clothes except for the jeans and shirt she was wearing.

Holding the baby, he watched her ride away until she was out of sight, then he climbed back in his truck and drove home.

When the others in the *tipospaye* saw him alone with Tayhcawin and heard where Cori had gone, there were mixed reactions. Kate, who remained angry about the vindictive withdrawal of funds from the clinic, said it would be a good thing if Cori were encouraged to leave. 'Who knows what she'll see on her vision quest? But if the spirits don't tell her to go, we should. It will be better for her – and for us.'

Ada was more charitable. 'It will not be better for her. To make it easier on Abel's conscience if she leaves, she has told him her father will take her back. But from what we know of Mr Hartleigh, I believe Cori may remain alone. Without family, without her child, without us . . . what will sustain her? We can't be so cruel.'

'It was her choice to go to the vision pit,' Emory observed. 'What we think is beside the point. The *hanbleceya* will tell her what to do. The spirits will decide.'

Bessie Appearing Day joined the discussion. The old woman chattered rapidly in Sioux, often using words or phrases that had become unfamiliar to the others as the language was spoken less and less, but her general meaning was clear. It was hardly certain, said Bessie, that the *hanbleceya* would decide this matter. For one thing, according to tradition, the vision quest was always undertaken by chiefs and warriors, never by women. The spirits might not like seeing a woman in the vision pit, and would refuse to show themselves to her, or would tease her – and deliberately mislead her. There were tales, said Bessie, of young men who submitted themselves too frivolously to the intense experience of the vision quest and what they saw drove them mad. In her own youth she had heard of a young man who went to the vision pit, and when he did not return after a half moon, his friends found him there sitting upright, eyes open in terror – frightened to death by the spirits.

The story affected Ada. 'Perhaps you should go and get Cori,' she told Abel.

'No. This is her choice. I must wait until she returns.'

On the morning after her second night away, Cori didn't return as she had told Abel she would. Uncertain about whether it would be wise to intrude on her private spiritual journey, he waited. At last, as the sun began to go down, he could no longer sit still. Old Bessie's stories were going round in his brain, heightening his anxiety. He left Tayhcawin with the *tipospaye*, took his truck and drove fast along the roads to a point where, after walking a mile, he could climb the hill to the vision pit.

The sun was setting just as he reached the top of the hill. He climbed down into the shadowy recesses of the sacred cave. It was empty, except for the blanket folded neatly on the ground and the empty tin canteen. Abel thought at first she must have headed back to the *tipospaye* while he was on his way here; since she was on horseback, he wouldn't have passed her on the road. But if she had been returning home, he realized then, she wouldn't have left the blanket and canteen. They were here because she had wanted him to find them.

Any doubt he had misread the signs were erased when he stopped at the ranch of Michael Strongheart Bear and found that her horse had been returned.

Driving back to the *tipospaye*, Abel's eyes did not scan the landscape. There was no point in searching for her. The spirits had spoken, and whatever vision they had given her, it had been so vivid and uncompromising, she had not paused to say goodbye.

So Tayhcawin was his now, his alone. Without a mother, he thought, she was a child of fate, born out of a moment

163

when he had been brought together briefly with a white woman whose conscience compelled her to imagine she could love an Indian.

But it was no love if it could be killed so easily. A surge of fury went through him, quickly curdling to hatred. He had thought he could understand her leaving, had reasoned through it with her. But now he could only feel betrayed – as his people had always been betrayed by the *wasicuns*. Well, then, she was out of his life. He would not bring up his daughter to honor her – to honor any part of herself that was not Indian.

If he had his way, Abel thought, the child would never even know her mother's name.

BOOK II

Cankpe Opi
Wounded Knee

12

October 1969

Standing on the sidewalk in front of the stationery store, Emory Fast Horse counted out ten single dollar bills into the open palm of the twelve-year-old-girl he regarded as his niece.

'That'll pay for everything on the list, Tay,' Emory said, nodding to the slip of paper in the girl's other hand, 'with a couple dollars extra. Use that to get something for yourself.'

'You mean it, Emory?' Tay was incredulous. Money was desperately needed for too many other necessities.

'Sure. When you're finished here, walk down the street and buy some candy and ice-cream.' Emory's gaze rested on the girl; though only twelve, she was rangy for her age and, even though she wore the durable workshirts passed down from the men to the women to the girls, it was possible to see that her body was starting to develop curves. Already it was apparent to Emory that Tayhcawin would grow to become a singularly beautiful woman. Often, though, the straight jet-black hair that grew down almost to her hips was gathered so close around her face, held by the beaded headband except for a curtain of long bangs, that it was hard to see what she looked like. Today, perhaps because they had come off the rez, she had left off the headband and her hair was held back with a blue plastic beret.

'Maybe you'd even like to get a little bottle of cologne,' he suggested. 'Seems you're gettin' old enough to wear perfume.'

Tay smiled modestly and glanced along the short main street. High Rock was a very small town, even so the choice of places to go seemed enormous compared with what existed on the rez.

'It's not my birthday, Emory,' Tay reminded him, still puzzled by this burst of extravagance, 'not even near.'

Emory laughed. 'Do you think I don't know when your birthday is, Tayhcawin? But birthdays are not the only things that deserve a little celebration.'

'What are we celebrating today?' She had noticed when they left home today that Emory was freshly shaven and better dressed than usual, wearing his good silver, and the black hat with the eagle feather stuck in the brim. And all the time they'd been in the truck, he'd kept whistling and singing along with the radio.

Emory hesitated. 'Let's just say,' he replied after a second, 'we're celebrating who we are.'

Tay nodded at him gravely, though the cryptic answer only heightened her curiosity.

Emory said he would meet her by the truck as soon as he was done buying some other supplies, then he went off down the street.

Tay pushed the money into a pocket of her jeans, and scanned the list of items to be purchased in the stationery store. She recognized the handwriting on the paper as her father's not Emory's. A dozen pencils. Two large boxes of blank paper. And a typewriter ribbon. Emory had already told her that it was mainly to get the ribbon that they had come off the rez, since none of the stores there sold any. What would her father want with a typewriter ribbon? Tay wondered. He didn't own a typewriter.

Just over the threshold of the stationery store, she stopped to gawk at the display of goods around her. Along with shelves of stationery and art supplies – a rainbow of paints and chalks and colored paper – there was a selection of gifts and toys. Tay rarely saw such a bright selection. The reservation stores sold only staples of food and hardware, and when trips were made to the 'border towns' – the more affluent white communities outside the reservation boundaries – young children weren't usually taken along. Tay had been to a border town just twice before.

The man who owned the store came out from behind a counter and asked if he could help. He was middle-aged, gray-haired with spectacles pushed up on his forehead, and his manner was friendly and solicitous, though Tay knew from hearing her relatives talk that many *wasicuns*, especially those living near the reservation disliked and distrusted the Indians. But she was aware, too, that she didn't have all the classic characteristics that would instantly identify her background. Her hair was a thick ebony black, but her eyes were a pale luminous turquoise. There was also a certain delicacy to her features, a fineness in the bones, that suggested the word 'patrician'. Most significant, her skin was not the reddish caste of the rest of her family, but tawnier, more like a *wasicun* who'd spent a day in the sun. When she looked at herself in the mirror, Tay always thought of her face as being bleached out, the features weak and undistinguished compared to the strong definition and nobility she saw in the faces of her relatives. But she knew that her blood was – as she thought of it herself – impure. Her father's mother had been a *wasicun*, so had her own. And her father had told her that both women had died not long after giving birth, which seemed the proof they came from a more fragile breed than the one Tay wished to regard as her own. Life on the rez was hard, but Tay had been impressed by tales her father told of their tribe's history, and she was proud to think of herself as one of the original

Americans. She rejected that part of herself that was white, all the more because she knew from Abel that her white mother had rejected the part of her that was Indian. Embittered by that rejection, Abel never talked about Tay's mother, nor did Tay care to hear more than he would say – that she was a woman who had not meant to get pregnant, and whose love he had come to doubt. If she had not died soon after Tay was born, Abel said, he was sure she would have left him anyway.

Tay told the store owner the items on her list and he led her along the aisles, pointing out where pencils and paper were stored. Tay was amazed by the variety – not one brand of pencil, but several; paper with lines, or blank. Typewriter ribbons were available in nylon or silk, black, or in colors. On the rez, the stores carried only one kind of anything, take it or leave it.

She lingered over each choice. 'I'm sorry to take so long about this,' she explained, 'but I'm buying for my father, and I'm not sure exactly which he'd like best.'

'No hurry,' the store owner said. 'Pretty little lady like you, ain't no hardship for me just standin' and lookin' while you make up your mind.'

Tay smiled, though his flattery made her uncomfortable. She wasn't used to getting the sort of compliments she'd heard on television when men and women were being romantic – and certainly not getting them from old men. She tried to make her choices a little faster.

Having assembled the items on the list, she brought them to the counter and had the man add up their cost, so she would know how much extra money she could spend on herself. There was more than two dollars left over. But not, she decided, for candy, or ice-cream or even perfume. The moment she'd seen the array of art supplies, Tay wanted nothing more than a sketch-pad and a nice paintbrush or two and some tubes of watercolor. In the reservation school, where she had discovered how much she loved to draw, she always had to settle for using scraggly old brushes or broken pieces of colored blackboard chalk and scrap paper covered with writing on one side. The US Bureau of Indian Affairs that provided the budget for the reservation schools didn't think art supplies were a necessary tool in educating Indians. Let them draw in the sand, or pick dry grass to make baskets, they have their own ways. That was the attitude.

With the drawing materials, Tay was stumped again by the number of choices. She walked along the shelves, picking up and putting down tubes of paint and boxes of lovely pastel chalks, as though feeling them might help her decide.

'You're an artist, huh?' the store owner said, as Tay paused by a box of fine-tipped paintbrushes, picked out two with different size tips, then paused to scan piles of sketch-pads.

'That's going too far,' she replied, 'but I love to draw and paint.' She turned back the cover of a pad, and looked at a sheet of the paper. 'Wow, it's so thick,' she remarked.

'That's a professional-quality folio.'

It would be nice to have what the professionals used! 'How much is it?'

'Seven dollars.'

She replaced it quickly on the stack. 'I've only got two dollars extra . . .'

'Each of those paintbrushes you've already picked out costs more than that.'

'These?' She stared in disbelief at the brushes in her hand.

'Genuine sable tip.'

Tay returned the brushes to their box. 'I never realized it cost so much to be an artist,' she said sadly, backing away from the display of art supplies. 'No wonder they're always starving.'

The owner eyed her. 'You really like drawing, huh?'

Tay gave only a small nod, keeping her head down to conceal a film of tears in her eyes. It hurt now to show enthusiasm for something it seemed she couldn't afford to love – well, of course, she could always draw, just never like a professional.

'Tell you what,' the owner said. 'Nice kid like you – I'd like to encourage your interest in art. Pay me what you can afford for the folio and brushes, if you'll agree to bring back some of your drawings—'

The door from the street opened suddenly, and the owner broke off to turn and see who had entered.

It was Emory. 'What's takin' so long, honey?' he said, walking over to Tay. 'You only had a few things to buy.'

'But there's so much to choose from, Em'. Never saw most of this stuff before. And then I decided to spend the money you gave me right here. You know how I like to draw . . .'

Emory nodded, and looked to the store owner. 'She's damn good at it, too.'

The owner stared coldly at Emory and said nothing.

Tay went on excitedly. 'The stuff's all more than we can afford. But this man said if I bring him back some drawings—'

'Never mind what I said,' the owner broke in. 'Just go on, get out. And I don't want you comin' back.' His manner had changed completely from avuncular and encouraging to plain nasty. He started pushing Tay and Emory toward the door.

Tay moved automatically, stunned by the sudden reversal.

But Emory bristled. 'Leave your hands off us, mister. We're goin'. But if the girl wants to buy somethin' to draw with, you might be decent enough to sell it.'

'Doesn't have enough money. Thought she'd con it out of me. Would've fell for it, too, if I didn't find out in time that she's a 'skin. Damned if you people ain't always tryin' to get something for nothing. C'mon, move out.'

Emory clenched his fists. Tay could hear him breathing so hard he was almost snorting like an angry bull.

'Forget it, Em',' she said quickly. 'There's nothin' I need

that bad.' She had a particular terror of the possibility of violence erupting. More than once she'd heard the story of how a beloved cousin of her father's had been murdered in cold blood, shot down by a *wasicun* who all but walked away.

Emory hesitated another moment, then started out with her. They left behind the supplies they needed.

'Hold on!' the owner erupted suddenly, striding after them. Tay and Emory stopped and turned.

'Just occurred to me,' the man said to Tay, 'all that stuff you were handlin' before . . . wouldn't been hard for you to sneak a few things inside that shirt. Maybe the whole reason you came in.' Because Tay's hand-me-down shirt was overly large, its bagginess did make it appear that something could easily be concealed within. The owner thrust a hand out at Tay. 'Let's have it.'

Tay glanced helplessly between Emory and the store owner. 'I didn't take a single thing, I swear.'

'Never mind swearin' – pull up your shirt and turn out your pockets!' He reached brazenly to start plucking at her shirt.

Emory knocked his hand away. 'Mister, she already told you—'

But there was no reasoning with the man now, his fury spiked by Emory's swipe at him, however harmless. Dashing straight out to the sidewalk, he started hollering along the street. 'Police! Get the police!'

Tay clutched Emory in panic. 'Oh, God, Em', believe me I didn't do anything wrong.'

'I know,' Emory said softly.

'So let's go,' Tay urged. 'Let's run!'

Emory shook his head slowly. He seemed oddly relaxed suddenly, his arms hanging loosely at his sides, fists no longer clenched. 'We cannot go now, or we will look more guilty. We must stay and explain to the police.'

In a minute, the owner was back. He stood blocking the

door. 'Be a cop in here any second,' he warned, 'so you better not move.'

Tay was too frightened to say anything.

'We were never in a hurry to go,' Emory said, giving the owner a thin smile.

Moments later a policeman arrived, panting from a dash along the short main street. A five-year veteran of the town's four-man force, that had been long enough for the cop to get out of fighting trim, so he stood panting for breath all the while the store owner's related how he had stopped the two 'skins from leaving when he 'realized' the girl was shoplifting. Emory kept a stoic silence, but Tay tried several times to correct parts of the shopkeeper's report.

'I was just having trouble making up mind,' she burst out when the owner told the policeman he'd become suspicious because the girl was handling so many things she obviously couldn't afford. 'He wasn't at all suspicious right then. He said he'd *give* me stuff cheap if I'd do a drawing for him.'

The policeman wasn't interested in what she had to say. Having ignored Tay's first couple of interruptions, after finally catching his breath he snapped at her, 'Shut up. You'll get your chance when he's done.'

It took only a couple of minutes more for the storekeeper to finish stating his case.

'Well, we should be able to settle this real quick and easy,' the policeman said then. 'Can I use your back room, Sam?'

'Sure,' said the store owner.

'C'mon, kid.' The policeman gripped Tay's arm and started pulling her toward a door at the rear of the store.

Terrified, Tay submitted meekly. But Emory moved quickly to block them. 'What are you going to do?' he demanded.

'If she didn't lift anything, she shouldn't mind being searched,' the policeman said gruffly. 'Now get out of my way.'

Emory stood his ground, legs spread and arms folded. 'It

should not be done like this. Not here. Not by you.'

The policeman smirked. 'Well, here's your choice, scalphunter. We can settle it here with a search, or I'll toss you and the girl in the lock-up until you go before a judge and he sets bail.'

Tay saw Emory's fists clench again. 'Let him search me,' she said quickly. She couldn't even afford a paintbrush. How long would it be before they could make bail?

Emory took a deep breath and finally stepped aside. As Tay passed him, he lowered his eyes, ashamed he could not better protect her.

The rear door led into a messy store room. A fluorescent fixture dimly illuminated a jumble of cartons stacked against the walls, and a damp concrete floor littered with old labels and wrappings. The policeman motioned Tay to the far side of the open space. 'Okay,' he said. 'Let's see . . .'

She stood trembling, not certain exactly what to do next.

'C'mon!' he snarled. 'Strip!'

'Please . . . believe me, I have nothing,' she stammered.

The policeman leered at her. 'I wouldn't say you've got nothing, little squaw, whether or not you stole anything. Now, you want to do this the easy way . . . or would you rather I take your clothes off for you?'

Glinting in the room's dim bluish light, his eyes looked especially cold and cruel. Suddenly Tay realized he hadn't really brought her in here because he cared about establishing her guilt or innocence. He just wanted to humiliate her, see her naked. The blood in her veins seemed to freeze. She stood paralyzed as he took a step toward her.

'Don't touch me,' she pleaded.

'I don't have to . . . if you cooperate.'

Her hands clawed her shirt loose from her jeans. 'There's nothing, see?' she begged, shaking the shirt when the shirt tails were hanging out.

'I'm not going to ask again,' he said in a threatening growl.

The choice, she saw, was to be forced – or be thrown in jail with Emory. So if it had to be done, all right, she would let him look and not give him the satisfaction of acting weak and slavish. Riveting her gaze on his face, she undid the buttons of her shirt.

He wasn't satisfied by seeing her in her underwear. There were still places, he said, where she might have hidden some small stolen article like a tube of paint. It had to be a full-body search. He made her take off the bra she had only begun to wear two weeks ago, then her panties. He made her stand with her legs spread, and told her to bend over and pull her buttocks apart, then he walked slowly around her.

As the ordeal continued, her hatred only burned hotter. Like a furnace in her guts, it consumed every other emotion – shame, despair, self-pity, terror. Today she could not escape, but no one would ever humiliate her like this again.

He was behind her when she felt his hand reach between her legs, and clutch at the tender cleft of her crotch. Shocked and terrified, she jolted upright and tried to bolt from him, but his other hand went around her waist and held her.

'What'sa matter, little squaw?' his voice growled in her ear, so close she could feel the heat of his breath on her neck. 'Doesn't that feel good?'

She couldn't move, couldn't summon a sound from her throat. Maybe she would have screamed, but it struck her that Emory might come running – and the cop could shoot him down.

She felt his fingers moving up inside her. A desperate trembling whisper came out of her. 'Please . . . oh, please, don't . . .' She hated herself now for being so weak and sniveling. She wanted to be strong against the white man, to conquer him.

He withdrew his hand. A wave of gratitude swept through her. She had moved him somehow. He was going to spare her.

The policeman walked around in front of her again. As soon

as she could see his face, she knew she was wrong. She hadn't reached him at all. The terror flooded back into her, too strong to overcome for all her furious loathing. As he raked his eyes over her body, she tried to forget her nakedness, to cloak herself so completely in her contempt for him. But now she was aware of it again, felt her skin crawl as his eyes traveled over her body and his hand came closer. She wrapped one arm around herself, and put a hand between her legs, as she darted glances around the room, looking for escape – or for a weapon.

Then she saw him smirk again, as if he knew what she was thinking. Tay understood then that the more her fear showed, the more it excited him.

'And now for something better, little squaw. Down on your knees. You're gonna suck my dick.' He began to move toward her, unzipping his pants.

With no other defense, she retreated to the only resource left – she closed her eyes and prayed that *wakan tanka* would protect her, would summon all the mighty spirits to her rescue.

And now, from some mysterious place at the core of her, Tay felt a gathering of will unlike anything she had ever experienced. She believed – no, she *knew* – she could keep this animal at bay in the same way she might stare down a vicious dog.

He was only a few feet away, his penis in his hand, when she abruptly uncovered herself and brazenly turned her bright turquoise eyes to meet him in a direct unflinching stare. He reacted almost as though he had collided with a wall, coming up short, freezing with an expression of surprise stamped onto his features.

Tay felt a surge of triumph and, without thinking – almost as if someone else was speaking – she heard herself challenge him. 'I will not do what you want,' she said. 'Try to make me . . . and I'll bite it off.'

'Real injun talk,' he said, and chuckled. 'Well, I'd move

too fast to let you. But if you even tried, I swear I'd choke you to death right here. Say I found some stuff on you, and you tried to run. Nobody'd doubt it – nobody who counts. So you choose, little squaw. But just don't be stupid, you might even like the taste. It could turn out to be a few minutes pleasure – instead of being dead forever.'

He started to reach toward her shoulder, as if to push her down.

'Touch me again,' she said, her voice edged with every bit of the contempt and rage possessing her, 'and the spirits will steal your manhood. I warn you. Go now, or you will be a sad, weak dog for as long as you live.'

He hesitated, and it looked as though he was trying to laugh again. But then his hand went down and he retreated a couple of steps. 'You're some crazy little bitch, aren'tcha?' he said. Suddenly he was the one who looked frightened.

'I guess you are through,' she said, still staring at him defiantly.

'Yeah . . . guess I am,' he muttered at last in a dry rasp. 'I wouldn't want you touchin' me. Must be something like syphilis got at your brain. Get dressed.' He whirled, and slammed out through the storeroom door.

When Tay returned to the front of the store, the scene was so normal it was eerie. The policeman was gone and the owner was back behind the counter, intently puttering, marking prices on some small items. Through the glass-paneled door, Tay could see Emory waiting alone on the sidewalk.

She was free to go, she realized. But she went to the counter first. The bag of supplies she had originally come to purchase was still sitting by the cash register. As she stepped in front of the owner, he avoided meeting her eyes.

'So,' he mumbled. 'You want this stuff?' He pushed the bag toward her.

'No. I want nothing from you.'

'Then, go on, git,' he said impatiently. 'Cop told me I was wrong.'

'Wrong about a lot of things, mister,' she said firmly.

Caught by her firm tone, he looked up sharply. 'That so? In what way?'

'Well, for one thing,' she said with a jauntiness that surprised her, 'you're never gonna get one of my drawings. And I really am darn good.' She went out the door.

Emory received her into an embrace. As soon as he was holding her, the raging woman was transformed back into a young girl. All the taut control she had kept over her emotions snapped and unraveled as though invisible steel cables had been cut. She broke into wracking sobs.

'What did he do?' Emory asked. 'If he touched you, I'll kill him.'

'No, he didn't touch me . . .'

Emory's protective embrace tightened. In a voice choked with remorse, he repeated over and over that he was sorry, that he wished he could have helped her. Finally, he said, 'But it won't be like this much longer. We will soon make them respect us.'

Caught by his tone of fierce resolve, Tay eased back to look at him. 'You're planning something, aren't you? What is it?'

'Never mind, Tayhcawin,' he said. 'It's not something children should know about.'

Not wanting to say anything to revive Emory's threats of vengeance, she did not insist. But to herself Tay thought that she wasn't a child, not anymore; now, sooner than she would have liked, she was a woman. The child in her had been killed during those few horrific minutes in the back of the store.

Her tears stopped, and at last they were ready to go. Not home. They would have to drive to the next border town, another fifty miles away – too bad they had to use the extra gasoline, but it couldn't be helped. Abel needed that typewriter ribbon, Emory said – needed it now more than ever.

As curious as she was, it was several days before she thought to ask her father about it. In the meantime, whenever Tay was with him or anyone else from the *tipospaye*, the conversations always centered on the way she had been treated by the policeman.

When told, Abel was instantly enraged. Though he abhorred fighting – he had not raised his fists again since the night Black Eagle had been shot – he wanted to drive straight to High Rock, find the policeman and settle with him.

'And how will that help?' Ada said, physically planting herself in front of the door of the main lodge to keep Abel from leaving. 'Will Tay be better off, if they throw you in prison for forty years?'

Emory said, 'If you want to go to prison, my friend, at least pick one where they've stopped locking the doors.'

Tay noticed that Abel flashed an odd look at Emory, as though angry at him for not keeping a secret. But the strange remark was enough to make Abel turn from the door and sit down again.

It was something else, Tay thought, she'd have to remember to ask her father about. A prison where they stopped locking the doors – could that be Emory's way of talking about the rez?

But Tay put this question aside while Ada and Kate and even Bessie spent the next few days fussing over her, each of them taking her aside to talk kindly with her about what had happened, encouraging her to talk out all the confused feelings about men and sex and her body that had been stirred up by the humiliating incident, bolstering her wounded psyche with their loving advice. Kate Highwalking, whose nursing at the clinic had involved her in treating many women who had been raped – by their own men as well as *wasicuns* who came onto the rez – was particularly intent on reassuring Tay. Two nights after the cruel body search Tay awakened from a nightmare in which she was surrounded by ape-like men who were pawing at her. She leapt from bed and went into the big room of the lodge to make a comforting fire, beside which Kate found her a while later, still sobbing. Kate knelt behind her, and wrapped her in an embrace.

'It is unfortunate that there are men who cannot control an animal side of themselves,' Kate said quietly as she held Tay. 'But since such men exist, you must learn to be aware of the way you will affect them. You are very lovely, Tayhcawin. Like the little fawn who gives you your name, you will be hunted. Simply because you are a prize – more beautiful than most women. That is not something to be ashamed of. If it makes many men desire you, and among these are a few whose desire makes them lose control, never blame yourself. It is because those few are evil – or weak . . . or just stupid. For there are *wasicuns* who still believe they have a right to take whatever they wish from an Indian. So when you walk among the *wasicuns*, Tay, like the fawn you must be especially careful. And whatever the *wasicuns* try to take from us – we must keep our dignity. With that, we may even, someday, take back everything else . . .'

With the loving support she received from the *tipospaye*, the trauma faded. She remembered then the little things she'd been curious about. Seeing her father alone by the riverside, under the tree where he liked to sit doing the beadwork he sold, she went and sat down beside him. At last she asked him why he needed the typewriter ribbon.

'It's very simple,' he replied. 'A friend of mine has an old typewriter, and it needed a new ribbon.'

'Which friend?'

'Joseph Two Bulls.'

Tay knew Joseph, who lived only a short way along the road with his own *tipospaye*. A large man with a face that was always set in an angry frown, he had a small forge and eked out his own living by shoeing horses and doing other odd jobs of metalwork. Tay liked him least of the men her father called friends, especially after she heard that, as a young man, he had stabbed a BIA agent in the arm and had spent five years in prison for attempted murder.

'But if you are buying the ribbon, not Joseph,' said Tay, 'it must be because you are the one who uses the machine. For what?'

'I am teaching myself to use it,' he said.

'Why?' she persisted. 'What are you writing?'

When Abel took a few moments to answer, Tay felt it was not just to continue concentrating on the moccasin he was beading, but because he was deciding how to answer.

'Letters,' he answered finally. 'That's all. Just letters.'

Letters to whom, she would have asked, and why teach himself to type these letters instead of using a pen and ink? But before the words were out, he looked up from his work to gaze at her. And there was something in his eyes like a silent warning, a plea to ask no more because it was a dangerous subject in some way.

So she said nothing more about it, though the mystery had only deepened.

13

The uniformed governess herded the two boys and their little sister into the huge living-room of the penthouse, and lined them up facing the wall of picture windows like soldiers arrayed for review. Straight from their evening baths, the boys in freshly laundered pajamas and the girl in a fresh lace nightie under her small velvet robe, they were indeed ready for the most exacting inspection. For all the bustle of the children's arrival, it went unnoticed by the woman who stood by the windows facing out toward the view of a lavender dusk settling over the misty bay and the majestic bridge that vanished away into a cloud of fog. Her slim figure was tightly sheathed in a shoulderless evening gown of midnight-blue silk cut to reveal her smooth straight back.

'Mrs Patterson . . .' the governess said.

Lost in reverie, the woman at the window still failed to respond.

'Mrs Patterson,' the governess repeated. 'The children are ready to say goodnight.'

'Oh, yes . . .' the woman said as though coming awake from a deep sleep. Turning, she extended her arms languidly; the children went forward to exchange hugs and kisses with their mother.

The older of the two boys, who was almost nine, lingered to ask a question. 'Does Grandpa know I'm not coming?'

'Of course he knows, Scottie,' Cori answered. Her son's claim that he was old enough to go to tonight's lavish birthday banquet had been the source of arguments and tantrums for weeks. But Cori was not moved. In her mind, the banquet to celebrate G.D. Hartleigh's seventy-fifth birthday and his fortieth year at the helm of Hartleigh Mining Company was a thoroughly dishonest piece of theatre; she felt her children deserved better than being made to play parts in such a gross deception.

The boy sulked off, and the governess led the three children away to bed. Cori Patterson turned again to the view. The bridge, the near half of it anchored to land, the other half disappearing into the fog, seemed such an apt symbol for her life. The starting point had been so solid and strong, the half extending from that point was still clear and easy to see in her mind's eye . . . but then at some point it had faded away into a fog.

'Ready, darling?' Frank Patterson entered the room carrying a white ermine coat. 'We should be going.' He moved up behind his wife to lay the fur over her bare shoulders. Gazing with her at the view over San Francisco bay, he added, 'I know tonight isn't going to be easy for you. But it would be hard in other ways if you didn't go. Count on me, I'll be right beside you. Okay?'

Cori turned around finally and laid her hand on her husband's cheek. 'Dear, dear, Frank, you've always saved me, haven't you?'

'I've always tried,' he said, offering his arm to lead her out of the room. He couldn't fail to be aware – even if he'd never been able to learn the whole truth – that there were many problems and heartbreaks he hadn't been able to spare her.

* * *

It was only six weeks ago she had returned home from spending four months at an exclusive mental hospital for the very rich. Along with a dining-room that served gourmet meals, a health spa, suites of rooms decorated with antiques – and sometimes with priceless paintings brought along by the owners who were required to make this a temporary home – were also the medical facilities and personnel required to administer intensive therapy for chronic depression including two rooms equipped to apply shock treatment. Cori had, in fact, received a course of these high-voltage jolts to her brain. At first, Frank had been furiously opposed to such a radical measure, but he had assigned the science editor on the newspaper to report to him all the latest developments and statistics, and had learned that, carefully done, it often showed good results in curing the sort of absolute despair that had overtaken his wife in the eleventh year of their marriage.

Finally, he had agreed, and Cori's doctors felt quite satisfied it was the most beneficial step they had taken, even if she had suffered the side effect of losing certain areas of memory. Some had recovered, not all.

Her condition had not come without any forewarning. There had been years of sleeplessness, relieved by pills. And periods when she had suddenly turned reclusive, unable to face the parties that for Frank, being in the business of communicating, were so important to him. She had also been stricken by acute post-partum depression each time one of their three children had been born. If he had to pick any one point that had marked the beginning of Cori's steady downward slide, Frank thought, it was probably the birth of their first child two years into their marriage.

About the deeper roots of her unhappiness, Frank could only guess. Having been totally in the thrall of her powerful father through all the years of her youth, there had finally been a total break with G.D. Frank didn't know the reason, had never been able to get anyone in the family to talk about it. If he got near the subject with Cori, she became agitated, and retreated into sullen silences that lasted for hours – and, later into the marriage, for days. So he had learned to leave the topic alone. The one thing he did know was that, whatever had happened, it had occured at precisely the same moment, twelve years ago, when he felt himself falling in love with Cori, and was already thinking seriously of asking her to marry him.

One day she had been there for him – an ever-delightful, ever-supportive presence, daily becoming a more indispensable part of his life. Then, overnight, she was gone. After the closeness they'd shared for years, and the newly developing intimacy, he was stunned she had left the city without making mention to him that she'd be away. Intent on finding out where she had gone, and why, his first phone call had been to G.D. As soon as Frank explained he was seeking information about Cori, the old man had brusquely stated he didn't know where she was, didn't give a damn, and had hung up. Frank had immediately made calls to Pamela Hartleigh and Bren and Cori's brother, Chet. They weren't as angry or short with him as G.D., but none were any more revealing. 'I'm sorry, dear boy, there's really nothing I can say,' Pamela told him – though he detected that her voice was as heavy with grief as if her child had died. Bren revealed only slightly more. 'Let it alone, Frank,' she said. 'If you did find out, you wouldn't like it. Let's just say she's run away and it's for the best. It's not as if a man like you needs to pine and sigh. Call a date, and close the file on little sister. Come to think of it, maybe you and I should get together next time I'm there. Or if you're ever in Washington . . .'

But, of course, he couldn't so easily 'close the file'. Frank knew no one whom he regarded as a closer friend than Cori, no person who was sweeter or more decent or generous or sensitive.

Despite her family's unwillingness to disclose anything, Frank had gone on trying to learn her whereabouts. The school where she had taught, the garage that kept her car, the various Hartleigh vacation homes, he had contacted them all, but no one could tell him anything. The only small consolation came from a worker at the Jackson Hole ranch, a man named Stovall, who told Frank sympathetically that Cori was certainly alive, and it was by her own choice that she had disappeared.

'I reckon if she ever wants you to know anymore than that,' Stovall told Frank, 'she'll find a way to tell you herself.'

As weeks passed into months, Frank came to his own conclusions about why she had vanished so abruptly. Obviously there had been a battle of wills between Cori and her powerful father, and she had seen cutting herself off as the only way of escaping from his smothering control. Though he missed her, Frank saw it as a positive step for Cori to demonstrate her absolute independence from G.D.'s tyranny. Once she had gained confidence in herself and could deal with her father without crumbling, Frank believed she'd be back. Yet he wondered if they could ever pick up where they had left off. Their exploration of romantic intimacy was a fragile, tentative phase that would probably not survive her absence.

Yet Frank did not enter any other serious involvements. He had begun working harder, moving up to the position of city editor as he was groomed to take over the reins of the Patterson newspaper. Then one late night a week before Thanksgiving of 1957, while he was at his desk racing to finish a story before deadline, he was vaguely aware of his name, uttered softly over his shoulder.

'Frank . . .'

When he swiveled his chair around, she was standing there. 'Hello, Frank,' she said tremulously.

How long had it been – nine or ten months? Except for idle wonderings about her every so often over a solitary cup of morning coffee, she had faded from his thoughts. Now, having her here, he felt like some place inside of him that had been hollow all this time had finally been filled. 'Good God, Cori, where have you been? When did you get back? What made you leave like that?'

As the questions tumbled out, his eyes took in all the details. Whatever she'd been through, it hadn't been easy. Her blue eyes were shadowed by dark circles, her high cheek-bones were defined more sharply in a face that seemed more gaunt. She had a bruised, beaten aspect. Yet somehow none of it damaged her appeal. Whatever strength and color had waned from her features, the effect was to transform her beauty from the delicate into the ethereal.

She did not shrink from his questions. She had been back two weeks already, she said, confined to her family's mansion because she had been particularly afraid to see him and apologize for the way she had left. But at last the thought of avoiding him for the rest of her life became even more unbearable than the prospect of facing him.

For the rest of the story, she waited until after he put the early-bird edition to bed, and he took her to a reporter's hang-out around the corner from the newspaper building where they sat talking until dawn while she explained it all.

Yes, she had fled to free herself from her father's absolute domination. She had wanted to continue with her education, take a masters degree that would better prepare her for a teaching career. But there had been a violent argument: G.D. said that teaching children wasn't the sort of career a young woman of her wealth and standing should be involved in; teaching was for poorer women who couldn't do anything else or find husbands. Though hell, if she insisted on teaching kids – until she married and settled down – she should have learned enough of the three r's to pass on to the brats without going back to graduate school, so he certainly wasn't going to foot the bill for that.

As Cori described it, her father's behavior didn't sound very rational, but Frank had no trouble believing that the issue had easily blown up beyond any reasonable proportion as soon as G.D. felt the authority to rule any of his children's lives at stake.

So Frank accepted Cori's lie that she had gone east to apply to graduate schools while attempting to find the means to pay for it herself. If she seemed sad and beaten, he believed, it was because she hadn't been able to manage it. A life of privilege hadn't prepared her to meet such a challenge. So she was back now, in her father's house, resigned to the compromise: as long as she was an obedient daughter, she would always be extremely comfortable.

Frank could see that her self-esteem had suffered from the defeat of returning to her father, and he imagined that it would continue to decline the longer she had to endure being his vassal. His impulse to rescue Cori from that psychological imprisonment was reinforced by a physical attraction that had only been intensified by a loss of girlish dewy innocence, and her evolution to a woman with an air of tragedy. Within two days of her reappearance, Frank brought Cori back to his apartment and made love to her, finally consummating the romance that had begun a year earlier.

For Cori's wedding to Frank in the third week of May, G.D. Hartleigh spared no expense to have his daughter married in the most traditional way and ensure it would be *the* social event of the spring season. The church service was performed by the Episcopal bishop of San Francisco, Cori wore a white silk gown with a long lace train. An afternoon reception followed aboard G.D.'s two-hundred-foot yacht, during which it cruised around San Francisco bay. Then there was a grand evening banquet and ball at the Fairmont. Cori went meekly along with everything her parents had prescribed. She understood that the festivities, so lavish as to be unforgettable for everyone present, were intended to blot out forever after the fact that she had once veered just as extremely outside the boundaries of social convention.

After honeymooning on the yacht with a cruise down the Mexican coast, Cori returned to the life of a socially prominent married woman as designed by Pamela – overseeing a household staffed with servants, volunteer activities, planning dinner-parties to enhance Frank's business standing and their joint social position. Frank could see Cori was left bored and listless by this routine, but she didn't respond to his suggestion to return to teaching. He could only hope that when they began to have children, the need to nurture and the challenge of parenting would revive her spirit. Accordingly, they had been married only a year when he urged that they start their family.

Fifteen months later their first child had been born . . . and Cori's more serious downhill slide had begun.

While more responsibilities at the newspaper were shifted to Frank, making him managing editor, then having co-publisher added to his title, he was immersed in his work. His efforts increased the success of the *Observer*, which in turn added to demands on his time outside the home. The newspaper became his 'mistress', distracting him from the disappointments of his marriage. Later, when Cori became even less functional, and had to be institutionalized, he had allowed himself the relief of brief affairs with ambitious trainees and interns on the paper – women who would be moving along in the search for advancement. But for all the difficulties, he had never stopped loving his wife.

Now, at last, he had reason to hope that the worst of her illness was past. She had talked about going back to teaching, had recently shown an animated interest in talking with him about his work, had been willing to go out with him in public – had even shown sparks of her old vibrancy and humor in some small dinner-parties with friends. Most telling of all, since her shock therapy, she had exhibited an appetite for sex that had been missing completely for the past few years. Indeed, she had seemed even freer about expressing sexual desires than at any time in her marriage. The only worrying aspect of this was that she talked about desperately wanting another child. She certainly wasn't too old, but Frank feared that the downward drift of her psyche might be activated again if she suffered post-partum depression. He had let her know he was opposed to enlarging their family, though trying not to make it an issue. Didn't she want to return to work? Why jeopardize that with all the inconveniences of a pregnancy, then the need to care for an infant? His gentle pressure seemed to be working.

He had noticed a small setback, however, after Bren informed them she was planning a gala testimonial dinner where all G.D.'s family and friends would gather to honor him. Cori had told Frank initially that she had no intention of going. For one thing, she knew Bren's gesture was motivated more by political expediency than familial love. For nearly twenty years Bren had devoted herself to HMC. Even after marrying eight years ago, she'd had no children. Bren had clearly demonstrated that the company was her first priority, and she had shown she was vastly more capable than Chet to assume leadership whenever G.D. stepped down. Cori believed that Bren had conceived the celebration to make a point of how long G.D. had headed the company, and nudge him into using the sentimental moment to acknowledge officially that Bren would be his successor. But Cori's greater reason to boycott the event, she admitted, was that she had no desire to celebrate G.D.'s long happy life. 'Why should I?' she said to Frank. 'I'd have been a lot better off if he'd died twenty years ago.'

In all the years since she had cut herself off from her father and then returned, Cori had been passively cooperative where her family was concerned. Frank wondered now if this show of bitterness was one more sign that her spirit was being restored, or an indication that her mental condition was backsliding.

'Don't churn up the waters now,' he appealed to Cori. 'Whatever you feel about G.D., go for your own sake – go if only to prove that you're strong enough, that it makes no damn difference. Don't you see, darling, if you have to keep yourself away, it's only another way of giving him control?'

Cori agreed she would join her brother and sister in attending the gala. But she stipulated to Frank that their children would stay home. 'He doesn't deserve to have any of my children there,' she proclaimed angrily, 'not one of them.'

Tonight, as they set out for the short trip to the Mark Hopkins where the gala was being held, Frank couldn't fail to notice that Cori was more moody and withdrawn than at any time since her total breakdown. But under the circumstances he didn't feel unduly alarmed. Though she had agreed to go dutifully through the motions of honoring her father, from the start Cori had confessed she wouldn't be happy about it.

G.D. was at the door of the ballroom personally greeting every arrival. Pamela stood at his side, a personal nurse on her other flank. Two years ago, a growing difficulty with remembering appointments and other such memory lapses had been diagnosed as 'early onset senility'. Now she was having trouble always putting names to faces, even to the one she saw in the mirror.

Pamela barely reacted when Frank and Cori greeted her with kisses, but G.D.'s eyes lit up with genuine delight.

'Well, this makes the evening almost complete,' he said, grasping Frank's hand warmly. Then he bent to give his daughter a kiss on the cheek. Cori stood like a statue to receive it. 'I wish your children could have been here, too,' he added to Cori.

'All of them?' she asked with a sharp edge as she stared coldly back at G.D.

The reply puzzled Frank, though it seemed from the way G.D.'s mouth set in a hard line that he understood her meaning perfectly. Frank asked Cori about it when they had left the receiving line.

'Is there some problem between G.D. and one of the kids? What you said to him back there—'

'There was a problem,' Cori said passively, 'but it's over.'

Frank was upset. 'Why don't you tell me about these things when they happen? I'm their father, after all.'

Cori turned a curious opaque glance on Frank and said nothing. He could sense that he had touched a nerve, but he dropped the subject. In Cori's vulnerable state, the aggravation of being pressed for details might be enough to cause an explosion.

Bren came up to greet them. 'Fabulous gown,' she said, taking Cori's hands then holding her at arm's length to admire her. 'Givenchy, right? I saw it at Magnin's. Almost bought it myself, but I knew Charles would go nuts if I spent that much on a dress, even for tonight.' Bren shot an angry glance at Charles Nordling, who had stopped several yards away to chat with other friends. A tall man who held himself with almost military erectness, handsome in a severe way, Nordling was the heir to a real-estate fortune that had been started when his grandfather bought downtown land at distress prices after the earthquake of '06. He was Bren's second husband, after a marriage in Washington to a White House television correspondent that had lasted only four months. Bren constantly complained about how cheap Nordling was. Her gown tonight, a cascading skirt of blood red chiffon with a red silk bodice cut daringly low, had no doubt been her own purchase.

'Frank,' Bren gushed on, leaning into him, 'you are a divine man, so good to our little Cori.'

'She deserves it,' Frank said.

'Oh, yes,' Bren said wryly. 'She's a saint, isn't she?'

Bren was being bitchy, but Cori didn't take the bait. 'You've done a beautiful job tonight,' she said, glancing around at the crowded ballroom, bedecked everywhere with garlands of flowers and extravagant bouquets.

'All in a good cause,' Bren said with a wink that seemed to acknowledge the ambitions behind the gesture. Then she spotted the Governor of California, Ronald Reagan, making his entrance and she darted straight away to join G.D. in welcoming him.

The evening designed by Bren was the ultimate balm to G.D.'s mammoth ego. Seated on the dais near G.D. along with Reagan, were the Republican Senator, George Murphy, and the Mayor of San Francisco. After dinner, Reagan himself gave an amusing testimonial, then Murphy – also an ex-movie star, who had tap-danced in film with Shirley Temple – joined Reagan in singing 'He's a Jolly Good Fellow' to G.D. Finally the lights were turned out for a screening of the filmed birthday message that had been sent by President Richard Nixon. After starting out with a jaunty 'Hi, G.D.!' and apologizing that he could not attend in person due to a need to monitor new developments in the Vietnam War, Nixon paid tribute to tonight's guest of honor 'as one of America's most outstanding citizens'.

At last G.D. rose to respond. He professed to be overwhelmed by the outpouring and spoke of the blessings of his long life – not least of which were his wife and son and his two wonderful daughters, and their families. The audience responded to this fine example of family closeness with heartfelt applause. When the ovation died down, G.D. went on to extol the particular satisfaction of seeing his family business grow and prosper under his forty years of guidance.

'But after four decades of being a miner,' he said, as though he had actually gone down into the shafts, 'maybe it's time to come up for air, and smell the roses. I'd especially like to spend more time with my dear wife, Pamela—'

Another break for applause, which Pamela sat through with a blank expression.

'—and also with my grandchildren.' He beamed a smile at the table where Chet's five children were seated then continued. 'It's particularly gratifying to know that I'll be able to leave the business in the hands of the Hartleighs. I suppose this is as good a time as any to tell the two children who've joined me at the company that they'd better get ready . . . because I'm planning to retire from my position as president. While I will remain as chairman of the board, my son Chet will continue the tradition of having a Hartleigh man as president and chief executive, and his beautiful and brilliant sister will be there to provide the faithful right hand that she's always been for me.'

From the smiles Bren and Chet flashed at G.D. there was no outward clue to the audience that there was any quarrel with the arrangement.

But as G.D.'s speech proceeded to the closing expression of humble appreciation, Cori's eyes never left her sister's face. It was admirable, Cori thought, that Bren could maintain such a perfectly pleasant façade when she must be seething inside. Cori knew how much Bren had counted on being the one to take over. Just as in the Washington days, Bren had put her devotion to the company ahead of everything. Several times, at the larger family gatherings, Bren had watched her nieces and nephews at play and expressed some regret about not having any children, but Cori believed any poignant emotion was a passing thing, quickly forgotten as soon as Bren was back at her desk.

G.D.'s speech was given a standing ovation, then a huge cake was wheeled in, and the entire crowd sang 'Happy Birthday'. At last, tables and chairs were pushed back and the

Count Basie orchestra played, and Tony Bennett made a surprise appearance to sing 'I Left My Heart In San Francisco'. Bren danced gaily along with everyone else, her smile as dazzling as ever. But whenever Cori caught her eye, the underlying truth came through, and a flash of understanding passed between them. *Yes, he's done it to me now*, Cori could feel Bren silently convey, *I know what it feels like and I'm sorry I didn't fight for you when I should have . . .*

Before long Cori told Frank she wanted to leave, though she was absolutely firm in insisting he must stay and enjoy the party. No telling how it might help the newspaper if he could spend a little time with Governor Reagan and Senator Murphy.

For herself, Cori could take no petty satisfaction in seeing Bren forced to endure, as she had herself, the sting of their father's blind loyalty to narrow old-fashioned ideas. Racist in her own case, sexist in Bren's.

What Cori felt instead as she left the party was a mix of exhilaration and a rush of optimism. For so long she had been the lone outsider in her family, with no hope of ever righting the wrongs done to her by G.D. But now maybe she and Bren could be sisters again.

More important, maybe they could be allies.

14

At noon two days later, Cori made one of her rare excursions out of the house. When she arrived at the small *dim sum* parlor off Battery Street in Chinatown, Bren was already seated at one of the many small tables. Wearing a fitted white wool suit and a cloche hat with a rim curved to match the fall of hair above her eye, she was dressed for an uptown corporate lunch, not a step-down Chinatown dive. Cori had dressed in a plain black cotton shift and a lined raincoat to keep out the November chill. It was because she disliked dressing up that she'd been glad Bren suggested this place, but Cori realized now it had been chosen because they wouldn't be seen here by anyone they knew.

Cori had barely sat down opposite Bren before a waitress came to the table carrying a large tray. A variety of bite-sized specialities on small plates were displayed from which diners could make a selection.

'Get whatever you like,' Bren said. 'I'm not hungry.'

Cori picked out a number of dishes and the waitress went away. 'It's all very good,' Cori said, encouraging Bren to try some. 'Frank used to bring me here in the old days.'

Bren flicked a wry glance at her. 'The old days – you mean

before you were married? Or just before you fell apart?'

It hardly came as a shock that Bren could be so blunt, yet Cori wasn't prepared. When Bren had asked to meet, Cori was certain the purpose was to commiserate over what she viewed as G.D.'s betrayal, not to ambush her.

'Excuse me for asking,' Bren went on quickly when it seemed Cori had taken offense. 'But, well, it hasn't gone completely unnoticed that one small side-effect of your recent therapy was to . . . shall we say, leave some places in your memory a little blurred. And I can't deny it, Cor', I'm curious about what you remember and what you don't.'

'I don't remember how much I've forgotten,' Cori said ruefully. 'But I think most of it's there. The important things.'

Bren nodded. 'That's good. If you remember that – the *most* important things – then I'm sure you'll want to help me.'

What she wanted, Bren continued, was to overturn G.D.'s decision to make Chet the operating head of the company instead of her. Cori's support was all she needed. Over many years, Bren explained, G.D. had been transferring blocs of company stock to the various trusts he'd set up for his wife and children. He'd never mentioned it to them because the maneuver was strictly for tax reasons, to pare down future inheritance levies, not because he had any inclination to divest generously. Even with the transfers, the share he retained outweighed any other single holding; he had also installed provisions that gave him certain powers of attorney allowing him to vote the stock.

Bren grabbed up the alligator purse she'd left at one side of the table and plucked out a folded paper. 'I got this from a young associate in the law firm that handles our estate papers. It lists the stock belonging to each member of the family. Take a look.' She handed the paper to Cori.

Cori ran her eye down the figures. There was one column showing the number of company shares held in each name.

Another column defined the amount in terms of percentage. Currently G.D. held thirty-five per cent, Pamela twenty-three per cent, each of the children's trusts fourteen per cent.

Cori shrugged as she handed the paper back. 'What's the significance? You said G.D. still has control over our shares. Even if he didn't, what you and I have together doesn't equal his – never mind that Chet and mother will always vote with him.'

'I've spoken to the lawyers. We can revoke the power of attorney that permits G.D. to vote anything in our name.' Now a smile curled across Bren's voluptuous mouth. 'As for mother, she's on my side.'

Cori regarded Bren dubiously. 'Bren, she's no longer capable of comprehending this. She doesn't even know you from me – half the time can't remember her own name. Her votes will automatically go with G.D.'s.'

Bren gave a sly shake of her head. 'She's given me a signed, authorization to vote her shares.'

'It won't hold up. She's been ruled mentally incompetent to govern her own affairs.'

Bren smiled archly. 'That would be a problem . . . except the document is dated four years ago. And it was notarized.'

Cori eyed Bren suspiciously. Four years ago was long before their mother's problem had set in. And there was no doubt that, while still fully cognizant, Pamela would never have made the slightest move against G.D. If she had signed the paper Bren described, she had scribbled her signature without full awareness of what she was doing, and the date had been added later.

'Who was the notary?' Cori asked.

'A partner in the law firm that oversees the trusts, Daniel Kinwood. Know him?'

Cori shook her head.

'Awfully nice, attractive, divorced a couple of years ago.

You'll be meeting him soon,' Bren added brightly. 'He's a few years younger than I am, but I'm going to marry him – as soon as I get my own divorce from Charles.'

Though Bren had made no previous mention of a rift with her husband, Cori felt no surprise. Bren's appetite for a new mate made even more sense in view of who he was, and how he could help accomplish her ends. Clearly the lawyer's reciprocal desire had been so aroused that he had been willing to throw aside all professional ethics to provide her with a fraudulent document.

'Bren, you're going over the line. It's not worth the risks you're taking.'

'Isn't it?' Bren said blithely. 'Cori, darling, the value of Hartleigh Mining's ore deposits was recently appraised at two billion dollars. Gold's only the half of it. Our uranium is a major source for the government, for weapons, all those nuclear subs they're building. One of the things I'll do much better than Chet is build up that side of the business. The Russians are going to be around for a while, and with the contacts I still have in Washington, I can lobby for more defense spending – not to mention nuclear-power plants, just so nobody call us war-mongers. Worth it, sweetie-pie? It's worth controlling if you want to see it really grow.'

'But you'll never get away with it,' Cori said. 'G.D. will see right through that phony authorization. And daughter or not, he won't think twice about sending you to jail with your new husband.'

'Poor G.D.,' Bren said with a mock pout. 'He'll have a tough time making his case. Aside from Dan and me, only you and mother know – and, well, she doesn't really *know*, does she? Even if you testified against me, there are reasons whatever you say might be . . . judged unreliable. Though I was naturally hoping, when I shared my little secret, that you wouldn't ever give me away.'

Cori looked down at her uneaten food. She had lost her appetite. 'I wish you hadn't told me.'

'I had to if I was going to bring you in with me.'

'Bring me in?' Cori echoed in shock. 'I *can't* go along knowing what I do!'

Bren's tone hardened as she leaned closer across the table, her green eyes lit by fiery determination. 'Cori, baby, look at those numbers I showed you. Mother's shares joined to yours and mine total fifty-one per cent; G.D. and Chet would have only forty-nine. You're the key. Having you on my side might also make it harder for G.D. to convince anyone I coerced mother.'

'I can't do it, Bren,' Cori replied in anguish. 'I'd like to see you get what you want. I know how much it means to you. But this way – it's not right, not honest.'

'Right? Honest?' Bren hurled the words back at her. 'For godssake, what fairness do you owe G.D. after what he did to you?'

Cori sat back from the table suddenly and looked away, desperate to pretend she hadn't been reminded.

But Bren wouldn't let up. Her hand shot across the table to grab Cori's wrist in a painful grip. 'This is your chance to settle the score,' she insisted. 'You've been punishing yourself ever since it happened. But you were innocent, you did nothing wrong. He could've helped you, made it easy. Instead he made it impossible for you to hold on to a piece of your heart, to a man you loved . . . and to your child. The same narrow-minded meanness made him deprive me. I don't have kids, Cori. I'd have liked to, maybe, but I've been wrapped up in the company too long . . . and now the company's my substitute, my "baby". G.D. knows how much it means to me, knows damn well I deserve to take his place, could do the job better than Chet. But he won't give it to me because I'm a woman. That's all it is. We're women so what we want doesn't matter. He took away our babies, both of ours.' Her frenzied grip became even tighter. 'Pay him back, Cor',' she pleaded. 'Pay him back! He's got it coming.'

Cori sat very still for a long time, refusing to look at Bren. At last she said, 'I thought I'd want to if I ever got the chance, but . . .' she trailed off.

Bren released her grip finally and eased back. She wasn't resigned to failure; she felt the anger she'd stirred up in her younger sister needed to be left alone to ferment.

There was a long silence. Neither one of them moved.

'What about the Indians?' Cori asked finally.

Bren shot a worried glance across the table. Where had this come from, what part of Cori's bruised psyche? Perhaps the pressure put on her had upset her delicate equilibrium.

'What do you mean?' Bren said.

'If I helped you, that would be my only reason. To get the company's policies changed, things worked out so the Indian's lives are improved.'

Bren smiled thinly. 'After all this time, you're still crusading.'

'G.D. wouldn't let me keep my daughter,' Cori said grimly, 'but she had to go on living by his rules anyway. It's too late to have my child back, I've already told too many lies. If Frank learned the truth, it would be the end for us, I think. But I can still do something to make life better for my lost child.'

'Any specific suggestions?'

Cori shrugged. 'I don't know. Maybe let them have some of the land back, or give them a share in the profits.'

Bren bowed her head in a pose of thoughtful deliberation. When she looked up again, she said decisively. 'All right.'

'Promise,' Cori demanded.

'As long as you do your part,' Bren said, 'I promise to do mine.'

'I haven't said I would yet,' Cori observed cautiously.

'That's all right. Take your time. G.D.'s not handing anything over for a year.'

'I don't like breaking the law,' Cori murmured, as though debating aloud with herself.

'But for such a good cause . . .' Bren said coyly.

Cori fell silent.

But there was no longer any doubt what she would do, Bren thought. Cori would go along, right down the line, and vote all her shares with Bren's and their mother's, never breathing a word of their criminal manipulation.

And once the votes were cast, then of course everything was open to reconsideration. If Bren had learned nothing else during her years in Washington, it was that promises could be freely made during the campaign, and just as freely broken as soon as the election was over.

It had been traditional for all of the expanding Hartleigh clan to fly to Jackson Hole to spend the Thanksgiving holiday there together. Some extra excitement would be added to the trip this year by the fact that G.D. would take delivery of his first private jet plane just in time to make the Thanksgiving junket its maiden flight.

The holiday had been the brightest spot in Cori's calendar, the only time each year when she returned to the place that had given her so much pleasure when she was younger. She would have liked to go to the ranch occasionally by herself, but since the bouts of depression G.D. no longer allowed it because, he said, he was anxious about her safety. Cori imagined G.D. really wanted to keep her away from the environment that had once stimulated her sympathies to the frontier culture of the native Americans. She would have fought the ban if she could have seen Buck, but years ago he had left the ranch and moved on. He'd sent a short note apologizing that he couldn't stay around to teach her kids about horses, but since she rarely came now it wasn't worth putting up with 'the bullshit of being a show-window cowboy'. He'd promised to keep in touch, but so far there had been nothing more than a postcard every year, each from a different place.

This year as the Thanksgiving approached, Cori dreaded the prospect of gathering with the family. Bren might have no trouble going through the charade of celebrating with G.D. and Chet even while secretly scheming to take over the company, but Cori's control over her own emotions was too tenuous to manage the pretense. A week before Thanksgiving she told Frank she planned to stay in San Francisco for the holiday. Though he always tried to accommodate her special needs, this time it led to an argument.

'The kids are counting on it,' he said. 'You, of all people, should know how much the kids love going there.'

'But I can't face it,' Cori said.

'Face *what*?' Frank demanded. 'The scenery? The people? Cori, all you have to do is show up for the turkey dinner. The rest of the time you can spend alone.'

'Then let me be alone here. You and the children go—'

'You know I can't do that. You've got to fight this urge to lock yourself away. It's a symptom, you must see that.'

At times that had been true. Not now. Though how could she explain? For her there had always been a degree of hypocrisy in playing happy family with G.D., and Frank knew it. To tell him the reasons it had suddenly become intolerable would require exposing Bren's scheme. Frank was too decent to condone the fraud and betrayal – never mind that she didn't dare reveal to him why she would even consider participating in it. Cori was left feeling that if she retreated from this obligation, Frank would regard it as a sign she was seriously regressing, possibly even recommend a return to intensive therapy.

The evening before they were to depart for the ranch, Frank

called to say he wouldn't be home for dinner, and might be tied up at the paper until late. It was even possible, he said, that he wouldn't be able to leave for the ranch. 'There's a big story breaking,' he explained. 'I need to cover this one myself.'

She erupted angrily. 'You practically ordered me to go, and now you want to stay behind? If you're staying then so am I!'

'All right. We'll all have Thanksgiving here. The kids can stand it, I guess. A little disappointment builds character, doesn't it?'

Her anger was instantly submerged in the flood of relief.

He encouraged her to tell the children it was his fault they weren't going, and that he'd make it up to them with some extra treats over the holidays. He was just starting to say goodbye, when Cori interrupted for an afterthought. 'The story, Frank, you didn't say what it is. Must be awfully important for you to cover it yourself.'

'It's Alcatraz again.'

'What do you mean?' Alcatraz, the notorious island prison in San Francisco bay, had been closed and unused since 1963.

'Don't you remember what happened five years ago?'

She thought only a second before it came back. In 1964, a small band of Sioux already living in San Francisco had gone out to Alcatraz and claimed possession of the abandoned island under the provisions of a treaty dating from 1868 in which the US government guaranteed the tribe the right to claim ownership of any parcel of federal land which was 'not mineral land, nor reserved by the US for special purposes other than Indian occupation'. The incident had briefly grabbed the national spotlight, dramatizing the grievance of native Americans who felt promises made to them long ago by the government had never been properly honored. After just one day, federal marshals had raided the island and forced the protesters to leave. At the time the event had stirred up a lot of memories, regrets and other confused feelings in Cori. When it was over, she had been glad to block it out of her consciousness.

Frank's voice cut through her recollections. 'The Indians are back, a larger group this time – local students joining some militants off the reservations. They've claimed the island again, and they're digging in. Even got weapons out there. These Indians are the biggest story in the country right now. Even if they hadn't asked me to cooperate, I'd want to stay with this one.'

The remark revived her full attention. 'Who's asked you to cooperate? In what way?'

'This bunch at Alcatraz wants the media to publicize their grievances. They've specifically demanded that my newspaper publishes a proclamation they've prepared. I'm going to meet with someone from the group to see what they've written. I'll be taking a boat out there tonight with a couple of other editors and some television people.'

'You mentioned that they have weapons,' Cori asked anxiously.

'Don't worry, sweetheart. They don't seem violent. If they're not attacked, there's no danger.' He told her not to wait up for him, and said goodbye.

Unable to face dealing with the children, Cori had the governess give them dinner, while she lay in her bedroom with the lights out, watching memories unfold on the screen of a dark ceiling. The thought of the Indians only a few miles away raised up again all the ghosts of her past, inspired her to relive all the sympathies of conscience and the yearning for justice and the passionate impulses of the heart that had seized her and shaped her fate after Black Eagle's murder. The memories that haunted her most were the birth of the baby, and her leave-taking. What sort of existence had her daughter been forced to live? What had Abel told her to explain the absence of her mother?

She anguished once more over whether she had made the wrong choice. Ten thousand times she had told herself the alternatives were worse. She couldn't have asked Abel to leave his people, or taken the baby with her into a life disconnected from any family or tradition. Always, though, she came back to blaming herself. If only she had been braver, stronger, smarter, she could have found a way to defy her father. He was a man, not a god – even if he had been known to joke that G.D. was practically the same word, with zero missing in the middle. But she couldn't have defeated him, she would decide again, not when he was in his prime. Now, though, he was older, vulnerable . . . and Bren was offering her a chance. Maybe, Cori thought, she could have her daughter back.

Cori sat up and watched the late local news on her bedside television. The Alcatraz takeover was the lead story. The lights of the television crews caught images of the militants, some in native American garb, waving improvised victory banners as they stood on the rocky shores of the desolate island, or in the old guard towers of the abandoned prison. The local anchorman reported that a delegation of newsmen had landed on the island earlier in the evening to meet with leaders of the militant group and receive a proclamation they wanted publicized. In taped coverage of a launch landing at the dock, and men disembarking, Cori spotted Frank accompanied by a couple of *Observer* reporters. They were shown walking, with other media executives, to the prison gates where the militant leaders waited. The camera zoomed in to show the tense faces on both sides, then panned across the determined faces of the island's occupiers as one of their leaders held up a piece of paper with lines of typewriting faintly visible. Then Frank was seen accepting the paper from the militant leader.

As the camera held the picture of the two men for just a second or two, Cori let out a gasp, then sprang forward, her hands pressed to the screen as though it was a window she was desperate to open, to call to someone passing by. The man pictured handing the paper to Frank, Cori was sure, was Abel.

The taped coverage ended, and the anchorman was onscreen saying that the delegation had now left the island. The news continued with today's reports from Vietnam. Flares of napalm and faces of young army men passed by the electronic window. But in her mind's eye Cori was still seeing him, him now as he had been long ago. Her lover.

Then the doubts came. Could she trust her mind not to play a trick? Would Abel ever involve himself in something like this? She remembered a tranquil, quiet man who would sit under a willow by the river applying his deft hands to doing lovely beadwork. Not a warrior. But of course she couldn't quite trust her memory anymore, not all of it.

Cori turned off the television and lay back in the darkness. So many years ago she had taken a journey to find him – and it had ended in losing herself. What would she find if she could make one more journey, just a short one, to that desolate island prison?

15

In the newspaper reports printed the morning after the occupation of Alcatraz, Abel Walks-Through-Fire was credited with being a member of the 'action committee' from the Rosebud Sioux reservation who had prepared the angry proclamation handed out to the media. The late edition *Observer* a maid brought to Cori on her breakfast tray quoted the typewritten manifesto in its entirety:

> We feel that Alcatraz Island is more than suitable to be an Indian Reservation as determined by the white man's own standard. We mean it resembles most reservations in that: it is isolated from modern facilities, and without adequate means of transportation; it has no fresh running water; it has adequate sanitation; there are no hospitals or other modern health care facilities . . .

The list of grievances went on, adding up to a brutal irony intended by the writers of the manifesto: Indian reservations were no better than this prison island abandoned by the government as too inhumane an environment even for the worst criminals in society.

Having read the proclamation, Cori no longer had any trouble believing that the gentle man she'd once known could have been transformed into a warrior. And if he had lost the gentility that had once made her love him, then how had her child fared, spending her formative years in those same dehumanizing conditions?

In the early afternoon, Cori left her home, and took a taxi to Fisherman's Wharf, not only a tourist mecca, but the center of the local fishing industry. Several dozen men in waterproof overalls and heavy sweaters milled around on the sunny wharf at the foot of Jones Street, companionably exchanging stories after they had finished hoisting the crates of fresh fish to the pier. Cori scanned the crowd of fishermen and picked out one old salt who struck her as more kindly than the rest, perhaps because he resembled Spencer Tracy in *Captains Courageous*.

His reaction to her proposition wasn't kind at all, however. 'Take you out to "the Rock"? Lady, you think I'm out of my mind? There's a bunch of wild fucking Indians out there who'd sooner shoot anyone than give 'em an autograph, and a dozen police boats circling around the place. I'd get a stiff fine even for trying to get through.'

Alcatraz was under siege, access rigidly controlled by the San Francisco police and federal agents. The number of occupying militants had been established as more than seventy, and it was feared a direct confrontation would provoke massive bloodshed. The strategy decided upon was not to storm the island, but simply keep the occupiers cut off. They weren't expected to hold out for long.

Disregarding any logic, Cori continued to move through the crowd of fishermen, telling others what she needed, offering each more money. Most laughed at her outright, a few dismissed her as a foolish thrill-seeker or told her off angrily.

She thought of going next to the St Francis Yacht Club. There were friends of hers and Frank's who owned boats . . .

But at last the reality sank in. Her problem wasn't limited to finding a way past a strict cordon; she had to do it in a way that could preserve the secret she had kept from Frank through all the years of their marriage.

The stand-off stretched into weeks. Cori's desire to talk to Abel and learn what she could about Tayhcawin, her child, became more of an obsession. Not being able to fulfill it corroded her morale. She stayed home, slept away the days. She vowed to leave the house only to see Abel. Observing Cori's mysterious deterioration, Frank feared she might have to be institutionalized again.

When the siege went on into the new year, some of the students started to give themselves up and leave Alcatraz. But Abel remained with a hard-core group who swore never to let the whites take back this new 'Indian territory'.

Bren was the one person who had known the effect of the Alcatraz occupation on Cori right from the start. After seeing Abel's name in the first reports, she had telephoned Cori. At the time she had discouraged making any effort to see Abel.

'What the hell's the point? You'd be running all kinds of risks. Just thinking about it is bad for your health, Cor'. Get it out of your head, or it could push you over the edge.'

'If I could just know my baby is all right,' Cori said.

'She's not a baby anymore, and she's not yours.'

'You've never had a child. How can you understand? Being without her . . . if anything's been wearing me down it's wondering, all these years, what happened to her, what's she like . . .'

From subsequent conversations over the past couple of months, Bren could tell that the frustration of having Abel so near yet unreachable was becoming more than her sister could bear. And Bren had her own selfish reasons for wanting Cori

211

capable of proving herself mentally sound and able to make responsible decisions.

On a wet, foggy afternoon in early February, Bren stopped by the house one afternoon for a visit without bothering to call ahead – Cori was always home these days, she knew, and Frank would be at work. Bren had decided to suggest a way Cori might satisfy her longing.

Pulling a chair up close to Cori's bedside, Bren began by pointing out that both sides in the stand-off were still allowing news reporters to have controlled access to Alcatraz. The Indians craved free attention to their cause, and the police let them have it, thinking they might surrender when they had enough.

'Members of the press can climb right on a police boat and get ferried across the bay,' Bren observed. 'It should be easy for you to get some kind of press clearance. You can get on the island and talk with Abel under the guise of doing an interview.'

'That's your brilliant idea?' Cori said mockingly. 'Frank knows everything that goes on at the paper, including who gets issued press cards. There's no lie I could tell him that would explain why I'd pulled such a stunt.'

'Honey, forget about lying. You need to try some other vices. Like bribery. There must be a reporter who'd take you with him? You might not need your own press card if he'd pass you off as an assistant or a photographer. Hell, there's got to be some run-down second-stringer on the *Observer* who'd take a pay-off to do nothing more than play the shill. Isn't it worth a thousand bucks to you?'

Of course it was worth anything to Cori – if she could be sure Frank would never know. 'But shouldn't I try to use someone on another paper—'

'No, you couldn't trust them. They might report it to embarrass Frank. But find an *Observer* man who can't resist the money: he'd never want his own boss to know how corrupt he was.'

Cori felt a curious admiration for Bren's twisted shrewdness. 'You know a lot about how to use people, don't you?'

'I worked in Washington, remember.'

At first Cori hadn't imagined she could go through with it. Then she had thought of Forsetti. Vince Forsetti had wangled his way onto the *Observer* as a copy boy after dropping out of high school eighteen years ago. Learning the ropes the hard way, he had eventually become a reporter, and currently he was covering the seamier side of the local scene – accidents, crime, domestic violence. Forsetti was known to have insight into such subjects; he had come from a broken home, and his father had been shot to death under mysterious circumstances. Over years of the annual Christmas parties Frank gave at home for his reporting staff, Cori had often encountered the reporter. He was darkly attractive, and when he played up to her, regaling her with stories of his adventures in the San Francisco underworld, she enjoyed it. She knew he was slickly cultivating her because she was the boss's wife. Yet his flirtatiousness was finely tuned to be complimentary, never too brash and offensive.

This past Christmas, however, it had crossed the line. Not merely compliments on her beauty, but questions: did her husband appreciate her enough? Cori realized he was probing to see how easily she might be seduced into becoming someone who'd advance his interests at the paper.

A week after talking with Bren, Cori phoned Forsetti in the city room. Too nervous to give her name, she claimed to have information that might interest him for a story, and he agreed to a rendezvous by the sea-wall on the Golden Gate promenade that afternoon. When he arrived, he appeared only mildly surprised to see Cori there.

'So that's what all this is about?' he said after she explained her proposition. He had hoped it was something different – that she had taken the bait for an extra-marital affair. 'You want me to get you out to Alcatraz so you can speak to one of the Indians, and it's got to be done without Mr Patterson finding out.'

'You can do it, can't you? What's going on out there would be the kind of stuff you cover.'

Forsetti paced along the sea-wall. 'Sure, I've been covering it right along. And I can probably pass you off as a nameless assistant. But I don't like it.'

'If a thousand dollars isn't enough—'

'I don't want any hush money. But you'll have to tell me why it's so important to you. What the hell's going on between you and this Indian?'

'I'm not going to tell you that,' she said flatly. It would give him too much power, she realized; knowing what Frank didn't, he would be able to pressure her into anything.

He thought for another minute. 'All right, I'll give it a whirl.'

'If you don't want money, then . . . how do I show my appreciation?' He was not a man who would do something for nothing.

'One of these days I'll have a chance to move up to editorial. There'll be competition, though, and it'll all come from these dudes who've gone through journalism school. I'm as good as they are, but it won't matter. That's when I'll need you to put in a word with Mr P. on my behalf.'

'He won't listen to me on a decision like that.'

He gave her a long look. 'Well, if that doesn't work out, maybe I'll think of another way you can settle your debt.'

That was the future, she thought. Right now her need to see Abel was all that mattered.

The following Tuesday was overcast, with a blustery wind

that whipped up high choppy waves in the bay. Plumes of icy spray broke across the bow of the rented skiff Forsetti piloted toward the gray island at the middle of the bay. As Cori stood in the open cockpit, freezing droplets stung her cheeks and battered at her eyes but she never turned her face away from their destination.

'You'll be more comfortable if you sit down,' Forsetti called over the sound of the engine. He was himself seated at the wheel.

'I'm fine,' Cori shouted back. It would take a lot more than getting warm to be comfortable. She hadn't felt her nerves so close to the brink of shattering since Black Eagle's murder. It wasn't getting past the police patrol boats that frightened her so much as facing Abel again. Forsetti had arranged an interview, ostensibly to explore the state of mind of the remaining militants as their occupation headed into a fourth month.

At the foot of the old cement quay where Machine Gun Kelly and Al Capone had once disembarked to spend the rest of their lives behind bars, a police launch was stationed. From his long stint as a crime reporter, Forsetti was well known to the police, and they passed him onto the island without asking to see his press card. Cori was accepted on his word as his stenographic assistant. In a raincoat and a hat with a large brim, she was an anonymous figure.

From the quay, they climbed up concrete steps to a door in the walls of the prison. Along the way, Cori saw a number of men walking the pathways or just passing time sitting on rocky outcroppings, but Abel was not among them.

They passed through the walls, and crossed the bare yard where prisoners had milled during the scant hours they were allowed outside. A young Indian man dressed in denims, his black hair worn long and tied back, intercepted them at the entrance to the old administration building and led them inside, along corridors dimly lit by kerosene lanterns placed at intervals. Acquainted with Forsetti from previous visits, the two men casually chatted about the results of recent football games as Cori tailed along. By an open doorway, the young man stopped and pointed them inside. 'I'll tell Walks-Through-Fire you are here,' he said, and left.

'Would you please leave me alone now?' Cori said to Forsetti before entering the room.

'This guy you asked to meet is one of the chiefs – could be a tough customer. You might want protection.'

'I know him, he won't hurt me,' Cori said. But her voice was quavering as she spoke.

'How do you know him?' Forsetti asked. 'Why were you so desperate for this meeting?'

'I told you right at the beginning, Vince, I'm not going to answer those questions.'

'I'm sure it's a hell of a story. Can't help wanting a scoop.'

'Please go . . .'

The reporter shrugged and walked back along the corridor while Cori went through the door. The room inside appeared to have been an office for some prison official. A row of filing cabinets still lined one wall, empty drawers pulled out. A metal desk and a couple of chairs left behind by the prison regime were spaced randomly around the room. Cori went to the window and looked out through iron bars. It struck her that she was a prisoner, too, had been one ever since she had let G.D. lock her into the existence he dictated for her.

Behind her, she heard someone enter the room and close the door. Her heart began to hammer so furiously in her chest, she thought it might explode.

'Where is Mr Forsetti? I thought he'd be doing the interview.'

His voice. It sounded no different than the last time she'd heard it, gentle, without anger. Tears sprang to her eyes as all the emotions of their last parting were reborn.

'Miss . . . did you hear me?'

Closer. Yet still it was impossible to turn and face him.

'I was told Mr Forsetti—'

She wrenched herself around.

He stared at her a moment, then rubbed a hand over his eyes, brushing back the hair that shaded his brow, as though trying to clear an illusion brought on by fatigue or fever.

Too overcome to speak, Cori inventoried the damage that time had done to him. Gone was the lean boyish aspect evident even in his thirties when she had known him. He was still thin, still attractive, but there was a tired, wasted air about him. His thick hair was shot through with gray streaks, his face drawn and lined, his shoulders were stooped. Of course, she reminded herself, he was in the middle of a taxing ordeal. When it was over, he would certainly look better. Yet she felt, too, that there was a deeper spiritual fatigue that would not be so easily cured.

He took a step nearer. Though he remained out of reach, his hand floated up as if to caress her face. 'You are still very beautiful,' he said, as his hand fell back to his side. He squeezed his eyes shut for a second, blocking out what he had just admired. 'But why have you come?' he added, not just a question but an expression of pained regret.

'I need to know about Tayhcawin. Tell me. Please, Abel.' Saying his name sparked a fresh surge of feelings she had thought long dead. She moved to close the distance between them. 'How is she? What is she like?'

He hesitated, then turned and opened the gap again, walking away to face an empty wall. 'Isn't it better if I don't tell you? She's a ghost for you now, an event in a distant past.' He turned to her again. 'Why make her more real? Don't you see it will only make it harder for you, that it would be better by far if you hadn't come? Go away, Miss Hartleigh.'

The formal address stung no less than if he had slapped her. It wiped away all their intimacy in a stroke, reincarnated her as one of the oppressors he was rising up against.

'I'm married now,' she said. 'My name is Patterson. You've met my husband, in fact . . .'

'Patterson,' he said thoughtfully. 'The newspaper publisher?'

'Yes. We were married not long after I came back to San Francisco.'

He smiled faintly at the twists of fate. 'He seems a very decent man. You told him about—'

'No,' she cut in. 'None of it.'

Abel looked down a moment, reflecting on the significance of her reply. 'All the more reason, then, for you to put everything else behind you.'

'She's my *child*, Abel,' she pleaded. 'Yes, it would be better if I could forget. But I never will. I can't forgive myself for leaving her.'

'There wasn't a choice.'

'As if that mattered a damn to my conscience.' Cori sank down into one of the office chairs. 'Oh, Abel, listen . . .' It began to flow out of her. Staring at the floor, she spoke of the inner torture she had endured over the years, her breakdown, the institution, shock therapy. Listening, he leaned against the wall, then slid down to crouch on his haunches Indian-style, watching her with an expression of anguished sympathy.

'I was better for a while,' she concluded. 'But now . . . since I've known you were here . . .' She raised her eyes as she made her final plea. 'It would help so much just to know she's all right.'

There was a long silence. Then Abel rose from his crouch and pulled the other chair over to sit down opposite, his knees almost touching hers. Quietly, he said, 'Our daughter is . . . is a miracle. She is a sun that lights the darkness all around her.

She is kind, and loving, and wise beyond her years, and she has all the beauty of her mother. But more, she has been given the strength of Tunka, the rock, eldest of all gods. With that strength, she has been able to keep growing solid and straight and be happy with herself, even while the rough life we have grinds others down to dust. And I believe one more thing may be true: her goodness and strength has been recognized by Wakan Tanka, the great mystery, so she has been given some of the powers of the *yuwipi* that belonged to her ancestors. When other children cry, Tayhcawin will go to them and make them smile again. In our *tipospaye*, even the older women when they feel ill, will go to her, and they say her touch can make their pains vanish. A year ago, when Bessie Appearing Day was at the end of her life—'

He hesitated when he noticed the sadness pass over Cori's face. 'Yes, Bessie went to the spirits. But she lived long, and there was sickness only at the end. Then it was Tay she wanted to nurse her. She said that when Tay sang to her or just held her hand, it would chase her pains even quicker than the potions of Nellie Blue Snow.' He leaned back. 'So let your mind be easy about your child. She is blessed. The very best of what you are is in her, *ohitika win.*'

The best of what I *was*, Cori thought sadly. Hearing again her Indian name after so many years, she could only reflect how little she deserved it now. Brave woman? How could she be called brave if she still concealed so much of the truth?

'Thank you, Abel,' she said, rising from her chair. 'I've been so afraid that she was suffering.'

He rose with her. 'I'm sorry that it's been so hard for you.'

'What you've told me will make everything easier.'

They stared at each other, acutely aware of what they had shared that was no longer possible. There was nothing to do now but leave. Cori could almost hear the ghosts of prison guards cruelly shouting out that visiting time was over. Then, as words of goodbye were almost on her lips, an idea seized her. Something she hadn't dared conceive until the depth of his love for their daughter was revealed by the way he'd spoken about her.

'Abel, I swear it wasn't in my mind when I came here. But . . . the way you've spoken about Tayhcawin, there's no doubt how much you love her and want what's best for her.'

He nodded attentively.

'She's obviously extraordinary, and would make the most of any opportunities if they were given to her.' Cori started to speak more rapidly, the idea exciting her more as it took shape. 'Where she is now, she can't get the kind of education that will help develop her full potential. I remember what it's like, Abel. She has to cope with so much deprivation. Imagine what it would be like if Tayhcawin had the best schooling, access to good libraries, museums.' The idea possessed her now. She reached out to him, one hand grabbing onto the edge of his leather vest like a salesman collaring a prospect. 'Think of what could be done for her here, Abel. Let her come. I'm offering this for *her*, don't you see? Not for myself.'

He put his hand over hers, grasping it tightly, as a rescuer might hold the hand of someone clinging to a ledge. 'It's impossible, Mrs Patterson, you must see that. Bringing her into the middle of things when you've never told anyone? What you told me about your own health . . . you're not up to dealing with that situation. It would destroy your marriage, and you with it.'

It stopped her only an instant. Her mind, in overdrive, seemed to have a solution for every problem. 'My sister will take her . . . accept her as her own. Yes, I know Bren will do it.' Bren needed her as an ally in taking over the company? Then this would be the price. Bren would not say no. Nothing was more important to her than taking G.D.'s place. Aloud, Cori thought it through. 'She can say it's a child she's adopting

– a philanthropy. Or else claim it as her own. She's had dozens of men. They'd have no trouble believing that she had the child, and gave it up. The rest of my family believes I came back home after our baby died – even if they suspected she was mine, my family would never say anything. It would be between Bren and me. Oh, Abel, it would be easy. And so much better for her – for our child. Let Brenda take her. You must.' Her pleading was taking on an edge of hysteria. She was almost ready to fall to her knees. 'Please. Say yes. She'd be near me, safe, but no one—'

'*No*!' He roared out abruptly, casting off all concern for her fragility. 'Why do you think this would be better? Because you are a *wasicun* and you think the way you live, the ideas you teach, the things you value must be better!' He brought his voice down, but his eyes still burned with righteous fury. 'And like all *wasicuns* you wish to take away whatever the Indian cares about and reduce him to nothing.' He pushed her away. 'Well, you will not have her. Neither you nor your sister. No.' He retreated from her, backing toward the door to be the first to leave. 'I will not teach her to feel shame in what we have. I will not let her be turned into one of *you*!'

Cori was shattered. Not by his rejection of the idea, but of her, the burning flame of hatred for all whites that had suddenly flared out of him. 'But a part of her *is* me,' she countered, mustering only a whisper. 'Even a part of you is . . . a *wasicun*.'

'No. I could not live divided, and neither can she. We must be on one side or the other. And the choice has been made. Mine . . . and hers.' He strode to the door, then paused to look back once more and capture a mental picture of her.

'*You* chose for yourself,' Cori cried out. 'But you won't let her.'

'She doesn't need to.'

'Of course she does. She must know she's – ' the word for a mixed blood came back to her – '*iyeska*.'

'It does not matter to her. She has no attachment to the white.' He paused for a moment. 'Tayhcawin knows that her mother didn't want her – that she left her and went away . . . and died.' His gaze lingered another second, then he turned and walked out.

So in a way they did not exist for each other, Cori thought. Mother and child were both falsely dead to all around them. She spun back to the window, and stood looking out through the bars until Forsetti came and took her back to the boat.

It did not matter that she was leaving the prison island. She was not going free.

16

The Month of Falling Snow – 1973

Perspiration streamed down Tay's body as she sat in the circle
of sixteen others who had come to cleanse themselves
physically and spiritually in the *oinikaga tipi*. Like the others
in the sweat lodge, men and women of various ages, she was
naked. The steam rising off the pile of white limestone rocks
at the center of the circle raised the temperature in the confined
space to a level that would not be bearable to anyone clothed.
Beneath the rocks, an earthen pit had been scooped out and
within it, heating the rocks, burned *peta owihankeshni* – 'the
fire without end'. As it was, the temperature inside the low
dome-shaped enclosure was not easy to tolerate. Tay's whole
body throbbed as her system strained to adjust to the extreme
temperature. Her long hair, sweat-soaked, stuck to her shoulders
and breasts, the moisture dripping like heavy rain from the
tips. She was acutely aware of the rivulets running slowly down
over her nipples, the curve of her stomach, across her thighs,
into the sensitive cleft between her legs, touching her almost
like caressing fingers. Tonight she had been slow to shift into
that phase where she lost all sense of real time and place, felt
herself wafting up into the air like the steam.

She thought back to the first time she had been to an *oinikaga tipi*, only a few days after her father had returned from his mission in San Francisco, two years ago. Most of the other Alcatraz activists had given themselves up long before; Abel had been one of just fifteen who stayed to the early summer of 1971. At last federal marshals had raided the island, seized the holdouts, and Abel had been sentenced to four months in jail for civil disobedience. By the time he returned to the rez Tay had turned fourteen, and when he learned from the other women in the *tipospaye* that she had begun having her moon-time, he had brought her along with him to the next sweat lodge. The purpose of the ritual was not so much to cleanse the body as to induce the feeling that the flesh had almost literally melted away and what remained was pure consciousness, the sense of being in tune with nature and the spirits. It was too intense for the young. Usually girls didn't come until after their first period. Participating in the experience was a rite of passage.

That first time, when she had been completely unprepared for the heat, the hot steam going down into her chest, the heady aroma of the green cedar sprinkled into the fire, she had quickly felt faint. But seeing her father across from her, unflinching as he sat with his back straight, Tay had said nothing, made no move to go. And soon she had the illusion of her body becoming weightless, floating up, a sense that she could look down on herself sitting there. Her mind became an entity on its own. What appeared in front of her was something she saw only within, visions from far away – of her father, not with her, but when he had been alone inside the high stone walls. Perhaps the images were only memories, things he had told her about the many months he had spent on Alcatraz Island. Yet, at the edges of what she saw in her mind's eye, was a vague shadow of something she was certain he had never mentioned at all – a *wanagi*, a ghost: the spirit of her mother.

She said nothing to Abel about it. The experiences of the

sweat lodge were stronger and more meaningful if they were kept private, not to be spoken about as though they were sights seen by a mere tourist in the spirit world.

She had been to a few sweat lodges since. The *wanagi* had never returned, but there had been other vivid illusions when she felt herself not only rise into the air of the lodge, but fly away outside, soaring over the land like *wanjbli*, an unspoiled land that from horizon to horizon belonged to her tribe. She felt herself carried back in time, becoming a maiden who was sitting in a sweat lodge amid warriors in the time of the great Sioux chief, Red Cloud.

Tonight, though, she could not free her mind from her body, could not leave the reality of the lodge for another time and space. Partly it was because she was so worried about her father. Since his return from the occupation, and the months in jail, he had not been as robust and vigorous as before. Tay believed that some illness was eating at him, leaving him weak on some days, something too serious for her to cure, even though, he said, she had the ability to take away his headaches when she would lay her hands across his brow. It occurred to her that it might be an illness of the spirit. He asked her so often if she forgave him for leaving her alone all those twenty months to pursue his crusade. 'I never thought it would last so long,' he would explain apologetically, again and again, 'but once we were there, we couldn't give up.'

Each time she told him there was nothing to forgive. 'I only wish you would have let me go with you. I believe in what you did then, and what you are still trying to do.' He had taken no militant action since returning to the rez, but he still wrote dozens of letters to Congressmen, and the councils of other tribes, and people in the arts who might help the cause of the native Americans. How could he doubt that she was proud of his commitment?

No matter how often she gave her assurances, however, he

would ask her again. He worried a lot, too, that she was not happy. 'I wish so much I could give you more,' he often said lately. 'You are so lovely. You should have fine clothes, a nice house. I would like to know you will always have the best of everything.'

It seemed odd to her. She never complained about the lack of material things. She always felt pride in being a part of this place, this tradition; she loved the legends and beliefs that told the story of all time and her people as they understood it. The *Paha Sapa* – these Black Hills – were her home, and she felt that the caves in these hills were rightfully called by the Sioux *wamaka og'naka icante*, 'the heart of everything that is'. It was from these caves that *we-ota-wichasha* had first emerged – 'blood clot boy', the first man, formed from a drop of menstrual blood that fell to earth and clotted on the ground in the moon-time of the first woman. What a wonderful, sensible belief – that woman came first, man was made from her; not, as the *wasicuns* believed, woman was only an afterthought, formed out of one useless rib of a man.

Tay knew that others on the rez could no longer look around them with any pride; they saw only poverty and despair, too much alcoholism, too much illiteracy, too many babies born to young women – no more than girls sometimes – with no men to support them. But Tay would not surrender to the idea that the tribe was doomed to decline and ultimate extinction. The Sioux were a great people with a great history; the hope of renewal lay in never letting go of the belief that they could be great again. Infused with that conviction, Tay never thought of herself as merely part Indian.

Less steam was rising now, the rocks were cooling. As the mist thinned she could see through it to the other side of the circle. She was conscious of the dark eyes of the young man seated opposite her as they roamed her body. His name was Edward Nightsong Bird, and she knew him from the rez school where he had been a couple of years ahead of her. As she stared back, he looked up boldly to meet her gaze, then his eyes flicked down again, then back up. It was generally understood that such brazen looks were forbidden to invade the ritual of the *oinikaga tipi*. Tay's eyes flashed at him furiously and he bowed his head. Quickly, she leaned forward and picked up one of the bowls of cold water that were regularly passed into the lodge from a man who remained outside. She tipped it onto the rocks and the 'breath of grandfather' rose thickly into the air again, curtaining her from the young man on the other side of the pit. Yet Tay sensed he was still looking in her direction. She could not cut herself loose from the overwhelming awareness of her body, the sensitivity to the beads of sweat creeping so slowly over her skin. She couldn't give herself over to the spirits. Grabbing up the blanket that was bunched around her on the earthen floor, she wrapped it around herself, leapt to her feet and left the lodge.

The cold air of the clear winter night collided with the hot, perspiring skin of her face and hands, immobilizing her for a second. Tilting her head back, she looked at the star-speckled sky and breathed deeply.

The water man, who sat huddled in his parka just outside the low beehive-shaped sweat lodge glanced at her. She knew him, an old man named Billy Turning Bear. 'Are you all right, Tayhcawin?' he asked.

'I will be, Billy. But it isn't working for me tonight. I'm going home.'

'Greetings to your father,' he called softly as she walked away along the narrow path formed of the earth that had been scooped out of the fire pit, symbolic of the presence of 'grandmother earth' at the ritual.

She walked across two low hills to reach the road. There was only a sliver of moon, but with the light of the stars it was enough to follow the ribbon of asphalt leading toward home, two miles away. She saw distant headlights approaching, and while they were still a quarter of a mile away she could hear a radio playing and raucous laughter. She covered her head with the blanket, and changed to a slow stooped walk so she would appear to be an old woman. Soon a dilapidated pick-up truck sped past in the other direction, eight or nine young men in the open back along with those in the cab. Tay saw one of them holding a fifth of whiskey to his lips as they passed. They were all obviously drunk. A couple of them shouted out to her.

'Hey, Grandmother, want a ride?'

'We'll make you feel young again!'

But the truck didn't slow down, and the sound of the music and their drunken laughter quickly faded. What a terrible shame, she thought, that so many of the young men felt their lives were hopeless and turned so quickly to alcohol to dull the pain.

After half an hour, Tay arrived at the *tipospaye*. It had grown to a cluster of five separate small houses around the main lodge as children who had been only six and seven when Tay was born gave birth to children of their own, often as soon as they reached their mid-teens. They were either unmarried, or the men went away so the mother and newborns could collect aid money from the Bureau of Indian Affairs. Sometimes the mothers went, too, knowing their children would be cared for by the extended family of cousins and grandmothers and aunts.

When Tay stepped through the door of the one-room tar-paper shack she shared with Abel, he was at the old pine table working at the typewriter. He was surprised to see her; the sweat lodge was supposed to last until dawn. When he asked why she had come home, she sat down in the chair facing him. 'I was worried about you,' she said.

'Me? Why?'

'Because you are worrying so much about me. I feel there

228

is something bothering you that was never there before. All my growing-up time, you told me that no matter what is missing in our lives, there is so much that is special and good I do not need to envy anyone. You taught me to love the open space, the sky, the animals, and to feel how we are part of them, and they of us, in a way that the *wasicuns* will never feel or understand.' She leaned into the table, her hands reaching toward him though he was too far away to touch. '*Atie*,' she went on – she always used the Sioux word when referring to him as her father, 'you have made me proud of who I am . . . who *we* are. You have given me never a moment's reason to doubt your love for me. I have known, too, that because my mother died in giving me life, you have always tried to make up for the loss, to show the gentle care of a mother—'

Abel looked away, embarrassed. Tay leaned out farther, and grabbed his hands, pulling him around again. 'Yes, *Atie*, you have been mother as well as father. So why do you ask again and again, if I forgive you for that time you were away. As much as I missed you, I never thought to blame you because you were not here. You went for good reason. Don't you know I share in my heart all the yearnings in yours that made you leave me?'

He gazed at her fondly through eyes that had taken on a faint silvery sheen. His voice broke when he said her name. 'Tayhcawin, what you say is like cool water to a thirsty man. Of course, I do not doubt your feelings. But as I have watched you grow, I see you coming to what may be a crossroads . . .' He spoke haltingly, careful with his words. 'Turn one way, you might have a magical life, with every opportunity in your grasp. Another way . . . and there is no certainty you will ever have more than you have now.'

'I have all I want,' she said earnestly. 'I'm not unhappy, *Atie*. Especially since you've returned.'

'But you are almost . . . you *are* a woman,' he said. 'We

must think about how to make a good life for you in the years to come. What about your schooling? You can't get a good education here.'

'I've already had the most wonderful education! Our ways, our songs and ceremonies, the things that Nellie Blue Snow has told me about the things that grow in the fields and the messages of our dreams, the things you have told me about the way *wanjbli* and *mato*, the bear, and the other animals guide us and speak to us. These mean more than anything I would study in a fancy school. If they are not learned, they will die away as our people die.'

Abel nodded. 'Of course they are worth saving. But learning the old ways must not keep you from learning other things – from "playing the game", as the *wasicuns* say. Even to help our people, you should have advantages I did not.' There was a strained yearning in his voice. 'I want you to go to college, Tay, to have all the benefits a young white woman would have.'

'I know you want that, *Atie*. Isn't that part of what you've been trying to get with all your work? Isn't it to win a better life that you made all your protests, wrote all your letters to Governors and Congressmen, campaigned for—'

'Listen to me, Tay!' he broke in impatiently. 'No matter how hard I work, you can't depend on what I'm doing, or what you're dreaming, to get you the better life you deserve.'

Tay sat back and gazed at him with some disappointment. If she had dreams, it was because he had encouraged her long ago to believe they could be fulfilled. Now he was discouraging her.

'What did you mean before,' she asked warily, 'about being at a crossroads – having a magical life depending on which way I go? What roads are these, *Atie*, and what must I do to choose?'

He was silent for a long moment, looking away into a shadow. 'It's not what you must do,' he said. 'It's a choice I should make for you.'

He was talking so strangely, Tay thought, there was such sadness in his voice, the kind of heaviness she'd last heard when he told her on the phone that he'd been sentenced to prison and it would be another few months before he came home.

'What is it?' Tay asked, suddenly fearful. 'What sort of choice are you talking about?'

He turned from the shadows to face her. He seemed on the verge of speaking again when the heavy silence was broken by a sound from the night outside, a woman's voice excitedly yelling his name repeatedly, rapidly coming nearer.

A moment later Kate burst through the door of the shack on the run. ' . . . white sonofabitch killed a Sioux man over in Buffalo Gap . . .' she panted. 'Leonard's on the phone, wants you . . .'

Abel dashed straight out through the open door to run up to the main lodge.

Though she had never met him, Tay knew that Leonard was the name of one of the leaders of the group of native Americans who were fighting to get more recognition for their rights as citizens, as well as making the government honor the old treaty promises. If he was calling Abel, there was probably some plan to organize a new protest in the attempt to see that proper justice was done in the murder of this Indian.

Tay went to the door, and watched her father as he sprinted up the moonlit hillside. As tired as he had seemed in recent days, he was charging ahead quickly, spurred by the need to lend his will and his talents to the ongoing crusade.

How long would he be gone this time? she wondered. And when would she have a chance to hear his answer to her question? What sort of choice had he been talking about?

The dead Indian was named Wesley Bad Heart Bull. He had been stabbed to death in a bar by a white service-station attendant who had then been taken into custody and brought to the courthouse in Custer, a small county seat in the heart of the Black Hills. At court, the accused was charged with involuntary manslaughter in the second degree and released on five thousand dollars bail.

Outraged by one more example of the state's callous disregard of fairness where Indians were concerned, the murdered man's mother had contacted some of the tribal activists involved with organizing past protests to tell them what had happened. These men had quickly assembled a group that would travel in a caravan to Custer and demonstrate against the low bail and the relatively light charge. If an Indian had killed a white, they all knew, no less a charge than murder would have been lodged – and the bail would have been many times higher, impossible to pay.

The morning after Abel received the phone call asking him to join a caravan of protesters to Custer, he said goodbye to Tay and climbed into his ancient pick-up truck. Ada and Kate sat with him in front, Emory and eighteen other men and women were clustered in the open loadbed.

Tay had been begging to go along since last night, but Abel continued to refuse. 'We're headed for a town called Custer, after all. Maybe they'll think it's our turn to be massacred.'

'Then you mustn't go,' she pleaded.

'Forgive me, Tay – that was a very poor joke. There could be some local resistance, but nothing so terrible. Still, it will be no place for a young girl.'

'Yet you think I'm old enough to stay here and take care of the little ones,' she complained.

'Exactly. Someone must look after them.' He started the truck engine. 'Now, don't fret. It's only a couple hours' drive from here. We'll all be home by evening.' He put his hand out the window and touched her cheek, then he drove off.

It was late afternoon and Tay was in the main lodge giving

dinner to the young children she'd been left to care for, when she received a visit from Wanda Mountain Tree, who lived with the next *tipospaye* along the road. Wanda brought news. At Custer, the demonstrators had marched *en masse* at the office of the state prosecutor. At first, they had been able to state their demands in a peaceful exchange, but then police controlling the crowd had man-handled Sarah Bad Heart Bull, mother of the murdered man. After that, as Wanda put it, 'war broke out'. The Indians had rioted, fistfighting with the police and destroying a couple of patrol cars with home-made firebombs before they had been subdued with billy clubs and tear gas. Both sides had sustained injuries, though fortunately there had been no deaths. Twenty-seven Indian men had been arrested, Abel among them.

Tay slumped down at the long dining-table. She assumed it would mean another long separation from her father, and she had an ominous premonition that she might not even see him again.

But less than an hour after Wanda departed, the phone in the lodge rang. When she answered, Tay heard her father's voice: 'I don't want you to worry, but I won't be coming back tonight.'

'How can I not worry?' she cried. 'I know you're in jail. *Atie*, I'm scared for you!'

'Honey, I'm not in jail—'

'I heard you were arrested.'

'I was, many of us – and we're all out on bail. There's actually some lawyers on our side this time.'

'If you're free, then why aren't you coming home?'

' 'Cause we're all driving straight on to Rapid City to demonstrate there.'

'*Atie*, no!' Rapid City was still supposed to have the largest concentration of Indian-haters in the region – and it was the place where Abel's beloved cousin had been murdered seventeen years ago.

'We must go, Tay. We're gonna wake up this whole state – this whole country before we're through. They're not gonna beat us down anymore. We've all had enough, damn it.'

Through the phone, Tay could hear her father's voice quivering with a rage she'd never known in him before. He was such a gentle man, his righteous anger always sensibly controlled. The way he sounded now, he seemed to want to achieve overnight all the victories that their people had dreamed of for centuries. And yet, Tay recalled, less than twenty-four hours ago, he'd been advising her that she couldn't count on her life improving as a result of his efforts. She couldn't help wondering if his outburst of rash impatience hadn't been somehow triggered by that exchange. Was it for her that he felt impelled to keep rushing on to the next confrontation?

'*Atie*, last night – you were about to tell me something when that call came – about a choice you had to make for me. What did you mean?'

'Never mind, Tay. I was feeling weak. The choice would have been a kind of surrender. Today, I feel very different.'

'So . . . you won't tell me?'

'There's nothing to tell. I was being foolish, and you spoke wisely. Your life is here . . . and here we will make it as fine and promising as it would be anywhere else. Good night, Tayhcawin. I'll see you tomorrow.'

'Be careful, *Atie*, be very careful,' she said before hanging up. 'I love you.'

Long after she had put the young ones to bed, she sat by a fire, puzzling over the unanswered riddle of the crossroads. From his final remark, it sounded like the choice involved sending her away. But to where? Maybe he'd meant only sending her off for a better education. But how in the world had he thought they could pay for that? It was all they could do to spare the extra money for gas so he could drive off to these protest demonstrations.

Anxiety plagued her as she thought of him marching again so soon after being arrested. The situation between the Indians and the *wasicuns* was plainly growing darker and angrier than it had for a long time, no doubt as a result of the greater determination of Indians like her father not to let their rights be denied any longer. It seemed certain that, as in the Indian wars of old, before there would be any new treaties, blood might have to be spilled.

Tay rose from her place by the fire, pulled a blanket down from one of the pegs by the door, wrapped herself in it and went out into the cold clear January night. Looking up at the vast blue-black sky and the million pinpoints of light, the wisps of cloud lit by mother moon, she murmured the traditional phrase that preceeded prayers and rituals, '*Mitayuke oyasin*' – all my relatives – a quiet call to all of nature to listen. Then she prayed silently that her father would be protected and returned to her safely.

She wondered, too, as she looked at the heavens, if her mother could have also heard the prayer.

17

The situation heated up in the weeks following Abel's renewed involvement with the protest movement. The march on Rapid City exploded into a riot with police and local citizens. Dozens of Sioux demonstrators were injured and arrested. Many were held several days before bail was accepted and arranged, but Abel and the others from the *tipospaye* returned the next morning. One of Emory's eyes was closed and blackened as a result of being punched by a policeman, Kate was limping on an ankle twisted while running from an outraged drunken cowboy, and Abel had a bad bruise on one arm from a billy club. Yet the entire group was elated rather than beaten down. They had brought home a victory. The furious two-day uprising of so many native Americans had put the entire Black Hills region on notice that their demand for justice could no longer be shrugged off or mildly placated case by case: without a general recognition of their rights, there might be a return to the full-fledged hostilities of frontier days. The state's attorney dealing with the case of Wesley Bad Heart Bull had promised his killer would be vigorously prosecuted.

While Abel continued working on the new crusade, Tay noticed that he took no carpentry jobs, did no handicrafts, even ignored the tasks he'd always performed around their shack and community land, such as splitting firewood or doing plumbing repairs. When he wasn't preparing a new pamphlet or writing letters to state and local bureaucrats, he was off attending meetings with other Indian activists. As the movement gathered momentum, cooperation was growing between groups from different reservations.

In the middle of February, a small delegation from the Pine Ridge Sioux came one evening to speak with Abel in his shack. Eager to know more of what went on in these meetings, Tay was pleased when Abel did not ask her to leave but allowed her to continue homework on her bed while he sat with the visitors at the big table in the center of the room. While pretending to focus on her geometry problems, she heard the visitors tell Abel that winning justice for the Rosebud Sioux as well as themselves was not just a matter of dealing with *wasicuns* who took unfair advantage, but of rooting out corrupt members of any tribe who did the bidding of the whites to undermine the Indian cause. The man who held the elected position of tribal leader of the Pine Ridge Sioux, they said, was such an 'apple-man', red-skinned outside, but white inside; he had not only appeased government people in Washington, but had stolen tribal funds for his personal benefit. The visitors told Abel they wanted to remove this corrupt leader from power, but they needed the help of their 'brothers' from other reservations. A trial by the tribal council was already scheduled to decide whether to impeach the man, but since the council's members had all been appointed by him, there was little doubt they would vote to keep him in power. To remove him they would need a threat of rebellion, the bigger the better. Anticipating this insurrection, the Nixon administration had already dispatched sixty-five armed federal marshals to Pine Ridge to keep order and support the tribal leader who had been their valuable 'puppet'.

Tay heard Abel agree that, when the tribal council voted on the impeachment a few days hence, he would go to Pine Ridge and bring along other Rosebud Sioux to join the demonstration.

When the delegation left, Tay moved to sit at the table where Abel had resumed working on a pamphlet he was writing. 'How long can you keep this up,' she asked, 'without being hurt or sent back to jail?'

'I can't think about that,' Abel said.

'Then think about me. *Atie*, you're all I have.'

He rose and came around the table to her. Crouching beside her chair, he took her hands in his. 'Tayhcawin, I have many dreams lately in which my murdered cousin comes to me. Black Eagle says nothing, but he stands and looks at me, and I know the meaning. He is telling me he might still be alive if we had taken our stand earlier – if we had earned back the respect we had lost. Our people have been quiet too long; while we remain quiet we lose respect even for ourselves. I must raise my voice now. I must fight if it comes to that. But, of course, I am always thinking of you. I do this for you, as I should have done it for Black Eagle long ago.'

It would be pointless to object further, Tay knew. Though the fear did not leave her. If her father kept putting himself at the center of this new war with the *wasicuns*, he was bound to be hurt. All she could do to protect him was to stay near him. Though if she asked to be part of the fight, she knew he would refuse. So she said nothing.

But as she leaned over to embrace him, she was already making plans.

A week later, Abel left the Rosebud reservation to drive west to Pine Ridge. Again, his pick-up truck carried a full load of other men and women participating in the protest. Ada went along, but this time Kate stayed behind. Her sprained ankle hadn't recovered, and being unable to run would put her in jeopardy if federal marshals came after the demonstrators. With Kate available to take care of the children, Tay was free to join the caravan. Knowing her father wouldn't permit it, she waited until his truck had left, then went out to the road and hailed down one of the other trucks joining a caravan to Pine Ridge.

Like other central reservation settlements, Pine Ridge town consisted of a few run-down stores, a couple of gas stations and some churches clustered near a complex of buildings that housed the US Bureau of Indian Affairs, a government health-services clinic, and offices of the tribal council. Arriving at the town, demonstrators gathered in front of the tribal council offices where the impeachment trial of the despised leader of the Pine Ridge Sioux was being held. A decision by the council was supposed to be announced during the afternoon. As the crowd waited it kept growing until there were several hundred. Federal marshals moved into place to barricade the building.

Abel was at the front of the crowd, one of several men who gave speeches chronicling the long history of the government's broken treaties, and demanding it was time to obtain all that had been promised. Tay stayed at the fringes, where it was easy to stay out of Abel's view.

The crowd was in an angry and excited mood when one of the protest leaders interrupted a speech to announce that the impeachment trial had ended, and by unanimous vote, the council had voted to keep the leader whom all the rank-and-file members of the tribe had been trying to remove. The result was regarded as proof of the control Washington continued to exert over the lives of Indians without any concern for their wishes or best interests.

Though outraged, the crowd was still disciplined enough not to provoke the well-armed marshals into a fight. The demonstrators marched in protest behind their leaders to a community meeting hall where the local Sioux recounted abuses they had suffered and debated steps to end them. Hearing these stories, all the unforgivable humiliation Tay had felt at the hands of that white policeman four years ago came back to her. She felt inspired to join the struggle against the oppression of the *wasicuns*.

When some elders near the front of the hall spoke in voices weakened by age, Tay moved up closer along one of the outside aisles to hear.

'If we are going to end this once and for all,' one old man said, 'let us all return together, today, to *Cankpe Opi*. Our dreams should be recaptured in the same sad place where they were lost.'

The old man's suggestion immediately struck a chord in the crowd. Voices were instantly raised to second the idea. Groups of protestors started moving to the doors of the community hall, already heading eagerly for the next battleground.

Cankpe Opi meant Wounded Knee. Among all the places where the Indians had fought the *wasicuns* in the past, none held more symbolic meaning than this small settlement. It was at *Cankpe Opi*, in 1890, that the Indian wars had been brought to an end with one final burst of inhuman savagery when the seventh cavalry, the unit once commanded by George Armstrong Custer, had massacred three hundred Sioux men, women, and children from the tribe of Chief Big Foot, camped there not with any hostile intention, but simply waiting to make peace. The spot was marked today by the place where the victims had been buried there in a mass grave.

On a platform at the front of the hall, Abel stepped forward behind other leaders who announced that the caravan to Wounded Knee was unanimously approved, and all who wanted to go should wait in their cars and trucks to depart together. As he surveyed the crowd from the platform, he suddenly spotted Tay. Furious, he jumped down to the floor and rushed over to her. 'What the hell are you doing here?'

'The same as everyone else! I want to be part of this.'

'Tay, this isn't just a demonstration anymore. I'm not sure anyone can control what will happen next. I couldn't bear it if you got hurt.'

'Then we will protect each other. Because it will be no easier for me if anything happens to you.'

He gazed at her, his expression like a changeable sky moving from stormy to fair and darkening again with the fleeting passage of clouds across the sun. Then abruptly he swept her into an embrace. It lasted only briefly before he broke away. Emory had moved up beside Tay.

'Take her home,' Abel commanded, tossing Emory the keys to the truck. 'I'll ride with the others and you can join us later.'

Emory took a tight grip on her arm, and started pulling her away.

Tay struggled against Emory while shouting at Abel who was already moving in another direction. 'So you'd take me against my will – force me to give up fighting for what I believe in? If you do that, *Atie*, then how are you different from the rest of our enemies?'

He stopped to look at her again. Defeated by her logic, he could not reply. But after a second, he motioned Emory to keep going. She gave up struggling. If he did not feel she belonged with him, then the very heart of her conviction was already deadened. It was because she was part of him – because no matter what blood had been mixed to conceive her, she was Indian – that she felt this was her fight, too. But he wouldn't let her share it with him. Because he loved her, he said. But there was something missing from that love if he couldn't understand how important this was to her.

Cankpe Opi remained a desolate spot. On a knoll, near the marker for the mass grave, stood a wooden church with a white steeple visible far across an open plain. At a distance below the church there was a large trading post. Built after the massacre, the church and the trading post were regarded by the Indians as twin flags planted to proclaim the white man's victory, symbols of the society that continued to exploit them.

It was evening when a line of fifty-four cars drove into Wounded Knee bringing two hundred and fifty Sioux. Upon arriving at the scene that epitomized all the savage mistreatment they had long endured, their fury boiled over. Several men, armed with rifles and revolvers, shot out the settlement's few street lights. Then they entered the trading post, made hostages of the white owner and his helpers, and ransacked the place for guns and ammunition.

Some of the older Indians, deploring the violence, got back in their cars and left. Abel tried at first to prevent the rampage, but he soon realized that the flood of emotions that had broken loose could not be contained. Anyway, one more peaceful demonstration might only lead to one more empty promise. So he let the younger hotheads have their way, and became a follower rather than a leader. Along with those who remained, he followed the young men up to the top of the knoll where they all started digging trenches and constructing bunkers around the white church and the grave where their massacred ancestors lay buried.

Word soon reached the authorities that Wounded Knee had been occupied, and hostages taken who would be released when a list of Indian demands was met. Within hours, a massive force of BIA police, federal marshals, FBI and agents had descended on the scene, supported by armored vehicles and heavy weapons from the National Guard. Roads were blocked, shipments of food stopped, electricity turned off.

The authorities expected the renegades to yield quickly once they were surrounded, all access cut off. But as one day passed into the next, the will of the Indians did not waver. During the first week of tense face-off, frayed nerves caused one side or the other to start shooting, and two of the occupiers were wounded. Truces were arranged so that the injured men could be removed to hospitals, but no one else left their positions. No less than in the wars of the old west, these warriors seemed ready to die rather than surrender.

Tay continued to brood on what she felt was a kind of betrayal by her father. By keeping her away, he had denied her the chance to share in fulfilling the destiny of her people. She resented the powerlessness she felt as she sat down each night in front of the television set at the Rosebud community hall to watch the latest scenes of the confrontation being broadcast on the news.

'I should be there,' she said repeatedly to Kate.

'We are all there in spirit,' Kate said. 'You do not have to starve or get hurt or die in order to be part of the struggle.'

But being a spiritual ally was not enough for Tay. She contemplated hitch hiking to Wounded Knee, then decided Abel would only have her forcibly sent away again.

A week went by, then another. It became clear that sympathizers were managing to smuggle food and other supplies past checkpoints to the blockaded Indians. In fact, the longer the siege went on, the more the conscience of the country seemed aroused to express solidarity. Members of sixty-four different Indian tribes made their way to Wounded Knee, sneaking through the government blockade to join the original occupiers in a show of support. Blacks, whites, and chicanos also came. Church leaders gave sermons declaring that it was time to recognize and apologize for the national shame of depriving 'the first Americans' of their rights and their property.

As a condition of releasing their hostages and abandoning the occupation, the militants were demanding that the government honor the terms of a treaty that had been made between the United States government and the Sioux in 1868. Curious to know the exact nature and extent of these terms, Tay went to the library at the reservation school and tried to locate a book containing the information. Amazingly, she could find nothing about the treaty anywhere on the shelves. True, the library was small and poorly stocked, yet what reference work could be more deserving of a place here than documents relating to Indian history?

Kate suggested that copies of the treaty would probably be printed in books kept at the offices of the Rosebud tribal council, and offered to drive Tay there the next day.

Long neglected on a shelf of a common room at the tribal council, Tay finally found a set of old law books with broken spines containing the terms of the treaty. She knew as she read them that there was no hope they would ever be fulfilled. A little more than a hundred years ago, at a time when settlers were still crossing Indian lands by wagon train, the government in Washington had agreed that each and every tribe would be recognized as an independent sovereign nation. The lands they had agreed at the time to regard as inviolable Indian territory, if turned over today, would consist of most of South Dakota, and five other western states.

So what sense was there to the stand being made at Wounded Knee? Certainly there were wrongs that ought to be righted, but that could be achieved only by taking sensible steps, acting responsibly, not by making impossible demands. The occupation had started at the end of February, now it was nearly April. There had been a purpose at the beginning, a point had been made. But continuing the long siege now was senseless, Tay thought, all the more since the occasional outbreaks of gunfire continued between the opposing sides, and people were getting hurt.

When she expressed this opinion to the other women at the *tipospaye*, they argued with her. 'For the first time the whole country is paying some attention to our problems,' Ada said. 'If we surrender, that will end. And nothing will have changed.'

'Our people can't stay surrounded there forever,' Tay said. 'If the men came out now, voluntarily, they could still negotiate some gains. If they're forced out, they'll just be treated as criminals.' Tay felt an urgency in getting her point across because there had been news reports recently that the police, FBI and the National Guard were losing patience with the stand-off, and might soon make a full-scale assault to overwhelm the Indians and free the hostages.

'Whatever we think is right or wrong,' Kate said, 'makes no difference. Only those who are there can decide what to do.'

It was especially frustrating to hear this since Tay had wanted to go, and had been prevented.

That night the local television news showed taped coverage of a brief firefight that had erupted at the siege. Through telephoto lenses aimed at the knoll where the occupiers had dug their trenches, figures could be seen putting their heads up, shooting back, or darting across open spaces between the protection of the trenches and the church which had become their central shelter. Tay strained to recognize her father, but she could discern nothing more than anonymous dark shapes. Yet she was filled with a sense of foreboding more powerful and more terrifying than anything she had ever experienced before.

An hour before dawn, when the others were all still asleep, Tay put on a backpack stuffed with a few changes of clothes and left the *tipospaye*. Having heard that the siege lines at Wounded Knee were regularly being crossed by sympathizers smuggling in supplies, she was hopeful of being able to reach her father, to persuade him to leave the occupation and use his influence to get others to lay down their weapons. She knew he wouldn't have approved of the violence and hostage-taking, that he must have been swept along out of his desperation to make some gains.

She walked until sunrise, then hitch-hiked a lift to a highway junction with a delivery truck. On the highway, she was picked up by a woman driving an expensive two-seater European convertible who told Tay, after hearing her destination was Wounded Knee, that she was also headed there. A trim plain-spoken blond in her early thirties, the driver introduced herself as Sherri Martin, and explained that she was one of the news producers at a television station in Rapid City. The station had kept a crew covering the siege since it began, but they were no longer sure it was worth the expense.

'The feds have been saying all along they're going to storm the hill any minute and finish this thing off,' Sherri Martin said. 'We didn't want to miss the pictures if all hell was going to break loose, but our guys have been there a month and not much has changed. I'm going to appraise the situation. We're starting to think it could remain a stalemate for another month or two. What about you?' she asked then. 'Why are you going to Wounded Knee?'

'To see my father, if I can,' Tay answered. 'He's also been there since the siege began.'

The news producer gave Tay a sharp glance, already sensing a story. 'Oh? He's a cop?'

'No.'

'Not one of those poor hostages!'

After a moment, Tay said, 'He's one of the militants.'

The news producer drove on silently a minute, flicking a few more curious glances at Tay. 'I never would have taken you for an Indian,' she said at last.

'If you had, would it have made a difference?' From the woman's reference to the hostages, it seemed she might be opposed to the occupation. 'Do you want me to get out?'

'No, no, of course not. I didn't mean to sound unfriendly.

It's just . . . well, you don't look at all like them.'

'Well, I am one of *them*,' Tay said defiantly. 'I am a Sioux of the Rosebud tribe. My name is Tayhcawin Walks-Through-Fire.'

For the rest of the journey, Sherri Martin made an effort to show herself as sympathetic and open-minded to the problems of the Indians. Near midday, she stopped at a roadside café, and insisted on paying for a sandwich and soda for Tay. But Tay felt that the newswoman's gestures were meant to win her over, to pry out some angle for the news. Unwilling to be put under a microscope, Tay told nothing about herself or Abel, restricting her answers to general information about the tribe, or parroting things Abel had written to explain the quest for Indian rights.

When they arrived at the outskirts of Wounded Knee, they were stopped at the first of a ring of police checkpoints. Sherri was already known to many of the police from previous visits and they passed her straight through. When a policeman asked about Tay, Sherri passed her off as an assistant.

'Thanks,' Tay said after they had been waved through the roadblock.

'You'll need a lot more help to get to your father,' Sherri said. 'There are more checkpoints closer in – then there's a firing line, and several hundred yards of open ground with a lot of nervous guns covering it on both sides.'

'People have been crossing over at night.'

Sherri nodded. 'It's very dangerous. There's often shooting. Maybe I can arrange something for you, safe passage across the lines. The police might agree . . . if they thought you were going to talk your father into coming out.'

Tay eyed the newswoman curiously. How had she guessed the very reason that Tay wanted to talk to Abel? Or was it simply logical to assume that a daughter would want her father to be relieved from danger?

Tay assumed that Sherri Martin would want something in exchange for her offer to intercede, but why not give it to her? It could mean some sympathetic coverage of the Indian point of view. She agreed to let Sherri Martin explore arranging a safe passage for her, and they drove at once to a parking lot outside a trailer which had been brought in to serve as the command post for the FBI and other authorities involved in the siege.

'I know a lot of these guys, too,' Sherri said as she stopped the car outside. 'Let me go in alone, I'll bring you in to meet them after they've been softened up.'

In an oblique way, Tay thought, she was being told that the men running the siege were, like most white lawmen in the region, not particularly sympathetic to any Indian.

As she waited outside the trailer, Tay could see toward the hill about half a mile away capped by the Sacred Heart Church. At the base of the hill, near the trading post, several armored military vehicles were in position. Against the kind of weapons arrayed against them, the militants would stand little chance. Their best defense at the moment, Tay realized, was the conscience of the nation.

The door of the trailer opened, and Sherri reappeared looking grim. Tay instantly assumed that permission for a safe passage to see her father had been denied.

'Tay, your father's not here anymore,' Sherri said.

Tay stared back, paralyzed by disbelief. Where else could he be? Then she heard the woman's voice cutting through her thoughts.

'He was hurt a week ago in an exchange of gunfire. Not a bad wound. He wanted to stay, but yesterday he was moved to a hospital . . .'

Not a bad wound. Tay clung to those words. Yet it was serious enough that he had been forced to leave . . . serious enough that he hadn't been able to let anyone at the *tipospaye* know. And he had been hurt a week ago.

'Please,' she said, not caring in the least what the woman might ask in exchange, 'would you take me to see him?'

18

Abel lay in a ward with four other comatose patients, all hooked up to tangled tubes and wires leading to electronic monitors. Tay pulled a chair from a corner to his bedside and sat down. It might be a long wait before he could speak to her.

A doctor had given her the prognosis before she had been allowed to see him. The original wound had not been serious; a bullet had passed through his shoulder. But during the week Abel had stayed with the siege, the injury was treated superficially and a bacterial infection had set in. Carried in the blood, it had gone to the vital organs, evolving within days to a condition that was ravaging his system. He was fighting for his life.

Glancing around the hospital room, surfaces of sterile white everywhere, Tay couldn't help wondering bitterly if everything possible would be done in this white hospital. He was, after all, only an Indian.

Sherri Martin looked into the room and apologized that she had to leave, but said she would return. Through the rest of the day, into the evening, Tay sat watching her father, remembering the hundreds of days they had spent together. Often he had told her about his own father, a *yuwipi* man who supposedly had the power to cure. He'd said that maybe the power had been passed down to her; there were times that her touch had been said to relieve the pains of others. If only, Tay thought, it could be true. She moved her chair closer to the bed, took his hand and held it. He didn't open his eyes. As the room darkened with the onset of night, she drifted off.

'Tayhcawin.'

She came awake to his feeble call. His hand was still grasped in hers. 'Oh, *Atie*,' she cried softly, 'why didn't you take care of yourself?'

He spoke haltingly, in an old man's croak. 'I was busy . . . trying to take care of our people.'

She lifted his hand to press it against her cheek.

'Listen, daughter . . . I have had a dream . . .'

Another of his dreams! She didn't want to hear it. Dreams always seemed to foretell a destiny it was better not to know. It was his dream of Black Eagle that had put him on the road to Wounded Knee. 'You should rest,' she said. 'We'll talk later.'

'No, we cannot.' Despite the weakness of his voice, his tone was urgent. 'Tay, in my dream *hinhan* came to me—'

She lurched back from the bed. 'Stop, *Atie*. You pay too much attention to these—'

His grip on her hand tightened. 'Listen! *Hinhan* called to me from high in his tree, then flew down onto my shoulder. Do you know what this means?'

'Yes, I know,' she said quietly, surrendering to his need. She had often talked with Nellie Blue Snow about the lessons to be learned from the animals, their importance and meaning as symbols, the messages they brought. To hear the hooting call of the owl in a dream was a foretelling of death.

'*Atie*,' Tay pleaded softly, 'forget what you saw when you were sleeping. Dreams are tricks of the mind.'

A faint smile touched his lips. 'What have you learned, my

daughter? Our dreams are messages from the spirits, and we must heed them. I am going to die,' he said flatly.

'No, no, no,' she insisted in a whisper.

'I am prepared. But I must prepare you.'

She started to protest again, but he summoned all his strength and pulled himself up on the bed, his eyes suddenly blazing with ferocious determination. 'Stop! Don't waste the time we have.' The command silenced her. She sat up like a pupil taking a lesson. He sank back. 'You asked me a question I have yet to answer. Remember?'

Oddly, for so much time had passed and the context was lost, she knew instantly what he meant. She recalled his worry about her education, the lack of advantages available to the *wasicuns*. 'The crossroads,' she said. 'You were talking about a choice you had to make for me.'

'Yes. To keep you with me . . . or let you go to a place where your life would be better. After we spoke about it, I decided it would be wrong for you to go. You convinced me you were happy and content with what we have.'

'I am,' she said fervently.

He continued as though he hadn't heard. 'But my decision has changed. Because I will not leave you alone, Tayhcawin . . . yet I am not able to stay with you.' He spoke in such a tone of absolute certainty that she could not argue. 'I will send you to someone who I know will care for you.' His eyes switched away from her, rolling upward. She was afraid he might be going into a faint, but then she saw that there was a searching expression on his face. He was staring at the ceiling as a man might pray to the heavens for strength. 'When I join the spirits,' he said, 'you will go to your mother.'

She didn't believe she could have heard correctly. If he went to the spirits, *he* was the one who would join her mother. 'Where?' she asked. 'I will go where?'

'To your mother. She is alive in California.'

Tay sat unmoving for a moment, then shook her head, still refusing to believe. He couldn't have done this . . . told *this* lie. Not her father, who always valued the truth so much. He would never have forced her to shape a whole lifetime in the shadow of such a falsehood.

He turned to her again. 'When I was there she came to me. She didn't want you when you were born. But this last time, she asked to take you, so you would have—'

Tay sprang up and went to a corner of the room. He had seen her – two years ago, and had said *nothing*! She stared into the shadows unable to look at him now, her trust shattered. 'Why did you do it, *Atie*! Why did you tell me she was dead?'

His voice came quietly over her shoulder. 'I thought it would be easier, simpler, than the truth.'

'What truth? You told me long ago she didn't want me. Now you say she *does*. Did she always?'

There was only silence from behind her. When Tay turned around, his eyes were closed again. A chill passed through her. She moved back to his bedside. Looking down at him, she was surprised by the warring feelings that ran through her – and oddly relieved. Hating him for the lie made it so much easier to lose him. '*Atie*?' she whispered.

His eyes opened again. 'Where are my clothes?' he said, suddenly anxious. 'My things. Find them. In my wallet I've written it down . . . her name, where to find her . . . and there's money to get you there . . .'

She was turning to start the search when the night-duty interne entered holding a couple of syringes with medications. He looked at Tay as he gave injections to Abel. 'You look beat. Wouldn't hurt if you went and got some rest.'

'I can't leave,' Tay said. 'He told me he's going to die.'

The interne glanced to Abel. 'Did you say that?' he asked, with a wry bedside charm.

Abel's eyes were closed again. He lay motionless except

for the rhythmic rise and fall of his chest.

'He's not going to die,' the interne said to Tay. 'It's serious, but the worst is over. I'd still recommend for his sake and yours that you get a little sleep.'

'*Atie*?' Tay said, 'do you want me to stay?'

Silence. He had lost consciousness.

The interne guided Tay to a room along the hall behind a nurse's station where there were a couple of cots provided for visitors. She lay down, but she couldn't sleep. Her mother was alive, *wanted* her! His revelation had unleashed a storm in her mind. A hundred things Tay had never wanted to know – not when she believed this woman had completely rejected her – now piled up on a list of things she couldn't wait to learn. *Who was she? What was her name? What did she look like?* Tay got up, and walked back toward the room. He'd said the answers were written down.

As she headed along the corridor, Tay saw Sherri Martin coming toward her with a tall young man beside her, and two other men following with a camera, and sound equipment.

'How's your father, Tay?' the news producer asked as they met.

Tay shrugged. 'He's sleeping now.'

'Tay, this is Neil Rocklyn,' Sherri Martin motioned to the tall man beside her. 'Neil's a reporter at my station. He and I . . . well, we know this is a very difficult time for you, but we're hoping you might give us a short interview.' She glanced at a wall clock in the corridor showing a few minutes past nine. 'If we get it down soon, it'll go out on our late news broadcast.'

Tay retreated a step 'I couldn't . . . no.' What sort of news did they think she could give them? Still in shock from her father's revelation, she wondered if they had learned somehow her mother was alive – if that could be a story they wanted.

'Of course, it's your decision. But think a minute: you've

got a chance to win support for what your father wanted to accomplish at Wounded Knee.'

It was the reporter talking. Tay took her first good look at him. He seemed awfully young to be on television, older than herself, but not by more than a few years. He was very nice-looking yet a trace of an impish quality in his features undercut the cool reserve she would have expected to go along with his handsomeness. His twilight blue eyes sparkled, and his dark brown hair fell in a boyish shock across his forehead.

'How could I make a difference?' she said. 'I've got nothing to tell you that hasn't already been said by him or the others who've taken a stand.'

'No, you have something more, Tay,' Sherri said. 'You can tell us your own feelings.'

Tay looked between the producer and her reporter. How could her feelings be news? She was no longer even sure what they were. Did she love her father or hate him? Was she white or Indian? Suddenly she couldn't identify so totally with Abel's crusade.

The reporter stepped closer to her. 'Tay, this is for television. It's what people see that will move them. In this case, what they'd see isn't a bunch of furious Indians waving flags and shooting guns at cops, but a young girl whose father has been hurt badly fighting for what he believes in. It'll put a human face on a story that, until now, has been too many faceless gun-toting silhouettes, and issues so old everybody thought they went out with the covered wagon.' He came closer. 'We're a local station, but this piece might be picked up, shown around the country – even in Washington. You could gain more ground telling your story than the men at Wounded Knee did with all their battle cries.'

He had a nice voice she noticed, mellow, soothing. Lulled by the sound, she forgot for a second that she no longer felt so allied to the cause. 'Maybe later,' she said. 'Right now, I'm too upset.'

'Of course you are, dear,' Sherri said – then kept insisting. 'We've come an awfully long way for this, though. Maybe we could just get a quick shot of you at your father's bedside . . .'

'No—'

'C'mon, Tay,' the news producer cajoled, 'I know it's tough for you, but you want to get people on your side in this whole Wounded Knee thing. If we can show you reacting to what's happened, it'll give the viewers the sort of emotional kick that'll win 'em right over.'

'No,' Tay repeated. Whatever her feelings about Abel, she'd be damned if she'd let their sorrows be exploited so a television station could deliver a 'kick' to their viewers.

'Tay, just thirty seconds—'

'Forget it, Sherri,' Neil Rocklyn cut in firmly. 'Take the crew, get a shot through the door of the room – that'll be enough.' He turned to Tay. 'Only if you don't mind . . .' She shrugged indifferently, and Sherri led the camera crew away. Neil stayed with Tay. 'Sorry,' he said. 'We get so wrapped up in reporting the news, we tread a little hard on people's feelings, but we're not really such ghouls.'

She accepted his apology with a faint smile. 'I'm sure you're not. Fact is, one reason I wouldn't do that shot is I doubted I could act the way you wanted.'

'What do you mean?'

'I just couldn't cry on cue.' She realized as soon as she said it that all her bitterness toward Abel was about to overflow. But it was too much to explain to this stranger. Avoiding any more of his questions, she moved along to where the crew had set up their lights and camera, the lens aimed through the open doorway of the hospital room. As she looked at her father lying oblivious in bed, Tay was reminded again of the last thing he'd told her – the wallet containing her mother's name. She started toward the door, then realized she'd better wait until the news people were gone if she didn't want them scavenging more details of her life.

A doctor came and curtly told the camera crew they were disrupting hospital routine and their taping had to stop. Sherri Martin said goodbye to Tay. Rocklyn seemed to have left after Tay wouldn't answer any more of his questions.

Tay moved into the hospital room. What was in his dreams now? she wondered as she stood by his bed. Was *hinhan* calling to him? In a way, the prophecy had already proven right. The man she knew, the father she had loved, had died when he confessed to concealing the truth from her all her life.

She searched the room and, in a small closet, found the clothes Abel had been wearing when admitted, jeans, a denim work shirt, and a vest of leather he had tanned himself. Buttoned into a pocket of the shirt was the wallet, a leather folder covered with his beautiful beadwork. In one compartment of the wallet, Tay was astonished to find three hundred-dollar bills and six tens, evidently the money he'd mentioned for travel expenses to California. How long had he been carrying it around? He couldn't have gotten money after he was in the siege. So had he always believed he would die, and would need to send her away?

In another compartment, she found a couple of business cards, one for a lawyer in Rapid City, another for a South Dakota Congressman – people Abel had probably contacted in connection with the Indian rights crusade. Then, stuck behind the cards, she found a piece of note-paper. In the center, written on the same old typewriter Abel used for all his speeches and correspondence, were three lines – a woman's name, and below it the place in California where she could be found. After reading the words, Tay realized this must only be another contact he'd made, or intended to make, in connection with his work. She went back to rifling the wallet. But there was nothing else. Tay stared again at the three lines on the note. It seemed impossible that this could be the truth her father had finally wanted her to know. The address was given simply as: Hartleigh Mining Corporation, San Francisco, California.

On the line above was the name: Brenda Hartleigh. Her mother.

In a daze, Tay drifted back to the bed where her father lay. Could it possibly be true? The Hartleigh's mines were still the largest employers of Indian labor in the Hills. The doctor had said Abel would survive. When he woke again, she would have to ask him how it could have happened.

Looking down at him, tears began to fall down her cheeks. Suddenly she wished he had told her nothing – that she didn't have to learn anything that changed her love for him.

A nurse came in, pulled curtains around the beds of the other two comatose patients and turned out their bedside lamps. 'No more visitors in here, hon',' she said.

'I have to talk to him.'

'The doctor gave him something that'll keep him out for a while. If you want to stay in the waiting-room, or go back to the cots, we'll get you if there's any change.'

She walked back to the waiting-room clutching the wallet. A hand on her shoulder wrenched her out of the mist of preoccupation. 'Will you be all right?'

She looked around to see the handsome young television reporter. She brushed her eyes dry as she nodded.

'Look, I know the way we put you on the spot you might think nobody gives a damn about anything but getting a story. I couldn't leave without clearing that up.'

'You already apologized, Mr Rocklyn.'

'This is about more than an apology. The others have gone back to the station, but I stayed hoping we could talk. Maybe I could buy you a sandwich or something – there's a little coffee shop in the hospital lobby . . .'

She hadn't eaten since before she'd started hitch-hiking. She agreed to accompany him to the ground-floor coffee shop. Before taking the elevator down, she told the nurse where she'd be if there was any change in her father's condition.

The coffee shop was half-filled with groups of nurses or relatives awaiting the outcome of an operation. Tay sat down with Rocklyn in a booth. A waitress came and Tay ordered a hamburger and a glass of milk. Rocklyn asked only for coffee.

'I did some research into your father's background,' he began, as they waited for their food. 'Digging into news files that went back almost eighteen years I came across the story about a bar fight in which his cousin was killed. You know about that?'

She nodded. 'A bar fight doesn't describe it. His cousin was shot point blank when he was ready to walk away.'

'Yes. I know. And the man who pulled the trigger never spent a day in jail, while Abel Walker – as he was known then – was sentenced for contempt and assault. Do you think that's where it started – his involvement in the protest movement?'

Tay hesitated. What was he driving at? 'When I agreed to talk to you, Mr Rocklyn—'

'Call me Neil,' he put in.

She went right on, 'I didn't realize that all you wanted was to continue your interview.'

'I'm sorry, that really wasn't my intention.'

'Then why all these questions?'

'Part of it's professional – I'd like to understand so I can do a better job of reporting. But there's something else, something personal.' Her milk and his coffee arrived at the table. He took a sip, wincing as the hot liquid touched his lips. Tay watched him. With his eyes crinkled at the corners, he looked friendlier, more vulnerable. 'As it happens,' he went on, 'I grew up right near Rapid City. I remember what it was like twenty years ago. I'd guess there wasn't a worse place in this country when it came to the way Indians were treated. As a kid, I always felt bad about it, seeing the Indian men get kicked out of bars, women who weren't allowed into the shops. But when you're a kid, and your elders do things that seem nasty and stupid, it's not always easy to speak up. All you're likely to get for your trouble is a smack across the mouth.' A rueful smile touched his lips. 'I got a few of those smacks as a kid because I had an uncle who ran a bar in town, and I can remember being in there when I was too small to climb up on the barstool by myself – and now and then I'd be there when an Indian man came in, and he'd be thrown out, and I'd pipe up and say it was lousy. Got a smack every time. Maybe it made some difference, though. Later my uncle sold the bar, and started up a better place with food – and he didn't keep anyone out of there.'

He paused and fixed Tay with a long serious look. It gave her the feeling that he'd told her something significant, but to her it had sounded like nothing more than nostalgic ramblings.

He went on, 'The restaurant my father owned was called the Last Sunset. Mean anything to you?'

Tay had only the vaguest sense she might have heard the name somewhere. As she mulled it, the waitress brought her hamburger. Tay didn't touch the food. 'Should it?' she asked Rocklyn.

'It's where Black Eagle, your father's cousin, was killed.'

It was one of his earliest memories, he went on, hearing his parents talk about what had happened in the restaurant. But he hadn't realized the connection to Tay's family until he had gone back in the news files earlier today to do his research.

'It made me feel that I have a special responsibility to help him . . . help you. That's what I wanted you to know – that I'm serious about doing whatever I can to get your message across. Using the news is one way. But if there's anything else you need, I want you to feel you can ask me. Think of me as a friend.'

'Thank you,' she replied flatly. 'That's very kind.' If this young man felt himself to be a friend to the Indian cause, it made him seem even more stranger to her now – because her own identity had become blurred since her father's confession.

He looked disappointed by her flat reply. But before he could make any further appeal, a waitress behind the counter picked up a ringing phone, then called out. 'Is there an Indian girl here?'

'I guess that's me,' Tay answered.

'The doctor says you'd better get back upstairs.'

Tay bolted from the table. Rocklyn hurried to catch up after tossing some money on the table.

Dashing out of the elevator on the ward floor she almost collided with a pair of nurses and the interne who were talking together in the corridor. 'What's happened?'

'He was conscious,' one of the nurses said, 'calling for you.'

Tay started to run from them, but the interne grabbed her arm and held her back. 'That was ten minutes ago,' he said. 'Then he . . . he slipped away, and we couldn't save him. I'm sorry.'

Slipped away. What he meant, Tay realized, was that her father was dead.

Neil put a consoling hand on her shoulder. She shirked off his touch, and walked along the corridor. Through the door of the ward, she could see Abel lying on the bed, his eyes closed. He had heard the call of *hinhan*, she thought, and he had answered.

And before going he had confessed to a lie, and told her a truth he could no longer explain. A welling torrent of grief and love began to rise in her – and clashed almost instantly with her rage and disillusionment. She could not forgive him. *Damn you, Atie*, she cursed him silently, *you even stole away all my tears*. And then the last thing he had done, the worst crime of all, was to abandon her, to leave her completely adrift from every anchor of culture and history and family she had grown to depend on.

She whirled away from his room, unable to look at him anymore. Neil was close by.

'You still want me to do an interview?' she snapped at him, her bitterness erupting. 'Get out your tape recorder, I'll give you some news.'

'Take it easy,' he said in his soothing voice. 'I can see this isn't the time—'

'I thought you wanted to help me get my message across.'

He yielded, and took a small pocket recorder from his jacket. As soon as he pressed the button to start recording, she grabbed his hand and yanked the recorder near her mouth.

'He was a liar,' Tay said. 'A fraud and a liar, and I wouldn't want anyone else to make the mistake I did by believing in him or anything he said.' She stopped. The words sounded so vicious coming from her mouth, she regretted them. But before she could even be tempted to take them back, she pushed the recorder away and ran. Somewhere, she thought, if she kept running, there might be a place where she could no longer hear the echo of the owl's call.

Rocklyn stood watching her flee. Tayhcawin, he thought to himself: young fawn. He had never seen a more beautiful young woman, and he was shaken by the brutal words that had burst from her. In the shock of death, she had not reacted rationally, he knew. She was not ever going to ask his help, he realized; she would not regard him as a friend. But perhaps there was one thing he could do to help her anyway.

As he watched her coltish figure vanish into an elevator, his finger pressed down a button to erase the tape.

19

Brenda Hartleigh strode into the mahogany-panelled boardroom of the Hartleigh Mining Corporation, and the sixteen male directors of the company, led by her brother, Chet, rose together from the long black granite conference table to give her an ovation. In the HMC financial report distributed before this afternoon's meeting, the latest quarterly profits were shown to have taken yet another upward leap. Part of the improvement could be traced to a steep rise in the price of gold, but there was also no question that Brenda Hartleigh had proven to be a skilled corporate manager. All the doubts and criticisms leveled against her when she had wrested control of the company from her own father three years ago had been laid to rest. Even G.D., while publicly displaying the most intense bitterness after Bren's *coup*, was said to have acknowledged before his death last year from a stroke that she had a grasp of developing the company's modern potential that far exceeded his own. Since Bren had taken the private company public, and the stock's value had quadrupled, the directors were unanimous in feeling that, at today's meeting, she should be voted the salary increase she had requested.

'Be seated, please, gentlemen,' Bren said briskly, while she remained standing herself. 'Before we get down to business, there's one sentimental duty I'd like to perform.' She moved to a pedestal at the side of the room over which a silk sheet was draped. 'No matter how HMC may grow, or what new directions we may take, I feel strongly that we must never cease to honor those who laid the foundation. That's why I've commissioned this for the boardroom.'

With a theatrical flourish, she whipped away the sheet to reveal a lifelike bronze bust of G.D. The sculpture came as a surprise to all the directors except Dan Kinwood, the corporate attorney who was also Bren's husband. For the three years Bren had been at the helm of HMC, she had never allowed any mention of her father to be made in the offices of the company, and all pictures of him hanging in the building had been taken down. Apparently Bren's fear of operating in G.D.'s shadow, even the shadow of his memory, had at last been conquered.

'I expect this to serve as a constant reminder of the high standards set by my father,' Bren said, 'a symbol that he remains here in spirit.'

The sentiment was accorded more applause, and Bren sat down to call the meeting to order. First on the agenda was the matter of 'compensation for the president'. Dan Kinwood posed the motion, Chet Hartleigh seconded, and the directors thereupon voted unanimously to raise Brenda Hartleigh's salary to six hundred thousand dollars per annum.

Bren promptly moved on to the next item on the agenda. With the price of gold per ounce rising to new highs, she said, the company was building an enormous cash fund. She had been developing a program to spend this money in ways that would ensure the future growth of Hartleigh Mining. The first step was to increase the output of the company's uranium-mining operation in the Black Hills.

'As long as the Russians are a threat,' Bren observed, 'the

Pentagon will want more bombs and missiles with atomic warheads, so they'll purchase as much nuclear material as we can supply.' Capitalizing on her strong connections in Washington, Bren announced, she had also lobbied successfully for the building of two new nuclear submarines, as well as for government action to stimulate use of nuclear power for generating electricity. In years to come, Bren predicted, power plants might all be powered by fissionable materials.

Spending money to increase uranium production would thus yield even greater profits which could be used to invest in defense contractors and power companies. Influence could then be exerted to shape policies that would keep the demand for uranium strong.

The meeting was opened for discussion. The younger directors all spoke immediately in support of Bren's plan.

But then John Stanmore asked to be recognized. Stanmore was in his late sixties, a gray-haired banker who had advised G.D. and was a holdover from his regime.

'Brenda,' he said in his stiffly formal manner, 'you opened this meeting by reminding us how important it is not to lose sight of our foundations. Gold has always been the primary resource for HMC – and this happens to be a time when the value of gold is going up. I don't see why we're not putting our efforts into getting more gold out of the ground, instead of shifting our emphasis to more dangerous endeavors.'

'Uranium mines are no more dangerous than our gold mines,' Bren replied. 'We haven't had any mine accidents in either in the last ten years.'

'The danger I speak of,' Stanmore came back, 'is not in the mining process, but in the character of the ore itself – and the financial future it promises. Gold has kept its value since biblical times. Uranium has yet to prove such an enduring source of revenue.'

'Atomic power is the wave of the future,' Kinwood said.

'All you need to knock the bottom out of that market,' Stanmore argued, 'is for one of these nuclear power plants to blow up—'

'What they do, actually,' said another of the older directors, 'is melt down.'

'The so-called "China syndrome",' Kinwood said with a mocking edge. 'So named because a nuclear core might get so hot as to go right through the earth to China. That's nonsense. Nuclear-generated power is perfectly safe.'

'So far,' Stanmore agreed. 'But if there ever is a serious accident, there goes your wave of the future. And suppose the government stops making nuclear weapons?'

'Can you really imagine that happening?' said another of Brenda's partisans. 'The Russians will always be a threat. Right now there's talk of a missile gap between our stockpile and theirs. Our missile production will be increased to keep up.'

Bren spoke to unite the two factions. 'I'm not talking about developing one part of the business at the expense of the other. We'll mine gold as long as we have it. But one of the ways to maintain the value is to keep it scarce – the way the DeBeers ration their diamonds. The price of gold and diamonds depends on psychological factors more than any real need. So we can't over-produce. But the amount of uranium we sell will depend on the defense and industrial markets we build for it – and if we do that well, the sky's the limit. Gentlemen, for HMC to keep growing, our uranium provides the best opportunity.'

The younger company directors all continued to voice their enthusiasm for Brenda's forward-looking policy, and the resistance of the few holdovers from G.D.'s time fell away. Bren's expansion plan was approved, with only John Stanmore voting a loud 'nay', and two other elderly directors abstaining.

At the end of the meeting, Bren took up her customary position by the door of the conference room to say a personal goodbye to the directors as they left.

'I hope there's no hard feelings, Brenda,' said John Stanmore as he went out.

'None at all, John,' Bren said to her father's old ally. 'I welcome an honest difference of opinion about what's good for the company.'

Watching Stanmore walk away, Bren resolved that she would have him replaced with someone younger and more malleable before the board met again.

She could see Dan standing in the corridor, still amiably chatting with the men who would be on his committee, so she went through the door that connected her office to the boardroom. The sweep of windows that went around a corner offered a majestic view from the twenty-sixth-floor perch. Bren went to the window and basked in the golden light of the sun setting across San Francisco bay. At this moment even the sun itself looked to be made out of the stuff her company mined. Yes, it was *her* company now; she no longer worried that there would be any confusion on that point. She could afford to be magnanimous and let the image of G.D. reappear again within these walls.

Her husband came in and walked up behind her. 'A home run,' he said.

'Just one thing I need to top it off,' she said, turning to him.

'What's that?'

She smiled seductively. 'A good fuck. Power always makes me feel hot and horny.'

Kinwood glanced over his shoulder. 'The secretaries haven't gone home yet.'

'Never stopped you before.' It wasn't at all uncommon for Bren to call her husband into the office during the day for sex. It had been a part of their 'contract' from the beginning of their relationship that he would oblige whenever she felt the urge. Indeed the affair that had preceded their marriage had begun when Kinwood had kept an office appointment with

Bren at a time that she was G.D.'s vice-president, and he was an associate with an outside firm. That day, while they continued to talk business across her desk, Bren had slipped off her shoe, extended her foot through the kneehole to plant it in his crotch. After the meeting, they had gone straight to a hotel and stayed for six hours. As Bren got older, and her authority over her domain had grown, her desire had become even more insatiable. But they didn't go to hotels anymore. Bren saw no reason not to do it on her desk or on the floor, have a quick shower in the luxurious adjoining bathroom, and get right back to work. When there was a bed available, it never seemed as exciting to her.

'It's so near closing time,' Kinwood remarked. 'Don't they always come in to say goodnight?'

Bren went to the door of her office, closed it and turned the bolt. 'Problem solved.'

Kinwood frowned, still reluctant.

Bren sashayed toward him. 'What's wrong, Danny? Is it bad etiquette to lock out a secretary? Or are you just getting tired of me?'

'What I'm tired of, Bren,' he erupted, 'is being treated like I'm nothing but a possession, one more corporate perk here to serve you any time you call night or day, like the company jet.'

She kept coming toward him. 'I'm sorry, Danny. I suppose I ought to send you roses more often, remember "the little things".' Her voice hardened. 'But I'm too goddamn busy to worry about hearts and flowers. That's the way it's been with us from day one, remember? And when you were one of two dozen associates pushing a pen in a law firm, you never minded being ready for me day or night because that was your way to get out, and go along for a much better ride with me.'

'I went out on a limb to help you take over this company. You used to appreciate that, treat me more like a partner.'

'And how do I treat you now?' She came up next to him.

'Like I'm nothing but your goddamn office-boy.'

Bren gave him the same shrewd measuring appraisal he had seen her use in negotiations when she was weighing which of many possible responses to give. She chose to be diplomatic. 'Forgive me, Danny,' she purred as she slipped her arms around his neck. 'I have been inconsiderate of your feelings lately, but I get so wrapped up in the business nothing else matters.'

'You've got control now, Bren. You should make room for other things in your life.'

'I'll make more room for you . . . right now.' She had one hand on his fly, unzipping it.

Bren's touch had always been expert. Dan forgot his temperamental objections. 'What about having a family?'

'I'm too old.'

'It's been done at forty-three. There are new—'

'Forget it, Danny. It's too late. I'm content with things the way they are, and if you're not . . .'

She didn't bother spelling out the alternative, and he didn't need to hear it. By now she was massaging him vigorously, and he was in the throes of excitement, aware again that he could not expect to live by the normal rules as long as he was with Bren Hartleigh – she had even refused to follow the custom of taking his name in marriage. Yet she had the ability to arouse his passion, even if he wasn't sure he had ever loved her – probably none of the men who'd been with her had loved her – so he would stay with her until the day when his discontent reached an intolerable level. He knew already that when he left her she wouldn't miss him, she would simply find another man to give her what she wanted right now.

Yielding to his own urges, he made her ready to have it the way she liked it, pushing up her dress, tearing her panties down while she pulled his erect member free from his trousers. In a minute he had shoved her backward onto the desk, and he was inside her, plunging down, giving it to her rough and hard without preliminaries, and she was encouraging him with her moans and whispers to be even rougher and wilder. He slowed down only when he feared he might come too soon, because that angered her whenever it happened. Soon he knew from the rhythm of her panting pleas that she was near climax, and he picked up his pace again.

There was a momentary halt in their momentum when they heard the door rattle as someone tried the knob. Then a knock, soft but no less interruptive.

'Bitch,' Bren complained in a throaty growl, her legs vicing even more tightly around his waist, 'she ought to know better . . .'

'Ignore it,' Dan said softly. 'She'll go away.'

There was another series of soft raps. Clinging to each other, the couple barely breathed. Even when Bren was motionless, Dan could feel her inner muscles contracting and releasing, keeping him stimulated. The silence went on for half a minute. Evidently the secretary had gone. Soon they recovered their rhythm, Kinwood raising her with his hands beneath her buttocks so that he could reach even deeper into her. At last she cried out in release, and he came only a second later, with one last surging thrust that pushed her body halfway across the desk.

They lay together for a few seconds, recovering.

'Well done, lover,' Bren said finally. 'You're the best fucking corporate counsel this company ever had.' She levered her hands under his shoulders. 'Now get off my desk. There's a little more work I want to do before calling it a day.'

Kinwood straightened himself while Bren went into her adjoining bathroom. In a minute she was back, hair combed, looking as if he'd given her no more than a memo since entering the office. 'What's got to be done now that can't wait 'til morning?' he said.

'It's three hours later back east, the best time to get my Washington friends – at home after a nice dinner. When we discuss the little favors we can do for each other, they don't like talking on their office phones. And I'd like a couple to know soon as possible that I expect their help to sell our nuclear materials.'

Kinwood conceded with a nod. 'I'll be in my office when you're ready to go.'

'Don't bother waiting around. I'll see you at home.'

The way she dismissed him brought back the humiliating feeling that he was merely her servant, flicked away once she was satisfied. He ought to remind her, he thought, that he still held the key to the power she claimed as solely her own: if he ever let it be known that she had only been able to seize control of the company by using a fraudulent document, he could bring her down overnight. Pamela Hartleigh was still alive, even if *non compos mentis*, and Bren was still controlling her interests on the strength of the same bogus authorization.

But exposing the fraud was a threat to save for a much rainier day. 'See you at home, then,' Dan said lightly, going to the door. He stepped out closing the door behind him.

As he started heading for the elevator, he stopped in his tracks. In the large waiting area outside Bren's office, an unfamiliar young woman rose from her seat on the couch. Being past office hours, some of the lights had already been turned out, but even in the gloom, and despite the rough western-style clothes the visitor was wearing, Kinwood could see that she was breathtakingly beautiful. The play of shadow accentuated her high cheek-bones, and the low light shone off her black hair in a way that brought out the bluish halftones, and made her turquoise eyes glow like jewels.

'The office is closed,' he said automatically when he found his voice. Now he noticed the ragged backpack on the floor near the couch.

She came toward him. 'I know. But I met one of the secretaries on her way out, and she told me Miss Hartleigh was definitely in her office. So I waited.'

'Was that you knocking at the door?'

'I'm sorry if it bothered you. I thought, if she was there alone—'

'No bother at all.' He had moved nearer too, and he realized that she was younger even than he'd first thought – nearer eighteen than twenty-one – evidently innocent enough that it hadn't occurred to her people might have sex in an office. 'What did you want to see Miss Hartleigh about?'

'It's personal.'

He said nothing, taking pleasure in looking at her and at the same time wondering what business Bren could have with this young woman that would exclude him. Some new kind of sexual adventure? Anything was possible with Bren. 'I'm her husband,' Kinwood said, 'you can talk to me.'

Before Tay could answer, the office door opened. 'I thought I heard you out here,' Bren snapped at Kinwood. Her jealousy aroused by the glimpse she'd had of the look on her husband's face, she turned on the young woman. 'And just who the hell are you?'

The hostile tone of the question reassured Dan, even as it shocked Tay, almost stealing her courage away. But she reminded herself she was here because Abel had said this woman wanted her to come. Pulling herself up straight, Tay gave her reply.

'I'm your daughter.'

Bren stared back while Tay remained braced for anything. After a long moment, a very thin smile touched Bren's lips. 'Are you indeed?' she said drily. Then she tossed a glance at Dan. 'Run along, lover,' she said. 'I may be staying late tonight.'

'Just like that?' he objected. 'You don't want me to be—'

'Go home and I'll see you later,' she said more harshly. 'My daughter and I have a lot to talk about, and we need to be alone.'

Kinwood spun away and continued toward the elevators.

Bren extended her arm to Tay. 'Come in, dear,' she said silkily. 'It's about time we got to know each other.'

BOOK III

Pejuta Win
Medicine Woman

20

San Francisco – March 1976

Near the stretch of Post Street where the best stores were located, the burgundy Rolls-Royce slowed down. 'I'd suggest Gumps or Shreve and Company, Miss Hartleigh,' the chauffeur said to the passenger riding beside him. 'You're bound to find something suitable at either one.'

'Which do you like better, Carl?' Tay asked.

The black chauffeur laughed amiably. 'I don't do my shopping at either, Miss. But your mother prefers Shreve – if you're planning on getting a really special gift.'

'I am. I hardly know my aunt, but she's had such a bad time, I would like to give her something really nice for her fortieth birthday.'

The car stopped in front of Shreve and Company, the city's oldest and most fashionable jeweler, and Tay let herself out. She never waited to have the door opened for her; even after three years of living in the luxurious surroundings provided by her mother, Tay had yet to feel comfortable with having servants make her bed, cook her meals, launder her clothes, or lay out the choices for what she should wear each day – a service Bren had instituted in the early days when she was determined to break Tay's habit of dressing always in jeans and sweatshirts. Schooled now in dressing more stylishly, Tay was left to choose her own clothes. For her shopping expedition, she wore loose beige linen slacks, an amber cashmere jacket worn with a long knitted black scarf and a red tam, colors that made her jet-black hair and turquoise eyes all the more striking. Her independence did not extend to going downtown alone, however. Bren had decreed that the chauffeur must always take her – Carl wasn't merely a driver, after all, he was an ex-marine and trained pistol marksman who also functioned as a bodyguard.

He got out of the car now revealing his impressive bulk. 'I could come in with you, Miss Hartleigh,' he offered.

'With all the jewels in there, Carl, there must be guards all over the place, I'll be fine.'

As she crossed the sidewalk Tay spotted a newsstand, and went over to scan the front pages. The jury in the Patricia Hearst case was expected to deliver a verdict any minute. Yes, there it was, in the headline: Patty, an heiress to the Hearst publishing fortune, had been convicted of bank robbery. Her sentence was light, though, taking into consideration she'd been kidnapped from college and presumably brainwashed into helping her abductors. It was the Hearst kidnapping that had made Bren so nervous about Tay traveling around on her own.

When Tay had started college the autumn after arriving in San Francisco, Bren had urged her to go to nearby Berkeley. The choice had suited Tay well enough, too, since it was well known as a place for independent thinkers. At Berkeley, Tay had found off-campus rooms in a house on the same street where Patty Hearst also had a student apartment. Since Patty had been taken from there by a small group of revolutionaries calling itself the Symbionese Liberation Army, Bren had expressed a fear that Tay might someday suffer a similar fate. Tay hated being put under the stifling protection, but she endured it. She suspected, though, that it wasn't only protecting her that concerned her mother, but keeping a watch, making sure she didn't step out of line.

From their first meeting, Bren had made it clear that certain conditions would have to be met if Tay was to live with her. That first night after Tay had shown up at the offices of Hartleigh Mining, Brenda had talked with her until midnight, moving from the office to a nearby restaurant, interrogating her like an attorney questioning a witness on why Tay had suddenly emerged from nowhere to reclaim their relationship.

At the end of that first long night's conversation, Bren had taken Tay back to the mansion on Nob Hill, her own home since G.D.'s death and Pamela's move to a special care facility. Bren's accepting the role of Tay's mother was not done so much out of familial loyalty as out of cool pragmatism. If the girl were allowed to roam free, might she not someday expose her tie to the Hartleigh family in a way that was damaging, at the least embarrassing? By taking Tay in as her daughter, Bren knew she would always have a trump card to play against her sister – a threat of exposing that the girl was actually Cori's bastard – if Cori ever tried voting her company stock in a way that jeopardized Bren's control. Tay would be an asset in other ways, too. Exquisitely beautiful and obviously intelligent, she had the potential to marry very well and advance the financial and social interests of the Hartleighs. Bren also felt she might mold Tay into a loyal ally. Wouldn't this mixed-breed, raised in abject poverty, be overflowing with gratitude for being taken into a world of wealth?

While telling Tay she was ready and willing to accept her as her daughter, Bren also demanded that certain conditions be met. All ties to Tay's past must be irrevocably severed, and her true background obscured. She could keep the name Tay – without letting anyone know its Sioux origins – but she would legally assume the last name Hartleigh. The official story to account for their kinship would be that Tay was Bren's daughter by a man both would refuse to name. Brenda had no reason to fear being contradicted by anyone close to her. G.D. was dead, Pamela's memory obliterated by Alzheimer's disease, and Chet had been spared by their parents from ever learning the truth. Finally, Cori was too emotionally unstable to deal with all the complications that would arise if her husband learned she'd had a secret love affair that had yielded a daughter by a half-breed Indian. As understanding as Frank could be, Cori had always been terrified that exposing the secret would destroy her marriage, as it had shattered the loving relationship with her father.

When Tay pointed out there were numerous people on the rez who knew her father's identity, Bren dismissed it as insignificant. 'You're a thousand miles from those people now, and light years in terms of that life and this one. If we're careful, these worlds won't ever have to meet again.'

Agreeing to Bren's terms, meant Tay had to amputate a part of her identity, assume a new 'self' almost as though she were a fugitive trying to avoid recapture. But such was her disillusionment with Abel that it did not seem too extreme to her. After his death, she had accompanied his body back to the reservation. Still in a haze of confusion, she had stayed two more days until he was interred in the tribal burial ground with a traditional ceremony, his body wrapped in a handmade star blanket, sheaves of sweetgrass burned over the grave. But as she watched the burial ritual, she already felt cut off from it. Having lost her trust in her father, she could no longer vest her belief in the importance and integrity of the culture in which he had raised her.

Whatever lingering qualms Tay felt about transforming herself according to Bren's dictates were overcome as she was seduced by the comforts of her new life. No more crude unheated cabins to sleep in, no more tattered hand-me-down clothes. She was given her own large bedroom, new clothes in the latest styles, servants who brought any food she had a yen for, not to mention a flood of new amusements – the restaurants and shows and concerts Tay attended with Bren and her stepfather, the sights of the city to explore on her own, the luxuries she could buy on charge accounts.

At times, memories of her past life welled up. She would think of Kate and Ada and the children of the *tipospaye* whom she had loved, and of the magical lessons about nature she had learned from Nellie Blue Snow. She would have pangs of guilt for renouncing it all so completely. But embittered by Abel's betrayal, and faced with her mother's ultimatum – that she could live in one world or the other, never both – Tay never thought of going back.

From their first long conversation, Tay had recognized that Brenda Hartleigh was smart, dynamic, sophisticated, and absolutely dedicated to the family business. These were admirable things, things Tay didn't mind thinking were reflected in her own nature – intelligence, grit, energy. But what Tay had not seen that first night, nor ever since, was any sign of maternal warmth. Even with the passing of time and growing familiarity, Tay never felt the kind of closeness she'd known with her father. Even the story Bren told to explain how Tay had been conceived involved no love, only a free unbridled spirit. She had been traveling across country by car on her way to vacation at the family's ranch in Jackson Hole, Bren told Tay. On a road in South Dakota, her car had overheated, Abel had stopped to help, and she had been sufficiently attracted to spend the night with him. It had been done on a whim, for a thrill. By the time she realized she was pregnant, Bren was involved with an attractive young Congressman in Washington . . . and she'd had the wild idea that keeping the baby might help her pressure the man into marriage. The rómance had ended, but by then she was into her second trimester, and she could no longer contemplate abortion. There was no place for a child in her life, however; as soon as Tay was born she had arranged for a lawyer to track down the father. Abel had agreed to take the baby rather than give it up for adoption. From what Tay saw at once of Bren's selfishness, ambition and self-indulgence, the story rang true, and she never questioned it afterwards.

It was her Aunt Corinne who struck Tay as being warmer and kinder, though it was an impression Tay had been able to gather only through the most fleeting contacts – since Bren made a point of avoiding family gatherings. When Tay asked why they didn't see more of their relatives, Bren's answer was that family relationships had been strained since the company fight in which she had won control. Her brother, as G.D.'s male heir, resented that the mantle of power had not passed to him. As for Cori, though she had sided with Bren in company matters, she was otherwise so jealous – and her emotional balance so delicate – that Frank Patterson felt contacts between the sisters should be kept to a minimum.

For the two and a half years since Tay had come, Bren's explanations had worked to keep her segregated from the rest of the family. But now Cori's fortieth birthday was approaching, and Frank had decided that the best antidote to her depression would be to celebrate with a party, nothing too crowded or noisy, just a supportive gathering of family and intimate friends. When Frank called Bren's house on a weekend to confirm her cooperation, Tay had taken the call because her mother was out. Dan Kinwood wasn't around either; he and Bren had separated a few months after Tay's arrival and were now divorced.

'Of course, we'll help you celebrate,' Tay told Frank. 'We'll be there with bells on.' She wanted a chance to get closer to her aunt and uncle, and couldn't imagine her mother would object.

Bren's reaction when Tay told her about Frank's call came

as a shock. 'You never should have agreed to go without talking to me,' she said crossly.

'Why not?' Tay shot back. 'Why can't we end this idiotic family feud? I'd like to know Aunt Cori and Uncle Frank. With or without you, Mother, I'm going to that party.'

Bren had backed down then and agreed that Cori's birthday was an occasion the whole family should celebrate together. If Tay was going to be around Cori for even an hour or two, Bren didn't want them unmonitored.

Now, having come to buy a present, Tay hoped she could find something that would have meaning, somehow convey her desire to forge a personal link. But as she browsed through Shreve and Company she saw that everything was far too expensive for her budget. Tay had always been given a liberal allowance, and the purchases she made on her credit cards were rarely questioned when Bren came to paying the bills. But for this present, Tay was resolved to spend only the money she could truly call hers – two hundred dollars that remained from the money Abel had left for her in his wallet. Touched hearing about her aunt's fragile psyche, the time spent institutionalized, the inability to find some rewarding work for herself, Tay felt there was no one she would rather give something meaningful than her aunt.

Finding nothing that appealed to her in all the luxuries at Shreve, Tay left the store. Carl was waiting on the sidewalk by the Rolls.

'I'll walk, Carl,' Tay said. 'Gumps is right nearby, and I can window-shop on the way.'

'Miss Hartleigh, your mother gave me strict orders—'

'She keeps me as much a prisoner sometimes as if she was a kidnapper. I'm tired of it, Carl. Trail along in the car. I'll be fine.' Tay set off before the chauffeur could object.

Tay continued along Post Street to Gumps while the car trailed along. She saw nothing in the second store that appealed to her until she came to a glass counter displaying a selection of hand-crafted silver jewelry set with turquoise stones, necklaces and bracelets worked with etchings of animals, and symbols with meanings she understood. The Indian jewelry aroused a nostalgia for the culture she had left behind. To give one of these things, Tay thought, would be to give something of herself.

A saleswoman came over, and Tay explained she hoped to find a gift among the things in the case.

'All this is American Indian,' the saleswoman said. 'Some of these people do lovely things.' The note of condescension in the way she said 'some of these people' was unmistakeable.

Relief that she was no longer one of *these people* mixed with Tay's shame at her own defection. Suddenly it seemed all the more important to let one of these pieces represent her as the gift to her aunt. As she searched the case, she noticed a bracelet of heavy silver, worked around the perimeter with a design of zigzagged parallel lines along which five fine stones of turquoise were set at intervals. From her familiarity with Indian symbols, Tay knew the lines represented a river, itself a symbol of the continuity of time, and the stones were intended to mark different phases of life. Perfect for a fortieth birthday present, and the cost was just one hundred and ninety dollars.

At dinner that evening, Bren asked what Tay had done that day.

'I bought Aunt Cori a birthday gift.'

Bren frowned. 'Oh? Let me see . . .'

Tay realized suddenly that the nature of the gift might annoy her – representing as a violation, however slight, of Tay's promise to cut the ties to her past. 'It's a surprise,' she said.

'Of course. But you can show *me*.'

'It's already gift-wrapped. You'll see it at the party.'

Bren suspected there was more to Tay's secretiveness than relishing a surprise, but she shrugged and let it go. She adjusted less easily, however, to the possibility that Tay's gift-giving might lead to a greater closeness with Cori. There was always the risk of that leading to Tay discovering whose daughter she truly was. And by now Bren thought of Tay as her own, though she was honest enough about her own character to know affection did not enter into it. Tay was a possession, an investment – but this one Bren was determined always to keep and profit by.

From her office the next morning, she called Cori at home. 'What's going on between you and Tay?' she asked.

'Going on?' Cori echoed, mystified. 'Nothing.'

'Then why is she suddenly so damned eager to please you? Snapped up the invitation from Frank, now she's bought you a surprise birthday gift.'

'Well, it's not a surprise anymore, is it?' Cori said. It was deliberately petty of Bren, she thought, to mention it.

'I still don't know what it is. Wouldn't tell me. That's what made me wonder how cozy she's gotten with you at my expense.'

'I haven't seen her, Bren. I've always agreed with you it would be better if I kept my distance.' Cori's voice quavered; the conversation was clearly upsetting her.

'Remember that,' Bren said threateningly. 'I couldn't forbid Tay to come to your party without making her suspicious, but don't take it as an opportunity to start getting intimate – unless you're ready to have Frank and everybody else find out who's child she really is.'

'No! I'm not!' Cori said desperately. It had been hard enough for Cori to deal privately with the guilt of having abandoned her child at birth, she could not face it if she were ever forced to account for that decision directly to Tay.

'Good,' Bren said calmly. 'Then they won't.' She hung up, confident that the situation was firmly under control.

* * *

287

The Patterson penthouse sat atop the Brocklebank Apartments, the elegant cream-colored high-rise that had appeared in Alfred Hitchcock's film *Vertigo* as the home of a wealthy woman played by Kim Novak. Frank could remember seeing the film with Cori in 1958, at the time they were evolving from friends into lovers. Because of the associations with the film, he had thought of moving to a new home after the onset of Cori's depression. But her doctors had advised that unless she clearly displayed a suicidal disposition, it could be equally important to stay within the home that had been her familiar anchor throughout her married life. Of course, Cori should not be left unobserved when depressed, high guard-rails and glass panels could be added to the penthouse terraces. But, the psychiatrists observed, a suicidal woman living on a ground floor could still find a dozen ways to kill herself.

Tonight, festooned with plants, flowers and fairy lights brought in by the party planners, the apartment made a glittering setting for Cori's birthday celebration. As Tay stepped out of the elevator directly into the gallery of the penthouse and a maid took her coat, she felt more eager anticipation than at any time since starting college. At last, she was getting past the barriers between herself and the rest of the Hartleighs that her mother had erected.

Eager to make the best impression, Tay had charged a new dress at Magnin's, a bare-shouldered ivory silk sheath. Worn with a four-strand necklace of inexpensive black beads, the pale dress contrasted strikingly with Tay's tawny complexion, turquoise eyes and long shining obsidian hair. As soon as she entered the already crowded living-room, heads turned. Tay was no longer oblivious to the effect of her beauty. On the reservation, because there she had been ragged and unkempt – and perhaps because she had been the odd one out – she had not often been the focus of men's stares. But since coming to live with Bren, learning how to dress and apply make-up for maximum effect, she always stood out in a crowd. The boys at college, sales clerks, young men in the street, were always asking for dates or making propositions. Except for a few months of dating a Berkeley senior, however, she had yet to let herself become involved. Even in that short-lived romance, she had not let physical intimacy go beyond kissing. She wasn't sure why she remained so guarded. Perhaps the disillusionment with her father had left her with an overall distrust of men. Or it might be a reaction to the traumatic encounter with the policeman when she'd been only twelve. Or perhaps it was only reasonable to wait – however long it took – for a man she could truly love and depend on. On the rez she had seen too many young women, even girls in their early teens, whose impatience to experiment left them prematurely saddled with babies.

Frank Patterson broke away from other guests to greet Bren and Tay. 'The Hartleigh women have always been known for their beauty,' he said, 'but the new generation has even managed to improve on the last. Tay, you're a vision.'

Tay blushed modestly. 'Thank you, Uncle Frank.'

Frank motioned to a trio of teenagers, two older boys and a girl, who had been waiting off to one side. Frank introduced them as his and Cori's children, Scott, Dean and Lynne.

'You're really our cousin?' said Dean, at fourteen the younger of the boys. It was clear from his wide-eyed gaze that he had developed an instant crush on Tay.

'So they tell me,' she replied.

'Where's Cori?' Bren asked, impelled by vanity to divert the focus from Tay.

'Still getting ready,' Frank said, before sending the kids off on party errands, an obvious pretext to put them out of earshot. 'Cori's been looking forward to tonight so much,' he said then. 'Now that it's here, she's hiding in her bedroom – a nervous wreck about facing everybody.'

'It would've been better,' Bren remarked, 'if you hadn't put her through this kind of stress.'

'As a matter of fact,' Frank said tightly, 'this is just what the doctor ordered – *all* her doctors. They've been telling me she needs to face real situations, not avoid them. Having a party for an occasion like this was the real thing to do.'

'I wonder,' Tay said, 'whether it would help if I went in and brought her out?'

'Sure,' Frank said. 'You might be just the one to ease her over the hump.'

Bren caught Tay's arm to hold her back. 'They hardly know each other. I'll go.'

'No, Cori would enjoy a chance to talk with Tay,' Frank said. 'She was so glad Tay was coming – mentioned it a few times.'

It might look suspicious if she insisted, Bren thought. She'd have to rely on Cori to realize how self-destructive it would be if she let herself get too honest with Tay. Bren let go of Tay, and Frank pointed the way to the bedroom wing.

'She's a knock-out,' Frank said, watching Tay walk away. 'But so nice and unaffected.' He turned to Bren. 'It's no secret I've never admired the way you behave, Bren. But by God, whoever you went to bed with to have that kid, you got lucky once.'

'Thanks for the kind words,' Bren said sarcastically.

'I can't help wondering what the story is? I mean, what went on between you and Tay's father? You could have had an abortion, but you didn't – and yet you gave up the child, then waited so long to take her back. None of it seems characteristic of the very independent, very selfish woman you've always been . . .'

'I guess, dear Frank,' Bren said drily, 'there's more to me than you realize. Now, excuse me for slipping away, but I ought to mix with the other guests.'

Frank watched Bren wade into the crowd, as always playing her looks and power for all they were worth. He had to judge her more charitably if for no other reason than giving birth to a child like Tay. But as a newspaper man, he still hungered to get the story on how it had happened.

Tay knocked lightly at the closed bedroom door.

'A little longer, Frank,' a voice came back weakly. 'Please.'

'It's not Frank, Aunt Cori. It's Tay – your niece.'

There was no answer. Tay wondered whether to knock again or just leave. Then the door swung open. Cori stared out, dressed in a slip, her eyes red.

'I . . . uh . . . Uncle Frank said you felt shy about . . . facing the crowd,' Tay stammered in embarrassment. 'I thought . . . if I could give some moral support . . .'

Cori kept staring at her. Groping for a way to fill the awkward pause, Tay remembered the little gift package she'd kept with her, and held it up. 'I brought you a birthday gift.'

Cori's eyes flicked to the package, but she seemed hesitant to take it.

Until tonight, seeing her aunt at close range, Tay hadn't fully realized the delicacy of her mental state. 'If you prefer,' she said, 'I can leave it outside with the other gifts . . .'

'No,' Cori said abruptly, and took the package from Tay's hand. 'Come in. Stay with me.'

Cori went back to her mirrored dressing-table, and Tay followed, taking a seat on the end of a chaise nearby. While Cori started to unwrap the gift, Tay glanced around the huge bedroom, sumptuously carpeted and decorated in tones of rose and beige. The bed was on a stepped-up platform that faced toward large windows giving onto a view of the bay and the Golden Gate Bridge. Tay was distracted from the view by hearing her aunt gasp. She turned to see that Cori had removed the bracelet from the box, and was holding it up, tears in her eyes.

'It's an Indian design,' Tay said, filling the silence. 'I chose it because . . .' Tay halted abruptly, uncertain of how much of her background she could expose even to her aunt without violating Bren's conditions. The two sisters were so estranged, so different, it was hard to tell how much, if anything, they knew, of each other's separate lives. 'Well, it's something I liked,' Tay went on, 'so it's giving you a piece of myself in a way. I've been hoping we could get to know each other better, Aunt Cori. I know – the way it is between you and my mother – it's been difficult to know each other. But . . . I have a feeling we'd . . . like each other.'

'Yes,' Cori replied, very softly, her eyes still on the bracelet. 'I think we would.' Her eyes shifted to Tay. 'But I . . . I don't know if . . .' Whatever she had intended to say was lost as Cori bowed her head and began to sob.

Tay moved to kneel in front of her. 'Aunt Cori, I was sent in here to cheer you up and help you get ready. Please don't cry – you'll get me fired from the job.'

Cori lifted her face and forced a smile. 'Dear child,' she said softly, 'dear, dear girl . . . you're so very lovely.' Her arms went out to encircle Tay, who returned the embrace. The desperate way that Cori clung to her astonished Tay. It was as if her aunt feared she would plummet into an abyss if she let go.

'Well, what a touching little scene this is!' Bren's harsh voice shattered the moment of intense closeness. 'What the hell's been going on in here?'

Cori pushed back from Tay and swiped the tears from her eyes. Tay turned to see her mother in the doorway. 'I gave Aunt Cori her birthday gift,' Tay said.

'Obviously it was a big hit.' Bren advanced into the room. 'Suppose you give me a look?' Cori didn't move. Her hands remained closed over the bracelet as Bren came up to her. 'Let's see it!' Bren commanded.

Tay looked between the sisters, baffled by the hard tone

her mother was taking, particularly with Cori's condition so tenuous. When Cori still didn't move, Bren reached down into her lap and pulled the bracelet away.

'Beautiful,' Bren said as she held up the piece of jewelry. 'Indian stuff. Perfect.' She flashed an angry glance at Tay, before rounding again on Cori. 'And did she give you a little history with it? Did you have a nice little talk about Indian handicrafts and culture, or perhaps about the way of life—'

No longer able to tolerate Bren's bullying, Tay sprang to her feet. 'What's the matter with you? I gave her a gift, that's all. We've hardly talked about anything.'

Bren kept looking coolly at Cori. 'Is that right, Cori? Perhaps I came in too soon. Would you like me to leave so you and Tay can talk – get to know each other better?'

Cori raised her face to look at Bren, then she shook her head. 'No,' she said, in a voice curiously vacant of emotion. 'I should get ready for the party. You should go, both of you, and let me get ready.' She turned to Tay. 'Thank you so much for the present.'

Tay stared back. She wanted to apologize for Bren's harshness, wanted to stay and talk more with her aunt, but her will was defeated by the expression of implacable coolness that had come over Cori's face. Tay felt that a wall had now gone up between herself and Cori that could not again be so easily penetrated. Some other time, perhaps. She left the bedroom with Bren.

'I don't see why you had to act like that,' Tay said as they walked back to the living-room. 'The last thing she needs is to be scolded and picked on.'

'So you know what she needs, do you?'

'Oh, Mother. Is it so hard to see? She's a sick woman. What can help her is constant love and support.'

'She has her husband and children. She can do without you or me to hold her hand.'

Tay grabbed at her mother's arm, and pulled her around. 'Why are you so angry at her? Something must have happened between you, something she did that you can't forgive. What is it?'

'You're quite wrong,' Bren said casually. 'If I have any problem with Cori, it's only that I don't think she appreciates quite enough all I've done for her.'

Tay appraised Bren curiously. But before she could even form her next question, Bren had moved off into the crowded living-room, smiling broadly at some old friend of the family as she struck up a conversation.

Tay found Frank and pulled him aside. 'I'm sorry, Uncle Frank. I went in to Aunt Cori, but then mother joined us – and, well, I'm not sure we didn't leave her worse off than before.'

'Don't blame yourself, Tay. Cori's unhappiness runs very deep. I'd go in myself now, but she hates it when I hover around her too much. Says it makes her feel like a cripple.'

'She said she'd get ready and be out soon.'

Frank gave a despairing shake of the head. 'I wish you could have known her before she got sick, Tay. She was . . . like a candle flame. Fragile, glowing, sometimes blown this way or that by a passing breeze – I mean, she'd get swayed by some instant enthusiasm, then it would pass. But she was so lovely, so . . .' His voice faded, but not the shine in his eyes. Tay could see how in love he must have been when he had married Cori.

Frank caught her looking at him, and shrugged off his reverie. 'You never know, maybe she'll bounce back. For now, let's concentrate on the positive things – one of which, I might add, is having you join the family.'

'I'm very fortunate to be taken in.'

'It's hardly a matter of luck,' Frank said. 'Being here, Tay, is your birthright.'

True, she thought; she ought to get over feeling like a mere foundling who'd been adopted. Bren had a responsibility to her. And yet Bren's treatment left her so insecure about her place in the family that she was left with the sense that, any time Bren wished, she might be banished.

Frank pulled her out of the reflection. 'Speaking of which, has your mother spoken at all about taking you into the business?'

'Oh, I don't think that's up my alley,' Tay said. She had only negative associations with Hartleigh Mining – memories of people on the rez blaming the company for taking advantage of them, stealing their mineral rights, underpaying for their labor.

'What would you like better?' Frank asked.

Tay shrugged. 'I don't know yet.'

'Come to the newspaper sometime and let me show you around. I could give you a job there. It's interesting work, Tay.'

She was touched by the offer, the sort of tangible recognition of kinship she hungered for. 'Thanks, Uncle Frank. I will come.'

'Good. Call my secretary and we'll set up—' He was interrupted by a maid scurrying up to murmur something over his shoulder. 'Oh God,' Frank sighed. With a hasty 'Excuse me' to Tay, he hurried from the room.

Within minutes the news had traveled through the gathering. Cori had been noticed standing on one of the terraces, dressed only in a slip, as she gazed out at the view. It was hard to be certain, but it was believed that the guest who had coaxed Cori back inside had stopped her from jumping. The story had hardly finished making the rounds before one of Cori's doctors was seen arriving.

Frank brought the party to a quick sad end, announcing to the crowd in the living-room that Cori had been taken ill. 'Thank you all for coming,' he concluded. 'I'm sorry it ended this way, but I know your prayers are with Cori, and we all hope there'll be another opportunity to show how much we love her.' He disappeared before Tay could speak to him again.

In the days that followed, Tay kept thinking back over the few minutes she'd spent alone with her aunt, remembering how sad and vulnerable she had seemed. Many times she reviewed the few words that had passed between them, wondering if there was anything she had said or done that was connected somehow to the way Cori had acted immediately afterwards. Of course, it wasn't logical to feel responsible; Cori had been a desperately unhappy woman for a long time. Yet Tay couldn't shake off a sense that there was some kind of link. Cori's emotional response when they were alone together had been so intense.

Bren did nothing to soothe Tay's vague feelings of guilt. When Tay openly expressed her concern about Cori, Bren suggested there was no telling what might drive her sister into a deeper and more destructive depression. 'The best thing for you and me is to stay away,' she said.

Still, Tay couldn't accept the idea that withholding love or friendship from Cori would be better than giving it. Though she guessed her mother wouldn't approve, Tay called Frank to ask about Cori. The news Frank gave her was not good. Cori had spent the next two days after the party in her room, often crying, until her doctors increased the dosage of tranquilizers. Reluctantly, Frank had returned her to the institution and new shock therapy was being considered.

'Do you think,' Tay asked, 'I might visit her? I . . . I'd like to do something to help. Anything . . .'

Frank paused for a long moment. 'That's very sweet of you, Tay, so I hope you won't misunderstand this. But I'm beginning to realize that one of the things that Cori has trouble dealing with – perhaps the most trouble of all – is her sister, anything that involves Bren, or brings them into contact. Anything at all . . .'

'Including me,' Tay supplied.

'I know it's not your fault. I should have realized it sooner, shouldn't have invited Bren here the other night.'

Tay could only agree as she reflected on Bren's harsh treatment of Cori as she had witnessed it.

'So,' Frank went on, 'I think it would just be better—'

'I understand, Uncle Frank.'

'Maybe it won't always be like this. It doesn't have to change my relationship with you, either. I'd still like you to come down and visit the newspaper.'

'Thank you,' Tay said. She realized, though, that as decent as her uncle was to restate the offer, accepting it would be unwise while Cori considered her an unwelcome reminder of her volatile relationship with Bren.

As they ended the phone call, Frank included one afterthought. 'Cori told me to thank you again for the bracelet, by the way. She loves it.'

'Really?' What Tay remembered was that the gift had seemed to be a catalyst in the whole unpleasant exchange between Bren and Cori. Having brought the gift had been an element in her guilt.

'Oh, yes,' Frank said. 'She's got it with her all the time. In fact, she refuses to take it off.'

21

Spring 1980

A clammy mist hung over the city this Monday morning in
May as Tay gunned the black Ferrari onto the streets of Nob
Hill heading toward downtown San Francisco. The expensive
sportcar had been Bren's college graduation present two years
ago. Tay would have preferred something more practical and
less conspicuous, but by now she understood that Bren took
perverse pleasure in contrasting the extreme luxury she could
provide with the abject poverty Tay had left behind. And Tay
had since discovered she wasn't immune to the thrill of driving
the Ferrari, just as she had also gotten used to living in the
mansion. A year ago, when she had talked of moving out to
her own apartment, Bren had promptly called in a contractor
and turned several ground-floor rooms into a spacious
maisonette with a separate entrance. Tay felt obligated to stay.

It was not the only way in which she had failed to free
herself from Bren's control. A month before graduating from
Berkeley, Tay had been summoned to a solitary lunch with
Bren in the HMC executive dining-room, and told that she
was expected to go to work for Hartleigh Mining.

Unknown to Bren, Tay had already let Frank give her a
tour of the newspaper, and she had found the atmosphere

stimulating. Faced with Bren's announcement, Tay revealed her wish to accept Frank Patterson's offer to become a reporter trainee at the *Observer*.

Bren threw a tantrum. 'This is the way you thank me for all I've done?' she raged. 'How the hell do you know what I'm offering won't be better than a job with Frank?'

No matter how far behind she had left the rez, Tay could never forget that the mining company was regarded there as among the worst of white entities that had always exploited the Indians. But she tried to frame her objection more diplomatically. 'Mother, it's better if I don't get involved with the company. That would push me back into contact with . . . things you want me to leave behind, and that's bound to stir up problems between us.'

'There's plenty you can do without ever going anywhere near the mines. You'd be working with me here at the head office.'

'Doing what?'

'I was thinking of public relations? You're bright and beautiful, just the kind of person we should have as a spokeswoman.' Bringing Tay into the company, Bren thought, might provide the solution to one of its most serious problems. Many years ago, tribal councils in the Black Hills had launched legal claims that the company's mineral rights had been acquired unfairly. These cases were still grinding their way slowly through the courts, and as the Indian rights movement gathered momentum, they had become mingled with the whole question of whether the US government had honored past treaties guaranteeing the sanctity of Indian lands. There was a danger that someday Hartleigh's rights to rich lodes of gold and uranium ore could be rescinded. The image of the 'paleface' mining company exploiting the red man might be neutralized, however, if one of the principal executives of Hartleigh, a member of the founding family, was herself partly native American.

But Tay remained resistant to joining the company. 'I don't want a job where the work consists of batting my eyelashes at any man who might start attacking the company so that he'll back off. I'm a lot more interested in telling the truth, and I could do that in journalism easier than public relations.'

'There's something else that makes you even more valuable,' Bren persisted. 'You can understand better than anyone the problems of the people who are fighting us in the Black Hills.'

'I've moved too far from that world, Mother. That was the way you wanted it, and I couldn't fight you. But I still sympathize with my – ' she caught herself – 'with those people. I couldn't work to take advantage of them.'

Bren's approach softened. 'Tay, dear, I'm not blind to the handwriting on the wall. Sooner or later Hartleigh Mining will have to sit down and negotiate directly with the tribal councils. When that time comes, having someone on our side who also understands the opposite point of view would help resolve things in the most sensible, peaceful way. That's why I'd like to bring you into the company.'

From Tay's pensive silence, Bren could tell the appeal had made a dent in her resistance. Now Bren spoke to close the sale. 'I know we still haven't gotten as close as a mother and daughter should be. And I realize it's my fault. I've been too wrapped up in the business. If you'd join me now, it would give us another chance to find common ground. I'll start you at a good salary, more than you'd get as a newspaper trainee. Try it for . . . say, two years. After that time, if you still want to work for Frank, all right. Just give this a chance. Don't you owe me that much?'

Still, Tay sat thinking.

Impatient for a decision, Bren took a gamble. 'What do you think your father would want? Did any newspaper do so much to help him, or the cause he cared about? Your own uncle was one of the first people Abel wanted to see when the Indians took over Alcatraz. And what did Frank's newspaper or any other do to help your father in his fight? Nothing more than report his protests, and battles – and his death – while everything went right on as before. You think Abel would want you to work for those people?'

'Whatever he thought about newspapers,' Tay declared, 'he believed the mining companies were the real enemies.'

'So he did,' Bren came back strongly, unfazed, 'and now I'm offering you a chance to join "the enemy" – take it over someday, and work from the inside to change things for the better.'

When Tay remained silent, Bren knew she had taken the bait. But, of course, changing things was not at all what Bren had in mind.

Tay's first months with the company were a training period during which she rotated through different departments, learning the operations. Hartleigh Mining Corporation was revealed as a vastly more complex enterprise than she had imagined. Under G.D., the business had consisted only of mining, refining and selling the metals. But Brenda Hartleigh had foreseen and capitalized on a much greater potential. Gold, after all, remained at the heart of the international monetary system, while uranium was the basic strategic material by which the balance of power between super-nations was determined. Controlling a large supply of these two elements gave HMC a central role in the world's political and financial machinations. One whole floor at company headquarters was occupied by a department that traded gold on commodity exchanges around the world. This was linked to a department on another floor that traded in gold-backed currencies. Profits from these activities were siphoned into other investments overseen by a separate division. Another subsidiary supported and encouraged the development of nuclear power for public utilities. There was also a large department dealing with the defense industry – and within this unit a confidential group that worked directly with the military, filling requisitions of material for nuclear weapons' testing and research.

Tay saw several opportunities for intriguing work, but she yielded to Bren's urging to try public relations. Its purpose, as Bren described it, was to educate the uninformed about the business of the company, let people know the ways in which Hartleigh Mining was actually serving their interests. Nuclear generating plants, for example, made cheaper electricity widely available. Uranium bi-products were important in medical technology. Gold wasn't just coveted by the rich and greedy, but recognized universally as a metal of unique beauty. What else did people everywhere use for a wedding band?

In the past year, Tay had found satisfaction in serving as spokeswoman for Hartleigh Mining. Though she had started at trainee pay, her annual salary had moved up to a hundred thousand dollars. She wouldn't have been earning nearly that amount, she knew, if she had gone to work for Frank Patterson. Frank wasn't the kind of man to be so openly nepotistic as Bren. Yet Tay was confident she did her job well, and was worth what she was paid. She had proven it in the first weeks after she had started working on the company's public relations.

One day last March, news had flashed around the country that a nuclear generating plant at a place called Three Mile Island in Pennsylvania had malfunctioned. A 'meltdown' of the nuclear core had contaminated the facility with lethal radioactivity, and dispersed radioactive steam into the air, threatening the surrounding communities. At the time, HMC's public relations was being overseen by an outside firm with whom Tay was expected to collaborate. Their advice to HMC was to ignore the accident. Making any public statement about its own facilities would only arouse fears, and tie it closer to the disaster.

But Tay perceived that any nuclear accident must not be dismissed or ignored. The days might be past when schoolchildren were instructed about how to survive an atomic blast and every large American city had a network of public shelters to be used in a missile attack, but nuclear power even for peaceful purposes remained an emotional issue. Most people still lived in terror of a doomsday scenario arising from the Cold War arms race, and the insidious genetic damage that could stem from atmospheric fallout. Rather than let Three Mile Island spark further opposition to nuclear power, Tay advised that HMC acknowledge its role as a supplier of nuclear fuel to electric utilities, and defuse fears by educating the public about how unlikely such an accident was, and how safe and economical nuclear power was compared to conventional technology. With Bren's approval, Tay conceived a series of full-page newspaper ads to make this point. One of the most effective showed a stark news photograph of a huddled group of Pennsylvania women, their faces etched by grief and worry. Across the top the photograph was boldly captioned 'Three-Mile Island?' Underneath, the text identified the women in the picture as wives of coal miners from a different Pennsylvania community waiting outside the collapsed shaft of a coal mine for word of survivors. Implicit was the message that nuclear power was far safer.

As dramatic as the meltdown had been, Tay's public relations campaign helped soothe away the alarm of the public. The outside firm was dismissed, and she took over all of Hartleigh's PR.

Tay left the Ferrari in the underground garage of the HMC building and rode the elevator to the top-floor executive suite where she had a large-window office guarded by a small outer office for her own secretary. To reinforce her hold on Tay, Bren had done everything possible to provide the most appealing work environment.

The secretary, a sedate older woman named Claire Wilson, was already at work when Tay walked in. 'Your mother wants you to come straight to her office,' she said.

These days, Tay and Bren never traveled to the office together. Bren was a workaholic who rose at dawn and was chauffeured downtown to be at her desk within the hour. Tay kept a standard schedule, drove herself, and often started the day with a meeting out of the office. Moving into the maisonette had so far allowed her a satisfactory degree of independence. She and Bren ate dinner together once or twice a week, but otherwise saw each other only in the normal course of business.

Tay went along the corridor to Bren's immense corner suite, passing through a bank of secretaries to the inner office. Bren was at her desk, on the phone, the panorama of San Francisco bay visible through a wall of glass behind her. She wore a black wool suit with a short jacket, the sort of classic Givenchy that had made the designer Audrey Hepburn's favorite, set off by large diamond clips at her ears and a sapphire pin. Her blond hair appeared to have been given a fresh golden rinse and cut. Tay suspected that her mother had set her sights on a new man.

Bren hung up on her phone conversation as soon as Tay entered. 'I was at a dinner party last night,' she said without preliminaries. 'Charlie Benson was there . . .'

Benson was the owner of a string of radio and television stations up and down the West Coast, Tay knew.

'He was nice enough to prepare me,' Bren went on, 'to expect a call from some new hotshot TV reporter on his staff down in LA who wants to do a story on HMC.'

'What's the angle?'

'Old stuff. Our relations with the nuclear-power industry.

It's a tie-in for a story about the new nuclear-power plant being discussed for Southern California.'

'I'll meet with him,' Tay said.

'No,' Bren said, 'that's what I wanted to tell you: I'll handle this one myself.'

It was unusual for Bren to intrude in this aspect of the public relations, but Tay realized that her mother's experience as a lobbyist had amply equipped her to deal with it effectively and had no objection. Tay was curious, though. 'Why do you want to be bothered? This is what you pay me for.'

Bren gave a whimsical shrug. 'Since I was given the advance warning, I called the reporter myself to ask about his story. We had some rapport on the phone, so I invited him to fly up here. We're meeting for lunch today.'

So that explained why Bren had gone to the limit in dressing up. By now Tay was well aware that her mother's substantial sexual appetite was activated only by very attractive men. In as much as this one reported television news, she must have had an advance look, and liked what she saw.

'Sounds like everything's under control,' Tay said. She wondered if she should ask if Bren had already bothered to check if the reporter was married or not. Getting too aggressive with a man who was still in love with his wife might have a disastrous effect on any willingness to report a story sympathetically. But when it came to handling men, Tay decided, her mother knew the ropes better than she did herself. She started out of the office.

'Just one more thing,' Bren said as Tay reached the door. 'If this man or his station does contact you or your department for information, make sure the request is passed on to me.'

'Of course. Better tell me the station, and who he is.'

'It's KNBS. His name is Neil Rocklyn.'

Arriving home at the end of the day, Tay noted the compact

sedan with a rental company sticker in the rear window standing in the circular drive. Lunch must have gone so well, the reporter had accompanied Bren home. Just for an extended interview? Tay wasn't sure she wanted to know.

When she'd first heard the reporter's name, she hadn't made the connection. But this afternoon, she had abruptly looked up from her desk, struck by the memory – the young man who had interviewed her the night Abel had died. She remembered that Rocklyn had been considerate, intervening sympathetically on her behalf when other people were pressuring her. Tay also recalled he'd seemed ambitious, anxious to get an interview with her because it would transcend local interest and be broadcast nationally. Evidently that desire for wider exposure had taken him from a small television station in Rapid City, to a job in Los Angeles.

She walked around to the side of the mansion, and went through the separate door into her maisonette. The apartment had a bright, modern sheen without being too glossy or antiseptic. As always, Bren had been indulgent about allowing Tay to have her own taste – as long as it didn't compromise the general air of luxury. Tay wanted classic modern furniture with simple lines, and had taken time to go hunting with the decorator Bren called in to assemble a mix of wooden pieces by Frank Lloyd Wright, Bauhaus chairs of chrome and leather, and Noguchi lamps. Against a background of pastel linen curtains, and floors of burnished quarry tile covered with area rugs of Persian, Turkish, and South American origin, it had a haphazard effect that came together due more to Tay's innate sensibility than a decorator's.

Tay picked up the mail left for her on a table in the small entrance hall by one of Bren's household staff, but as she started flicking through the envelopes, her thoughts wandered back to that hospital hallway where she had met the young reporter. Suddenly, without logic or warning, she was overtaken by a welling of grief more intense than she had ever felt. Glancing around at the luxury in which her mother had ensconced her, she was seized by the realization of how far she had come. She knew she ought to feel grateful for her good fortune, the security and comfort she had found, yet she was oddly more upset by a sudden remorse for what she had lost. Here she was cradled in luxury . . . but until that night when she had forever lost her father – lost her trust in him – she'd had even greater treasures. She'd been cherished, her heart filled with love given in return. With that emotional bond had come her sense of belonging to a unique culture and system of belief. Now she lived without belief, trust, love. All at once, she understood why she had been unable to respond to any of the many men who had shown an interest in her over the years. Feeling she had nothing to give, she had felt nothing could be received. If only her mother had been able to replace even a part of what had been lost, then her own heart might have been warmed back to life. But the mother she had found was incapable of loving, so Tay had remained frozen in indifference, emotionally numb.

She understood, too, what had brought all this into focus: hearing the name of that reporter, remembering that night – the night when, in a sense, she had died along with Abel.

Tay went into her bedroom, stripped off the expensive wool suit she had worn to the office, and changed into the jeans and one of the Berkeley pullovers she liked to wear at home. She washed off all her make-up, and touched a brush to her long black hair a couple of times. Gazing at herself in the bathroom mirror, she felt as though she was looking at a stranger. But perhaps seeing someone who had known her in the last moments of that past life would help her to pick up the thread again.

An interior door connected the maisonette to a stairway leading up to the main rooms of the mansion. Tay climbed up to the mansion's marble foyer. She could hear voices in quiet conversation coming from the nearby library. With its wood panelling, floral upholstered chairs and fireplace, it was Bren's favorite for intimate entertaining. The door was ajar, a flicker of firelight visible as it bounced off a span of polished mahogany. Tay paused outside, listening. The reporter was talking. She remembered his voice, mellow and smooth, perfect for a broadcaster.

' . . . to bring a crew next time, after I've filmed some segments around the mines. Assuming you have no objections . . .'

'Why should I?' Bren answered. 'Have I been at all difficult to deal with? I'll give you my complete cooperation, Neil – in any way you ask.'

Tay could hear Bren was exercising her wiles to the hilt.

From Rocklyn's next reply, it seemed he had taken the hook. 'I just might shock you with some of the requests I make.'

'Try me,' Bren said, her voice falling to a throaty purr.

There was a pause. Tay was on the brink of retreating, but the impulse to connect with her past urged her forward. She entered the room. Bren was curled in a chair near the fire, shoes kicked off. She had removed her suit jacket, and the top buttons of her ivory silk blouse had 'slipped' undone. She turned sharply toward the door, startled and annoyed by the intrusion.

Neil Rocklyn set aside a glass he'd been holding and rose from a sofa that faced the fire. He looked at Tay directly, admiring her beauty, but without apparent recognition.

'I'm not interrupting anything, I hope,' said Tay.

'Not at all,' Rocklyn said.

Bren made a grudging introduction. 'Neil, this is my daughter.'

'A pleasure to meet you, Miss Hartleigh,' he said. As she moved further into the room, his eyes stayed on her, then he squinted as if working to bring something into focus.

'We're not meeting for the first time,' Tay said.

Bren shot her a stinging look. She knew in a flash that Tay hadn't stumbled in casually.

'You look familiar,' Rocklyn said. 'But remind me—'

'Wounded Knee. At the hospital – the night my father died.'

'Your—?' His voice failed as the facts linked up in his mind. 'Yes . . . I remember now.' He turned astonished eyes to Bren. 'And she's also *your* daughter?'

Bren turned from glaring at Tay, to arch an eyebrow at the reporter in a way that not only acknowledged the relationship, but defied him to question it further.

Rocklyn shook his head in amazement. 'Well . . . this certainly gives me a fresh angle on the Hartleighs.'

Bren slipped her shoes on and got quickly to her feet. 'I've promised to cooperate, Neil, as long as you want news about the company. But I'd expect you to respect our personal privacy. The story you want has nothing to do with . . . a brief and unfortunate moment in my past. So leave this alone. If you don't, it will create many unnecessary complications.' She rose now, and touched her hand lightly to Rocklyn's arm. 'I've known you only a short time, but I feel . . . we've become friends. Can I rely on you?'

Watching the performance, Tay was impressed by the combination of earnest sincerity and seductive sensuality her mother could project. She was ten years older than Rocklyn, but that didn't seem to matter; she was a very beautiful woman and he appeared to have fallen under her spell.

'If that's the way you want it,' Rocklyn said to Bren, then he looked to Tay, assuming it was a shared wish.

Tay had reached a moment where she wanted exactly the opposite – to stop hiding, stop feeling ashamed – but this was Bren's call. Rather than battle it out with her, Tay said nothing.

'Well, I've got a plane to catch,' Rocklyn said. He glanced

to Tay. 'Nice seeing you again, Miss Hartleigh.'

'I'll take you to the door,' Bren said quickly. She slipped her arm through the reporter's and guided him out of the room.

Tay lingered, staring into the low flames in the fireplace. The countless times in her youth when she had sat by different fires burned in her thoughts. Campfires with her father. Fires in the sweat lodge.

Bren returned from the farewell with a smug smile on her lips. 'I like him,' she said. 'Don't you?'

'I hardly know him,' Tay said.

'But you met him before . . . and you wanted to see him again.'

Tay didn't answer. The impulse she'd had was too complicated to share, though it had nothing to do with the kind of attraction she knew her mother imagined.

Bren had moved to stand directly in front of Tay. 'I don't know what you wanted,' she said. 'I don't care. But from now on, you leave him to me. Understood?' She didn't wait for an answer, but turned to leave the room.

'Strictly as a public-relations matter,' Tay said, 'I think you'll be making a mistake to pressure him too much.'

Bren stopped by the door. 'I can handle that. Anyway, what interests me this time are private relations.' She went out.

Tay turned back to the fire. The burning memories were still there. She recalled sitting by the fire in the *tipi* of Nellie Blue Snow, listening to the old woman's wisdom about nature, healing, the symbolism of the animals.

How had she dared to hope she could find her way back to that rich past simply by touching this tiny fragment of it – seeing this man who had been there at the moment she had broken away?

It was all much too far gone for such an easy fix.

22

When Tay arrived for work the next morning a message was waiting that Mr Rocklyn had telephoned. She didn't call back and told her secretary that any further calls were to be referred to Bren's office.

Near the end of the day, the secretary came to the office door. 'Miss Hartleigh, that TV reporter is on the phone again,' she said with obvious exasperation. 'I've done what you asked, but he keeps calling. This is the ninth time, and he says he'll start again in the morning unless he talks to you.'

Tay agreed to take the call.

'You've been avoiding me,' he began.

'Strict orders from the president of the company. She wants to deal with you personally.'

'From what I learned yesterday, Miss Hartleigh, I doubt the president would fire you even if you disobey orders.'

'Don't be too sure, Mr Rocklyn. These orders were practically written in blood.'

A soft laugh came through the line. 'I saw the problem shaping up. But attractive as your mother is, I can't be seduced into veering away from a story I intend to investigate fully. I'm sorry if it creates difficulties within your family.'

Tay was glad to hear he wasn't so easily manipulated by Bren as she'd thought yesterday. 'You mentioned investigating. Sounds like you're looking into more than HMC's involvement with a nuclear-power plant . . .'

'Will you see me if I come back to San Francisco? I'll explain when we meet.'

She hesitated only a second. 'It has to be confidential. And I want your pledge that anything I say will be off the record.'

'That's a hard bargain for a newsman to accept: you'll give me a story only if I can't use it.'

'Those aren't exactly my terms, Mr Rocklyn. I may give permission – but first I want to know what story you're chasing.'

'On that basis, I accept.'

They made the arrangements, and said goodbye. Tay told herself that her only interest was in hearing about his investigation. It was her job to deal with such matters, attending to the company's public relations.

But then why the hell did she have to feel so damn guilty?

Two days later, after telling her secretary she'd spend her lunch-hour shopping, Tay took a taxi across the Golden Gate to the hillside community of Sausalito.

Their rendezvous, a vegetarian café called the Fruit 'n Grain, had been Tay's idea. She had no particular fondness for health food, but it was the least likely place to encounter anyone remotely part of her mother's private or professional circle. The café was on Bridgeway, Sausalito's shoreside boulevard, across from the tidal basin where houseboats of all sizes and description were docked. Inside, walls hung with bunches of dried flowers and herbs defined a long narrow room filled with rough-hewn redwood tables that were all crowded at lunch-time. In her beige silk business-suit, Tay felt instantly out of place as she searched for Rocklyn over the heads of young men with pony tails, and girls in tie-die dresses and love beads.

The '60s were still alive and well in this part of San Francisco.

She spotted him at a rear table, no less a fish out of water with his prime-time haircut and sleek gray flannel blazer. A tieless navy silk shirt made some concession to informality.

He stood and gave her a welcoming smile as they shook hands. 'Thanks for coming.'

Tay slipped into her chair, and picked up a menu. 'Forgive me for choosing this place,' she said, 'I'd guess nutburgers and tofu salad aren't your usual diet.'

'Got me pegged for a real meat and potatoes man, have you?'

'When we first met, you told me you came from cowboy country. Out there it's steak and eggs for breakfast, steak sandwich for lunch, and steak and fries for supper.'

He laughed. 'Yep, you've just described what my mother fed me 'til I left home. My habits have changed, though. Reporting the news brings in a lot of data on what's healthy. Nutburgers, no, thanks – but I haven't had a steak in a year.'

The rest of it suddenly came back to her. She stared at him. 'Wasn't it your uncle who owned the bar where—'

'That's right,' he cut in, as if embarrassed to hear her speak of Black Eagle's murder.

'And your father? What did he do?'

'He was a rancher.'

Tay raised her eyes to study him over the menu. She wondered what other cowboy attitudes he'd left behind – or kept.

A pretty waitress came to take their order. She was wearing a buckskin tunic, with her long blond hair cinched tightly under a beaded band worn around her forehead. Tay had seen Indian-style dress worn by hippies for years, but for some reason it irritated her today. The trivialization of the larger, richer culture into a mere fashion trend reminded her of how disloyal she had been herself to that heritage. She asked for a garden salad

315

and apple cider. As though to demonstrate how wrong Tay might be about him, Rocklyn ordered a vegetarian burger with a side of fried tofu, and carrot juice.

'If this kills me,' he said when the waitress left, 'I'll come back to haunt you everytime you eat fiber.'

She laughed, but let the repartee die. She was impatient to learn what he was investigating.

But he diverted the conversation again. 'You could've knocked me over with a feather when you showed up the other day. It stretches the imagination to think of your father getting together with a Hartleigh to make beautiful music.'

'They weren't together long enough to make more than a couple of notes, and sour ones at that.'

'How did it happen?'

'The way I hear it, plain bad luck. She was driving cross-country, her car broke down, and a nice-looking man stopped to help. My mother was a liberated woman before anybody knew what that meant . . . so she showed her gratitude in a way she could also enjoy. They spent one night together. Just one. End of story.'

'And how did you get from there to here?'

Tay lost patience with his probing into personal matters. 'Listen, Mr Rocklyn—'

'Call me Neil.' They were interrupted by the waitress arriving with their drinks. Neil took a sip of his carrot juice, and mugged a face that was meant to be amusing. But Tay wouldn't be charmed into forgetting her purpose.

'I came here to talk about the story you're researching,' she said. 'You've hinted it could have a negative impact on the company I work for.'

'Your family's company,' he corrected. 'Which is why family history seems fair game for the story.'

She bristled. 'You told my mother you'd respect her privacy.'

316

'I also gave you my word that anything you tell me will remain confidential . . . unless I have your permission to reveal it. That still goes. But I have a hunch, when you hear my end, you won't want to hold back.'

'Then let's start with your end.'

'Okay. But I'm sorry if it ruins your appetite.' He picked up a slim leather brief from beside his chair, and pulled out a black-and-white photograph which he set in front of her. It was a middle-range shot of a young Indian woman, attractive, but obviously marked by a hard life. In her arms, she held a pretty little girl of three or four. Child and mother faced the camera, strands of black hair trailing across their faces so that the wind blowing off the low hills was almost palpable. It was a striking photograph, but Tay saw nothing which might invite a hostile journalistic inquiry beyond the familiar signs of poverty – the frayed faded clothes, the side of a rusty mobile home visible as background. Her eyes roamed over the detail. A typical embrace, the little girl's legs dangling from the cradle of her mother's arms, one hand laid lightly against the side of her mother's neck, the other—

Tay breathed in sharply as the defect leapt out at her. The small hand resting on the far shoulder of the woman was connected to the stub of an arm, wrist and elbow linked directly together. Tay lifted stricken eyes to Rocklyn, but said nothing when she saw he was already holding out another picture. She took it, a clinical photograph taken in a hospital. A naked baby lay on its back staring up; the head was malformed, without a lower jaw.

The reporter was already extending another across the table. One more, she told herself, that was all she could take. This time she was relieved to see a normal-looking, handsome Indian boy of five or six standing upright by the door of a building – a school or clinic – smiling.

'Douglas Lonetree,' Rocklyn said. 'He's been diagnosed

317

with acute lymphoblastic leukemia, one of eight kids in his community with one form or another of the disease. Given the population density, about eighteen times the normal percentage. Luckily, it's a form of cancer where there's been a lot of progress. Five years ago Douglas wouldn't have had more than a ten per cent chance of living another six months. Right now, they give him a sixty-forty edge on two years.' His hand moved to the brief again.

'No more,' Tay said softly.

'I know its rough. That's why I was trying to ease into it with a little more small talk.'

'Where does my company fit in?' Tay asked.

'All the people in those photographs live in a settlement on the Standing Rock reservation called Upper Horse Jaw. Ever hear of it?'

Tay shook her head. She knew of the reservation, of course. The Standing Rock tribe was one of the six main branches of the Lakota Sioux, but as with Rosebud there were dozens of little settlements on the reservation familiar only to the locals.

'Upper Horse Jaw is three miles from the reservation's western border – which puts it about fifty miles from Victory Four.'

Victory Four. That name Tay knew well – Hartleigh's largest uranium-producing mine, so called because it was the fourth shaft dug in the search for uranium at the time the first atomic weapons were being built, and tons of its ore had been refined to produce the radioactive material that had gone into the 'victory' bombs dropped on Hiroshima and Nagasaki.

Neil went on, 'I'll give you a third landmark. The mine is about seven miles from two hundred acres of scrub land with nothing much on it but a deep ravine and a couple of trickling streams – land just a couple of miles outside the reservation, land owned by Hartleigh Mining.' He eyed her, checking for any sign of recognition. But this was also unknown to Tay.

'What gets regularly dumped into that ravine, we think, are tons of waste from the processing of uranium ore into weapons-grade fissionable material. The streams flow from there onto Indian land.'

Tay got the connection now. She answered with the truth, but filtered through the habit of an experienced company spokesperson. 'Hartleigh Mining owns a lot of land, Neil, hundreds of thousands of acres. I don't have any personal knowledge of the piece you've mentioned, but I'll certainly take a look at the records and—'

He cut her off. 'Were you listening, Tay? I didn't just say your mineworkers are littering the landscape with used coffee cups or cigarette butts. I'm telling you people are dying and suffering horribly because of what your company has probably been doing for years. And you want to fob me off with the usual PR bullshit? How many more deformed babies will be born or conceived while I wait to get at the truth?' His voice rang with indignance. 'I'd have expected a polite brush-off from some run-of-the-mill company hack. But Tay, those are *your* people, aren't they?'

The question hung in the air while he went on staring at her. Right here, right now, she was being forced to choose again, to redefine her identity as one or the other, the rich *wasicun* or the poor Indian. She tried to hold back the choice. 'You said you suspect nuclear waste is going into that dump site. But you don't actually *know*.'

His tone hardened. 'The property is surrounded by a locked chain-link fence, opened only when trucks go in or out. We have samples from downstream, not actually on the property, that show high radioactivity. We've also followed the trucks from Victory Four, and sent a photographer over in a helicopter; he came back with pictures of trucks dumping loads into the ravine.' He tapped the photographs he had already shown her. 'Put that together with this and it's not hard to add up. But proof? Documents that show the company is *knowingly* guilty? No, we don't have that.'

So this was what he was hoping she'd provide. Yet Tay couldn't exercise one loyalty without betraying another. And there was a matter of basic fairness: before conspiring with a stranger, didn't she owe her mother a chance to respond to the charges?

His sky-blue eyes were fixed on her, waiting. Now she realized, too, how reluctant she was to disappoint him.

The waitress returned with their food.

Neil leaned back and looked at the plates in front of him. 'Health food,' he said wryly. 'Of all things to eat while we're talking about this.'

In the crowded little restaurant, Tay suddenly felt hemmed in, suffocated. She pushed her chair back from the table. 'I'm not hungry anymore. Can we get out of here?'

He gathered up the photographs, left money on the table, and they walked out into the sunshine. Tay crossed over Bridgeway to walk by the waterside, and he trailed along. For a while neither spoke. They came to a place where a space between the houseboats gave a view out to the bay, and she stopped to lean on a dock railing. The breeze off the glittering water blew strands of her gleaming jet-black hair across her eyes; she thought of the mother with the malformed little girl. 'Tell me, Neil,' she said, 'did you also show those pictures to my mother?'

'No. I'm fairly sure she's already aware of the problem, so I took a different approach. Played dumb, just asked a lot of general questions, said that problems with toxic waste are becoming an important issue, and I'd like to know how HMC dealt with the problem. She promised cooperation . . . at a later date.'

'But with me you thought you'd try the shock treatment right away, go for a quick knock-out punch to the conscience.'

She looked at him. 'Because, as you said, those are "my people".'

He looked back squarely. 'Aren't they?'

She turned away again to look across the water to the mainland. 'My father was not pure Sioux, but *iyeska*, a half-breed. He never thought of himself as any less an Indian, as far as I know, but maybe it was because the whites – the *wasicuns*, as they're called – were less willing to have him belong with them. Me? I grew up proud to think as he did – until he was dying, and he told me who my mother was, and that she wasn't dead. Right up to then, he'd lied.' She paused to let the anger settle, amazed at how easily it could still grip her after all this time. 'I've lived with my mother now almost seven years. I see her for what she is – smart and beautiful, but also cold, selfish, power-hungry. She took me in, though, gave me a secure home, educated me.' Tay faced him again. 'If what you're telling me about the company is true, of course it must be stopped. Who or what I am is beside the point. But I have to do this in a way that's fair to both sides – and to myself. I won't be your spy. And I resent your trying to recruit me by manipulating my emotions.'

He frowned, plainly affected by her indictment. 'I'm sorry, Tay. But I care about this story more than anything else I've done – as a penance, maybe, because my people did so much to hurt the Indians. So I'm pushing hard and fast to get at the truth instead of using finesse because there are lives on the line – and I can't deny I was hoping to get the real reporting done before I had to turn it over to someone else.'

'Why would you turn it over?'

'The network wants to give me a promotion. Told me yesterday – I'm going to be head anchorman in LA.'

'Congratulations,' she said automatically, though she felt let down. She guessed it would tie him to a desk instead of leaving him free to do field investigations, and it struck her that she didn't want to see this man vanish so quickly from her life. 'When do you start?'

'Middle of next month.'

'I'll see what I can find out for you, Neil,' she said.

'I can't tell you how much I appreciate it, Tay.' Impulsively, his hands had come up to grasp her arms.

In the next second, they were both acutely aware of having no more to say, yet needing no words to speak volumes. His eyes locked on hers as questions and answers traveled between them silently. He brought his lips slowly down to rest lightly on hers. His mouth parted, and they breathed each other in, enjoyed the warm teasing touch of tongues. Tay felt the heat rising through her body, a flood of sensation new to her. When she pulled away, it was in her mind to tell him what she was feeling, to say she was ready to give herself . . .

But as soon as the contact was broken, the memory of a warning flashed through her mind, and desire died. If her mother had been willing to play the game of seduction to conceal the facts, could she be sure the reporter would be any less crafty to expose them?

She held him away, shaking her head. 'No . . .' she said quietly, refusing her own impulses no less than his.

He gave her a searching look, but the emotions denied had been so fragile, he could not fight for them. Still, his other passion remained. 'Does that mean you've changed your mind about helping?'

The question persuaded her – his heart was more set on a story than anything else. A good cause, whatever her disappointment. 'No, I'll help,' she said, 'as long as I can act within my conscience.'

'I wouldn't want you to do it any other way.'

They were back to silence.

'I have a car,' he said. 'I'll take you across the bay.'

She shook her head. 'We each came alone, it's best if we leave that way.'

He nodded, and she left, breaking into a run when she saw a taxi just leaving someone in front of a store on Bridgeway.

Back in her office, she sat staring out the window, reliving the hour she'd spent with Neil Rocklyn – those vividly pathetic photographs still floating before her eyes . . . and the feel of his lips on hers. Why did she even doubt that his attraction to her was sincere? She'd come so close to something new and phenomenal, why had she pushed it away? The question echoed over and over through her brain. Was she possessed by the normal confusions of a captive heart?

Or was she a 'skin who would always have trouble trusting a *wasicun*?

23

Early Sunday morning, when Bren was still sleeping, Tay went to the HMC building to search the deserted offices for anything to confirm what Neil had told her. She soon realized there were so many departments, so many files and computer tapes that might relate to land use or the handling of mine materials, she could prowl for weeks before finding relevant documents. The quick route to an answer would be to ask Bren what truth there was in Rocklyn's charges. But it would be obvious her knowledge came through meeting with the reporter, and Tay was reluctant to face her mother's jealous fury. In fact, she had been guiltily avoiding Bren completely.

She couldn't keep Neil out of her thoughts, couldn't forget the physical sensations that had overtaken her when she was with him. But she kept wishing it could have happened with someone else. As much as Tay felt an obligation to help Neil, she also knew that joining in any effort damaging to the mining company would pit her irrevocably against Bren, and probably be the end of all she had left of a family.

Held back by the threat to the secure status quo implicit in being involved with Neil, when he called at the start of the next week, Tay told her secretary to take a message. Later, when she looked at it and saw he'd wanted to talk to her before going on a trip, Tay regretted her timidity. She called Los Angeles, but he had already departed to cover the last story he would be doing as a field reporter. Tay was told he'd be gone several days, and difficult to contact during that time: the story was the eruption of a newly active volcano in northern Washington named Mount St Helen's. The mountain had blown its top yesterday in a cataclysmic blast estimated to have five hundred times the explosive force of the Hiroshima atomic bomb. First reports said twenty-five were dead, many more missing.

That evening, Tay watched the NBS affiliate in San Francisco and saw Neil's report, flown out from the area of devastation. Seeing him walk through the wasteland of volcanic ash dressed in an army field jacket, she cursed herself again for not seizing the chance earlier to talk to him. As a correspondent in the war with nature, he had gone where the same unpredictable forces that had been unleashed yesterday might at any moment erase another two dozen lives. Seismologists said there was a strong possibility of additional eruptions occurring at any time. Tay vowed not to be so timid with her feelings when she saw him again. Meanwhile, she resolved to help get the facts behind HMC's dumping.

Still, she thought, if the company had handled nuclear waste in such a deadly way, it was doubtful Bren would admit it. Tay went instead to the one other person who could understand the need to balance family considerations with a quest for truth.

'But you've found no proof?' Frank Patterson said, leaning back in the worn leather chair at the head of the long table in the *Observer*'s editorial conference room.

'I've hardly looked,' Tay said. 'I didn't want to do it when I might be seen.' It was her lunch-break again, and she hadn't told her secretary where she was going. 'I haven't felt I could talk to anyone in the company, either. The records would only get buried deeper, if I happened to go to any of the wrong people.'

'Does that include your mother?'

'I know it's awful to say, Uncle Frank – I owe her so much – but I don't trust her to be honest with me.'

Frank nodded, and they shared a thoughtful silence.

Since turning down the offer to work for the newspaper, Tay had rarely seen her uncle. She was fond of him and her aunt, and had wanted to keep up the contact, but the long-standing tensions between Bren and Cori made the connection hard to maintain. Looking at Frank now, however, Tay knew that coming to him had been the right thing to do. In his shirtsleeves, reading glasses pushed up atop his graying brown hair, he was the very image of the incorruptible crusading newspaper editor.

'Since you feel this debt to your mother,' Frank said at last, 'how do you want me to proceed?'

'I'm ready to let you decide. Of course, I understand if you want to stay out of it.'

Frank rubbed his chin. 'It's a tough call. I could raise questions in the paper that put the heat on. But I'm against printing unfounded speculation when there's no evidence to back it up. The company could be needlessly damaged, millions in value knocked off the stock. Large as our own holdings are, I'm not thinking of how we'd be affected: there are thousands of small stockholders who'd suffer much more. Should we stir up hysteria before we know we're on firm ground? The best course is probably to let Rocklyn keep carrying the ball and see what he turns up.'

'He's depending on my help,' Tay said. 'I'd feel very bad if I let him down.'

'Oh?' Frank cocked his head, and gave a knowing smile. 'I've seen him on the evening news doing those reports from

Mount St Helen's. Attractive fellow . . .'

Tay looked down, trying to hide a blush. 'All right,' she said, 'I do like him.' She lifted her eyes. 'But that's not why this is important.'

'Take some advice, Tay, speaking from my experience as a newsman. You couldn't do anything to make Rocklyn madder than handing this story to me. If he nails down the proof it would be a feather in his cap, maybe Pulitzer prize material. I don't like passing up a chance to let my paper get the credit, but I'd sooner do you a favor. For the sake of your feeling for this man, you don't want anyone else to break the story before he does.'

Tay fell silent. It was becoming more obvious that either she spied extensively on Neil's behalf, or she would have to confront Bren and ask for the truth.

Frank understood her quandary. 'Go to your mother, Tay. If anybody can get her to do the right thing, it's you.'

The meeting ended and Frank escorted her out through the bustling city room to the elevators.

'How's Aunt Cori?' Tay asked as they waited.

Frank gave a defeated shrug. 'Stays more and more to herself.'

'I've called a few times, asked to visit or take her out.'

'I know. She's mentioned it. She thinks a lot of you, Tay.'

'But she always makes excuses not to see me. It's odd, but I get the feeling that it makes her feel worse to talk to me.'

'Don't take it personally,' Frank said. 'She makes excuses not to see everybody. Even me, sometimes.' He suddenly looked so bereft, that when the elevator doors opened, Tay hesitated to go. Then he smiled as assurance that he'd recover. She gave him a quick kiss on the cheek and stepped into the elevator.

On her way back to the office, Tay brooded on the condition of her aunt. With all the blessings of a devoted husband, healthy children, wealth, beauty and intelligence, how could such sadness take hold and make her want only to withdraw from the world?

At the end of the day, Tay went to Bren's office to ask if she was busy that evening and propose spending it together.

'I've got to attend a Republican fund-raiser,' Bren said. 'They want money to put Ronnie Reagan in the White House. Be good for us to have a Californian man as—'

'I need to talk to you,' Tay broke in.

Bren caught the note of urgency. 'Let's do it now?'

If she was going to get answers, Tay felt, she'd have to make her pitch outside the framework of the company, away from this castle of Bren's where the first instinct would be to defend it with every weapon. 'I hoped we could spend some time together,' Tay said. 'Share a bottle of wine and talk in a way that's . . . more open and honest than we usually are with each other.'

Bren appraised Tay with a shrewd penetrating glance. 'Quality time, eh, a real heart-to-heart? Hey, you're not pregnant—?'

Tay laughed. 'No.'

'Well, I suppose if I mail in a check for twenty-five thousand dollars, the Grand Old Party won't mind if I don't show up.'

'I'll cook dinner,' Tay said gratefully. 'Come down to my apartment at—'

'No, dear. My turn. Shall we say seven o'clock – cocktails to start? From the sound of this, it might help if we loosen up a little even before the bottle of wine.'

It wasn't uncommon for Tay, whenever a couple of weeks went by without seeing much of Bren, to suggest having dinner together. Occasionally Tay prevailed on Bren to come down to her maisonette apartment, and they would have supper family-style – recipes Tay cooked, eaten at the oak table in a corner of her living-room. But Bren was uneasy with such informal intimacy. What she preferred – needed – was to have the servants around, and to eat the more elaborate cuisine prepared by her full-time chef.

When seven o'clock came, Tay went up the stairs leading to an alcove of the mansion's formal entrance hall, an imposing space that rose two stories above its checkerboard floor of black and white marble. Deferring to her mother's strict rules about dressing for dinner, Tay had changed out of her at-home jeans and pullover to the scoop-necked red velvet cocktail-dress Bren had given her last Christmas.

Tay had lived so much of her life in rudimentary poverty, that she had never ceased to be intimidated by the size and the opulence of the mansion. The larger part occupied by Bren was furnished with a mix of the antiques, folk art, and paintings acquired by G.D. and his wife. Since inheriting it, Bren mixed in her own collections. G.D. had favored the western-theme sculptures of Frederic Remington, rare Navajo rugs, and such one-of-a-kind memorabilia as the chair Billy the Kid had been standing on when he was shot in the back; Pamela favored beds and divans and bureaus made for the palaces of French kings and dukes; and Bren bought paintings that told the history of art from Monet to Warhol. These diverse tastes came together in one of the most eclectic but elegant interiors in the city.

Tay went to the room where Bren usually gathered guests for a pre-dinner drink, a large den overlooking the rear garden. Most of G.D.'s collection of western memorabilia was here, including a section of a long bar that had been the favorite drinking stand of Wyatt Earp and Doc Halliday in the frontier heyday of Dodge City. One of the mansion's staff, a handsome Mexican houseboy named Joaquin, was already behind the bar, mixing a shaker of the vodka Martinis that were Bren's favorite. Seeing Tay, he picked up an intercom to let the butler know that Bren should be informed her daughter had arrived. Then he asked Tay what she wanted to drink.

Tay requested a Martini. She didn't like hard liquor, usually, but tonight her nerves needed some medicine.

Bren swept in gowned in a long blush-pink silk brought back from her recent trip to see the Paris couture shows. The full formal wear further eroded any feeling of an intimate evening at home for mother and daughter. Bren took a Martini from the bar while making diversionary small talk about the dinner she was missing and Republican efforts to put Reagan in the White House. When she'd had a good swig, she told the houseboy to leave.

'So,' she said at last, waving Tay to a leather club chair, 'don't keep me in suspense. It's so rare you want to talk like this, something earth-shaking must be in the works.'

Tay sat down, taking the moment to compose herself. She hadn't wanted to jump into the crux so quickly, but of course it was Bren's habitual strategy to keep others off-balance. 'We need to clear the air about a couple of things. One's personal, the other is business.'

Bren took a chair opposite, and fortified herself with another long sip from her glass. 'Lead off with business. We ought to be able to settle that one quickly.'

'What can you tell me,' Tay said, 'about the way the company disposes of its radioactive waste – especially from Victory Four?'

Bren's eyes flashed. 'You ungrateful little bitch,' she burst out almost instantly. 'So that's the personal part, too, in a nutshell. I asked you to stay away from him, but you couldn't. You went right ahead—'

'He kept calling. When he told me why, I wasn't going to chase him away.'

'Chasing him away,' Bren said through clenched teeth, 'is what you get paid for.'

'No! Not if it means letting babies be born deformed, and children die of—'

'Indian babies, let's not forget,' Bren threw in, 'Indian children.'

'For godssake, that's beside the point. If we're responsible for systematically harming *anyone's* health, it's got to stop.'

Bren settled back in her chair, and took off some more of her drink, letting the atmosphere cool. Her sudden calm made her explosion seem deliberately theatrical in retrospect. 'There's nothing in what he says, Tay.'

'Nothing?' Tay answered. 'I've seen pictures of sick and—'

'I didn't say there are no sick Indians,' Bren interrupted. 'It may even relate in some way to nuclear materials. But HMC is not responsible. That part of the state is loaded with radioactive ground, or we wouldn't be mining there. Our own testing shows natural trace elements seep into the ground water. But we don't put them there.'

'It's a relief to hear that. Can I get copies of those tests, anything else that proves we're not responsible?'

'Isn't my word good enough?' Bren said.

Tay replied carefully. 'For me, it would be. But others have to be satisfied.'

'Like Neil,' Bren said tightly.

'There will be dozens if we don't kill this story soon.'

'I've just killed it, darling. I've told you there's nothing to it. But that's not good enough for you.' Bren lifted her glass again. Seeing it was empty, she went to the bar to refill it. 'You're still one of them, that's at the root of this,' she said as she poured from the shaker. 'Not one of us. I guess, as the saying goes, you can take the girl out of the tribe, but you can't take the tribe out of the girl.'

Bren's wounding offensive left Tay groping for a reply. 'Maybe it hurts more because I know how little those people have already, how much they've suffered. But why have you always made that an issue between us? To be with you – to love you – why should I have to reject another part of myself? Damn it, the mixed blood in my veins came out of your choice, not mine!'

Bren turned so abruptly from the bar that the liquid in her glass sloshed onto the floor. 'Wrong again, darling,' she shot back harshly. 'It wasn't my choice at all.'

'What do you mean?'

Bren stood absolutely still, like an aerialist in the middle of a wire who had unexpectedly lost her nerve and feared that the tiniest movement would send her fatally crashing down.

'Tell me!' Tay insisted.

Bren whirled back to the bar and downed her second drink. Then she murmured something inaudible.

'What?' Tay demanded harshly, moving up behind Bren.

'I said "let it go",' Bren repeated, practically shouting. 'Let's just leave things as they are, all right?'

'If I could do that,' Tay said, 'I wouldn't be here now.'

Bren faced Tay again. 'Nothing's going to change, dear,' she declared, retreating from the more damaging leap she'd almost taken. 'If you want to stay here, work for the company . . . and be a Hartleigh, then you'll back off. Stop pushing in anywhere I tell you not to go. Do you understand?'

'I can't live or work under those conditions. Not if it means people who could be saved go on dying and getting sick.'

'*Your* people,' Bren taunted her again.

'Yes! *My* people!' she shouted back, no longer willing to run from the challenge. 'That's part of me – a part you could never accept, always wanted to forget from the day I was born. But it's a fact, and if you can't live with it, then I don't belong here. Perhaps I never did.'

'Perhaps,' Bren said coolly. 'If you feel that way, get out.'

'I didn't have to be told,' Tay said, already starting out of the room.

'You'll be out of a job, too!' Bren screamed in her wake.

Tay kept walking without even a hitch in her step. As she neared the door, Bren took a couple of quick steps, as if tempted to bar the way. Suddenly she had the sense that something valuable could be lost if Tay left, though she could not exactly define what it was – a secret leverage over her sister, or one more beautiful possession? Or was it conceivably the chance for a kind of simple unselfish love she'd always nursed a hope she might someday develop?

Yet she couldn't bring herself to reveal even the slightest vulnerability. She stopped herself from speaking a word of regret or apology. She felt too angry and betrayed to care what misconceptions Tay would carry away with her.

At the door Tay paused, 'Goodbye, Mother. It's such a damn shame we could never love each other.'

It was even more regrettable, Tay thought as she moved on, that Abel had not let her go on believing the lies he had told her. At least then she could have gone on loving him.

She went straight down the stairs and into her apartment. In a whirl of nonstop movement, she packed a single valise with a small assortment of basic clothes, leaving behind anything of real value. None of it belonged to her, it had only been borrowed, now it was being reclaimed.

Outside, she walked past the sleek Ferrari, kept going with a purposeful stride until she had turned out through the gate, had left Hartleigh property. There she stopped. She looked one way, then the other.

Where did she go now?

24

The bus driver stopped where she requested, past the mailbox, after the bend in the road. She lingered there in the bright midday sunshine, looking up the bare dusty hill toward the tar-papered side of the main lodge. Had it been a mistake to come? When she'd bought the bus ticket, she had intended to go to the Standing Rock reservation and see for herself what was happening as a result of the policies of Hartleigh Mining. But during the overnight bus ride from San Francisco, she had decided on this detour. If she could connect here again – with Ada or Kate or Nellie Blue Snow or the children she had grown up with – if anyone would forgive her the complete rejection she had made of them and all that had come from being Abel's daughter, then she could forgive herself. Could belong here again.

Though if she was rejected, she would belong nowhere.

At last, she picked up her valise, heavy with the special equipment she had brought along, and walked up the hill.

You could go home to some places and be shocked by how much had changed. Here the shock came from how little, all the more because her privileged existence of the past seven years had enlightened her to the full extent of deprivation on the rez. At a glance, she saw only tiny improvements. A couple of sawed-off oil drums by the main lodge were planted with wild flowers blooming in the late spring sunshine. A pair of aluminum-framed windows had been installed where old wooden frames had rotted out. The rusting cars resting on their hubs in a field were newer than the ones that had been there when she was growing up.

A girl of about three-years-old wearing a faded dress without underwear squatted just outside the lodge's open door, shoveling the dry earth into a tin cup with a soup spoon. That was a big difference, Tay realized now. In the past, there were always many children running around, diverted from boredom by each other's company, throwing the ball around in games of *pte-he-ste*.

The child noticed her and fled inside the lodge, then a thin pretty Indian girl, a teenager, appeared in the open door, the small child timidly hugging her knee. She stared at Tay with her wide dark eyes and said nothing. Tay remembered now how unnerving it could be when a *wasicun* walked up to the door of any dwelling on the reservation. She smiled to put the children at ease, and introduced herself as the daughter of Abel Walks-Through-Fire.

'I have heard your name,' the teenager replied. 'I am Brightmoon Crying Wind.'

She was, Tay learned, a niece through marriage to Ada Crying Wind. She had come to live with Ada's *tipospaye* after having her baby. At the girl's account, Tay had to hide her dismay. The teenager in front of her was certainly no older than seventeen – and her child was already at least three. 'Where is Ada?' Tay asked. 'I'd like to see her.'

'She died the next season after I came.'

'Oh, no! How?' Tay was heartsick. She had loved Ada, who would still have been a fairly young woman.

'Walking on the road at night she was hit by a car – some

young men coming back from having a good time.' It didn't have to be said that for the young men a good time had involved getting drunk. The highways of every reservation were dotted with crosses marking the sad results of the young men's good times.

'What about Emory and Kate?' Tay asked anxiously. 'Kate Highwalking and—?'

'I know who you mean. Emory went away to find construction work in Denver. Kate still lives here. She's at work now.'

'She still works at the clinic?'

'Yes.'

Tay asked if she could come inside to change clothes, then leave her valise while she went to visit Kate. The girl named Brightmoon seemed reluctant, but stepped aside from the door.

The inside of the lodge had changed more than the outside. The sitting area had less ramshackle furniture, an electric refrigerator had replaced the old icebox in the kitchen and there was also a dishwasher.

Walking past open bedrooms on her way to change in a bathroom, Tay saw walls taped with children's drawings. She asked Brightmoon where all the other children were and was told that they were at the reservation day school. That at least was a significant improvement.

Before leaving the house, Tay asked Brightmoon one more question. 'You said you'd heard of me. I wondered how?' Her curiosity had been aroused by the reluctance the girl had shown to allow Tay into the house.

'From Ada and Kate,' Brightmoon said. 'They used to argue about you?'

'Argue?'

'Because you left and never came back. Ada said your heart was broken when your father died. She never blamed you for going away to find your mother and staying with her.'

'And Kate – what did she say?'

The girl's voice sank. 'That you were ashamed of being one of us – and we should have expected nothing better from an *iyeska.*'

The clinic was a one-story structure among a cluster of buildings at the administrative center of the reservation. Haphazardly expanded several times since first installed as an eight-bed infirmary in the 1920s, the disjointed collection of wings grafted onto the small boxey central core, was a reflection of the government indifference that had ruled over the reservations during the past fifty years. As she approached, Tay could see that even the most recently built wing was showing signs of dilapidation, its rain gutters rusted through, the concrete walkways leading up to it cracked and crumbling. No new additions had been made for many years. The kind of progress Abel had been fighting for was still very far from being achieved. It struck Tay that the irony of Wounded Knee – the stand for which her father had, in a sense, given his life – was that it seemed more of an end to what he had fought for than a beginning. At the time of the siege, the wave of public sympathy for the native American plight had risen to its height. When the siege was broken, the wave seemed to have broken with it. Leaders of the American Indian Movement were arrested for civil disobedience. Others were hounded by federal agents until, goaded to violence in self-defense, they were jailed. So here stood this jerry-built clinic to serve a tribe. If the dream of men like Abel had been fulfilled, the reservation would have its own new hospital, as well equipped as any in the white cities.

In the small front lobby forty-odd men, women, and children filled the plastic chairs and leaned against the walls. A woman orderly sat at a metal desk in front of double doors leading to the examining rooms, and other patient facilities. Occasionally she called out the name of someone to proceed through the doors.

At the desk, Tay asked to see Kate Highwalking.

'She's busy with patients,' the orderly said.

'When will she be finished?'

'Look around. She's the only one on duty. If you want to see her, wait your turn.'

Tay found a place to sit on the floor. The others in the waiting-room raked her with curious glances. She had been taken for a *wasicun*, and it was hard for them to comprehend anyone from off the rez coming here for treatment, or being willing to wait.

An hour had gone by when she glanced through a window of the waiting-room and saw Kate outside, smoking a cigarette as she strolled slowly with her arm around a young woman. Tay had spotted the woman in the waiting-room earlier. Now Tay could see the tears on her cheeks, sparkling as they caught the afternoon sun. Tay watched until she saw the conversation end, the woman walking away from the clinic. Then she hurried outside.

Kate was headed toward a side door when Tay called out her name. She turned and looked at Tay for a long moment without reacting. Tay waited, giving her a chance to walk away if she chose.

At last, Kate moved toward her. 'You look well, Tayhcawin. The white world agrees with you.'

'Not as much as you think, Kate.'

Kate drew deeply on the cigarette and gave Tay another long searching look. Her narrow handsome face was heavily lined around the mouth and eyes by fatigue, the hair once worn long was close cropped around her head, the body clad in a doctor's white smock was still discernibly tall and lean.

'I know you're angry at me for leaving the way I did,' Tay went on, speaking from the heart. 'But I was angry with you, too – you and Abel and everyone here who knew me. You must have all known who my mother was, knew she was alive, but you kept it from me.'

'It was Abel's wish. If he didn't want you to know, it was not for us to tell you. And she *was* dead as far as he was concerned. As you were,' she added, 'when you left us.'

Tay moved close. 'Am I still?'

Kate ignored the question. 'Why have you come back, Tay?'

'To find out where I belong.'

'As long as you even wonder,' Kate said, 'it's not here.' She glanced toward the clinic. 'I should be getting back.' She took a last pull on her cigarette, tossed it down and ground it under her cowboy boot.

It hurt Tay that Kate, once almost like a mother, could dismiss her so easily. But she didn't bother pleading her own case. 'I came for another reason, too. There are health problems at Standing Rock that may be caused by Hartleigh Mining,' Tay explained. 'I came to find out more.'

'You don't have to go up there to see the damage your company has done to the health of our people,' Kate said harshly. 'We have men with bad lungs from dust in the mines, and skin rashes from the chemicals used to leach the gold from the ore, and bones broken in accidents on the job that never healed well because the men got no benefits and went back to work too soon so their families could eat. I see all those problems here.'

Tay had no defense. She had ignored all this too long. 'I hope to do something to make it better.'

'It should be easy for you. You're a Hartleigh.'

Tay shook her head. 'Not anymore.'

The hard mask Kate had been wearing softened very slightly. 'Usually, I don't take such a long break from my patients . . . but I came out to spend an extra minute with a woman who was upset. I had to give her the news that her younger brother

340

is brain-dead in the hospital at Sioux Falls, hit a tree last night after drinking too much wingtip soup – that's what the kids call the stuff they make out of shoe polish and Lysol when they can't afford real whiskey. Anyway, I've left many people waiting inside . . .' She paused, and Tay could feel that a decision was in the balance. 'Come inside with me, Tayhcawin,' Kate said at last.

While Kate treated the constant flow of men, women and children, Tay joined her in the examining-room and assisted. Between patients, or while Kate was engaged in replacing a bandage or removing stitches or diagnosing a feverish child, they talked in snatches. Tay explained the events and feelings that had made her leave the reservation, and had brought her back, and Kate talked about her own life over the past seven years. She had started at the clinic as a self-trained nurse serving the white doctors who would visit the reservation two or three days a week. When funds for visits by outside doctors had been cut, Kate had taken on more patient-care herself, determinedly schooling herself through observation of doctors whenever possible, and by reading medical journals she ordered through the mails. She had made herself into a skilled caregiver, diagnostician, reader of test results and X-rays, and prescriber of necessary medicines. She had, in fact, reached the point where she could capably do everything but surgery – and even there she had made exceptions, like a tracheotomy to save a small child choking on a fragment of a plastic toy. In strict legal terms, she exceeded the limit of the tasks a nurse was allowed to perform, but even the doctors who came irregularly recognized that she was almost their equal. Aware of the need she filled, one of them routinely provided signed forms for any medicine Kate prescribed.

When Kate's stint ended at sundown, they rode back to the *tipospaye* in her pick-up truck. Finally Kate raised the subject of Standing Rock. She was aware there had been an increase in birth defects and certain other serious health problems; she knew a woman who did nursing for the clinic on the other reservation, and had heard from her about the situation. But she had never heard it blamed on the mining company. Some people thought it might be due to fallout from past nuclear testing even many hundreds of miles away. Others suggested it was due to a curse by angry deities – gods of nature who were offended by the way the environment was being spoiled.

'The second idea is closer to the truth,' Tay said. She shared with Kate what she had learned from Neil about the suspected dumping of nuclear waste contaminating water that flowed onto Indian land.

Kate became instantly livid. 'It's just another kind of massacre! The *wasicuns* won't stop until they've killed us all.'

'It's careless and stupid,' Tay said. 'But it's not a deliberate plot, Kate.'

'Maybe not. But so much of what has happened to us was simply because of carelessness and stupidity, and the end result is the same.' Gripping the steering wheel tightly as she drove, Kate's knuckles were white. 'What are you going to do to stop it, Tay?'

'I have to get evidence and give it to a friend of mine. He'll broadcast the story on television if it's substantiated. That would put pressure on Hartleigh Mining to stop the dumping.'

'I'll help you,' Kate said.

'You're needed here.'

'There are ways I can help without leaving.'

When they returned to the lodge, it was as overrun with children as Tay recalled in the past. Not all the mothers and fathers were present; but the ones Tay met remembered her from when they had been children, her contemporaries. They greeted her with a combination of awe and suspicion, then stayed to themselves while Kate took Tay with her to the phone and made a few calls. One was to arrange a borrowed vehicle

Tay could use to journey to Standing Rock. Another to Celeste Stillwater, who was Kate's counterpart at the Standing Rock clinic. When Kate explained Tay's mission, Celeste happily agreed to provide a place for Tay to sleep, and cooperate in any other way.

Dinner made by Brightmoon and another of the young mothers was the kind of basic meal Tay remembered, fresh vegetables grown in a garden behind the lodge, home-baked bread, and a small serving of tinned meat. Kate brought out a jug of *mni-sha*, and the traditional herbal wine nudged Tay even deeper into a nostalgic mood. After dinner, she went out alone and walked down to the small separate sleeping shack she had shared with her father. Looking through the window, she saw a couple of children getting ready for bed helped by one of Ada's grown daughters. She remembered how content she had been as a child, how unaware of the problems and injustices – how well Abel had shielded her, and encouraged her to find her pleasure in the things that were freely available. She hadn't known then what was missing, what only the rich could have – and hadn't cared.

Reminded of the past, the things she valued, Tay recalled Nellie Blue Snow, the old medicine woman who had taught her so much – lessons that had all but faded from her memory. When she got back to the lodge, she asked Kate about Nellie.

Nellie was still alive, Kate said, but no longer provided her own brand of native medicine to members of the tribe.

Tay was surprised. Men or women gifted with the knowledge and special sensitivity of native cures and healing methods were never supposed to give up practicing no matter what their age.

In Nellie's case, Kate explained, it had come about because the old woman's faith in her own medicine had been shattered in a collision with the white world. A Sioux man who lived with his *wasicun* wife off the reservation had a young daughter who was in hospital weakening with an illness doctors had been unable to diagnose. Believing that his daughter was possessed by evil spirits, the man had asked Nellie to come to see the child. At first, Nellie had insisted the girl be brought to her; for a medicine woman to practice off the reservation, and especially in a place of conventional treatment, could make her liable to serious penalties. The child had continued to weaken, though, her condition becoming so grave she was expected to die. In desperation, the father pleaded with Nellie to come to the hospital late one night, to bring her own cures and perform one more ceremony. Nellie agreed, but halfway through her ministrations, members of the hospital staff had entered the child's room and stopped her. The next day the child died, and Nellie had been prosecuted on a variety of charges that fell short of blaming her for the girl's death. Nellie had been given a suspended sentence, but since then she was unwilling to do any tribal medicine.

It had been a long time since Tay had experienced within herself a rage against the injustice the Indians suffered because of the *wasicuns*' ignorance and intolerance. But she felt it now. For what had old Nellie been punished? At the least she had brought some comfort by giving a grieving father the contact with his own traditions. Why were the *wasicun* doctors not prosecuted for failing to diagnose the illness that had killed the girl?

Before she left Rosebud tomorrow, Tay resolved, she would visit Nellie and try to inspire her to serve again. Kate could obviously use the help.

Nellie Blue Snow had already been quite an old woman when Tay was born, though her exact age remained uncertain. Not in doubt, however, was that she had already been alive at the time the original Wounded Knee massacre had taken place in December of 1890. Her father and mother had been among the nearly three hundred Sioux cut down by the army's seventh cavalry – the same outfit once commanded by General George Custer – two-thirds of the victims being women and children. Nellie had escaped in the arms of a young woman who was one of a few dozen survivors. The respect in which Nellie was held by the tribe, and their belief in her magic powers, were enhanced by the very fact that she had survived the deadly onslaught.

As she had for many years, Nellie still lived alone in a small mobile home, with the *tipi* where she performed ceremonies pitched in a field behind it. When Tay went the next morning, the old woman instantly recognized her and welcomed her warmly. Nellie turned off the television game show she'd been watching in the trailer's compact living-room, and offered Tay a cup of herb tea.

Tay marveled at the old woman's energy as she moved into the trailer's kitchen. Her face, the skin so extremely wrinkled, looked like a squashed paper bag with two raisin-like eyes set into the folds above her cheeks. The thick snow-white hair was still worn long with feathers attached to the tied ends that hung across her shoulders down to her waist.

'I expected you sooner, Tayhcawin,' Nellie said when they were seated together.

Tay was puzzled. 'I arrived only yesterday, Nellie. I came as soon as I could.'

'I was talking of the years. You've been gone almost ninety moons, isn't that so?'

Seven and a half years. Tay nodded.

'It should not have been so long. You were meant to be here. The tribe needs someone to replace me.'

'Replace you? Me?' Tay couldn't help smiling. 'Nellie, I'm the last person who would—'

'Your grandfather was a *yuwipi* man. The medicine way is in your blood. I have seen it from the time you were a child.'

Years ago, if Nellie had made such pronouncements, Tay would have been unnerved; she believed then that Nellie spoke with some special authority that came from her familiarity with the traditions – or even with the Great Spirit. Now she put it down to the eccentricity that came with age.

'There's no need for a replacement,' Tay said. 'I came to encourage you to keep the medicine way, Nellie. You're too valuable to give up. Kate thinks so, too. Modern medicine is not always enough to help our people – or even as good.'

The tiny black raisins disappeared as the old woman closed her eyes meditatively, and sat motionless as though listening to an inner voice. Then her eyes opened again. 'I know the need, Tayhcawin. But it takes strength I no longer have. What strength I have left, I have saved for you.'

The old woman's focus on her was becoming unsettling to Tay. 'I don't understand,' she said.

'I must teach you all that I know. So you will replace me.'

Tay pulled forward on her chair so that she could reach across a gap between her chair and the old woman's and grasp her wrinkled hands. 'Nellie, I'm honored you think I could ever do what you do. But I'm not so good or so wise. I haven't been as loyal to the tribe, either. I came back because a *wasicun* asked me to help him learn about what's happening to our friends at Standing Rock. I don't know how long I'll be there, or when I'll be back here.' As she said it, Tay realized how much she wanted to see Neil again. If she had to make a prediction for herself, it involved staying close to him.

Nellie was nodding as though at last she understood. But then she said. 'You will come back. Soon. You are needed here.'

It was uttered with such finality, that Tay felt it was pointless to discuss. Rising from her chair, she thanked the medicine woman for the tea, and ran quickly through the polite banalities of how wonderful it was to see her again, how well she looked, how much she hoped Nellie would reconsider her 'retirement'.

The old woman followed her to the door of the trailer. When Tay went down the two outside metal steps, she turned to wave.

'When you were young, Tayhcawin,' Nellie said, 'you could comfort those who were sick . . . you were known for that, being able to cool a fever or ease someone's pain with a touch. Do you remember?'

What came back to Tay was sitting by Abel's bedside the night he had died, listening to him talk about his father, the *yuwipi* man, and saying that he believed the power had been passed down to her. That night she had wanted it to be true; she had wished she could heal him. But no longer. Perhaps a woman like Nellie had a power that came from a combination of wisdom, and an energy derived from her unquestioning belief in an ancient tradition. Tay had no such pure belief. In this day and age, she was sure, no one, no one at all, could replace a woman like Nellie.

Before turning away, she said, 'I'll try to come back and see you again, Nellie.' But it was only an empty amenity. She never wanted to be subjected again to the medicine woman's unnerving assumption. Sadly, too, it was highly doubtful that Nellie would still be alive the next time Tay came this way.

25

On the Standing Rock reservation, Tay stayed at the house of
Celeste Stillwater, the local nurse Kate had phoned. Celeste
had also organized several men on the reservation who knew
the Hartleigh property, and could help Tay get past the fences
and guards to take photographs and collect other evidence.
Prior to her arrival, there had been only a vague feeling among
the reservation dwellers that the sickness and strange births
that had plagued the tribe in recent years were unusual. Health
problems due to poverty and substandard medical care had
always been common. Once the connection to questionable
practices of the mining company was made, many of the
Standing Rock Sioux were enraged, anxious to do whatever
was necessary to get the dumping stopped. One man who
offered help had a cousin who worked as a truck driver for
Hartleigh Mining. Even the driver hadn't known there was
anything dangerous about the materials he was handling.

The HMC property bordering the rez was enclosed by a
chain-link fence patrolled day and night by teams of armed
guards. It was large enough, however, that the full perimeter
couldn't be constantly watched. With the help of three local
Sioux who brought tools to cut through the fence, Tay entered

349

the property at night without a problem. She carried with her the special equipment brought from San Francisco: a geiger counter, several small lead containers, and a camera.

A road led through the property to the ravine where the nuclear waste was dumped. Tay and the three Sioux followed it, staying far to the side so they could duck easily out of sight when a patrol went by. As they approached the ravine, a convoy of twenty dump trucks drove up. The Indian who worked as a driver had alerted Tay to the time when the convoy would arrive. Concealed behind scrub brush, she watched the dump trucks line up at the edge of the ravine, and disgorge tons of slag and dozens of metal drums. Tay snapped two rolls of pictures using infrared film. After the trucks left, she climbed down the sides of the ravine with her guides to scoop samples of the slag into the lead containers, and took pictures of the drums, all marked with the three-bladed warning sign that indicated dangerous radioactivity. Geiger-counter readings showed levels of radioactivity so high that Tay hastened to complete the job, feeling that even the minimal exposure could be dangerous.

The following day she called Neil at the television station. As soon as he heard about her reconnaissance, he agreed to fly to Rapid City from Los Angeles the next morning.

Until she saw him coming down the ramp and walking toward the terminal buildings, she hadn't realized how keenly she had been longing to see him again. She'd been on the move so much, she hadn't given a thought to what clothes to wear when she dressed this morning. Since arriving on the reservations she had subsided into the style that had been common when she had lived here – hair done in braids, a headband, jeans, and a buckskin vest she had borrowed from Celeste. Neil was similarly dressed according to local custom in jeans, a plain white shirt, and a leather jacket lined with sheepskin. He carried only a small overnight bag: apparently he didn't plan to stay more than a day.

'Thanks for picking me up,' he said when he passed through the arrivals gate. A nice hello, but he was clearly reluctant to show any emotion.

Hiding her own eagerness, she gave him the same sort of restrained greeting. 'Thanks for coming so quickly.'

'If you've got the proof nailed down, I don't want to waste any time getting out the news.'

'I've got it,' she said confidently. They pushed through the doors to the sidewalk unloading area. 'I brought it with me.' She nodded toward her borrowed pick-up truck.

Neil looked concerned. 'From now on don't leave that stuff where anybody could get at it.' He glanced around, as if concerned that they were being followed.

'I didn't realize this was such a cloak-and-dagger operation,' Tay said. They reached the truck and got in, Tay at the wheel.

'Think again,' Neil said seriously. Even the government had a vital stake in Hartleigh Mining being able to continue its uranium processing without interference, he explained. It was hard to know where either company or government might draw the line in protecting the operation if they felt it was threatened. Recently, at another company which processed nuclear material under government contract, an employee named Karen Silkwood had begun agitating for improvement when she discovered hazardous work conditions existed. Her employers hadn't responded, so Silkwood had started collecting proof of the problem. On her way to a meeting with a newspaper reporter to present the evidence, she had been killed in an automobile accident – and the proof had never been recovered.

They decided to drive into the city and find an anonymous coffee shop where they could sit while she showed him the evidence she'd gathered. As Tay steered, she cast a few reflex glances in the rear-view mirror. No one seemed to be following them, but she remained shaken by the Silkwood story. 'I hadn't realized how dangerous this could be,' she said.

'I should have warned you sooner,' Neil said. 'I would have – if you'd let me know you were coming out here on a hunting expedition. Why didn't you call me first?'

'I didn't want to bother you until I had something concrete.'

'Bother me? Tay, I'd have been glad to hear from you any time. All the more if it meant insuring your safety. If anything happened to you, I . . .' He paused, then he burst out, 'Well, what the hell did you think it meant when I kissed you?' She glanced at him as he went on more quietly. 'Tay, I felt something very special happened between us the last time we were together. Though the next day, when I called and you wouldn't speak to me—'

'I was afraid,' she broke in, wrenching her gaze back to the road.

'Of what?'

'I knew, one way or another, getting close to you would mean a break with my mother. She did get furious as soon as I started pressing her for answers. She's fired me and cut me off.'

'I didn't realize—'

'It's not your fault. Now that it's done, I feel liberated. I always had the strangest sense I didn't belong there. Still, I was afraid of . . . of . . . I don't know, maybe it comes down to not having a roof over my head, being cast out, adrift.'

'If you're with me,' he said, 'you're not adrift.'

She turned to him again, and his eyes repeated the promise. She reached across the seat and took his hand.

'Hey! Better keep your eyes on the road.'

The truck had started drifting out of the lane.

Tay looked forward again, but she kept one hand in his as she steered the truck onto a shoulder and braked to a stop. As soon as she turned from the wheel, he reached out and she slid over into his arms. Her lips lifted to his, and they kissed deeply. When they pulled apart, breathless, she heard him say 'I love you.' She straightened and eased him away.

'Did I say something wrong?' he asked.

'Neil, I . . . I've been cut up in pieces for so long, waiting so desperately for someone to love me and make me whole, that I'm not sure—'

He got it now. 'You're afraid of pushing yourself into this too fast.'

She gave an embarrassed shrug. 'I know so little about you.'

'You know I grew up on steak for breakfast, lunch, and dinner.'

She smiled. 'I need a little more.'

'Here goes. I've never been married, I go to bed late and wake up early, I love my work, have no hobbies – hey, I'll sit down and write a six-volume autobiography if that's what it takes to convince you I'm the right man for you.'

'I don't think I'll be that hard to convince. I just . . . need to spend some time with you.'

'Fine. We've got some important work to do, anyway. Let's take care of business, maybe the rest will take care of itself.'

From the glove compartment, Tay pulled the envelope of photos, geiger-counter readings, and notes from a talk she'd had with the Sioux man who worked as a truck driver for HMC.

As she drove on, Neil riffled through the collection. After a few minutes, he said, 'No need to sit down over coffee. I can see already you've made our case. That hole in the ground is almost as hot as a bomb site. As long as water runs through it onto Indian land, there'll be no end of sickness and death.'

'I can't believe the company understood the consequences of what they were doing.'

'We'll see how fast they stop once we make it public knowledge.'

'They wouldn't keep going.'

'No? No matter how much proof there is that smoking causes cancer, the cigarette companies go right on selling the product.'

'That's hardly the same. People want to keep buying cigarettes. These Indians never asked to have radioactive water soaking their land.'

'But they don't own the land it comes from, which makes for all kinds of legal problems. That won't matter if Hartleigh Mining accepts responsibility, and stops the dumping . . . but let's see what happens when I broadcast the story.'

'Sure you have enough?'

He tapped the papers in his lap. 'This is all I need. Your interview with that truck driver – where he talks about the guys who load the trucks wearing lead-lined suits – that's better than pictures. You know, you've got extraordinary instincts for collecting news, Tay, on top of which you'd look great on camera. I think I could get you started at my station in LA.'

'I've been told before I could have a future in the news business,' she said, remembering Frank Patterson's offer.

'Maybe it's your destiny,' Neil said.

'I'll give it some thought.' For some reason Nellie came into her mind. Everybody seemed to have ideas about her destiny. 'Where do you want to go now?' she asked.

'It would add to the story if I can visit the reservation, do some interviews of my own. I'd like to go into the clinic, talk to the people who may be ill from radiation. You think they'd mind? A camera crew from a local station is standing by to meet me out there.'

'I'm sure they'll cooperate in any way necessary.'

'There's one other thing I'd like to do first,' Neil said.

From growing up near Rapid City, he retained a knowledge of the roads and he directed Tay to turn off the main highway onto a back road heading out into the countryside.

They went north through the rolling country leading to the Belle Fourche River. Along the way, she answered his questions about her youth, how it had felt to make the adjustment to living in the 'white' society after Abel had died. He wanted to know more about her, but also about the dilemma of native Americans in general – a nation within a nation that had struggled for centuries against extinction. As they talked, he mentioned that covering Wounded Knee had been the most personally affecting story of his career – so much that it had prevented him from doing his job.

'In what way?' she asked.

'I let my personal sympathies take over and held back a piece of the story because I thought it would look bad for the side I favored. There's nothing worse than a reporter covering up what he knows.'

Tay was shocked, ready to revise her opinion of him. It sounded like he was confessing to protecting the interests of the white authorities.

But he told her now about erasing the tape, the passage he'd recorded of Tay, standing in the corridor of the hospital after Abel had died, furiously denouncing him. 'The daughter of one of the siege leaders calling him a fraud and a liar . . . can you imagine the damage that might have done to the movement?'

It hurt to be reminded of her bitter words, all the more at this moment when she had come back to make peace with her past. 'What made you do it?' she asked.

He shrugged. 'Looking back, I'd say maybe I loved you even then.'

'And what would you have said at the time?'

'That it eased my guilty conscience?'

He had been raised, he told her, in a home where the prejudices of the pioneer generation still survived. His father had employed Indians on his ranch to do menial jobs because they were the cheapest labor available, but they had not been well treated. In his youth, Neil had seen Indian ranchhands abused, thrown out of work, their pay withheld.

'There's no defense for what my father did . . . except he'd been told a thousand times by his own father how his grandfather – my great-grandfather – was scalped during the Indian wars when he fought to keep his land, the ranch that came down to my dad.'

'You must've been told the same stories?' Tay said.

'If I'd stayed on the ranch, I'd never have shaken off the same stupid ideas. But I went to college, started seeing the world. Soon as I let a little light into my mind I was ashamed of the way we'd always treated native Americans. I've been trying to make amends ever since.'

They rounded a curve in the highway, and Neil suddenly pointed to a dirt road and told Tay to turn. A short distance from the turning, the road passed through a gateway with a sun-bleached wooden signboard suspended over it.

'This is it,' Neil said. 'The Rocklyn ranch.'

Tay saw nothing at first to mark a homestead. Then the road crested a low hill and dipped down into a rill leading to a narrow winding river, a stretch of shallow water skimming over silvery rapids. On the grassy bank about a quarter mile ahead, a simple frame house stood with a barn and a couple of smaller sheds, a fenced-off corral and animal pens, and an ancient standing windmill to pump water. It was a beautiful setting, even though the signs of neglect were everywhere, fences falling down, grass and scrub growing out of control, the house weathered to a dingy gray. Tay realized that the ranch was uninhabited, had probably been deserted for years. As she halted the car, she could hear the rusty squeak of the windmill turning, and the creak of hinges from an open barn door swinging slowly back and forth. A wave of sadness overcame her to see this lovely spot left derelict.

Walking to the house, Neil told her that during his first year at college, his father's cattle had been struck by hoof-

and-mouth disease which required destroying them all. Struggling to recover from this devastating financial blow, Neil's father had worked himself into an early grave, dying of a heart attack a year later while he was out on his horse one night looking for strays. His mother wanted to keep the ranch going with Neil's younger brother, but then the brother had also gone off to college in the east. When she had gone to see her younger son graduate, she had been seated at the ceremony beside a widower whose son was also graduating. The two had now been married almost ten years, living in Florida. His mother had sold the house and the twelve hundred surrounding acres for a good price, money she'd needed for a comfortable retirement.

'But why did the buyer leave it like this?' Tay asked.

'He's a city slicker who had a dream of putting it back the way it was, making it work again. But he's never had the time.'

'What a shame. It could be so wonderful.'

They reached the porch. Neil took her hand as he brought her up the steps to the front door. 'Want to take a look inside?'

'Isn't that trespassing?'

'I'm sure the city slicker won't mind,' Neil said, pulling a ring of keys from his coat pocket.

Her eyes widened. 'You?'

He smiled as the door swung open and he motioned her across the threshold. Inside, the sturdy house and its simple furnishings had been well preserved – Neil paid a caretaker to come periodically, sweep away the dust and keep the house weathertight. The Sears mail-order furniture, homemade hooked rugs, needlepoint samplers on the walls, and quilts acquired at church quilting bees constituted a vision of the way legions of ranching families had once lived. In its own way, it was a tradition and a culture that had suffered from progress as much as the Indian way of life.

They ambled together through the rooms lit by shafts of

sunlight pouring through calico curtains, while Neil spoke about his youth, painting a family portrait in which his father emerged as a kinder man than the bigoted mistreater of Indians described earlier. Except for his adherence to the narrow views of the old west, he had been a decent, hard-working rancher.

After they had toured the ground floor, Neil stopped and pointed up the stairway. 'Just bedrooms up there.'

By stopping, giving her the choice to go up, he had charged the moment with meaning. Tay's pulse quickened . 'Don't you want to show me?' she said.

'If you're sure you'd like to see . . .'

She started up the stairs first, extending her hand to bring him along. At the top, she could see through two open doors. One room was bare, but in the other was an old wrought-iron double bed covered with a quilt. She led him there.

When she turned to him, he embraced her gently, 'I want it to be right for you, Tay,' he said. 'I want to – how did you put it? – make you whole. If you have any doubts . . .'

Again she answered wordlessly with her eyes and hands and mouth, moving closer to kiss him as she began to remove his shirt. Had she waited long enough? *Too* long, if anything.

He began matching his movements to hers. When they had shed all their clothes, he lifted her onto the bed and they kissed for a long time, his body over hers. He laid a trail of kisses down her neck and shoulders, across her breasts and stomach. She was consumed by sensations she had kept locked away. 'Yes,' she whispered, 'yes, my darling, make me whole . . .' Then she could talk no more, gasping as his mouth moved lightly across her thigh and stayed at last at the center of feeling, sending electric tingling jolts of pleasure radiating outward to the tips of her limbs. At last, she couldn't stand another second without having him filling her. Clawing at his back, she urged him to bring himself over her, and in the next moment he was there. She wrapped her legs around him and his hard shaft speared down into her. He reared and plunged and a cascade of thrills fluttered within until she felt herself so filled with the ecstasy that it could no longer be contained within her. She clung to him as though to keep herself from flying apart. And then the explosion came, one after another, and, with her eyes closed, she felt herself rocketing away, out of here and now into some eternal boundless realm.

The rocket circled back to earth, she opened her eyes, and she was in his arms.

'How do you feel?' he said, his arms tightening around her.

'Almost whole.'

'Almost?'

'Keep trying. Maybe you'll get it right next time.'

They smiled at each other, and began again.

Later he telephoned from the house and arranged for a camera crew from a Rapid City network affiliate to meet them at the reservation settlement of Upper Horse Jaw.

They were there at mid-afternoon, and he had the cameraman take general footage of the community, then did random interviews, going into local stores and knocking on doors of the small houses to ask residents if they were aware of increasing health problems, and record their reactions when he informed them of the probable cause. Watching him at work, Tay saw the smooth professionalism Neil combined with sincere compassion. In momentary flashes, she would recall the lovemaking that had ended only hours before, and a rush of anticipation would overtake her for the next time they would be alone together.

Yet she kept remembering that every time he'd spoken of love, she'd felt impatient to shift away from the subject. It puzzled her. She couldn't imagine wanting anyone else, still she hadn't been ready to promise her heart.

They went at last to the clinic where Celeste Stillwater

worked. A husky broad-faced woman wearing a simple cotton dress she had sewn for herself, Celeste waited to greet them at the entrance to the flat-roofed wooden building. Newer and smaller than the clinic at Rosebud, inside there was only a single examining-room, a dispensary, and an infirmary with a dozen beds. As they entered the infirmary, Celeste explained that serious but curable cases were sent to the *wasicun* hospitals. Patients kept here were either those that could be treated and released easily and quickly – or the terminally ill, who wished to die on the reservation and rejected heroic life-extending measures. Lately the place had virtually become a hospice, all beds presently occupied by terminal cases.

Tay tried to hide her shock when she followed Celeste into the ward and saw that, of the dozen patients, only two were elderly. The rest were children, teenagers, or young men and women in their twenties. Celeste said that they had all been consulted about admitting the television crew, and had readily agreed once they understood the issue.

Neil made the rounds, trailed by a camera, and spoke with the young patients, asking the history of their illness, where they lived in relation to the stream that ran from the dumping ground onto their reservation, eliciting stories of their swimming in the poisoned water. Despite their grave condition, the young people participated eagerly.

Then Tay noticed one young boy lying face to the wall in a corner bed. Taking the cue that he didn't want to be disturbed, Neil circled past that bed without stopping.

Tay asked Celeste about the patient and was told his name was Jimmie Rae Niquant, and he had been at the clinic several weeks, diagnosed with progressive cancer of the spine. He was twelve years old, one of several children born out of wedlock by different men his mother had slept with before she had died of alcohol poisoning four years ago. Jimmie had been raised subsequently by an older half-sister, Celeste said, but the half-sister had several small children of her own, and after Jimmie had become ill she had developed some superstitious belief that *wanagi* were to blame for his illness, and the bad spirits might be passed on to her own children if the boy were not kept at a distance. In all his time here, he had received not a single visitor.

'Like most kids, Jimmie has an easier time believing in evil ghosts than in malignant cells. He believes the spirits have cursed him, and he's sure he must have done something to deserve it – doesn't blame the half-sister at all for not coming. But he can't figure out what it is he did wrong. He was the one kid who didn't want to get involved in these interviews because he thought it might make the *wanagi* madder, and they'd make his pain worse.'

Tay studied the small figure hiding in the bed. 'Would it be all right if I talk to him?'

'You can try,' Celeste said, 'but he's pretty closed off. I've been thinking, in fact, this probably isn't the best place for him, that he should be somewhere he could also get psychological counseling.'

'You mean a *wasicun* hospital,' Tay said.

Celeste nodded.

'Maybe not,' Tay said. 'They know nothing there about how to get rid of *wanagi*.'

While Neil continued his interviews at the other end of the ward, Tay went to the boy's bed. She spoke his name and asked if he would talk to her, but he continued to lie motionless, facing the wall. She lowered herself to the bed, still he didn't react at all. Tay wished now that she knew some of Nellie Blue Snow's ceremonial magic. Certainly a part of his sickness, the part that had so crippled his will he thought himself undeserving of attention and love, came from his traditional beliefs. With tradition, there could be at least a cure for his mind.

Ignorant of the true magic, however, all she could do was invent her own. In a soft steady voice, Tay told the boy that the spirits who had caused his illness had gone seeking bad people who deserved to be punished, but had gotten lost and had entered his body by mistake. They would only stay as long as he thought he deserved them, but if he trusted in his own goodness, then they would realize they were in the wrong place and leave.

The child gave no sign that he had heard, but Tay could see over his shoulder that he was awake. So she continued her 'ceremony'. There was a chant, she told the boy, that would help the spirits to flee, if only he kept telling them he did not deserve them and they must leave. Reaching into her memory, she began softly singing a chant Abel had sung to her many times when she was young – something passed down from his own father, the *yuwipi* man, to keep bad spirits away. While she sang, the boy rolled over and looked up at her with luminous dark eyes. Even though weight loss had sculpted the bones in sharp relief, he had a beautiful face. Tay was moved to put her hand to his cheek, and he pressed into it, as though starved for any consoling touch.

'Jimmie,' she said when she finished the chant, 'you don't deserve to be sick, or to be left alone. Believe that.'

His black eyes stared back with penetrating directness. 'Will you come again?' he said.

He was asking for proof that he did not deserve to be left alone, she realized. 'Yes,' she said at once. 'Very soon.' How much time did he have?

She was aware of the bright camera lights being switched off at the far end of the ward and Neil finished his interview. She saw him look curiously in her direction, and begin to lead the camera crew toward her. She stood quickly, anxious to save the vulnerable boy from being disturbed. 'I'll be back to see you, Jimmie,' she said before intercepting Neil. 'I promise.'

To herself she added something to the promise. Next time, she would come better prepared to do battle with the *wanagi*. Nellie would surely give her the weapons.

26

With proof in hand, and the moving filmed record of those who were suffering the effects of the dumping, Neil was impatient to broadcast his story. But he called the producer of his evening news program, and said he'd be delayed a day in bringing all the taped and written material back to Los Angeles. He wanted one more night with Tay.

They ate at the round oak table in the parlor of the ranch house. Outside the sun slid down slowly over the horizon, burnishing the river to flaming gold. Tay had prepared a simple supper of fresh greens and vegetables they had bought at a roadside market, and Neil had opened a bottle of California Chardonnay from a basement stock. From the presence of the wine, Tay realized that the ranch had not gone completely unused. It was a romantic spot. Neil had no doubt visited from time to time, bringing along the occasional woman.

Over dinner, Neil talked excitedly about what they had accomplished during the day. He felt certain the mining company would be forced to end its lethal practices once they were publicly exposed. 'And you get a lot of the credit,' he said, raising his wine glass to her. 'I talked about you to my news producer. I've got some real clout now, so he didn't argue when I made a request – to start you right away in a training program. I know you've got the stuff, Tay, you could be a terrific on the air. Go through the program, I can have you reporting within a few months. As for a roof over your head, I'd like you to move in with me. Or if you have any doubts about that kind of arrangement . . . well, I know it's fast, but as soon as you're ready – next week, next month, next year, I'd like—' He stopped short. 'Hey, let me get this right. I've never done it before, but I'm pretty sure I know the routine.' His voice softened. 'Tay . . . Tayhcawin, will you marry me?'

She had seen it coming, but his momentum was too great to stop. As he gazed at her expectantly, she found it hard to reply at all. No one else in the world was as important to her, she realized. Yet there were mysterious forces pulling her in other directions.

The hopeful light in his eyes dimmed. 'Too fast, huh? I told you I'm new at the proposal game, but even a novice knows it means trouble when an answer takes this long . . .'

She groped for the words. 'Neil . . . I wish I could say yes . . .'

'It's your wish to grant, isn't it?' There was a touch of irritation, as though she was letting him down easy with a mere excuse.

'I've always thought it should be,' she said. 'But something happened today that changed my mind.'

She described her encounter with the boy at the clinic, and the promise she'd made to return. It might have been dismissed as no more than a charitable gesture, a sentimental impulse. Except as soon as it happened, she had experienced a certain inevitability in the promise, and recognized it was part of a context that included her visit to Nellie, the old woman's prediction, even the blood relationship to a medicine man in a former generation.

Neil listened patiently through her explanation. 'Look, I

can understand your desire to help the people here,' he said then. 'I want to do that, too – that's what this story is all about. Being a friend to this boy, not letting him die alone, that's a beautiful thing to do.' He leaned across the table, and covered her hand with his. 'But giving up everything else to go back to Rosebud and – what? – study to become a medicine woman? Even if that was your lifelong ambition, Tay – if the idea hadn't popped into your head from nowhere – I'd tell you it makes no sense at all. But especially when it means keeping us apart.'

His intolerance for her aspirations could have bothered her, instead she felt only sympathy for him. 'I don't blame you for not understanding this,' she said. 'Three days ago, when Nellie told me I'd come back to her, it sounded as crazy to me as I must sound to you. What's happened between us makes it even stranger to find myself doing this turnaround. But . . . suddenly I need more than anything to be part of making sure that the beliefs these people have don't get lost. That by itself will be strong medicine. For them, and for me.'

He weighed it silently for a moment. 'You're sure it's not because you're running away? You said you were afraid . . .'

'I'm not anymore. I feel stronger, surer. And I owe that to you. Being loved cleared away some of the fog about who I am and where I belong.'

His face worked through a series of expressions as he engaged in an inner debate and came to its end. 'All right. Do what you feel you have to do,' he said at last. 'It can't hurt to give ourselves time. I've got this place, I can visit often. Maybe after you've been here awhile, you'll want to come to me.'

Gratefully, she seized his hands in hers.

Through the window, they could see the last faint pink and orange tinges of a spring sunset fading from the horizon.

'It's so lovely here,' she said. 'I'm glad you've been able to keep it in the family.'

He smiled, understanding. It was the Sioux – her people –

367

who had tried a long time ago to wrest it away.

When he stood, she rose with him, her hands still clasping his. They kissed for a long time in the dark, then they went upstairs. Again, she led the way.

When Tay went back to Nellie Blue Snow, it was not with any belief that she was actually fulfilling a predestined mission to replace the medicine woman. She submitted herself to the experience in much the same spirit as an anthropologist would welcome the chance to record and preserve the customs of an endangered culture. Beyond that, she felt that the pledge given to a lonely dying boy in a moment of overflowing emotion must be honored. She wanted to ease the final days of Jimmie Rae Niquant. Considering his own superstitious belief in the evil spirits inhabiting his body, she believed it would be most meaningful to return to him with a greater knowledge of the ceremonies Nellie could teach her.

To Tay's amazement, when she told Nellie about the boy, the medicine woman said she would make a trip to the Standing Rock clinic to perform a healing ceremony herself.

'But I thought you stopped doing your medicine,' Tay said.

'As long as you are beside me, Tayhcawin, I shall find the strength to go on. Because your learning can only be done by watching and listening and following when I am at work.'

At Nellie's insistence, however, they did not go back immediately to see the boy. Tay was unhappy about the delay – time could not be squandered, Jimmie's illness was terminal – but Nellie was adamant: if her visit was to be fruitful, there were other tasks to be done first.

For the next five days, the old woman led Tay on a meandering hike through miles of open land around her home. They took with them bedrolls, and some bread and beef jerky and *pejuta sapa* – 'black medicine' as Nellie called coffee. At night they slept wherever their roaming had taken them by sundown. During the day, they moved very slowly, not only because of Nellie's advanced age, but because the medicine woman stopped constantly – often every few yards – to educate Tay about the natural medicines that grew everywhere. Hour after hour was filled with Nellie pointing out grasses and flowers, digging up shrubs to display the roots, and showing Tay how to cut a slice from the core of this root or remove the pollen from the heart of that flower to use for making infusions and salves that could cure or alleviate one ailment or another. Many animal substances also had medicinal effects: Nellie mentioned things as odd as the slime from a young frog's back, and the urine of the wolf. She paused to pick up stray bird feathers, or the dried skins of snakes that had been shed, or other cast-off animal matter. These she placed, along with many plant samples, into several pouches that were sewn to the front of her buckskin skirt.

The old woman's knowledge of the cures to be harvested out of nature seemed endless. For almost every sickness, she told Tay, a medicine had been supplied by Unci – 'grandmother earth'. The only things Unci did not know how to cure were illnesses man had 'invented' by his own carelessness and disrespect. Yet for all Nellie's familiarity with hundreds of useful plants, she could supply the actual names of no more than a handful. The rest she was able to identify only by sight, and her way of educating Tay about them was simply to point them out while explaining their uses, and the way they should be prepared and applied. She also needed to lead Tay to the places where the rarer plants grew, often just tiny patches of them. So the long hike was a necessary part of the teaching. Indeed, Tay realized, many such walking trips would be necessary before Tay could absorb Nellie's vast store of knowledge. Even though Nellie walked very short distances at a time, and never complained of being tired, the hikes that would be an essential part of Tay's education had to be incredibly taxing for a woman of Nellie's years. Tay understood at last what Nellie had meant when she said she was saving her strength to pass along her knowledge.

To limit the need for covering the same territory more than once, Tay wanted to bring a notebook to record the information for future reference. Nellie would not permit it. The medicine way, she said, had always been passed along by tongue from one practitioner to the next; it was forbidden for the ancient wisdom to be written down, and those who wrote it down to sell, she pronounced 'phonies'. The rule was more important than ever, she explained.

'If the *wasicuns* understood the value of these plants,' she said, 'they would harvest them all for themselves – just as they have taken everything else.'

On the day after they returned from the first five-day hike, Tay drove Nellie to the clinic at Standing Rock. They brought with them some of the nameless medicines freshly harvested from the land. Tay went alone first to Jimmy Rae Niquant and explained that she had brought a medicine woman to chase the bad spirits from his body.

As the sun set, Nellie arrived at the boy's bedside wrapped in her painted elkhide robe. She brought with her the long feather fan, composed for this ceremony of hawk feathers for doctoring, magpie feathers to give understanding, and the feathers of small waterbirds that, said Nellie, helped to take songs out of the air. No lights were on, the only illumination came from two of Nellie's home-made candles. The other patients in the darkened dormitory watched reverently as Jimmie lay wide-eyed against his pillows while the old medicine woman tied pouches of tobacco to the corners of his bed, smudged his forehead with the ashes of burned cedar and sage, fed him some powdered herbs, and then played a long shrill note on her eagle-bone whistle. At last, while Tay sat cross-legged in a corner and drummed on a tom-tom the soft steady rhythm she had learned long ago from her father, Nellie began to chant.

She sang quietly at first, but gradually her voice rose, and the sounds emerging from her throat became quicker, breathier, turning into panting, howling cries. As she sang, she moved back and forth beside the bed waving her feather fan, and in this, too, she grew steadily more vigorous, until she was doing a kind of hopping whirling dance. As the shadowy figure spun through the dim light, it was impossible to remember that this was a very old woman. Her voice rang out with all the power of youth; she was transformed.

Nellie chanted until the last glow of dusk was gone from the night sky visible through the windows. Then she ended her chant and walked straight out of the dormitory.

Left behind, confounded by Nellie's abrupt departure, Tay was uncertain of what to do next. Celeste Stillwater turned on a few of the night-lights and came over to Tay. When they leaned over Jimmie's bed, they saw that the boy was asleep.

'At least it relaxed him,' Tay said. The result of Nellie's theatrics seemed anti-climactic to Tay. Though what had she imagined would happen? That the boy would rise from his bed, miraculously cured?

'It was just what he needed, I'm sure,' Celeste said. 'Someone caring, his own people. A cure was never possible. I am grateful to the medicine woman, and to you, Tayhcawin.'

When she walked out of the clinic, Tay found Nellie sitting in the pick-up truck borrowed from Kate for the trip. The old woman wanted to return to the Rosebud reservation that night. On the drive, she sat silent, cocooned in a blanket, unresponsive to all Tay's attempts at conversation.

They had been traveling for hours on the moonlit ribbon of highway, a country music station playing softly on the radio, when Nellie spoke up.

'There was no *wanagi*.'

Tay was slightly startled; she had thought Nellie was sleeping. Switching off the radio, she said, 'I know, Nellie. Jimmie is very ill.'

'There were no spirits at all, Tayhcawin.'

'None, I know,' Tay agreed softly. She had explained about Jimmie's illness, but the old woman was apparently having a lapse.

But then Nellie said, 'You have told me the boy is dying. This cannot be so. When the young are so sick, there are spirits around them, waiting to guide them. Always. And there were none. I gave my call to the spirits, and there was no answer. I searched the shadows and saw nothing. If the spirits are not there, this boy cannot be dying. I tell you he has no disease, surely nothing so strong and terrible it will kill him.'

'But he does, Nellie – he has cancer of the spine.'

'Heed me, *Takoja*,' Nellie said sharply – she had taken to addressing Tay as 'granddaughter'. 'A hundred *wasicun* doctors may say he is dying, but this does not make it so. The spirits are not waiting to welcome this boy.' The old woman pulled her blanket close around her, and pulled her head down like a turtle retreating into its shell. She did not speak again on the drive.

The next morning, Tay called Celeste Stillwater and told her about the conversation. The nurse said that she had reviewed Jimmie's medical records, and the opinions were unanimous and unequivocal. The boy's chronic pain and paralysis of one leg were also consistent with the diagnosis.

'How did he react to Nellie's visit?' Tay asked. 'Does he seem any different?'

'He does seem happier – sitting up, talking with the others, not just lying around in a funk. That would be a natural reaction to all the attention. Having a medicine woman come and dance just for him made Jimmie a kind of a celebrity.'

'Do me a favor, Celeste,' Tay said. 'It may lead to nothing . . . but can you get a specialist to re-examine Jimmie?'

The nurse sounded dubious. 'He'd have to go to Rapid City, and have all the tests again, and the costs for that are very high and—'

'—and he's just an Indian kid and a charity case,' Tay put in hotly, 'so nobody gives a damn. But if there's even a small chance he can be helped, he ought to be seen again!'

'Tay . . . what can I tell the hospital when I say the diagnosis is in doubt? That an old Sioux medicine woman couldn't get the spirits to speak to her?'

'Yes, damn it,' Tay replied, dismayed to hear the hint of ridicule coming even from the Indian nurse, 'you tell them exactly that. And if it isn't good enough, tell them this isn't a charity patient – I'll pay whatever it costs.' For all she knew, it would take all the money she still had, savings left from her work at Hartleigh Mining. But there could be no better cause.

It took dozens of phone calls, Tay cajoling and pleading with doctors who repeated with smooth certainty that the records left no doubt. But at last she prevailed in finding a man who ordered new tests. Tay drove Jimmie to Rapid City herself and stayed over for the three days he was in hospital.

When the new tests came back, the pain and paralysis afflicting the patient was now judged to result from an unusual calcium growth on a vertebra pressing on the spinal cord. Nothing to do with a malignant growth.

No one was able to provide a satisfactory explanation for the changed opinion. Perhaps X-rays and blood tests had gotten mixed up, or were carelessly analyzed the first time. It was possible, too, that the woman burdened with raising Jimmie along with her own brood after his mother's death was all too quick to believe the boy could be sent away to die, had even doctored records or misreported symptoms. Whatever the reason, the first diagnosis had been an error . . . and Nellie Blue Snow had been the first one to realize it.

Mortified by the mistake, the doctors in Rapid City operated on Jimmie Rae Niquant free of charge. He emerged from the surgery free of his pain and paralysis, and went to live with a different set of his mother's relatives.

Tay continued her apprenticeship with a strengthened commitment to learn everything Nellie could teach. She no longer regarded the medicine woman's wisdom as merely the folk customs of a culture worth preserving. Nellie was the keeper of a treasure that could be vital to the survival of their people.

And she herself, Tay accepted now, had been chosen to serve as the keeper when Nellie went to the spirits.

BOOK IV

Cante Ishta
Eye of the Heart

27

The Time of Grass Appearing – 1983

For the first two years Tay was back on the reservation, Neil continued coming to his South Dakota ranch weekends and whatever holidays he was given from anchoring the evening news. Whenever he was there, Tay left the rez to stay with him. They enjoyed their time together, doing the homey things any established couple would do – decorating and restoring the ranch house, putting in a garden, riding the land, quiet Sundays when he served her breakfast in bed. And making love. On the mornings when they parted to return to their separate lives, the goodbyes were wrenching, eased only by the knowledge they would be together again.

Neil remained tolerant of Tay's decision to stay at Rosebud and study 'the medicine way' though from the first he was not so awestruck by Nellie's feat with Jimmie Rae Niquant as Tay had been. 'Poor diagnoses are done all the time,' he had observed. 'There are all too many quacks who make these mistakes. It's not a miracle when a second opinion turns things around. That's exactly why people get second opinions.'

'But Nellie *knew* at once,' Tay countered. 'Without X-rays or blood tests or even taking a pulse . . .'

'Yes, because she's gifted and experienced, and she's seen

377

thousands of suffering people in her time, and this boy just didn't have the look of someone so sick and doomed. But you'll never get me to believe she realized the truth simply because she didn't see the usual rush-hour crowd of ghosts waiting around the bed for Jimmie to die.'

In the end, they agreed to disagree on how magical it was, and Neil went on quietly accepting Tay's desire to stay on the rez.

As time went on, Tay witnessed many more amazing successes of Nellie's – none of them miracle cures, but ceremonies performed, or medicines administered that strikingly improved the condition of people suffering from asthma and arthritis, eliminated the pain of cancer patients, or arrested progressive blindness. Several women, infertile for many years, conceived after they or their husbands visited the medicine woman. A young Indian man told by *wasicun* doctors he was suffering the wasting effects of multiple sclerosis started to recover strength and mobility after adhering strictly to a diet Nellie prescribed.

When Tay told these stories to Neil he expressed admiration for the old medicine woman, but he also said openly that nothing she did could not be done by a conventional doctor.

It was not, after all, Tay's study of Indian medicine that made it easy for him to accept her staying on the rez. In the two years since his series of broadcasts on the nuclear dumping, the mining company had done nothing but stonewall its critics while continuing the practice unchanged. Dedicated to ending the health hazard, Tay had become a leader in organizing demonstrations – work stoppages by Indian mineworkers, and rallies of the growing number of people bearing illnesses traceable to the nuclear waste.

Because she was highly photogenic, and a renegade from the Hartleigh family, the media often covered Tay's activities, and she was featured as spokesperson for the Indian position.

The coverage brought her a degree of national prominence. Neil himself was ordered by his producer on a routine assignment to interview 'that gorgeous Indian who's stirring things up in the badlands'. He and Tay had conducted their romance so privately, it had remained a secret from his employers, and he carried out the interview as if he and Tay were strangers, happy to give her the public forum to present her cause.

For all Tay's efforts, however, Bren went on running Hartleigh Mining as she pleased. With profits rising steadily, she had the full support of her board – as well as the encouragement of her contacts in Washington. Since becoming President, Ronald Reagan had stated that the Soviet Union was 'the Evil Empire', and the United States must not fail to win the arms race. Bren felt no pressure to ease back on the production of uranium. In this national mood, Neil decided at last, there was little Tay could do to affect the company's policies.

'How much longer can we go on like this?' he asked as she drove him to the Rapid City airport one Sunday evening. By now she had bought herself a used pick-up truck.

'We could stay together starting tomorrow,' she said, 'if you're ready to take up ranching.'

'Or if you'd come back to LA with me.'

'My life is here,' she said evenly.

After a silence, he said, 'Where's it leading for you, Tay? Your work for Indian rights is admirable, but it hasn't changed a thing. As for being a medicine woman, Nellie's still going strong, doing it all herself again—'

'Watching her is how I learn.'

'But from what you told me last night, even when she dies, you'll have to wait years to pick up where she leaves off.'

He was referring to a fact Tay had learned not long after she had begun studying with Nellie, yet had never thought to mention to Neil until yesterday: in the practice of Indian medicine, it was tabu for a woman to participate or be present at any ceremony during her 'moon-time'. A menstruating woman was believed to be possessed of an energy that would overpower any other magic, render it impotent. The subject had arisen with Neil because last night was one of those rare occasions Tay had not wanted to make love, and when she explained, it had led to talking about the Indian belief. Tay had then shared with Neil something Nellie had clarified more recently. Because of the prohibition on women in their moon-time participating in any ceremonies, it was only after she had gone through menopause that a female member of a tribe could become a true medicine woman. Neil had quietly observed that this meant Tay was pursuing an ambition she might not realize for another thirty years. Last night she had met his observation with a lighthearted joke – 'So I'll work around it' – and the subject had been dropped. But it was obvious now that Neil hadn't stopped thinking about it.

'I've tried to be supportive of everything you're doing,' he went on, 'because I'm in love with you, Tay, and I don't want to lose you. But it's getting tougher. If your life here is just leading up to a long wait until you can really become the genuine article . . . well, forgive me, but I can't see the logic of keeping us on hold.'

'I want to be with you as much as I can,' Tay said. 'But my ambitions are no less important than yours, and I'm not waiting at all to realize them. I'm helping people right now. And whenever I have to, I'll go on without Nellie – because I may be the only one who knows how, even if I can't meet every . . . job requirement.'

'Job,' Neil echoed in a tone of commiseration. 'Tay, have you earned a penny in the past year? I offered you a real job once. But here . . . I'm always worried about the way you live – whether you have enough to eat, if you're warm enough sleeping in that old trailer of Nellie's. You don't have to live this way.'

'I don't have to,' she said sharply, 'I *want* to. And you don't have to worry about me. I've still got some money of my own. The important thing is that when I lived in an ivory tower, slept on silk, wore it damn near every day and drove a car that cost as much as a nice house, I was plain miserable. Here I'm happy, Neil. I feel good. I love you . . . but I also love what I'm doing. Don't make me choose between the two.'

The argument died out when they arrived at the airport. Neil had to run to catch his plane, so they patched things up hastily rather than nurse grievances while apart.

During the week, Neil flew east to be on the scene for a space-shuttle launching, and then he stayed in Washington for a few days. As the highest-rated anchorman in Reagan's home state, he had extra clout with the White House and was able to get one-on-one interviews for his show with both the President and Nancy.

When Neil returned after his absence, he and Tay were hungry for each other again. They spent all of Saturday in bed, and through Sunday they worked determinedly to keep any harsh word or thought from spoiling the mood.

But the satisfactions of being together made it always more difficult for Neil to accept the compromise of constant separations. Tay felt an ultimatum from him was inevitable – make her life with him completely, or accept an end to their romance. How would she respond? She wasn't sure she wanted to lose him, yet she couldn't bring herself to abandon her tribe – all her people – when their problems were only becoming more desperate.

The clinic at Standing Rock was now receiving twice the number of patients with conditions suspected of being related to the Victory Four dump site as it had two years earlier.

'This can't go on,' Celeste Stillwater cried miserably in a

phone call to Tay. 'If we don't make the mining company stop, the sickness will be so deep in our blood and bones our people will still be dying generations from now.'

'I know,' Tay said. 'But we still haven't managed to prove our problems come from what they're doing. And all the politicians are on their side.'

'Yes,' Celeste agreed. 'The bastards let it go on because they don't care if we die. They *want* us all to die. That will be the end of their Indian "problem".'

Each time Tay had talked to Celeste lately she could hear the pitch of despondency coming through more achingly in her friend's voice. Year after year, the Indian nurse had dealt with terminal cases believed to stem from the radioactive ground and water to which her patients had been exposed. For every Jimmie Niquant, there were a dozen others whose cancers were real and deadly. Celeste Stillwater seemed to take each death as a personal failure.

'We'll stop them,' Tay said. 'I know it's hard for you, Celeste. But don't give up hope. We'll find a way . . .'

'They've also got to pay,' Celeste said. 'They should suffer, too, for what they've done.'

'We can think about that sort of thing later,' Tay said, assuming her friend was talking about suing for damages. 'What matters now isn't hurting anyone else as much as helping our own people.'

'Yes, Tay, I know you're right. I shouldn't think of hurting anyone else.'

There was a slightly odd note in the remark, Tay realized now, as though Celeste was agreeing to abandon some notion she'd been harboring of extracting vengeance. But Tay didn't pursue it. Whatever the idea was, at least it had been dropped.

The conversation ended with Tay promising she would find a way to turn up the pressure on the company.

Then next day, she called the HMC offices in San Francisco.

Bren's secretary recognized Tay's voice at once, and told her Bren was out and not expected back for the day. Still, Tay tried again later. The secretary was more truthful on the second call. 'I'm sorry, Miss Hartleigh,' she said, 'my instructions are very clear. I'm not to put you through. Not ever.'

The servants who answered the phone at Bren's mansion had the same message. She should have expected it, Tay knew, after the past years of pitting herself against the company. But she had hoped there might be some personal plea that would crack through Bren's indifference.

Should she call Cori? No, Cori was too weak to take on Bren.

Something more had to be done, though. Something that mobilized more than just the Indians against the company. Something that made people everywhere notice and care.

Celeste Stillwater obviously perceived the same need. The day after her phone conversation with Tay she went to her nursing job as usual. Like most Indians involved with health care on the reservations, she worked long hours to meet the demands of under-staffed, ill-equipped facilities overloaded with cases. At times, a nurse on the rez could work thirty-six hours straight. Celeste did only a 'short' shift, however, arriving at six a.m. and leaving twelve hours later when another nurse arrived to take the night shift. During her shift today, an eight-year-old girl had died of leukemia.

From the Standing Rock clinic, Celeste drove home and picked up a five-gallon jerry-can with only a small amount of gasoline sloshing in the bottom. She went next to the rez store and filled the can to the top with gasoline – enough, she thought, to take her on a very long trip. While at the store, she also made two phone calls. One was to the nearest *wasicun* newspaper, the other to the nearest television station. She told them both about the journey she planned, and explained her reasons.

At sunset Celeste arrived at her destination. She drove her battered Ford pick-up straight up to the chained-metal gates leading into the Hartleigh dump site and got out. Then she walked around to the back of the truck, and lifted out the jerry-can of gasoline. The reporter from the local newspaper had already gotten there, also the television camera crew. They watched – and filmed – as Celeste Stillwater poured out the five gallons of gasoline from the jerry-can, drenching herself completely, then sat down on the ground in front of the gates. They stood filming, and making their notes, as she removed a box of kitchen matches from her pocket and sang a ceremonial chant. Later they would explain that they were afraid to intervene, that they could only hope to stop her by persuasion, and to get near her would have endangered their own lives. But Celeste did not seem to hear any attempts to dissuade her, if they were even made. At the end of her chant, she struck a match and exploded into a human torch.

The camera crew kept their lens trained on the immolation until the burning figure was only a stiff black form that toppled over and broke into pieces.

'You've got to get that tape,' Tay pleaded in her call to Neil the next morning. 'Get it and run it. There's been nothing on the news but a few lines. "A disturbed Indian woman burned herself to death . . ." They don't say where, or why – what she was disturbed about! Neil, she died for nothing, unless—'

'Tay, calm down. I've seen the tape. So have the news directors at this station and every other station around the country. We can't run it. It's just too . . . too damn hard to look at, that's all. Too gruesome.'

Tay was despondent herself in the wake of her friend's death, not only because of the loss and the horror, but the way it had been discounted. A front-page story in the local newspaper, but elsewhere it was moved to the inside pages. A mention on local television, but no attention from the networks.

'Neil,' Tay said reasonably, 'you knew this woman. She wasn't crazy; she was just too tired to think straight, and too miserable about what she was forced to deal with every day, and she was sure she was going to a better world. But she died for a *reason*. To wake people up! Sure, it's a horrible thing to see – unforgettable. But that's the point.'

'Darling, I wish I could help. You know how much this story has always meant to me. But there are broadcasting standards, and these images go too far beyond the bounds. It's not up to me, anyway. Even if I was ready to run the tape, there are half a dozen other hands on the switch who'd keep it off.'

Tay had no more words. Desperate as Celeste's act had been there was an aspect of heroism to it, a touch of that wild bravery in the Indian character that sought pain as proof of strength, and believed that to die a warrior was to insure immortality. But it couldn't be seen that way by Neil or by any so-called civilized man. The news, the reporting of truth, had to be sanitized, cleaned up to make it fit within the bounds.

'Tay . . . ? You still there?'

Was she here still – for him?

'Tay, I'll be at the ranch soon. We'll talk then. I . . . I know how hard this is for you. But it shouldn't be something that comes between us. Tay . . .'

'No, it shouldn't,' she said quietly.

But long after they had said goodbye, she was still feeling that it had.

28

In the days that followed Celeste Stillwater's desperate end, Tay felt herself sinking into a numbing lethargic hopelessness, mourning not only for a lost friend, but for the lost dream of picking up where Abel had left off, helping her people to recover some measure of their lost pride and power. It depressed Tay to see that so few of Celeste's tribe came to her burial ceremony. The nurse's sacrifice was not regarded as an act of bravery, but as a public embarrassment, encouraging the *wasicuns* to regard all Indians as crazy savages who were more to blame for their own tragedies than anyone else.

The event had also crystalized the crisis in Tay's relationship with Neil. Their interests were too far apart; the only way she could make her life with him, was to cut loose from a part of her identity, and leave the battles behind. Neil seemed to be giving her room to make that decision. He had not come for Celeste's funeral ceremony, and the couple of times they had talked on the phone the conversations had been brief and awkward, small talk burdened by the unspoken weight of the things that were too painful or too risky to say.

At sunrise of a day just one week after Celeste's death, there was a knock at the door of Nellie's trailer. Tay rose at once from the sleeping-bag on the floor of the small lounge area built in to one end. It wasn't unusual for those who needed the medicine woman to come at all hours, though Nellie found it hard to rise early these days, and Tay dealt alone with those who came when Nellie was sleeping.

She opened the door of the trailer wrapped in a blanket to conceal her nakedness.

The sun breaking over the horizon shone straight through the door so that the figure in front of her was only a tall black outline against the glare. 'Yes, how can I help you?' Tay said – her customary greeting at the medicine woman's door.

'Actually,' the man said, 'I came to offer my help to you.'

'Oh? How?'

'My name is Gene Cheroux.'

Not the whole answer but enough, Tay decided. She stared, trying to make out more of the details of the man silhouetted against the new morning sky.

'May I come in?' he asked.

'Oh – yes. Please.' She led him into the small lounge area at the back where she slept, and explained that they must talk quietly so as not to disturb the woman sleeping at the front of the trailer.

Out of the glare, his tall, broad-shouldered form was seen to be dressed in a well-cut pin-striped gray flannel suit, worn with a black silk shirt open at the neck, revealing a silver and turquoise necklace resting on his chest. The next thing she noticed was his hair, a thick mass of fine gleaming silver pulled straight back, and gathered into a pony tail. The handsome face accentuated by this silver frame was creased only slightly at the edges of dark eyes and by smile-lines around the mouth, not the face of a man whose hair was silvered by age. The wide ring of silver metal that circled the pony tail was worked with Indian symbols, she saw, and he had the high cheek-bones and somewhat hawkish nose associated with noble Indian features. Yet his coloring seemed less like the reddish caste of the full-bloods than the ruddy tan of a *wasicun* who spent his days riding under the desert sun. And she'd never seen eyes like his before on an Indian, not black or brown, but an amazingly deep, dark green. Looking into them was like peering into the shady recesses of a wild, unspoiled forest.

Tay was suddenly acutely conscious of standing before him fresh out of bed wearing nothing but an old blanket. 'Do you mind waiting a minute?' she said. 'I'd like to dress before we talk.'

He graciously agreed and sat down. In the trailer's scaled-down furniture, he looked even larger and more impressive.

Tay hastily gathered some clothes and went into the trailer's tiny bathroom. While she dressed, she inventoried all that she'd heard about Gene Cheroux, and her amazement grew that he'd seemed so young – early forties at most – and that she'd never seen him before, even in a picture. In the past couple of years, Cheroux had built a reputation that had now reached near-legendary status among Indians who were politically aware. A Lakota Sioux from the Teton tribe, he was singular in the achievements he'd piled up since overcoming the many deprivations and shortcomings of a reservation upbringing. He had never known his father – his mother, whose name he had taken, had not known herself who it was among the many men she slept with in return for a few drinks. After his mother had died of alcohol poisoning, he had been raised by his mother's aunt in her *tipospaye*. Making the most of a remarkable athletic ability in football and track combined with a natural scholarship demonstrated in the rigorous learning program he had designed for himself – reading the classics and poetry, devouring every book he could find in the rez libraries, later hitch-hiking to work as a stockboy in a border-town bookstore to get free access to more knowledge – he had won a full scholarship to Princeton. When he'd gone on to Harvard Law on a special grant, it had meant passing up lucrative contracts being dangled by both professional football and major league baseball teams. Fresh out of Harvard, he'd clerked for a Supreme Court justice, then joined a white-shoe Wall Street law firm at a high salary, and resigned after three years to advise privately one of the new breed of merger buccaneers who were building instant fortunes. It had seemed he was on the same fast track of greed and opportunism when abruptly he had changed his course again. The way the legend went, he declared that he had now mined enough gold out of the white man's territory, so that he could afford to spend his time fulfilling a desire that had driven him since he'd begun ferociously learning, always planning to become a lawyer so he could use the law as a weapon to win back the land. Since then he had devoted himself to working on the case that had begun wending its way through the courts when he was still a boy – the Sioux claim, under an 1868 treaty with the US government reinforced by several later treaties, to own vast tracts of land that had since been taken from them. The claim had been dismissed, appealed, reversed, dismissed again, appealed again, upheld, revived on new findings, winding its way through level after level of the courts, and still a team of lawyers refused to give up. When Cheroux wasn't contributing his time to the team of lawyers representing the Sioux tribal councils, he did *pro bono* defense work, traveling all over the country to help Indians of any and all tribes. He covered the thousands of miles between his different cases in a jet plane he piloted himself. In the past two years he had won back valuable oil rights for Kiowas in Oklahoma, preserved fishing grounds for Passamaquoddies in Maine, and successfully sued so that Indians of several south-western tribes who claimed the use of peyote as a traditional part of their religious practice could not be charged with illegal use of drugs. He had also saved two Navajo men from being convicted of murder by demonstrating the evidence against them was forged by police, and in other separate trials he had won acquittals for Apache and a Tillamook and a Wyandot and a dozen others who were being unfairly prosecuted for robbery or murder – cases that others had called hopeless because the defendants were poor, and Indian.

And now he was here offering help. Yet Tay's reaction wasn't pure relief and gratitude. Two years ago, soon after reading about Cheroux in a newspaper article Kate had shown her, she had written the office he maintained in Washington asking for help in the fight against HMC. A brief letter had come back from a secretary saying that Mr Cheroux's schedule did not permit him to take on one more case at the time. Nothing more. It seemed to Tay that he might have judged this one unwinnable, and he didn't want to spoil his impressive record of always defeating the *wasicuns*. If he had changed his mind, of course she was glad. But she was still suspicious that there might be an element of grandstanding, choosing to join the fray when it was a safer bet.

She finished washing and dressing, brushed out her hair, and slipped on her beaded headband. Even before taking his measure, she found herself hoping she looked her best.

As she emerged, he stood to meet her. 'Forgive me for coming so early,' he said, 'but I have to be in Oregon later today. Since I was coming this way, I thought of stopping . . .'

He made it sound as if he had merely made a slight detour in a trip from his house to the store. But she guessed he'd probably been flying his plane across the country.

'That's very kind of you,' Tay said. 'I know how very busy you are.'

An edge had crept in. He smiled thinly to acknowledge it. 'You haven't forgotten that I refused you before, have you?' he said perceptively.

She shook her head. 'I was very disappointed. This seemed to be your kind of cause.'

They had been speaking in hushed voices not to disturb Nellie. He suggested now that they go outside where they could talk more easily.

The sun was up full over the horizon, and the last of the night's chill was off the land. They walked across Nellie's property, through the sage and rabbitbrush.

'You were right,' he resumed. 'This is my kind of cause. I looked into it when you asked before, and thought about joining in. But there are so many tribes who must fight for so many things in so many places, that if I give myself to this cause, some other one could be lost – one where there's nobody at all, nobody like you, to carry a banner. From what I'd heard about you, Miss Walks-Through-Fire, I believed you might succeed on your own. There's no strategy I could invent that could be as effective as you might be – especially if you could use your connection to the Hartleigh family. I hoped that would happen, while I went on working where there are people who are completely defenseless.'

What had changed his mind, of course, was the self-immolation of Celeste Stillwater. He had seen the small item last week on an inside page of the *Washington Post*.

'If things have become that bad,' he said, 'obviously you need some new ammunition.'

'The most powerful you can give me,' Tay admitted. 'My family connection isn't worth a damn. There's no love lost between my mother and me – if there was ever any love to begin with.'

What he was offering, Cheroux explained, was to begin a full legal offensive against Hartleigh Mining – suing the company for damage to the environment as well as a number of personal-damage suits based on the health problems of the most seriously affected Indians. 'You haven't been able to budge them with nothing more than humanitarian considerations, so we'll hit them where companies always feel it – in the pocket.' He would sue for a few hundred million dollars, he said, providing his own expertise without charge and personally bearing all the legal costs. 'I'm sorry,' he concluded, 'but I feel that's the most I can do.'

His apology confounded Tay. 'Nothing to be sorry about, Mr Cheroux. I know the record when you take on a case. This could make all the difference.'

'But it will take time, Miss Walks—'

'Tay,' she put in. 'Short for Tayhcawin.'

He paused to assess her. 'Young deer,' he said. 'A lovely name.' Then he returned to business. 'As I was saying, the legal fight I'm proposing could take a lot of time, Tay. When we bring cases like this at the lower level, they get appealed up to the highest courts. Don't forget, Hartleigh Mining is in business with the federal government.'

Yes, the miners always had been. That was why the Sioux had lost their lands. 'Maybe we'll get lucky,' Tay said. 'Anyway, getting you to join in is already a victory.'

He looked at her quizzically. A victory implied a fight.

'For Celeste,' she added.

They walked a while longer while he described in more detail the legal moves he planned to make. In view of the slow grinding of the legal wheel, he advised her to continue all her own efforts at the same time.

With their business done, she invited him to come back to the trailer for coffee, but he said he'd already stayed too long. He had filed a flight schedule that ought to be followed.

He climbed into his rented car for a trip back to the airport. As she said goodbye, Tay felt a sense of possibilities being cut short all too soon. She wanted to spend more time with him.

But she was content with the knowledge that they would have to see each other again now that they were fighting the same battle.

She stood watching until his car vanished over a ridge

and the tell-tale plume of dust had dissipated in the morning air.

The memory of the past hour seemed a surreal fantasy – walking beside him in the bright new day, an Indian warrior in a pin-striped suit who'd descended suddenly from the sky and vanished just as quickly. He could have been only a spirit in a dream.

She smiled at the thought. What interpretation, she wondered, would Nellie give to such a dream?

Pamela Hartleigh had died fifteen years too late. At the height of her reign over Nob Hill society, her funeral would have been a mob scene, attended by anyone in the city who mattered financially, politically, or socially. But she had died no longer able to remember her own name much less any of the names that once filled her engagement book, and the funeral cortège to the cemetery this sunny morning consisted of only three chauffeured limousines, each bearing one of her children. With Cori and Chet went their families; Bren, unmarried at the moment, rode alone.

At the large marble mausoleum where the casket was sealed into place beside G.D.'s, Pamela's children stood apart from each other as a minister intoned prayers. Communication between the sisters had completely broken down after Tay had left years ago. Cori blamed Bren for sending Tay away and cutting her off from the family.

'You want her so goddamn much, go after her,' Bren had goaded Cori in their last confrontation on the issue shortly after Tay's departure. 'I'll be damned if I ever will. Hell, she'd like to tear down everything I care about. And you think I should've let that ungrateful little bitch stay and work for me? She wasn't even mine to begin with. I took her in only as a favor to you.'

'No, Bren. Everything's business with you, never feelings.

394

You took Tay because that was the deal – my price to help you get control of the company.'

'Well, we all got what we paid for, didn't we? She was here more than long enough to know whether she'd ever fit in. And you had every chance to tell her the truth if you wanted.'

'You know I couldn't do that . . . for the same reason I can't go to her now.'

'Because you're afraid of losing Frank?' Bren said scornfully. 'He must be long past caring who fucked you twenty-five years ago. Matter of fact, it always looked to me like he had a soft spot for your pretty little Indian – maybe liked her even a little *too* much.'

Cori ignored Bren's vile insinuations. She had agonized endlessly over whether she might go to Tay and confess the truth. At this point, however, she would have to explain not only abandoning her in infancy, but the years in which she had allowed Bren to act as her stand-in, perpetuating the lie of not being Tay's mother. She had believed her reasons sound and unselfish. Wasn't Bren the better role model – strong, stable, successful, fearless? Cori couldn't have coped nearly as well with providing an example, helping Tay adjust to the white world she'd entered. Nor did she feel strong enough to stand up to the stress of a confession and a plea for forgiveness that Tay might reject. And there was no guarantee that Frank, kind as he was, wouldn't feel betrayed.

So she had left things as they were. Cori could not disagree, after all, with Tay's decision to return to her father's people. Because it was less painful not to have her daughter so close while being always untouchable, she had found the situation more bearable. In recent years Cori had even stopped hiding from the world. She decided to try teaching again, and though her applications for regular classroom situations never survived interviews at which her tremulous self-doubt was all too apparent, notices she tacked on school bulletin boards offering individual tutoring brought her a few private pupils each week. Feeling useful again, along with regular medication, kept her depression at bay most of the time. The rage Cori continued to feel toward Bren was also therapeutic. It felt right – felt *sane* – to be furious at Bren for banishing Tay. So she clung to her anger, refusing to speak to Bren even today.

The estrangement between Bren and her brother was more recent. Chet had resented Bren since she'd pushed him aside to seize control of the mining company, but for a long time he'd masked his feelings. The growth and success of HMC under Bren's guidance had made it impossible to argue with her leadership.

Ultimately, though, Chet could not choke down his disgust with the handling of the Victory Four issue. Two months ago, after that poor Indian woman had burned herself to death in front of the dump site, he had raised the subject at the next board meeting. 'I don't know how many of you are aware of it,' he told the board members, 'but the black-eye we're getting from bad publicity isn't the only upshot of that unfortunate incident. We've just had to respond to papers filed in the South Dakota courts by a very smart Indian lawyer. He instituted a class action suit against us on behalf of all the victims of our nuclear dumping – a suit for five hundred million dollars. In my opinion, we could lose. But even if we don't, the company suffers from being perceived as so insensitive.'

'I think everyone's well aware of what's happening,' Bren responded. 'I circulated a letter about this.'

Bren's cohorts nodded.

'And no one's worried?' Chet asked in amazement.

'Why should we worry?' said one man. 'We know about this man Cheroux. Good as he is, we have our own lawyers who are smarter. They'll keep these cases tied up in the courts for ten years.'

Chet surveyed the faces around the table looking smugly

back at him. 'For godssake, the point isn't whether we can use legal games to duck our responsibility. What we're doing is *wrong*! In the past, we didn't realize the serious effect it was having on the health of those Indians. But we can't pretend we don't know now.' He turned to Bren. 'If we go on putting nuclear waste into that land, Bren, it's nothing less than murder – premeditated destruction of people's health.'

Bren was unmoved. 'If it's murder, I've got no less an accomplice than the US government. They're our prime customer for nuclear material, and they're well aware processing creates . . . unpleasant biproducts. As long as they think it's all right to put them into the ground – our property, for that matter, no one else's – that's where it goes. As for what you call "evidence" we're hurting anybody, there isn't one iota of proof we've caused a single health problem.'

Strictly speaking, Bren was right: there was no mark on a malignant tumor or a leukemic blood cell to say who or what had made it cancerous. Bren was on even firmer ground in claiming the protection of the government. For the sake of national security, the government would support Hartleigh Mining in whatever it felt necessary to go on stockpiling nuclear weapons.

But Chet realized that Bren's attitude was formed less by concerns about national security than by a vendetta against Tay. It was Tay, after all, who had helped to expose Hartleigh's harmful practices, Tay organizing Indian protests at the Victory Four dump site. The more Bren saw the issue as a struggle of wills between herself and Tay, the more determined she was to overcome any challenge to running the company her way. Chet was reduced to sitting back and biding his time. In the meantime, he and Bren no longer spoke; all corporate business involving them was communicated by office memo.

But now their mother's death gave Chet hope Bren could finally be dislodged as head of the company.

As Cori stepped out of the mausoleum following the ceremony, her brother fell in beside her. They were alone on a walkway that led down a gentle slope between other tombs and memorial plantings of dogwood and flowering shrubs. Frank and the others had gone ahead to the car, Bren had already been driven away from the cemetery.

'We need to talk,' Chet said.

Cori looked at him questioningly. He was big, as G.D. had been, but he had always seemed less hard and threatening.

'Before the will is read,' he explained, 'I need to know where you stand on the company. I'm expecting mother's stock to be shared out equally between us. If you'll vote with me—'

'Oh, Chet, you and Bren will have to work it out. I can't deal with those things anymore.' She continued ahead.

Chet caught her arm. 'I need you to settle this one, Cori. Bren will hang onto the power unless you and I—'

'Don't drag me into this,' Cori said, pulling free. 'Please. I don't have the strength for a fight.' She was pleading as if her very life was at stake.

Chet paused, but he could not let this go. 'Cori, listen, if this was only about who runs the company, I'd lay low and try to organize a different way of working it out. But this is truly a matter of life and death. Bren's picked up right where G.D. left off, never caring a damn abut the people who live and work around the mines. She's just so twisted up by anger at her daughter, she doesn't care about doing what's right. But there are too many victims, Cori. You've got to help me end it.'

At the mention of Tay as Bren's daughter, Cori's concentration sharpened. She was reminded that her brother had never learned the true circumstances surrounding Tay's birth. At the time Cori had been banished by her father, Chet had been protected from knowing his sister was pregnant, allowed to think the rift with G.D. revolved around her desire to be independent of him. Later, when Tay had shown up at age seventeen, it had seemed entirely believable – and more in character – for Bren to have an illegitimate daughter abandoned at birth who now came seeking recognition.

'What has to end, Chet?' Cori said. Had he meant the feud between Bren and Tay, or all the pretenses?

Chet perceived her confusion. 'Haven't you been following the story on Victory Four?' he said.

It had been a long time since Cori paid any close attention to company business or even the news of the world. 'No. But it's Tay I want to hear about. Tell me about Tay!'

The intensity of her demand surprised Chet. He'd never observed any particular bonding between Cori and Bren's daughter. 'I'll tell you as much as I know, but it's all related to what's happening at the company . . .'

She listened intently as they stood in the shade of a white dogwood and he told her about HMC's disposal of radioactive waste products, the effect it was having on the people of Standing Rock, and the work Tay had been doing for the past four years to help the Sioux with their health problems and end the dumping.

'Yes, of course,' Cori said when he was done, 'it has to be stopped. I'll help in any way I can.'

Chet walked with her to the end of the path where their limousines waited. 'Thanks, Corker,' he said, embracing her. 'With the problems you've had the past few years, I know it takes guts for you to stand up to Bren. But I always thought you were a brave kid, more than you got credit for.'

Brave. Maybe she had been – once. When she had been called *ohitika win*. She only wished she could summon the courage – someday – to tell Tayhcawin how proud she was to be her mother.

29

Winter 1985

On the Thursday in November after Ronald Reagan's landslide re-election to the presidency, Neil arrived at his ranch for an extended weekend. In the last weeks of the campaign he had flown back and forth across country to cover personally the Reagan camp, and on election eve he'd been at Reagan's ranch in Santa Barbara to interview the President. Added to the traditional dusk-'til-dawn coverage on election day, the grind of the past month had left Neil feeling hollowed out, and he had begged his news producer for extra time off.

By this autumn, his romantic liaison with Tay had endured for more than four years but they had never spent more than a full week of living together, and that much only twice each year when he was given a furlough from the anchor desk. Several times, he had wangled assignments abroad on big stories – a Moscow summit, a Tokyo trade conference – and he had asked Tay to come with him. But she would not leave the reservation. Partly because of her work, but she was also plagued by an almost superstitious notion that if she allowed herself to stray again into the white world as she had before, she might not come back. And it was on the rez, more than any place else in the world, that she was needed. So it was only when Neil came to his ranch that they saw each other.

In the meantime, she had seen Gene Cheroux three more times when he came to South Dakota to make motions in the state courts connected to the suit he had launched against Hartleigh Mining. He was a dynamic presence, and she always hoped he would stay longer, that she would have the chance to know him better. But his visits were always short, a few hours at most, and their time together devoted mainly to talking about the case, reporting his progress or updating his own information. Explaining his hasty departures, he invariably told her that some other important case awaited his attention, and Tay had no doubt he was telling the truth. Yet she imagined he could make a little more space in his schedule if he wanted. She wondered if he thought she was targeting him as 'a catch', and he had stepped back to let her know a romance was not on the cards. She'd never heard or read anything about his personal life, but it wasn't unlikely that there was already a woman – or several. The next time she was with Gene, Tay thought, she ought to let Gene know she had her own romantic involvement, and all she desired from him was a closer friendship.

When she joined Neil at his ranch this time, Tay took great satisfaction in helping to restore him after the grueling schedule he'd just completed. She pampered and indulged him, making special meals, helping him unwind with long walks, giving him massages with the herbal muscle-relaxing oils Nellie had taught her to prepare. Even when they made love, she let him take it easy, undressing him, taking the lead herself, playing at being his loyal and willing concubine. Their first two days were idyllic, with none of the tensions that usually crept in as the time came closer for another parting.

On Sunday morning, while they were having breakfast in the parlor, the phone in the kitchen rang. Neil answered and stayed on for a few minutes, speaking in a voice too subdued for Tay to hear. When he hung up and returned to the oak table, he sank back into his chair heavily.

'Bad news?' she guessed.

'No. Good news,' he replied gravely. 'Very good.'

'Then you're the only man I know who opens a gift box and looks like he'd peeked into his best friend's coffin.'

'They want me to go to New York,' he said grimly. He was avoiding her eyes, staring out the window that overlooked the bend in the rushing river.

'That's not fair,' she sympathized, 'they've just brought you back from all that traveling for the campaign. And we were going to have a few more lovely days here—'

'Not now, not today,' he said. 'For good.'

The call had been from the president of the network to tell Neil he'd been chosen to take over as anchorman for the national evening news. One of the premier positions in television journalism, it carried an appropriately rich salary. But the broadcast originated in New York. Neil would have to move there.

'How soon?' Tay said. Her mood had deflated to match his. No need to ask if he'd accepted. Neil had been building to this since winning a scholarship to the University of Michigan and signing up for the college radio station.

'I'll have to leave in a week to help with the publicity. They want to give me a big build-up even before I go on the air.'

In the long pause that followed, their thoughts seemed to travel back and forth through the silence – angry, disappointed, loving outbursts jamming the air like the invisible radio waves of warring countries. Nothing was said, but the argument transpired anyway. Tay's failure to speak, to make an offer, was an answer in itself.

When Neil spoke again it was already to appeal a decision. 'I still don't understand it. I never will. If you love me, Tay, you should marry me. Be there in my life all the time, every day, every night, every minute – not just in my mind.' His hand shot across the table to seize hers. Looking at him through her own tears, she saw his eyes were also misty. His voice fell nearly to a whisper as he made his final appeal. 'Tay ... be mine. One hundred per cent.'

She knew he'd meant it only as a romantic plea, a fallback on the most hearts-and-flowers cliché. And yet the phrase 'be mine', with its connotations of surrender and ownership, incited her to remember the absolute core of what divided them. She sided with a people who had suffered because the 'tribe' to which he belonged simply assumed they were entitled to possess completely whatever they found and wanted. He seemed almost to be speaking out of that assumption now.

Slowly Tay shook her head. 'No,' she said, pride and regret mingling in her voice, 'I can't be yours ...'

They went on talking. They spoke of working it out. He assured her he would never sell the ranch, his family's heritage, and so he'd be coming back often. She told him she wasn't going anywhere, and she'd always be eager to see him.

As part of the valedictory to the wonderful feelings they had shared, they made love once more than night. And it was as tender, and torrid, and overwhelmingly passionate as it had ever been.

But they both realized there was a divide that could not be crossed.

It was two months into the new year before the children of Pamela Hartleigh were asked to come to the offices of the law firm that had represented the family's personal affairs for the past four generations to hear the reading of her will. There had been substantial confusion following her death because a number of conflicting documents had turned up, handwritten scrawls that appeared to have been written at times when the unfortunate woman's cognitive powers were already seriously impaired. The document finally judged to reflect her true last wishes went back to a time eleven years ago, soon after G.D. had died, and Pamela had already known she would be taking control of the estate.

Though Pamela had provided for her grandchildren and her son-in-law, Frank Patterson, of whom she was particularly fond, only the three immediate heirs were asked to be present today. They arrived separately and said nothing to each other as they entered the office of Gerald Marston, Pamela's personal attorney. Marston had no illusions about the state of relations between the three Hartleigh siblings, and he guessed the bequests he was about to reveal would do nothing to bring them together. He had set their chairs in a particularly wide arc in front of his desk, knowing it would be wise to have them well out of arm's reach of one another.

'I believe your mother has tried to be very fair and even-handed in assigning her world goods to the three of you,' Marston said when they were seated. 'I'm aware that relations between you three have been . . . strained recently, but I hope you can use your shared grief as a foundation on which to bring the family together again. It's obvious from what you're about to hear that your mother hoped family unity could be restored.'

Clearing his throat, the lawyer began to read through the clauses. As he had indicated, Pamela had taken the needs and personalities of all her children into account in making a fair distribution. The jewelry was given mainly to Bren, with a few special antique pieces put aside for Cori. Chet was compensated by receiving G.D.'s collection of western art and curios. The other valuable art and furniture was divided in thirds, as was cash and miscellaneous negotiables. As to the real estate, Bren received full title to the Nob Hill mansion she had already made her home, and Chet was given the New York apartment on Fifth Avenue – hardly ever used – and the beach home in Barbados, his favorite vacation spot. For her part, Cori was to have the Golden H Ranch in Jackson Hole, intact with furnishings and livestock, probably the most valuable single piece of real estate, though it had barely been used in recent years.

'This bequest is made,' Pamela had noted, 'in recognition of Corinne's particular appreciation for this part of the country, her fondness for horses, and for the culture of the west also enjoyed by my late husband. While my daughter's illness has made it impossible for her to spend time at the ranch in recent years, it is my hope that she may recover sufficiently to visit there frequently, and may even find in its tranquil, unspoiled serenity a place to rest and seek healing reunion. In the event she is unable to use it, or chooses not to, she is free to dispose the property as she wishes.'

Last to be read were the terms relating to the estate's major holding, Pamela's stock in Hartleigh Mining. As Chet had anticipated, this went in three equal parts to himself and his sisters.

With the reading completed, the beneficiaries rose and left as they had come, without a word to each other. Even though Chet had no axes to grind with Cori, neither wanted to provoke Bren by giving her any hint an alliance had already been formed. Hurrying ahead, Bren caught an elevator before the others. Waiting for the next down-car, Chet and Cori could finally exchange a few words.

'Mom seems to have known pretty well what we all wanted,' Chet said.

'Except for Bren,' Cori observed. 'Or she would have gotten all the stock instead of the jewelry.'

'What did you make of that thing Mom wrote for you – about the ranch?'

Cori smiled faintly. 'She was right. There's nothing I'd rather have. Maybe right, too, that I may never get to use it.'

'I was talking about something else – where she said it could be a place to – what was her phrase? – something about a reunion.'

'Seek healing reunion,' Cori provided. 'Obviously she was concerned about family unity, as Mr Marston pointed out. I guess she hoped we'd go there, you and me and Bren, and patch up our differences. Be a good place for it.' Her smile came back, brighter this time. 'Remember the old days – those big rowdy get-togethers, the games, that time we all went skinny-dipping at midnight, playing tag through the barn . . .'

Chet still looked mystified. 'But the thing is, Corker, that will was written eleven years ago. That's before Mom was ill. We were okay with each other then, remember, the three of us, getting along pretty well. Do you think Mom could've known what would happen later, how angry we'd be at Bren, and that we'd need to be brought together now? Do you really think she saw that far into the future?'

Cori stared at him, her own reasoning stuck on the question.

'And if she didn't,' Chet went on, 'then why would she put in that stuff about a "healing reunion"?'

Cori gasped audibly as the realization struck, but the sound was covered by the elevator door sliding open, and Chet didn't pursue the question.

More than anything else she had received from her mother, Cori thought as she rode down, this was the greatest gift. Forgiveness, even perhaps the hint of an apology for the choice her mother had made years earlier in forcing Cori to give up her firstborn. Pamela seemed to have perceived that forcing that choice was at the root of Cori's depression. Why else would she suggest that Cori might seek now to be joined again with her own child?

'You all right, Corker?' Chet said.

The elevator had arrived in the lobby, the doors were open, but Cori had not moved. She was still lost in the fantasy of reunion. Chet's voice spurred her ahead. 'I'm fine,' she said.

Yes . . . yes . . . she could do it. Go to the ranch, rest, get stronger, and locate Tayhcawin. And somehow find the will and the way to tell Frank.

They walked out of the Hartleigh building to where their limousines waited at the curb. 'I'll be calling you soon,' Chet said, as Cori's chauffeur opened the door for her.

She understood that he was referring to asking for her proxy to vote her newly acquired company shares in his favor, removing Bren from power.

'I hate doing this to her,' Cori said. 'The company is all she's got, her whole life.'

'I know, and Bren is a first-rate chief executive, except for one terrible blind spot. If she could only agree to operate more responsibly, and volunteer some compensation to her victims, I'd happily share the management with her.'

'Do you think there's a chance?'

'As soon as the stock is legally transferred, I'll talk to her. Once she realizes I've got the votes in my pocket, I'm hoping she'll feel there's no choice but to fall in line.'

'Let me know how it goes,' Cori said, and got into the car.

'You'll know,' he said. 'But I think Bren will probably call you first.' He leaned down to talk through the open car door. 'She can be very persuasive, Corker. Hang in there, and don't let me down. There's an awful lot of lives at stake. Maybe even Tay's.'

'*Takoja*!'

Tay woke to the cry in the darkness. She rose and went to the rear of the trailer where Nellie slept.

'*Takoja*?'

'I'm here, Nellie.' Tay knelt beside her cot. A full winter moon shone through the small rear window, its bluish light etching the wrinkled surface of the old woman's face in sharp relief.

'I will not be with you much longer,' Nellie said. 'I have heard *hinhan* calling to me.'

'You mean in a dream, Nellie? Or could it have been an owl hooting somewhere outside?'

Nellie Blue Snow smiled thinly. 'It does not matter. I have heard his call. I know that my time is near.'

'Is there anything I can do for you, Nellie?' Tay asked, accepting the prophecy. As she did, she recalled the death of her own father. Back then, she had not believed in the compact with nature, the interpretation of the signs and symbols. She knew better now.

'You are ready to carry on for me, Tayhcawin. Tell me you will.'

'I'll try,' Tay answered honestly. 'No one can really take your place.'

'Just do your best, *Takoja*. One more thing: do not forget to have a giveaway.'

'It will be done,' Tay said solemnly.

The giveaway was part of the Indian belief that there was, in fact, no such thing as ownership; all possessions, from the most trivial to the largest and most valuable, such as the vast, rich lands, were only 'borrowed' – like life itself – from the Great Spirit. They were meant to be shared, not claimed forever by any one man. It was a belief which, in their early encounters with white men, had made the Indians so vulnerable to having their land stolen; it had taken them a while to understand that another society felt free to write documents called deeds that carved the land up into separate pieces and gave perpetual ownership of these pieces to people who had never been there before. Yet the giveaway survived as part of the tradition of sharing that was customary among the Sioux. A few days after Nellie died, Tay understood, she would invite all who had known and loved the medicine woman to come and choose something from her possessions to take for themselves.

'But not the medicine things,' Nellie said quickly. 'Those are yours.'

'I know.'

Nevertheless, Nellie went through a careful recitation of the items to be kept by Tay. Feathers and pipes, the eagle-bone whistle, the buffalo skull that served as an altar at the sweats, the hide pouches full of *chan-chasha*, the red willow-bark tobacco used in sacred ceremonies, and the other medicines Nellie had gathered and prepared.

The moon had slipped away from the small window, the small area at the rear of the trailer was darkening. Tay wasn't sure, but she thought she had heard an owl's call from somewhere in the distance.

'*Takoja*,' Nellie said, 'I would like to have been able to walk beside you on your march ...'

'I know, Nellie.' It was a reference to a new demonstration Tay had been organizing, larger by far than anything in the past. She was hoping to have every Sioux tribe represented in the hundreds, perhaps the thousands, and other tribes from around the country, too, if they would come – all to walk in procession from Standing Rock to the Hartleigh dump site. If there were enough, it would have to receive national attention.

'But my spirit will be there,' Nellie added.

'I'm sure it will,' Tay whispered. It was becoming hard for her to speak without breaking down. She moved closer to the bed, and put her arms around the old woman. Nellie put her hand over Tay's and grasped it. Her grip, Tay noticed, was surprisingly strong.

'Look for me, *Takoja*,' Nellie said. 'I shall be flying over you, watching with the eyes of *wanjbli*.'

Tay nodded, and tightened her embrace on the medicine woman. A moment later, she felt Nellie's hand slide away.

Bren had flown to Hawaii for a few days to look at some

property for a new vacation home, and was attending a dinner party of some already entrenched San Franciscans when she encountered a friendly Republican banker who asked what was in the wind over at Hartleigh Mining – he'd heard from an acquaintance who was a company director that a special board meeting had been called.

'Oh, yes,' Bren said, feigning full knowledge. 'Nothing I can talk about, I'm sorry.' She hoped he'd be persuaded it was simply a matter of not breaking the law against divulging inside information. It would be ruinous if he detected that the head of the company had yet to be informed of the board meeting.

In a flash, Bren had the picture. Chet must be wheeling and dealing on his own, lining up support to push her aside. It came as no surprise that his ambitions to run the company had been renewed by gaining control of that additional percentage of ownership represented by his third of their mother's shares; she knew, too, that the possession of the shares was expected to be legally transferred before the end of the month. Yet Bren had completely dismissed the possibility of any real threat: with Cori's third, the majority vote would still be in her control. Surely, Cori wasn't going to switch allegiances, and risk the vengeance that Bren had vowed to extract . . .

But then where had Chet gotten the balls to start talking to directors on his own, calling a meeting without first asking her approval?

Leaving the party hastily, Bren returned to her suite at the Royal Hawaiian Hotel and placed a call to the Patterson home. With the time difference, it was past one a.m. on the West Coast, but Bren didn't think twice about jarring anyone out of sleep. She wanted Cori to know even the smallest mercies would be ignored if she failed to remember their deal.

It was Frank who answered the phone, still awake after returning from late work at the newspaper.

'No, Bren, and that's final,' he said stiffly after the third time she had insisted on talking to Cori. 'I'm not going to wake her up. I'm amazed you'd even ask, knowing her condition. You can damn well wait until tomorrow to talk to her, or I'll take a message and give it to her when she gets up at the usual time.'

Irritated by his tone, Bren played with the notion of saying something to shatter his smugness and rattle Cori's nerves – something that would open the door to the secret that had been kept from him. But she refrained. 'All right, just give her a message. Tell her . . . she's in my thoughts – along with you . . . and of course the children, *all* the children . . .'

'And that's what you called about in the middle of the night?' Frank said incredulously.

'Yes, that's all. I got worried suddenly – tell Cori this, too – something started me worrying and I thought it was important to tell her to be careful. Extra careful. After all, San Francisco is earthquake-prone.'

'Bren, this all sounds very strange. What's going on? Did you have a bad dream, or maybe a few too many *mai-tais*?'

Bren laughed, giving it a good-natured ring, as though suddenly admitting to her own foolishness. 'I am being silly, aren't I? But better safe than sorry. Just give her the message for me, will you, Frank?'

It was a good beginning, Bren thought after hanging up. When she got back to San Francisco she could reinforce the warning in person, and in a less subtle form. Perhaps, while Cori had been subject to Chet's sales pitch, she had drifted into thinking she was free to do as she pleased. But that was an impulse only someone strong and healthy could sustain. Cori was bound to retreat once she reassessed the avalanche of a new reality Bren would call down into her life as punishment for stepping out of line. Cori wouldn't have the guts to admit to Frank and her daughter the way she had deceived them both for twenty-five years.

* * *

A procession of more than eight hundred Rosebud Sioux had accompanied the horse-drawn wagon that took Nellie's body to the sacred burial ground where Tay led them all in a chant of mourning and a pipe ceremony, symbolic, of course, since the pipe couldn't possibly be passed among all those present. Now, at sundown, long after all the others had gone, Tay still sat in the burial ground communing with Nellie's spirit. To ask if the promise had to be kept.

The morning after Nellie's death, unable to think of anyone else who could understand the magnitude of her loss, she had called Neil in New York at his new offices. He had been sincerely empathetic and comforting, staying on the phone with her a long time though she could hear in the background that he was being constantly badgered by his producers or his assistants to continue preparing for the evening's news broadcast. But in the end he had explained that, as much as he would have liked to be with her, it was impossible. It was too soon after his debut to be deserting the anchor desk.

At the end of their call he asked Tay if there was any chance, now that Nellie was gone, that she might see her future differently. Thinking of Nellie's last requests, the answers she'd given, Tay could not encourage his obvious hopes. But she had not stopped wondering since if she was being fair to herself. Must she carry on for Nellie at the expense of her own happiness? If she and Neil were ever to be together, one of them would have to bend. Where did true happiness lie?

She put the questions to the spirits, though she expected no answers now. If there were answers to be had, they would come to her in dreams, always the time when those who walked the earth shared the spirit world. And if no dream told her, perhaps she would have to undertake the *hanbleceya* to determine her future.

Twilight settled, and Tay rose finally from beside Nellie's

burial place. As she turned, she saw him not far away, dressed for the weather in a shearling jacket and jeans, arms folded, leaning against one of the large rocks that bordered the ancient burial ground. Evidently he'd been waiting patiently for her to finish her meditation. How long had he been there? In the dusk, he seemed to be made of shadow, only a spirit.

'You *did* come,' she said. Yes, that was a sign.

'I'm sorry I had to be so late . . .'

Only as he straightened and she stepped toward him did her vision clear. It wasn't Neil.

'I didn't know she'd died until this morning,' Gene went on. 'I needed some information for the suit, and I called the tribal council. There were so few people in the offices today, I asked why, and that's when—'

'And you came,' she broke in, touched. 'You flew straight out here. But you hardly knew her.'

'I knew how important she was to you, Tayhcawin,' he said. 'That was enough.'

She had reached him. She could see his eyes only very faintly in the fading light, but the way they looked at her told her the reason beyond words.

He drove her back to Nellie's property, and instead of going into the trailer, she led him to the *tipi* in the land behind it where they made a fire in the pit and sat together speaking over cups of *mni-sha*. The sudden revelation of his feelings for her made her feel curiously shy with him, but he drew her out gently, focusing his concern on her grief for Nellie, and the effect of her death.

At last, Tay felt comfortable enough to confess that she had been hoping they might become close – 'friends, at least', she said – but she had completely misunderstood him, believing he was determined to keep their relationship strictly professional.

'You weren't wrong,' he said, 'even if you couldn't see the

truth. I was attracted to you when we met, Tay, but I talked to some Indian friends and they told me you were in love — practically married, even if circumstances kept you and your lover apart.'

'So you were being a gentleman,' she said.

'Perhaps. But not only that.' He paused to put another piece of stout wood into the fire pit. 'The truth, I guess, is that I was being a good Indian. I knew this man of yours was a *wasicun*. So I thought . . . if I try to take this beautiful woman for myself, am I not doing what we have always despised them for doing? Taking whatever they want, breaking the hearts of those who lose what they treasure most?'

After a moment she said, 'I'm not sure, any more, that I'm what Mr Rocklyn treasures most.'

'Perhaps not. When I came today, I expected him to be here, too.'

There was a silence. Across the narrow expanse of the *tipi*, they stared at each other. She understood now what he was waiting for.

'I'm not his, Gene,' she said. 'I loved him, but I've never belonged to him.' Softly she added, 'Being owned is not our way, is it?'

His arms went out to her then, and she lay back as he brought himself down over her and kissed her, perfectly gentle at first, caressing her lightly, treasuring her.

As he held her, she realized that the spirits had sent her an answer. But she didn't have to be asleep to see this dream.

On the first Friday in February, the board of the Hartleigh Mining Company convened in special session. The agenda for the meeting had been unanimously agreed on in advance, to consider a change in top management and take a count of the votes of the majority shareholders as to their preference.

Bren had made no attempt to block the meeting, nor had

Chet shown any inclination to call it off. When Bren had gone to see her sister at home several days earlier, she observed that her stern warnings left Cori visibly shaken and subdued. Cori hadn't even mustered the fortitude to come in person to today's meeting; she had sent an attorney with a sealed envelope stipulating the way her shares should be voted.

Yet Chet appeared equally unfazed. He knew that Bren, as expected, had been leaning hard on Cori. But he had sustained his own campaign, too. 'Don't let Bren manipulate you, Corker. We have to stay together on this.' And each time they talked, Cori's response had been composed, resolved and cooperative. 'I understand, Chet. Don't worry, I'll do what I think is best.'

Bren opened the meeting with a brief unemotional statement. Despite more than a decade of unparalleled growth and profitability for HMC under her guidance, there was a desire in some quarters for a change. She would willingly step down if so voted by those who represented majority ownership of the company.

Chet's pitch followed. Everyone at the conference table knew he had long been anxious to close the Victory Four dumping ground, but as he spoke now he expanded on his theme. There was more to his hopes for the company than just changing one old, bad policy. It was time to prepare for a new era in which the mining and processing of fissionable materials would be reduced to a minor, even a nonexistent factor in the balance sheet – at least, where earmarked for weaponry. Hartleigh Mining should take the lead, Chet declared, in working for a safer world by refusing henceforth to 'cash in' on the arms race.

Chet's speech provoked a lively exchange of comments by other directors. One praised it as visionary. The Cold War couldn't last forever, he said, no war did; the essence of planning good corporate strategy was to prepare for change. But another argued that there were rivalries and animosities between nations that had lasted for centuries, and no sign this one would end soon. A third observed that the point of business had never been anything but to make money, and right now the price of gold was half what it had been five years earlier while the value of uranium was holding steady.

At last Bren called for a vote. Chet seconded. Those directors who had accumulated significant holdings since the stock had sold publicly were polled on their choices. They broke evenly down the middle – actually a victory for Chet, since they were all Bren's hand-picked choices who had always sided with her in the past.

As expected, Bren and Chet each voted their own shares for themselves.

Attention turned to the sealed envelope which had been left at the head of the conference table, in front of Bren. The outcome of the vote would be determined by the disposition Corinne Hartleigh made of her shares. Suddenly there was a sense in the room that this was a more fateful moment in the history of the company than had been previously recognized. Chet's speech had raised the suggestion that the result could have a degree of global significance. And on the human level, there was Brenda Hartleigh to consider. In her mid-fifties now, she was still a beautiful woman, but not the irresistible *femme fatale* she had been in the past. Husbands and lovers had fallen by the wayside, while her devotion to the company had remained her one lasting marriage. What life could she have without it?

'Would you like to open it?' Bren asked Chet nonchalantly. 'Or should I?'

'It's the president's prerogative,' he replied.

Bren reached out and picked up the envelope. Weighing it in her hand, she smiled, quite confident of the answer that lay within. After a moment, she held it out to Chet. 'Why don't you do the honors?' she said.

It would be extra sweet, she thought, to have him see it first. She would be able to read it for herself from the expression on his face.

30

On this Saturday in June, the air was as clear as crystal, the sky a cloudless blue. A perfect day for a long walk.

At a point where the road curved gradually, Tay veered from the path she had been following down the middle white line to walk along the dusty shoulder. Looking back, she was able to see along the entire length of the line of men, women and children, almost four thousand of them, arrayed in ranks across the width of the two-lane highway, a procession stretching back more than half a mile. Moving steadily along the blacktop ribbon through the shimmering waves of heat, the most distant figures seemed to be materializing out of thin air, ghosts emerging out of the past to join with the angry victims of the present.

The Trail of Broken Health she had named the march, deliberately echoing the national caravan to Washington that had been organized by Indian rights activists back in 1972 called the Trail of Broken Treaties. After occupying the BIA building, that protest had dwindled without violence – and with nothing accomplished in the end. Of course its goals had been impossibly ambitious: to persuade the government to honor the old treaties, return the land. For this new march Tay's goals were more realistic, she wasn't trying to overturn a hundred years of civilized development, just a decade of criminal negligence.

In spite of the sharply climbing numbers of health problems on the rez, there was yet to be any response from the company management. At the beginning of the year, some Indian mineworkers had passed along rumors of a planned shake-up in company management that would lead to a change in policy, and Tay had called Frank Patterson to ask what he knew about it. Frank told her Chet had attempted to replace Bren as president, but had failed when Cori cast a tie-breaking vote of her own shares in support of her sister.

Tay was disillusioned in both her aunt and uncle. 'How could you let her do that?' she reproved Frank.

'Good lord, Tay, do you think I was happy about it? Up to the day of the vote, I was sure Cori was supporting Chet. She's been furious with Bren since you left, and I was sure she was appalled by the dumping, wanted it stopped. I found out only after the board had met and voted that Cori went the other way. I was stunned. I asked her why, but she just shut down, wouldn't say a thing about it. The more I wanted to understand, the less she was willing to talk. Frankly, it seemed so . . . so crazy,' he said, settling on the word with obvious reluctance, 'that it made me think I've been irresponsible not to have her business affairs placed under my control. I'm looking into that now.'

If Bren's power had been reconfirmed, Tay realized, the only hope that policies might be quickly changed was by stirring greater public sympathy and outrage. She had been determined to make the Trail of Broken Health the largest demonstration of Indian unity in the past ten years. Throughout the past few months, traveling repeatedly to the several Sioux reservations in the Black Hills she had urged the different tribes to cooperate. With the last of her own money, she printed posters and mailers that detailed the reason for the march and the statistics of the suffering, then paid young people on the rez and others to distribute the material and get it out to news organizations across the country. Ironically, the experience in public relations and media manipulation she had been forced to learn by working for Bren now became part of Tay's arsenal against her.

All the effort added up to this mile-long line today. Along the whole route they had been accompanied by reporters, photographers and camera crews. Overhead, too, flew helicopters rented by television networks. Good coverage, Tay thought – with only one exception: Neil was nowhere in the press corps. Even though he was the anchor of the national nightly news, she knew he went into the field occasionally to report the biggest stories, but this story hadn't been deemed big enough for the star anchorman, and his network had sent only a camera crew and correspondent. Though their affair was over, still his indifference hurt. His evening broadcast had become the highest-rated of the network news shows – his personal attention would have boosted awareness. She had hoped at least they might remain friends, but he hadn't even been back to the ranch once since he'd moved to New York.

Of course, Gene wasn't here either, but hardly because of indifference. He was in the state capitol right now, arguing that the repeated denial by state and local authorities of Tay's application for permits to hold a peaceful protest was a violation of the First Amendment. Not that they had expected otherwise. Hartleigh Mining contributed generously to the campaigns of all the local politicians and sheriffs.

'There they are!' A young man who had also been in the front rank of the march called out.

Tay spun forward again. About half a mile ahead a formation of county police cars had just loomed over a slight rise, creeping slowly in their direction, red warning lights flashing. Would they block the way, use force?

'What should we do?' the young man asked now.

'Just keep going,' Tay said. 'They're not going to stop us.' Though if they did, she knew, it would be an even better story. This was what the news gatherers really wanted to record, after all, a dramatic collision, not just a peaceful march. Tay hoped that no one would get hurt, but if there was a violent confrontation Hartleigh Mining would have an even harder time defending their actions.

'Sure looks like they mean business. Those cars are taking up the whole road.'

'Then we'll walk around them, Jimmie.'

Jimmie Rae Niquant smiled and kept walking. At seventeen, he had grown into a lanky good-looking young man without a trace of the condition that had once consigned him to a ward for the terminally ill. Fiercely devoted to Tay, he was also dedicated to her cause.

The procession and the phalanx of police cars moved steadily toward each other on a collision course.

Tay turned back to the ranks of people behind her, a few in wheelchairs, the younger children riding their father's shoulders, infants in pouches on their parents' backs or chests. Since noon, starting out after a mass pipe ceremony near an old vision pit several miles out of Upper Horse Jaw, they had walked fifteen miles. Another mile and they would be at the gates of the Hartleigh dumping grounds. Even if they were stopped now, it would be a victory. After coming this far, their progress televised and filmed and reported, public sympathy had to be with them.

'Don't be afraid!' she called out. 'Just stay behind me.' Holding up her hand, she waved them forward. Behind her she could hear the fading voices as the message was passed back farther down the long line.

The police cars started up their sirens, and began to come

on faster. Their intention was clearly to terrify the marchers, scatter them and break down the sense of order.

But Tay kept the pace steady, walking straight down the white line. 'Link hands and keep walking,' she shouted out, as she grasped the hand of Jimmie Rae Niquant at one side, and Kate's on the other.

The cars were moving at twenty or thirty miles per hour, she thought, only a few hundred yards away now. Tay tried to keep walking as though there was nothing between her and the horizon. The men driving those cars couldn't possibly just keep pressing down on the gas, wouldn't plough right into row upon row of men and women. It would be nothing less than . . . a massacre.

She realized then that to assume it couldn't happen was to reason only with the part of her that was *wasicun*, not Indian. She had heard Nellie talk about what it was like at Wounded Knee – the first time. Ninety years ago, when Nellie had been a small child . . . yet subjected to visions of horror that were burned forever into her memory. A cavalry detachment riding through a placid encampment, slashing at everything with their sabres, shooting point-blank at mothers and babies, killing every Indian they saw. Would Nellie have said 'keep going' if she could be here today? Or was she here? For a while this morning, Tay had seen an eagle soaring high in the sky over the route the march had followed.

The sirens wailed shrilly, the cars were close enough so that she could see the sunglasses on the men behind the windshields, implacable faces of the new cavalry. Tay felt Kate's hand squeezing hers tightening with fear.

'Don't stop walking,' Tay said. 'If we stop first, we've lost.'

They strode forward, and each rank took the next stride with them, all down the line.

The rubber squealed and smoked against the road as the brakes in all the oncoming police cars were stomped on hard, and the front phalanx came to a skidding uneven halt, the nearest car only seven or eight yards from Tay.

'Pass around them,' she said, veering toward one side of the road.

She walked past the cars with the same even stride, keeping her eyes forward. She expected a door to open at any second, a policeman to leap out and challenge her, but nothing happened as she passed the first row of police cars, then a second farther along, then one of the dark unmarked sedans she recognized as the type driven by federal agents. In rows three across, there were a total of at least thirty cars. Casting a glance sideways, she saw some of them contained as many as five men. Would so many have come just to sit idly by?

Still, nothing to do but walk on.

Then from somewhere behind her in the line she heard the screams and she knew it had started.

Now all along the line of cars doors sprang open and policemen and agents poured out, charging into the procession, swinging truncheons, shoving children and women aside, some with guns drawn as they grabbed men and pushed them to the ground to be spread-eagled and handcuffed. The orderly procession fragmented into a chaotic mob. Newsmen and camera crews waded in to get the story.

Tay whirled and ran back through the sea of scattered people, crying out a plea for calm. 'Keep going . . . don't run . . . there are thousands of us, they can't stop us all . . .' But how could she expect all those with children not to save them? Glancing around, she saw dozens of people fleeing away across the flat land flanking the road. She only hoped that none of the marchers who stayed would be provoked to retaliate too violently. Ten years ago FBI men had infiltrated the Indian rights movement, and in a raid on rights activists, two had been fatally shot. A Sioux named Leonard Peltier had been convicted of murder and sent to jail for life, but many believed

Peltier innocent, or at the worst guilty only of self-defense. Nevertheless, the killing had put the rights movement in a bad light, and the same could happen here if people didn't keep their heads. Tay kept making her appeal for calm.

Then, in the middle of the chaos she saw a young woman lying on the ground, her wheelchair tipped over in the mêlée. Tay knew her, Vonda Yellow Thunder who had been fighting ovarian cancer. Vonda had insisted on joining the march though Kate had said the toll on her waning strength might even be life-threatening.

Tay ran over, righted the wheelchair, and lifted Vonda back into the seat. 'I'll be all right now,' the Indian woman said – the tide of chaos had moved further down the road. 'C'mon follow me,' she shouted to some stunned marchers who were just standing in a daze, and she began pushing herself onward toward their goal.

Tay made a move to stop her, but was distracted by hearing her own name shouted out in a desperate burst. Turning, she saw nothing at first but the shifting screen of figures, shoving, running, fighting. Then a gap opened, and she had a glimpse of Jimmie being held by two policemen as they dragged him away. A line of blood trickled from his hairline down the side of his face.

Racing through the crowd, she came up behind one of the policemen, and clapped her palms onto his shoulders, fingers digging into the material of his shirt. The man was big and she had to reach up to grab him. 'Get your filthy hands off him!' she screamed. 'Leave him alone!' Powered by adrenalin, she had the strength to pull the large man off balance so that he toppled backward, almost knocking her over beneath him. She let go and stepped to the side as he caught his balance. They found themselves upright, three feet apart, staring at each other.

Panting, clenching his fists, his lips twisted in a snarl. 'Dumb red cunt,' he muttered. 'I'll tear you apart.'

As her eyes stayed on the policeman's face, a curious feeling swept through her. She felt no more fear, nor rage, only a cold determination to be the winner in any struggle that might occur with this man. For a second, she was perplexed by her reaction, so curiously isolated from what was happening at this place and time. Then it came to her: what she was feeling had less to do with this moment than something that had happened long ago. Because the man in front of her was the same racist bastard who had humiliated her when she was only a young girl forced to strip in the back room of a stationery store . . .

He came lurching toward her, his meaty hands extended to grab her. Ducking to one side, she swung her arm sideways with full force so that it cracked him across the face. He staggered momentarily, then changed direction to lunge for her again.

'Made me mad now,' he said, and threw himself at her, grabbing her in a bear hug so tight she thought her ribs were cracking as he lifted her off the ground. Raised her just high enough so that when she brought one knee up hard, it rammed directly into his crotch. He dropped her and went down onto one knee, holding himself as he grunted with pain. Looking up at her malevolently, he said in a low growl, 'Gonna be sorry, you stupid Indian bitch, I swear you're gonna be so fuckin' sorry . . .'

Still, Tay didn't retreat. She stood back and eyed him as she would a coiled rattlesnake, waiting for his move. She had never felt such capacity for violence within herself before. She could kill him, she knew. If the threat seemed serious enough – not just to her life or safety, but to her dignity – she could kill him.

He started to pull himself back up, slowly, still in pain, coming for her. It seemed crazy to Tay that he'd make another attempt to attack her when his reflexes were already so hobbled, but then she saw that his hand was moving back along his hip, reaching for the gun holstered on his belt. She gazed at the moving hand with a curious detached fascination. Did he mean to shoot her? A bizarre tumble of ideas went through her mind. If she let it happen, it would help the cause, make the story bigger, put more pressure on the company. It would fit so perfectly into her family history, too. Hadn't her father spoken so often of Black Eagle, a beloved cousin who had been shot in cold blood by a *wasicun*? Wasn't that what had set him on the road to becoming a fighter for Indian rights?

The policeman had his feet under him now, but he was still in a crouch, bent over as his fingers closed around the butt of the gun and he started to pull it free.

For one more second she watched, and then the oath she had sworn not to be his victim took over. Priming herself with two quick steps forward, she brought her cowboy boot up in a swift kick that caught the policeman under his jaw with such a force it nearly straightened him up, before he went over on his back like a felled tree.

Around her the melee had continued, but when the cop went down all the people nearby stopped moving and looked at the body lying inert on the ground.

Then an Indian man rushed to Tay's side. 'Go, get away from here or they'll send you to jail forever.'

Forever?

Had she killed the cop? Lord help her, she'd been ready to do just that. She leaned forward to look more closely . . .

And at that moment a blow crashed down on her head. The pain that went down her body was like a molten spike being driven through the top of her skull down to her feet, nailing her to the road. Then all at once she lost her footing, seemed to have stepped just an inch too far over a precipice, and she was hurtling down into a bottomless black chasm.

Abel woke her – his voice calling her to come up from the

river to have dinner in the lodge. She wanted to keep swimming for a while, but then she dived under the surface and hit her head on a log and scraped her body along the cutting edges of a sharp rock, and the water turned icy and made every wound throb with pain.

Abel called again, and she opened her eyes to the reality of the splitting headache and her bruised limbs, and the cinder block beside her marked with pencilled graffiti.

'Hey, lady, wake up!' the Sheriff's deputy repeated gruffly as he stood at the door of the jail cell. 'Your lawyer's here.'

She rolled over on the cot, still a little fuzzy on where she was or how long she'd been here. It took a few seconds to put it together. After being slugged unconscious from behind by a cohort of the policeman she'd knocked down, she'd been hauled into a car and taken to the nearest county police headquarters. Even though her consciousness returned quickly, a concussion kept her feeling nauseous and disoriented through a pitiless session of interrogation. She'd wanted to try reaching Gene, but they wouldn't let her. The policeman she'd defended herself against as he was pulling his gun, had recovered to join the interrogation. While the other men present – federal agents along with the police – had held him back from actually retaliating against her, the vengeful rage of the policeman Tay had beaten and embarrassed inflamed the general mood, and she'd been treated very roughly, manhandled in a way that left her bruised in several places. No thought had been given to furnishing medical attention of any kind, not even such minimal kindness as supplying an aspirin.

At last, barely aware of what she had said during the long hours she'd been badgered and deprived of food or any supportive contact, she'd been locked into this cell. By then it was night, and she was simply grateful for the silence and a place to lie down. She had collapsed onto the bare, thin mattress rank with the dried sweat of a thousand other desperate prisoners, and fallen back into the blackness. She had no idea how long she'd been asleep.

As soon as she sat up on the edge of the cot, the dizziness came back. Seeing she was awake, the deputy opened the cell door.

'Better not keep him waiting much longer, brighteyes,' he said. 'If he gets fed up and goes away, it won't be easy to find someone else to take your case.'

That at least made her smile. She could depend on Gene not to get fed up and go away. She fought off the dizzy feeling and stood, eager to be with him.

As soon as the deputy shoved her through a steel door into a visiting room, Gene hurried to her and held her.

The grip of shock and fear loosened at last. 'Thank God for you,' she said.

He leaned back and pushed the hair off her face. 'Looks like they've really put you through the wringer,' he said.

'Just what a girl likes to hear.'

He smiled and pulled her over to one of the two chairs by a table and knelt beside her. 'You feel okay? Sorry to harp on it, darling, but you really don't look very well. If you need a doctor—?'

'More than anything, I need to get out of here.'

'Okay. I'm working on it.' Quickly, he laid out the situation. Later this morning there would be an arraignment proceeding. She was to be charged with a range of crimes including felonious assault, resisting arrest and attempted murder. The full indictment sought by the prosecution wouldn't be revealed until they were in front of a judge, but he could guess bail would be set very high, maybe as much as half a million dollars.

'Where will I get that much?' she cried in dismay. Even getting a bondsman to put it up meant posting a percentage.

'You'll get it from me,' he said simply.

Filled with gratitude and love, she looked at him and

caressed his face. Abruptly, she burst out. 'But it's so damn unfair. All trumped up—'

'Tay. I'm on your side. But you did resist that cop pretty strongly. What happened?'

She remembered now the murderous rage she had felt against the policeman, the moment when she had believed she could kill him if she had to. 'He was starting to pull his gun,' she said.

'Policemen are allowed to pull their guns.'

'I was sure he was going to use it. I was protecting myself, that's all.' She searched herself. 'I guess I went a little haywire when I remembered him. I was trying to get even, maybe. But can they really call a kick attempted murder?'

Gene had taken a pen from his inside jacket pocket and was scribbling a note. 'Darling, if the weight of evidence indicates you had intent to kill,' he said as he wrote, 'it doesn't matter if the weapon's a gun, a toothpick or a foot. The evidence here consists of several law enforcement officials who say they were witnesses and that you appeared to go crazy when you attacked this guy, and there's no telling where you would have stopped if you hadn't been – "subdued" is the word they use in there.' He pointed to the report sheet atop an open file on the table.

'I was clubbed down,' she said.

The concern came back into his face. 'I know. I also know that a lot of what you told them when you were questioned ought to be thrown out, but that doesn't mean it will be.'

Tay looked at him with alarm. She thought back to those hours last night when she'd been too tired and sick to think. 'What *did* I tell them?' she asked.

'That you'd have been thrilled to see the cop dead – more or less a confession of intent to kill.'

She stared at him, as the gravity of the situation sank in. 'They really want to put me away for a long time, don't they?' With bail set so high, she realized, she might

430

have trouble getting out even before trial.

He shrugged sympathetically.

'I guess I went too far this time,' she said.

'No way,' he responded emphatically. 'Pictures of the cops beating up on your marchers have played on the news everywhere and won your campaign a lot of new support. It didn't hurt, either, to get the shots they got of you fighting back. And how about that woman in the wheelchair – Yellow Thunder? You think when people see the way she ended up, that doesn't get them all pumped to join the fight?'

'Oh, no, what happened to her?' Tay murmured in distress. She had thought that after she'd helped Vonda Yellow Thunder the ailing woman would manage on her own. But it sounded like the police had come after her again.

'I'll tell you what happened,' Gene said brightly. 'She finished what you started – kept rolling along that road and when the other marchers saw her, it shamed them into forming up again. The cops backed off a while, and the march went all the way to the dumping ground, where that woman handcuffed herself and her chair to the entrance gate.' He laughed. 'All the while they cut her loose, she was spitting and cursing. The TV cameras were there the whole time. It was the lead story on every network news show last night.'

Tay clapped her hands together, bursting with admiration.

'And you were the follow-up,' Gene added, his tone darkening.

She deflated with him. 'How strong is the case against me?'

He didn't answer directly, but glanced at the note he'd jotted. 'The policeman you fought with – you said something about remembering him, wanting to get even . . .'

She told him now, the memory coming back vividly as soon as she began. She was right there in that squalid dingy room again, naked and helpless before that leering sadist, twelve years old. She had worked so hard to hold back her terror then, crying hardly at all, forcing all the other emotions aside with rage. That was what had saved her. But she didn't have to hide the other feelings this morning, not with Gene, and she broke down as she described the humiliation, putting her face down in her hands as she wept.

Within moments, she felt his touch, a light caress moving over her hair. Lowering her hands, she saw him crouched in front of her. In his strong handsome face, and the steady gaze of the dark forest-green eyes, she saw the promise of rescue from the storm threatening to engulf her. 'It's going to be fine,' he said. 'Don't worry. No one's going to keep you locked up.'

She eased back to look at him, and he affirmed the pledge by leaning over to touch her lips with his. 'I just can't afford to lose this one,' he said.

31

Cori was lying down in her darkened bedroom when the evening news came on the screen of the muted television. She liked to keep the set on, especially after nightfall though most of the time she kept the sound off and rarely looked closely at any program. It made a window on the world reduced to a manageable size, kept in a box. And it was a form of companionship. The children were off at college, and Frank was always out these days, working at the paper, or at some function. Or perhaps with a lover. She couldn't blame him if that was the case. He was a wonderful man, considerate and caring, deserving of so many things that she no longer provided – gaiety, romance, intellectual stimulation, physical passion. Up to a couple of years ago, she had not lost hope in her own ability to recover. But then she had faced the choice of defying Bren, of letting the truth of her past be exposed to Frank and Tay if that's how Bren chose to retaliate for being turned out as head of the company. Facing that choice, Cori had discovered she didn't have the courage. After that, she had surrendered to the depression again, unable to believe there was any point in fighting it.

An image came on the television screen that caught her

attention, an unsteady close-up of a young woman, obviously tired but still very beautiful, surrounded by a mob of reporters as she came through a doorway.

Tay?

Because of her connection to a prominent local family, the San Francisco news broadcasts had all been featuring the story of her arrest yesterday and her release this morning thanks to the involvement of Gene Cheroux. On a number of stations she was described as 'the Hartleigh heiress' who had given up her life of affluence to 'go native'.

Yet this was the first time Cori had noticed. It took her a moment to reach for the remote control and turn on the sound. She wasn't sure that the image of her beautiful child floating in the gloomy air wasn't just a vision conjured out of her mind. Tay was in her thoughts so often, for so many years . . .

The sound went on as the picture changed to a wider angle framing Tay standing with a very handsome Indian man with long silver hair. The words Cori heard hardly made sense at first. Something about the police, a murder? The news segment ended with shots of Tay climbing into a car with the silver-haired man and being driven away, as the local anchorman said that a trial on the charges was expected later in the year.

Cori would have gone in search of a newspaper, but she had noticed a while ago that Frank no longer left them around, especially when there was any news that he thought might add to her anxieties.

She picked up the bedside phone and dialled the number for Frank's direct line at the paper. There was no answer after several rings, so the call switched automatically to a general message desk.

'I'm sorry, Mrs Patterson,' the woman at the desk said, hearing Cori's urgent tone, 'your husband left the office an hour ago. There's a reception for some sort of trade delegation at the Japanese Consulate. You might reach him there.'

'If Mr Forsetti is at his desk,' Cori said, 'I'd like to talk to him.' Vince Forsetti's driving ambition and street-wise cunning had lifted him to city editor some years ago without his ever calling on any help from her.

The message operator transferred the call and Forsetti answered in the clipped style of most newsmen when they were in the middle of getting out the next edition. 'Forsetti.'

'Vince, it's Mrs Patterson – Corinne. I need a favor, just a small one.'

'You know me, Mrs P – always glad to oblige.'

Cori explained that she had caught a little of the news about her niece on television, and now she wanted to know the details.

Like most people who'd worked at the *Observer* for any length of time, Forsetti knew that the publisher's wife had become a neurasthenic recluse who was said to drift in and out of contact with reality. He wasn't surprised it had taken her a day to catch up to the story, even though it concerned someone in her own family and had been making headlines.

'I haven't been following that one too closely,' Forsetti answered, stalling. Would his boss appreciate having his wife told something that would upset her?

'Then maybe you could just have a messenger bring me the clips . . .'

Forsetti thought about it. The woman sounded reasonable enough. Better if he obliged without bringing in a third party. 'Hang on a second. I'll pull the pages and give you a run-down right now.' He set the phone down on his desk, stood looking at it for ten seconds, and picked it up again. Of course, there was no need for him to check a file to be able to provide a complete summary.

'Thank you, Vince,' Cori said quietly when he was done. 'I'm in your debt.'

'Yeah – still. So tell your husband to make me managing editor.' But it was said with tongue-in-cheek. He doubted

Corinne Patterson had any influence left with her husband.

Cori lay back on her bed after hanging up. The story she'd heard revived all the feelings of that past time when her conscience had been so stirred by the injustice and persecution she'd witnessed that she had been driven to seek out Abel. And out of that impulse had come the child who was now herself a victim.

If only she could find the will and the courage to make one more show of solidarity, one more gift of her heart.

But minute after minute, she lay without moving, paralyzed by the very thought of how enormous a leap it was for her, a complete reversal of the path she had followed for thirty years.

It occurred to her finally that if she did not break out of the shackles now, then she might as well be lying sightless in the cold ground of her grave as immobile as on her bed in this darkened room.

Dead, beyond the reach of shame and regret and recrimination, she might even be able to help her daughter as she never had in life. She had already made a will that left her shares in Hartleigh Mining to her brother.

The minutes passed, the alternatives clicking through her brain in imagined moments like photographic slides illustrating a lecture. She examined them one after another, again and again – until it struck her that, whatever her decision, if she didn't act soon then Frank would be home, and she would have lost the chance. Spurred by that realization, Cori rose from the bed.

Once the decision was made, difficult as it was, she was surprised by how quickly she moved to carry it out.

As soon as Gene had arranged Tay's release on bail, he had taken her for a medical examination at a hospital in Belle Fourche, closest to the march site. He was worried about her after the hours she'd spent in jail, and he was also aware that the medical report might be important for her legal defense. The examination had, in fact, determined that Tay was suffering from a very slight concussion caused by the blow on the head she had received from a police truncheon. She would recover quickly with rest, the doctor said. Reassured that it was not serious, Gene was pleased by the finding since it would supply the grounds to have anything Tay had said to the police while in custody dismissed as unreliable.

After the examination, piloting his own plane, he had flown south, from Belle Fourche to Rapid City, to bring Tay home to Rosebud. Gene himself had to return to Washington where he was scheduled to appear at a Senate committee considering some new programs for aid to the Indians. He had wanted to take Tay with him, but her bail required that she stay within South Dakota. In any case, she wanted to be back on the reservation. Her presence would be reassuring to her supporters, and she knew the people who had once relied on Nellie now looked to her for cures and advice and ceremonies.

The morning after her return, they were indeed lined up outside the trailer. They brought sick babies, and the everyday pains that came with ageing, and problems with lovers . . . and they also came with serious health problems – the rates of diabetes and tuberculosis and other chronic diseases were five and six times as high among the Indians as elsewhere.

From observing Nellie, Tay had learned that while the medicine woman comforted those who believed in the old way by administering natural remedies, she had also used her position to influence sufferers to journey to the rez clinic or *wasicun* hospitals for more sophisticated treatments. It had been one of the earliest revelations of Tay's apprenticeship to see that Nellie herself did not rigidly insist that her traditional methods were necessarily better, or were in competition with the modern ways. Tay had once asked how Nellie could be a medicine woman, and yet recommend the white man's treatment over her own, and the old woman had answered, 'There are two missions of the medicine way. One is to make sure our customs survive, the other is to make sure our people survive. Most of the time one can be used to accomplish the other. But not always.'

Tay served those who came according to that lesson. She gave them the comfort of administering the native medicine they trusted. Whenever she recognized, or even suspected, a serious health problem she sent the sufferer to Kate Highwalking, or suggested a visit to the hospital in Rapid City.

Kept busy by her work as medicine woman, and by supportive visits from friends, Tay got little steady rest in her first two days home from the march, but she never had a moment of feeling tired or dizzy. Still, she was glad when the nights came, and there was quiet and solitude and a chance to be restored.

Gene called each evening, and they spent an hour on the phone. She listened as he kept her updated on anything concerning her case, and answered her questions about other things keeping him busy, and she told him how she was spending her days, the medicine work she was doing. She ached so much to have him with her, more than she had ever wanted to be with Neil. She knew now that what she had called love before – even if she had not misused the word – could not compare with what she had found with Gene. It was no longer unthinkable to consider changing her own life to share his.

But then what would be the result of all her study of Indian medicine? What did all these years with Nellie add up to? She had a promise to keep, too, that the knowledge would not perish or go unused.

She had been home three days when Gene called to say he would not be able to fly back for the weekend as previously planned. Some changes in a court calendar in Florida, where he was involved in defending a Seminole man, meant he might be appearing early next week and he needed the weekend to prepare.

'I wish I could fly straight back to you,' he said. 'And I would if there weren't so many people counting on me.'

'Don't worry,' she assured him. 'I'm yours – whenever you get here.'

'There's another reason, of course, that I don't like not being there. Someone should be staying on top of your case, Tay, getting depositions from all the witnesses, investigating that policeman. I'd hoped to start the ball rolling myself. Even if I'm not there, I don't want to wait any longer so – with your permission – I'd like to bring in a local lawyer. A very good man. He'll be able to get all the foundation work done when I'm not around, as well as collaborate with me on courtroom strategy. And one more thing: I'm so in love with you, I'm afraid of losing the objectivity I need to handle your case the best way. Having a back-up opinion will make sure I stay on the right track? Okay with you?'

'If you think it's best, I'm sure it is.'

'The man I have in mind is a *wasicun*, by the way, but he's got a long history of helping our people.'

Tay repeated that she'd go along with whatever he recommended, and wrote down the name and telephone number of the lawyer Gene dictated to her. She thought she recognized it – the head partner of a Rapid City law firm that had made a contribution of several thousand dollars to the march fund.

They stayed on the phone another twenty minutes trading endearments and fantasies, and saying goodbye so reluctantly that when the phone rang just a minute after they'd hung up Tay was sure it was Gene calling right back. She'd had the same hunger to hear his voice again.

'What took you so long?' she said as she grabbed up the receiver.

There was a long pause before a voice said, 'It's Frank, Tay . . . Frank Patterson.'

'Uncle Frank! I'm sorry . . . I expected someone else.'

'Actually, I'm the one who should be embarrassed. I meant to call days ago when I heard about the trouble you were in. I wanted you to know I'm ready to help in any way I can. But I'm afraid something happened that made me forget everything else – even important things.'

She noticed the ragged quality in his voice now – the sound of a man who was fairly distraught. 'What's wrong, Uncle Frank?'

'It's Cori . . .' Tay expelled a sympathetic sigh, fearing the worst, before he added, 'She's disappeared.'

Tay felt a lift of hope. From the sound of it, at least her aunt was still presumed alive. 'When?' she asked.

Frank spilled out the details. He'd come home a few nights ago and Cori was gone, slipped out of the house without their maid noticing. He had expected she'd be quickly located – she couldn't have left more than a few hours before – but the search continued in vain. There was speculation that she might have jumped in the bay, or met with foul play. Even though his own newspaper ran a picture of her on the front page, no one came forward to say they'd seen her. The police theorized, too, that she might have wanted to avoid being apprehended, and had disguised herself – at least worn a shawl or some other covering to avoid being recognized. There had been days of fruitless inquiries until a news vendor at the bus terminal, shown the picture the police were circulating, reported that he was almost positive he'd seen the woman buying a bus ticket.

'So the best guess is she got on a bus to go somewhere,' Frank said. 'But that's all we've pinned down so far. No ticket-seller remembers her. I've been calling around – anywhere Cori might go – to let people know the situation.'

'You thought she might come here?' Tay was astonished.

'She liked you, Tay, she often spoke about you, said she would have liked to know you better, wished Bren hadn't driven such a wedge between you.'

'I felt the same, Uncle Frank. But I can't imagine she felt it so strongly she'd have run away to come here.'

'I know. I've called thirty other people besides you. At this point every one seems like a long shot. But with Cori anything's possible. If she did come, Tay—'

'I'd let you know right away, of course.'

'Yes, right away,' he said. 'I'd come to get her. I'd do anything to have her back safe, and—'

He broke off, apparently overcome for a moment. No matter how her aunt's illness had frayed the conventional bonds of marriage, Tay thought, her uncle was still obviously deeply in love with her.

'She'll come back,' Tay said, eager to comfort him even if there was no assurance she could give that wasn't a cliché. 'Don't give up hope.'

He thanked her and hung up.

In the quiet lull after the disturbing call, Tay heard the echo of her own words. *Don't give up hope.* She realized then that she hadn't offered them simply as an empty ritual. She believed Cori would be all right – sensed that whatever journey her aunt had undertaken was not meant to be self-destructive.

Left with this slightly eerie presentiment, Tay had an impulse to step outside the trailer and clear her head with a few breaths of night air.

It was a cool, clear night, quiet except for the rattle of dried sagebrush, and a faint whistle that came from the breeze blowing through the stitching in Nellie's old *tipi* fifty yards down a slope. Tay looked around. Tonight she could almost feel the spirits gathering in the dark.

Or was someone out there, a person seeking medicine. 'Hello?' she called out. 'Anyone there?'

441

No sound came back, no sign of a presence, solid or spirit. Yet the chilling sensation of being watched persisted. A nervous illusion, Tay decided, a result of all the stress she'd been under. She felt better when she retreated into the trailer.

As her glance grazed across the telephone in the tiny sitting area, she was reminded of her uncle's call. Where, Tay wondered, could Cori have gone?

'I hope I didn't miss my appointment,' she said breathlessly, running into the reception area of the Rapid City law firm the next afternoon. 'I hate being late . . . but I had trouble parking.'

The last thing Tay had expected was to find the streets filled with cars. Rapid City had come a long way from being the easy-going western town it had been the first time Abel had taken her there, nevertheless it was rare to have anything like a traffic jam, and sidewalks lined bumper to bumper with cars from out of town.

'It's always like this on rodeo day,' the young receptionist said.

So that was it. There were a couple of big rodeos a year, and fans came from all around the state.

'No sweat,' said the receptionist, pressing a button on the intercom. 'Have a seat, and I'll tell the boss you're here.'

Tay sat and swept an appreciative glance around the waiting area decorated with good comfortable furniture and the western-landscape paintings that had come into vogue. Occupying the entire top floor of one of the nicer new downtown buildings, the law firm was apparently very successful. Tay had expected something rather more modest when Gene told her that the man he was inviting to help on the case was a *wasicun*, and also a longtime champion of Indian rights. She'd imagined then he must be a young, idealist working in a rickety backstreet walk-up. What other kind of white lawyer would care? Even if Gene also did *pro bono* work, he could only afford it because he had first made millions working on Wall Street mergers.

Her impression of the local lawyer had been reinforced by his evident enthusiasm for helping her. He hadn't waited for her to get on the phone to him, he had been first to call this morning, urging her to come straight to town this afternoon. Her case was in a hiatus at the moment, but that was no reason to sit back. 'Better to cut a cactus down before it grows too many needles,' he said.

'You sound worried about my chances,' Tay observed.

'You hurt a white policeman, and you're proud to call yourself an Indian. Around here that's never made too many friends on the jury.'

She had taken his suggestion to meet today. If he was the 'boss' of this firm, she realized, he must have made time to fit her into a very busy schedule.

'You can go in now,' the receptionist said. She pointed Tay toward a door standing open at the far end of a corridor visible to one side.

As soon as Tay passed through the door, he came out from behind his desk to greet her, a man in his early sixties with a medium build, receding gray hair, and a friendly aspect. He was in shirt sleeves, and the mound of a middle-aged paunch bulged between the suspenders holding up his pants.

'Come in, come in, Miss Hartleigh,' he said heartily. 'I'm Steven Nevelson.' He motioned Tay to the sofa in a sitting area at one end of the spacious office.

'How do you do, Mr Nevelson,' Tay said, adding, 'I prefer to use my Indian family name, by the way – Walks-Through-Fire. But you can just call me Tay.'

'Of course. Excuse me, Tay. In any case, I'm glad you could come so soon – and not just for professional reasons. I've been wanting to meet you.'

She took it as mere cordiality. 'It's kind of you to make time for me right away.'

'I'm always happy to help Gene Cheroux,' Nevelson said, lowering himself into an easy chair across from the place on the sofa Tay had taken. 'But that still isn't the whole story. In fact, I called the county police and offered to represent you as soon as I heard about your arrest. I would have jumped right in myself, but they said Gene was already on the case. I know you couldn't do better . . . not even with me, and I thought you should have the best. One way or another, I owe it to you to make sure you win.'

'You, Mr Nevelson? Why should you feel you owe it to me?'

'It goes back a long way. This isn't the first time I've been involved with your family, Tay. I was hired once to help your father.'

Tay leaned forward, intrigued. 'I never heard him say anything about it. When was this, Mr Nevelson?'

'Almost thirty years ago. And I'm afraid I didn't do much good for him. There was a killing involved, a tragic case. Maybe he just preferred to forget it.'

Thirty years. A killing. Now she remembered. 'No, he didn't forget. That was when his cousin Black Eagle was shot. Somehow he ended up being put in jail, and the murderer went free. He did speak about that – fairly often. But he never mentioned you'd represented him.'

Nevelson shook his head. 'I didn't exactly. I tried to help, but I was kept too much on the fringes. Your father didn't trust me enough, I guess, and your mother . . .' He shrugged regretfully. 'Well, she did a very brave thing by getting involved, but then it created too many problems for her.'

Tay's curiosity soared. She moved right to the edge of her chair. 'My mother? How was she involved?'

'She was the one who hired me.'

Tay stared at him, lost in confusion. 'To help my father?' she murmured. With everything she knew about her mother, this piece of information didn't fit at all.

'Of course, they were virtually strangers at the time,' Nevelson explained. 'That's why her willingness to become involved was so decent and kind. She'd been a witness to the killing, and it troubled her terribly. When she brought me in to help, she was simply being a good Samaritan. I suppose it was her interest in the case that must have led later on to her visiting the reservation and meeting Abel, and to, well, I suppose to . . . your being . . . conceived. I never even knew that part of the story until recently. When I read about you – that you were Abel's daughter, and your mother was a Hartleigh – I put two and two together.'

Still, Tay couldn't put it together herself. *Good Samaritan*? Tay had never imagined Bren could have a benevolent unselfish side. If the true genesis of her meeting with Abel had been so noble, why had she hidden it all these years – rewritten the history to make it nothing more than a chance encounter, a one-night stand? And more baffling, from being so concerned about the injustice to one Indian man she barely knew, how could she have evolved into someone who drove the mining company in a direction that would cause so much suffering to a whole tribe?

Tay would have brooded on the questions longer, but Steve Nevelson brought their conversation back to the purpose of their meeting. He was going to be cooperating with Gene, particularly in overseeing the day-to-day strategies of her defense, and he needed some detailed information from her.

'Gene told me there was a past incident between you and the policeman in this case, something that made you lose control when you recognized him. He thinks it may be the core of our defense but he wants me to judge the merits independently. Would you tell me about it?'

Having relived it with Gene, she was less emotional this time. And describing it matter-of-factly, moment to moment, somehow brought it back even more completely and vividly, with details that had escaped her before.

As she finished, Nevelson's expression reflected his own anger and contempt for the brutalization Tay had suffered as a young girl. 'You can't be blamed for what you did when you saw this man again,' he said. 'Rest assured, Tay, I'm not going to lose this time. I promise you.'

The lawyer kept her with him another hour, answering dozens of questions as he probed for any information that might be useful in constructing his defense, providing names of people who had been witnesses to what happened at the march, or could provide other useful information. If Emory Fast Horse could be located, she told the lawyer, he could provide some corroboration of what had happened in the stationery store.

At last Nevelson concluded the meeting, and walked her to the door of his office. 'When you see your mother,' he added as he was saying goodbye, 'Please give her my regards. We had only a brief acquaintance, but she made quite an impression on me. She was such a lovely woman . . .'

So perhaps he was another of Bren's easy conquests, Tay thought now. Couldn't an infatuation account for his skewed memory of how Bren had become involved with Abel?

'I don't expect to be seeing her any time soon,' Tay said. 'In fact, we haven't been on speaking terms for quite a while.'

'Oh. I'm very sorry to hear that.'

Tay gave him a puzzled look. 'You can't really be surprised, Mr Nevelson. How would you expect my mother and I to maintain a relationship? She's the one I've had to fight so bitterly over this nuclear dumping ground. Do you think the police would have broken up our march, if she hadn't used her influence to make it happen?'

He appeared even more confounded. 'Your mother? But I

thought it was Brenda Hartleigh who made those decisions at the mining company,' Nevelson said.

'It is,' Tay replied. 'Brenda Hartleigh *is* my mother.'

They gazed at each other through a brief exchange of silent questions. After a long awkward moment, Nevelson shrugged apologetically. 'My mistake,' he said. 'I jumped to the wrong conclusion. It was Corinne Hartleigh I knew, so I just assumed . . . I mean, since she was the one who'd been so concerned about the man who became your father, I was certain they . . . well, you can understand, that was as much as I knew . . .'

Tay nodded as she backed away. 'Of course, it was an easy mistake to make,' she said. 'I understand . . . I really do.' But she was talking to herself now more than to him. 'I think I do understand . . .'

As she walked away down the corridor, Tay's step quickened. Before she knew it, she was dashing out of the office, her heart pounding as she rode down in the elevator; then she was running into the street, racing to get to her car.

She wasn't even sure at first of where she was going, yet already there was a prayer in her heart that where ever it was, she could get there soon enough.

32

Driving, forced into the steadying task of keeping control, steering along a road, the jumble of thoughts and memories and puzzling discoveries began to fall into place, a path of logic she could follow like a white line down the middle of the highway.

It wasn't hard to see the whole quilt of motives that had been stitched together to keep her deceived for so long. Cori had been afraid to take her in because her husband didn't know she'd had a child before marrying him. Abel had wanted her to have all the opportunities that membership in a wealthy white family would provide, so he must have agreed with Cori to send her to Bren. And Bren accepted her because then she had leverage over Cori. That explained how Bren had been able to hold on to control of the mining company – it was the reason for the support Cori had given Bren that Frank had found so puzzling.

Going over the history in her mind, reconstructing the events according to this new reality, so many things that had never quite made sense before were suddenly comprehensible. She understood the distance Bren had kept between herself and her sister, her anxiety about Tay getting too close to Cori. Tay thought she understood, too, all the forces that had battered her aunt's – no, her *mother's* – sensitive being until all Cori had wanted to do was hide from life, past, present and future.

Finally, she grasped the truth of what her heart had known intuitively almost from the beginning. The woman for whom she had always felt a natural affection was indeed her mother – while she had never been able to call up more than a dutiful pretense of respect or love for the vain, selfish woman who had only been acting the part.

If only Cori could be found now, Tay thought. If she could be assured there was no blame, no shame, no sin, nothing beyond forgiving in all that had happened before. Years ago, Tay knew, she could not have learned the truth without damning Cori for abandoning her and perpetuating the lies, as she had damned Abel. But she had come to know there was no solace or healing to be found in merciless anger. Tay wanted only to embrace her mother.

Yet she was gone. And Tay no longer trusted her intuition that Cori hadn't harmed herself. There was no doubt that when she had left her home and her husband, it was because bearing the burden of keeping the secret had exhausted her.

As she sped past a row of roadside gas stations, Tay spotted several public telephones; it occurred to her to call Frank and tell him what she'd discovered. But she stopped herself. It wasn't her place to expose what Cori had kept to herself for thirty years despite the terrible cost to her peace of mind.

The sun was setting when Tay drove back onto the reservation. As much as she had tried to think of someplace else to go, something to do that might aid in the search or bring relief to Frank, in the end she could only head home. Gene would be calling, and she needed the steadying reassurance of his love. Nor could she desert those who looked to her as the substitute for Nellie. She knew that Delia Red Kettle, an unmarried sixteen-year-old girl, was approaching the time when her baby would be born, and Tay had taken over the midwife duties that Nellie had performed in the past.

It was deep twilight when Tay turned the car off the road onto the dirt track ending at the trailer. As she rolled to a stop and turned off the headlights, she became aware of the beautiful luminous glow of last light seeping in a line over the horizon. Enjoying the sight, Tay walked behind the trailer, where the view was unobstructed except for Nellie's old *tipi*. With all the scars of the land hidden by the gathering dark, it was easy to imagine how beautiful it had been before the invaders came. Tay stood looking out at the view until the light had almost faded.

As she turned to go back toward the trailer, she suddenly noticed the figure several yards away, only a silhouette against the twilight glow. A slight female figure – a young girl, Tay suspected, from the same *tipospaye* as Delia Red Kettle, sent to fetch the midwife. It seemed she had been waiting in the *tipi*, perhaps shy about interrupting Tay's contemplation of the sunset.

'Can I help you?' Tay said, taking a small step toward the girl. The slightly hunched posture of the visitor telegraphed her timidity. 'Come closer,' Tay said, extending her hands.

The figure moved nearer.

Tay perceived the face then. Not a young girl at all, though the illusion was preserved by the dark. It was possible to imagine she was merely a ghost, a vision of the young woman who had first come to this land so long ago.

'Tay . . . I've been waiting,' Cori said in a quavering murmur. 'Waiting so long . . .'

Tay nodded. 'I'm sorry,' she said. Her hands reached out, and Cori responded by raising hers. Their fingertips touched. 'But I'm here now . . . Mother.'

At the final word, Cori froze, staring in amazement. 'You know? But that's why I came.' She moved nearer. 'I came to

451

tell you.' Tay's fingers closed around her mother's. 'Oh, Tay, I thought it would be so hard,' Cori went on, hoarse with emotion. 'But all this time . . . you knew.' Half crying, half laughing, her voice failed.

Tay put an arm around her. 'No, not all this time. I learned only today.'

'But how? How could you—'

'I met the man you hired to help Abel – Steve Nevelson.'

Cori's eyes flared with recognition. 'Yes . . . he tried. But things were so different then . . .'

'Now he's going to help me,' Tay said.

Another long moment passed as Cori searched Tay's face for even the smallest hint of rejection. 'Oh, Tayhcawin, you understand, don't you?' Cori cried softly, tears starting to run down her cheeks. 'They wouldn't let me keep you, but I've always loved you. Always, always. Do you understand?'

Tay smiled forgivingly. She couldn't understand absolutely everything, not yet, but she was sure she would soon.

Cori smiled back through her tears. 'Oh, my baby,' she said in a grateful whisper. 'I have my baby back, don't I?'

The embrace Tay gave her, strong and lasting, was the answer.

Tay called Frank the next morning to say that Cori was safe, staying with her. She mentioned not a thing, however, to explain what had made Cori run to her. Talking with her mother all through last night, Tay had been able to fill in the blanks, and she perceived the power of the forces that had been working on Cori for the past thirty years, fraying her nerves, tearing at her soul. If Cori couldn't bring herself to tell the truth to Frank, Tay thought, perhaps the secret ought to be kept.

That same evening Frank arrived at the Rosebud Sioux reservation. By then, after Tay and her mother had spent the whole day together talking, Cori had defined for herself the need to reveal everything. Unless she did, Bren would always have the upper hand. And now that Cori could express her love for Tay, one of the first things she was determined to do was help her daughter win the battle she'd been fighting against Bren.

When Frank arrived at Nellie's property, Cori took him off on a walk while Tay remained at the trailer. By the time they returned, Frank had been told. Shocked as he was to learn that Cori had concealed a love affair and the birth of a child prior to their marriage, he had little trouble absorbing it and adjusting. If he was upset by anything it was Cori's failure to trust him, to realize that his feelings for her were rock solid, and he would not have stopped loving her if she had told him the truth long ago. Yet he proved that now. He didn't dwell on what might have been. It was far from certain that Cori could have been spared the years of depression even if she had not felt a need to keep her past hidden. What had obviously taken a greater toll on her sensitive psyche was being forced to abandon her firstborn. Realizing that, Frank perceived quickly that nothing would do more to repair the years of despair than letting her consolidate the relationship with Tay. When Cori asked to stay on the reservation, and Tay expressed the same desire for more time with her mother, Frank raised no objection.

'I'm just awfully glad to know I haven't lost a wife,' he said. 'And I've gained a daughter, I hope. I've always been impressed by you, Tay. Nothing would make me happier than having you look upon me as a second father.'

'That'll be easy,' Tay said.

'Good. I'll be waiting to welcome both of you home whenever you're ready.'

Staying with Tay over the next couple of days, Cori observed at close hand the involvement with the people of the reservation that Tay had taken over from Nellie. When Tay midwifed at the birth of Delia Red Kettle's baby, Cori was present. It seemed

453

entirely logical to Cori that her daughter felt drawn to the preservation and practise of the Indian medicine tradition. Abel's father, she remembered, had been a *yuwipi* man, an interpreter of dreams and spirit messages, a dispenser of medicines, a leader of ceremonies.

Yet Cori realized, too, that such an involvement could hinder Tay's ability to pursue a more normal life. She did not comment or pass judgment, however.

On the third night after Cori had come, they were sitting outside on a blanket under the stars, continuing the process of learning about each other. Cori had talked for a long time about the circumstances that had brought her together with Abel, and then had driven them apart. Talked about how G.D. had controlled her life, about how hard it had been thirty years ago for most genteel young women to defy their upbringing. When it came to reliving G.D.'s attempt to force her into an abortion, Cori broke down, and Tay held her comfortingly.

To help assuage Cori's guilt over abandoning her, Tay spoke in turn about all the wonderful aspects of her childhood, what a good father Abel had been, and the pride she took in her Indian heritage – which led to talking about the way she had spent the past few years with Nellie.

'I've wanted to do this,' she explained, 'because I don't want the traditions and the wisdom of the native Americans to be completely lost. It pains me to see that already so many of our ways are being forgotten or ignored.' She hesitated before adding a confession. 'Lately, though, I've realized that I can't stay here and give my life to it . . .' She had already told Cori about Gene Cheroux, whose work kept him elsewhere at the moment – work no less important than her own. She loved him and didn't want to be separated from him.

'So you'll be giving this up?' Cori asked.

'It will make me very sad to do it – Nellie Blue Snow trusted me with all that she knew, trusted me to use it and pass it along. But Nellie's life was to be a medicine woman. She never married, never had children, never left the rez to go anywhere else. I can't see myself making that kind of sacrifice.'

'The man you love,' Cori observed, 'you've said he's a Sioux. Couldn't he live here?'

'He's from the Teton reservation,' Tay replied, 'but in any case I'd never ask him to come back and live on this rez or any other. Not permanently. He does something more important for us by being out in the world – taking on the *wasicuns* on their own battlegrounds, showing his strength there, and winning. That's another very important way of gaining back lost territory.'

Cori was moved to hear Tay speak about her dilemma, the devotion to preserving the Indian way that conflicted with her love for a very special Indian man. She felt the maternal impulse to offer an answer.

And one solution did occur to her.

'Perhaps there's a place where you and the man you love could both be happy,' Cori probed, 'yet you could also go on doing the things you care about.'

'I'd like to believe there is,' Tay said. 'But I don't think it's here . . . and I doubt it's in Washington where Gene lives now.'

'I have a place in mind already.'

'Where?' Tay asked impatiently.

Cori told Tay about the Golden H Ranch, and her idea for the way it would be used.

'That would be wonderful!' Tay exclaimed. 'But it's a very big project. Would you help me with it?'

'In every way I can,' Cori said. 'I think I even have a name for it.'

Tay waited expectantly.

'*Cante Ishta*,' said Cori.

'*Cante Ishta*,' Tay repeated, trying it out. 'Eye of the heart. Mother, it's perfect.'

* * *

Eight months later, in a courtroom in Belle Fourche, Tay was acquitted of all charges brought against her for the incident on the Trail of Broken Health. Along with dozens of Indian supporters, Tay's mother and step-father, her Uncle Chet, and other members of the Hartleigh family filled the gallery and cheered Tay and Gene when the jury returned its verdict.

Bren, of course, was absent. In fact, she had hardly left her Nob Hill mansion for any reason since she had been replaced by Chet as the president and chairman of Hartleigh Mining. She had made one brief stab at clinging to her position, trying to intimidate the men she had appointed to the corporate board and to rally all the public shareholders for a proxy fight. But all support for Bren had been eroded by the public wave of sympathy that rose for Tay and the Indians in the wake of the march.

With the trial behind them, Gene and Tay flew together to Jackson Hole for a stay at the Golden H Ranch. It was time to begin shaping its future – and theirs.

They planned to build a home for themselves on the property, and they were going to spend the next few days riding on horses across the land and camping each night looking for the best aspect. They spent their first night on a secluded stretch of the river that ran through the vast acreage.

The night was so mild and clear they lay outside the tent Gene had pitched, and made love under the sky. The light of a bright three-quarter moon did its alchemy, turning the skin of his taut body to the color of gold, and hers to silver.

'You won't be going too soon, I hope,' she said, when they were done, lying quietly, naked in each other's arms. He still flew away whenever he heard that any Indian was in trouble – anywhere. But there had been fewer and less urgent alarms lately. And the case before the Supreme Court on which he had long labored had reached a major turning point. Regarding

Sioux claims that vast tracts of land awarded to them by treaty in 1868 had been illegally seized by the federal government – or taken by others the government had protected – the High Court had ruled in favor of the Sioux nation. Damages had been awarded to the native Americans in an amount that, with interest, currently stood at over three hundred million dollars. Those fines were still being held in escrow, however. The Indians did not want the money, the case had never been about financial loss or gain. They still wanted the land. The case would go on through the courts.

'My home is with you, Tayhcawin,' he said. 'But now as in the old days, I may have to leave now and then to fight.'

'Or maybe,' she said, 'you'll stay home while I do the fighting.'

'Or the third possibility. The fighting may end.'

She drew him close against her once more.

Looking over his shoulder as he stretched out on her body, she saw the gliding silhouette of a bird circling slowly and gracefully across the face of the moon, hurrying nowhere, fearing no one.

'Look,' she said, 'an eagle.'

'I don't think so. *Wanjbli* doesn't fly at night.'

But when he rolled over to look he could no longer disagree. 'It seems a spirit is watching,' he said.

Then, as they gazed upward in amazement, a second majestic winged shadow swooped out of the blackness to join the first in the moon's luminous arena.

'It must be a sign,' Gene said.

'Can you read it?'

He turned back to her. 'You're the medicine woman.'

She smiled and watched their soaring shadow ballet for a minute. Two spirits. In her mind, they were Nellie . . . and Abel.

'Eagles flying at night,' she said at last. 'I'd guess they

want us to know that we should never fly alone.'

He gave her a long adoring look. 'You must know your business,' he said, just before he began to make love to her again. 'I'm sure that's exactly what it means.'

33

Summer 1990

Right up to the last minute, Bren hadn't imagined she would come.

When she'd received the invitation two months ago in the mail, she'd dismissed it as more of a nose-thumbing gloat than a sincere gesture. The gulf between her and the rest of them was much too wide ever to cross, Bren felt, had probably become unbridgeable even before Tay and Cori had discovered each other and bonded so goddamn quickly and heart-warmingly as mother and daughter – though, of course, that was the torpedo that had finally and forever blown any hopes of full family togetherness out of the water.

In the years since she'd lost control over the company, Bren had emerged from solitude and had gone down many other avenues in search of some activity that would fill the vacuum left by the loss of power in the business she'd been born into – that, as she thought of it, was in her blood. She had made adventurous journeys to the world's backwaters, started new collections of art, taken and divorced another husband, engaged in numerous affairs. Over sixty now, she had yet to experience more than a slight diminishing of her libido. Sex remained important to her, perhaps because it had always been her substitute for love. These days she hungered for men decades younger than herself, and though she'd done all the advisable cosmetic surgery and could pass for twenty years younger on her best days – her best evenings, anyway – she no longer attracted them so much with her allure as she did with her money.

Yet none of it – cloaking herself in luxury, seeing the world, sex with the young men – ever gave her the kick she'd gotten from taking over the business and running it. She had taken it, after all, from G.D. Nothing would ever be as exciting as proving she had been as good as he was. No – better. Fair payment for taking Cori as his favorite, Bren had always thought, even though she'd been the one who emulated him.

The bitterness Bren felt not only to her brother but to Cori and Tay for depriving her of her reason for living was too consuming to be dispelled by any mere appeal to sentiment. Cori had made many attempts to close the breach, had written letters full of gratitude for the years Bren had sheltered Tay, had called many times. Tay had made similar efforts. Bren hung up on every phone call and ripped every letter to shreds, just as she had torn up Tay's wedding invitation straight out of the envelope. The same day she'd received it, she had called her travel agent to set up an itinerary for some exotic trip abroad – Fiji, perhaps, or the Kalahari or even Antarctica. Exactly where mattered less than the timing of the trip; she wanted to be far away when Tay was getting married.

Then, three weeks ago, when she'd gone to get all the necessary vaccinations and immunizations for the Nile steamer trip she'd decided on, her doctor had also done a quick routine examination. And he had been mildly concerned about the soreness she felt near her breast – not even a detectable lump, just a painfully tender spot.

Two days of tests had followed, second and third and fourth opinions, all hastily gathered – Bren pretending to herself every minute that the rush only had to do with getting away for her trip on the planned date. Within a week she'd gone in for the surgery, a partial mastectomy with removal of one breast and several involved lymph nodes under her arm. Chemotherapy was scheduled to begin as soon as she was fully recovered from the shock of the operation.

It terrified her – a new sensation for Bren. If she'd still had the company, she might have been diverted even now from focussing on her doom. With an outlet for exercising her power and strength over something vast and important, maybe she wouldn't have become obsessed with this disease over which she was so powerless as it took possession of her body. It would have helped, too, if there was someone who cared, even just enough to keep her company. But of course her body had always been a significant part of what she'd used to buy companionship, and now she felt that currency had been devalued by the loss of a breast.

So she was facing her mortality completely alone. The closest thing she had to friends were a couple of servants who'd remained with her over the years, an elderly housekeeper who had worked at the Nob Hill for her parents and had stayed on – and Carl, the chauffeur she'd hired at the time Tay was living with her, because he was also a bodyguard and Bren had developed a fear of kidnappers. Not because she loved Tay, but because she didn't want to be forced to pay a ransom.

It was Carl who had changed her mind about the wedding.

A few days after her release from the hospital, Bren had visited the surgeon so he could check her dressings. Until then, she hadn't been able to look at herself, to see the results of the operation. When she finally did see the wound, she could only feel that she had been mutilated, and any chance of ever being loved again – touched, at least – was gone. She emerged from the visit in a sullen silence.

'How'd it go?' Carl had asked with sincere concern as he

461

was driving her home from the surgeon's office. The chauffeur had always been taciturn, rarely speaking unless first addressed. But since his employer's cancer had been diagnosed, he'd seen the change come over her, and he'd begun to offer some quiet, solicitous remarks now and then.

'Do you like this automobile, Carl?' Bren answered him.

He followed along, though perplexed. 'The Rolls-Royce is an excellent machine, Miss Hartleigh.'

'Glad you think so. You might as well know now, Carl, you're in my will to get this car. And that's how it went today, since you ask. It looks like pretty soon you'll be able to hire yourself out to take sweethearts to the theatre in style, or pick 'em up at the church after they've been dumb enough to get married. Because I'll be dead.'

'I don't believe the doctor told you that, Miss. The sort of problem you've got, these days you don't have to die. There's an awful lot they can do to help.'

'Maybe I don't give a shit about being helped. It's been downhill for too long. Life used to be fun, Carl. Men, money, power. I did it all my way, as the saying goes. I had everything – and everyone – I wanted.' It flashed through her mind that the boast wasn't completely true. Tay had stolen Neil Rocklyn – but at least they hadn't ended up together. 'But now,' Bren concluded, 'I can't even buy most of what I used to care about. Feels like it's time to die.'

'Pitiful to hear you talk this way, Miss H,' the chauffeur said. 'There's so many people in this world fightin' hard as they can to go on living even though what they have, at best, won't ever come near one-tenth of what you'll always have at worst.'

Bren shrugged and looked out the window. This old-time religion crap about counting her blessings never did cut any ice with her.

The chauffeur went on. 'What you need, I'd say, is a little

therapy for your soul as well as for your cells.'

She showed him a smirk in the rear-view mirror. 'Well, lawsy,' she said with bitter mockery, 'maybe I should go along to one of those holy-roller churches with you next Sunday, Carl.'

'I had something different in mind, Miss.'

'What, exactly?'

'Thought you might make it up with your family.'

He had finally gone too far. 'I'd rather die first,' she snapped.

'Then you surely will, Miss. But I thought if you—'

'I've had enough of your opinions, Carl.'

He went silent, and she could see his eyes spark in the mirror though he kept his gaze aimed at the road. But abruptly he pulled the Rolls over to a curb, and turned around in the front seat. 'You can damn well take the car out of your will if you want, Miss H, but I'm gonna finish. Because if there's anything that might turn you around, it's going to talk with that niece of yours. There's an awful lotta people say she knows how—'

'Yeah, I know. But Indian chants and sweating my ass off aren't going to cure my cancer or give me back a complete pair of firm young tits. Now shut up, Carl, all right? Just be quiet and take me—'

'No, ma'am. What Miss Tay has been doing, I've read about it, even heard people talking. If only you'd give it a chance, I think it could change your—'

Bren's control shattered. 'I don't give a rat's ass what you think. You're just the fucking chauffeur. So face front, and get this car moving, or you're fired. Got it, Carl? No job, no car, no tomorrow with me as far as I'm concerned unless you take orders here and now.' The threat hung in the air, but she couldn't retract it. What he had suggested was the ultimate insult – that she should allow herself to think that her very survival could depend on Cori's ungrateful Indian bastard.

'Go right ahead and do what you want, Miss,' he said evenly.

'But I'm telling you just the same: I can see you having a chance of being saved if you could go to that place – what does she call it, some Indian name . . . ?'

Angry as she was, the words came automatically from Bren's lips in a tone of disdain. '*Cante Ishta*.' She had seen it on the wedding invitation.

'Yeah, that's it,' he said. He turned forward again, and smoothly steered the car back into traffic. Neither spoke for a few minutes. Nothing was said about his being fired.

'*Cante Ishta*,' he repeated at last. 'Now what do you suppose that means?'

Bren didn't answer. She didn't know. Didn't care.

Though, oddly, she found herself still wondering about it through the rest of the day.

Now here she was. It looked, Bren thought as the taxi drove in through the main gate, not so different from the last time she'd been here. (When had that been? Twenty-five years ago? It had never been one of her favorite places.) She'd imagined it might be much more tricked up, all kinds of hokey stuff to convince the 'tourists' they were getting their money's worth. But while some buildings had been added, they were even more plain and rustic than the original lodge and guest cabins and bunkhouses and stables G.D. had built. She noticed, too, the several dome-shaped *tipis* that were scattered around the far edge of one of the surrounding meadows. Otherwise, the only change was the name, no longer the Golden H Ranch – spelled out in bold brass letters on an archway over the entrance gate – but those two words of Sioux language plainly painted on a small placard nailed to a post.

When it had opened its doors four years ago as a center for teaching Indian beliefs and practices to all who wished to come, there had been no advertising or publicity, no effort to attract attention. Cori and Tay had agreed that the message should spread only through the work that it did, through the people who found their way there by whatever route. If they were helped, others would learn about it. Of course, that had made for a very slow, quiet beginning – which actually pleased Tay. She even turned down the chance for free publicity. Neil Rocklyn, too, having added a so-called weekly 'magazine' program to his news duties, had asked to do a piece about the new center, but Tay had refused. She suspected he was hoping for more than an interview, and she had to let him know they could never revive their romance, her heart was promised.

Once the new retreat was opened, almost all the first visitors were reservation dwellers invited by Tay, not just Sioux, but Indians from tribes around the country, poor and sick, in need of the same medicine they might have wanted at home, but able to have it here in more comfortable surroundings. The way Cori had set up her gift of the ranch, deeding it to a charitable foundation endowed by most of her holdings in the mining company, there was no need to ask for any payment; even travel expenses were provided to anyone in need. Bringing people of other tribes together enriched them of knowledge to be shared, and helped to build a sense of community among all native Americans.

From the first there seemed to be an uncommon magic about the sanctuary and its curative effect on people. Drawing purely from native American beliefs and customs and ceremonies, diet and exercise and medicinal preparations, dedication to nature and reliance on the messages of dreams, Tay had designed a program that quickly began to attract a broad spectrum of people seeking relief from the stresses of a society driven by greed, beset by increasing violence, and eroded by declining values. The early visitors from the reservations were soon joined by ordinary *wasicuns* – telephone repair men, bank managers, secretaries, anyone who heard of it and was interested – then the circle widened to include corporation heads, celebrities, Senators and Congressmen. What they had in common and what leveled them all, were the problems that brought them. Discontent, fear, a sense of having lost touch with the basics of life, a desire to perform better, to believe in themselves, to rediscover joy, to experience the simple pleasures of nature. They were men and women who had suffered breakdowns, or had been fired from high-paying jobs, or went on clinging to power without any pleasure in it, or were afflicted with depression, or having a crisis of conscience, or were dying from a terminal disease. They sat together through lessons in the legends, and discussions of the history, and instruction in legal procedures that related to achieving Indian rights, and shared revelations of their dreams, and sweat lodges and pipe ceremonies. No one was ever asked for payment, though those who could afford it gladly gave donations.

Eventually, with the spreading word of the renewal that many experienced, skeptics spoke up. There were critics who thought that this kind of popularization of the Indian culture demeaned it. Yet Tay felt no need to apologize or change course. On a practical level, the growing success of the treatment meant jobs for her people. They taught the lessons, built new facilities, maintained the old ones, guided visitors on nature walks, conducted the ceremonies. And the results of their combined efforts were consistently positive. Most who came to *Cánte Ishta* went away not only refreshed and restored, but with a new knowledge and respect for a way of life that had long been unappreciated and under attack.

Every single day, whether or not it could be seen or measured in acres or miles, Tay was winning back lost Indian territory.

Bren got out of the taxi by the porch in front of the large log house, but hesitated before telling the driver to unload her luggage. She had swept away all her proud enmities to come on this search for peace of mind. But now she was having last minute misgivings about whether she wanted to stay. What was she putting her hopes in? Indian mumbo-jumbo?

No one would miss her if she left now. She hadn't called ahead . . .

As Bren stood outside, Cori was coming back from a horseback ride with a group of teenaged boys, Hopis from Arizona who had all recently been in trouble with the law. In the past year, the retreat had developed a regular program with tribal councils to take in juvenile offenders and put them on a constructive track. Cori didn't spend all her time at the retreat. She was with Frank most of the year in San Francisco; their marriage was a full partnership again, all symptoms of depression behind her. But she came here often and aided Tay. Teaching and advising youthful offenders was the thing that gave her the greatest satisfaction.

After dismounting and giving her horse to one of the young riders to return to the stables, Cori walked toward Bren.

Bren was turning back to the taxi when she saw Cori. She shrugged and turned her hands up in a gesture of defeat. 'You're looking very well,' she said as Cori came near. Bren couldn't help being aware of the reversal of fates: now she was the sick one. 'But you always did think this was the best place for you,' she went on. 'I guess you would've been fine if you could've spent your life here.'

'I never think about what could've been,' Cori said. 'I'm all right, and it's even better here now than it was before. I'm very glad you came, Bren. Tay will be glad, too.'

'Will she?' Out of habit it emerged in her customary sardonic tone. But hearing it, Bren was sorry. She was here to be helped, after all, she needed them – perhaps needed Tay the most. 'Will she really?' Bren asked again, this time letting the note of hope come through.

'Weddings are times for whole families to celebrate,' Cori

467

said. 'And without you – we're not a whole family.'

Bren kept fighting the tug of sentiment. 'Actually,' she said candidly, 'it's not the wedding I came for.'

Cori studied her for a long moment, and then gave her a gentle smile. 'That's all right, too,' she said at last. 'We're just glad you're here.'

Bren's emotions teetered between rage and remorse. She hated nothing more than being in this position, needing to draw on someone else's strength. If she'd learned anything from G.D. it was self-reliance, that good old frontier spirit. That's what had won the west, made the Hartleigh's rich.

But what had worked in another day and age couldn't carry her through the dark valley she had entered now. Hard as she had fought to keep the barriers standing, they crashed down suddenly. 'Oh, Cori,' she murmured plaintively, 'I'm so damn scared.'

Cori didn't even ask the reason. She opened her arms, and enfolded her sister.

'You're too good, Cori,' Bren said as she let herself be embraced and tears fell from her eyes for the only time in the past forty-five years. 'Just too fucking good and kind. Damn it, you always were . . .'

Cori laughed lightly as she held Bren. 'I seem to remember,' she said, 'that's what got us in trouble.'

In the same way that the concept of possession and ownership was not so much a legal principle in Indian tradition as a compact with nature and the spirits, the ritual by which a man and a woman bound themselves to each other had never been one that called for elaborate pomp and ceremony, repetitions of vows, or a public exhibition of the material substance one party would bring to the other. A man did not 'own' a woman, nor did she need to promise herself to him. Lovers who decided to marry were bound by a private decision of the heart that was binding enough. The ceremony needed be no more than a kind of notification that a man and a woman had decided to make their lives together henceforth.

The wedding took place the next day when the sun was at its zenith in a special *tipi* erected for the purpose, a large oblong constructed of tall cedar poles with buffalo skins stretched over them, the many hides required loaned by the Indians who had come from the Standing Rock, and the Teton, and the Pine Ridge, and the other reservations of the Lakotas to honor both Tay and Gene for what they had done for the Sioux nation, and all native Americans. So many came that they could not be accommodated inside the *tipi*; they gathered outside, waiting to participate in the traditional feast that would follow the wedding. None felt slighted; celebration was no less important than ceremony.

Inside were only a few more than a hundred of the guests, the families of the bride and groom, their most honored guests and closest friends. All sat on the ground, except for some of the elderly for whom chairs had been provided.

Tay and Gene sat cross-legged facing each other at the midpoint of the *tipi*. Seated three deep along the edges of the open space were their separate parties. Gene's included the members of the *tipospaye* that had raised him, and people he had helped in legal cases who remained devoted and grateful, and friends from the Wall Street and Washington establishments – legislators and even one Supreme Court justice who had been notably sympathetic in issues of Indian rights.

As Tay looked around she saw Abel's *tipospaye*, and Jimmie, and many of the Rosebud Sioux she had helped when she'd worked with Nellie – and also Emory Fast Horse, who had reappeared after hearing about *Cante Ishta* and now worked there as the maintenance foreman. They were all together at one side of the *tipi*. But, by tradition, the Indians and the *wasicuns* were always separated so Tay had to turn to the other side to see the second strain of blood from which she had sprung – her mother and Frank and their children, and Chet with his five children, and Bren. The night before Tay had met with Bren and had learned about her illness, and had promised to help her. A promise Bren immediately misunderstood. 'If you can cure me, Tay,' she had said, 'I'll give you anything—'

'There's nothing I need,' Tay told her, before explaining her promise. The medicine she gave to Bren would not be only for her body, but her spirit. The ailments she believed she could cure, if Bren would only let her, would be fear and cynicism and vanity and discontent and stress and even physical pain that could derive from those other problems. 'I believe,' Tay explained, 'that your body can be healthy again if you let me cure all the rest.'

'And suppose it isn't? Suppose you teach me to love my life. That'll only make it harder to die.'

Tay had to smile at her aunt's negative logic. 'None of us really knows how far we are from crossing over to meet the spirits,' she said. 'Whether the distance for you is short or long, Bren – and, as tough as we both know you are, yours may be very long – wouldn't you rather enjoy the journey?'

Last night, Bren's response had been only silence. But as she caught Tay's eye today, she gave her a smile. Maybe Tay was being too quick to look for a change, but it seemed to be the first time Bren had ever smiled without that cynical tilt at one side of her mouth.

If the ceremony that followed was short and simple, it only gave a greater weight of emotion to the few gestures involved.

An elder always spoke first to remind those who would make a new generation that they had a responsibility to the past, to remember their traditions, and always honor Unci –

'grandmother earth', the source and sustainer of life. Tay had asked Emory to speak.

Then an earthen jug of water was brought and poured over the hands of bride and groom. In the old days, of course, the water was simply taken from the nearest natural source; there would never have been any reason to question its purity. But Tay had asked for this water to be brought from the stream that passed from Hartleigh land onto the Standing Rock reservation. By her efforts, the dumping had ended, and a purification system installed by Chet ensured that the once-deadly water was now clean and untainted. It was Jimmie who carried the pitcher forward and poured it.

Finally, a basket was set on the ground between the couple being wed. It was Kate who brought the basket. Separated into four parts within the basket were the corn kernels, the pollen of the corn plant, some bits of the husk, and maize – the ground corn meal. Both Tay and Gene took a bit of each with their fingers and swallowed it.

There was a pause then. Tay and Gene looked at each other across the basket.

'You can kiss now,' Kate whispered.

And they did, with an accompaniment of sighs from all the spectators.

'But we aren't married just yet,' Gene reminded Tay as they stood up.

And she remembered one more ritual had to be performed to make the union complete. She lifted her hand and gestured to the end of the great oblong *tipi* where all the Indian guests had been sitting. They rose and started moving to the other end, all carrying small baskets containing craft objects they had made, or food they had grown or prepared. By tradition, man and woman were not joined until their families were joined, too. And it was accepted custom where such a circumstance might exist that the joining was symbolized by the native Americans presenting gifts to the *wasicuns*. It had always been so.

Because in the home of the Indians, after all, the *wasicuns* had always been guests.

EPILOGUE

In January 1993, Ben Nighthorse Campbell took his place in the Senate of the United States representing the people of the State of Colorado – all the people. Nighthorse Campbell is the first native American ever to have a voice in this high chamber of the federal government.

Encouraged by this breakthrough, the chairman of the Democratic party in South Dakota, Steven Nevelson, in consultation with the many native American tribes in his state, is hoping that one of them may be nominated to run in the upcoming elections. He is currently discussing the possibility with two potential nominees who are very popular in the state, and may still technically claim residency. Due to the recent birth of their second child, neither Gene Cheroux or Tayhcawin Walks-Through-Fire is eager to leave home at present. But both have said they could not refuse to serve the party or the people if the opportunity is offered.

Polls are currently being taken to determine which of the potential candidates is the more popular.